Praise for
LINDA SANDIFER'S PREVIOUS NOVELS

The Daughters of Luke McCall

"Linda Sandifer has a nice way of filling a tale with the stuff that makes you want to read just one more page until you have finished the book. For those who like the real West, fans of Linda, and those who are just plain looking for a grand read."
Affaire de Coeur Magazine

Raveled Ends of Sky

"Many stories have been written about the covered wagon pioneers, but few have been from the woman's viewpoint. Based on actual diaries and reminiscences, [Raveled Ends of Sky] tells of a spirited young woman's hazardous trek to California in 1843 and the uneasy early years of American settlement there just before the gold rush of 1849. An excellent read."
Elmer Kelton, Spur award-winning author

"The author's expertise, both as a writer of romance and an astute student of history of the period, shines through in this epic adventure."
Abilene Reporter News

"Nancy Maguire, a spirited young woman determined to escape the stifling society of New England, sets off for California in this near-mythic tale of a quest for freedom and independence on the American frontier. . . .a gritty, realistic drama of early trailblazers."
Booklist

Books by Linda Sandifer

The Daughters of Luke McCall
Raveled Ends of Sky
Firelight
The Turquoise Sun
Desire's Treasure
Came A Stranger
Embrace the Wind
Mountain Ecstasy
Midnight Hearts
Heart of the Hunter
Pride's Passion
Tyler's Woman

The Last Rodeo

A Novel

LINDA SANDIFER

STRATHAVEN BOOKS

Printed in USA

This is a work of fiction. All the characters and events portrayed in this novel are either fictitious or are used fictitiously.

THE LAST RODEO

ISBN 978-0-9816332-0-6

Strathaven Books, PO Box 32, Iona, ID 83427.

Cover Design and Photo: Emily Sandifer

Typeset in Palatino Linotype 11 pt by Get It Together Productions

Library of Congress Control Number: 2008902868

First Edition: October 2008

Printed in the United States of America on permanent paper

Acknowledgments

I would like to thank the following people for their assistance and support throughout my long journey to see this book in print: Amanda Sabourova, Bonny J. Anderson, and Charm O'Ryan for editing and critiquing various drafts; Emily Sandifer Youngerman for the cover design and the photograph of that long Nevada highway; Bill Corbett for a male perspective and valuable insight; Irene Bennett Brown for her words of encouragement and seasoned advice; Kae Cheatham for the beautiful interior layout; and, finally, to the die-hards of the Blue Sage Fiction Writers—Karen Finnigan, Charm O'Ryan, Sandra Lord, Sherry Roseberry, and Maxine Metcalf—for many, *many* years of sharing not just their writing, but their friendship and their lives.

To Van, with whom I have traveled many miles and shared the peaks and valleys. Your hard work and unerring faith have always inspired me to take just one more step.

Thank you for believing.

Prologue

From the Journal of July Jones

The highway stretches as far as the horizon, diminishing to a fine line at the base of the distant mountains. For the most part, the highway is a straight, uninterrupted arrow, but occasionally it undulates with the curvature of the sage-brush hills, disappearing and reappearing like pieces of a twisted ribbon.

Regardless of the point at which you find yourself on this length of asphalt, there is the illusion that you can drive forever and never reach its end; that you will be able to see everything coming and going; that there will be no surprises, no hills nor valleys, no bumps nor detours; that you will be able to get off any time and change direction.

It's easy not to look back, to turn your rearview mirror to the sky. It's easy to take root in the highway's freedom and in its loneliness that fills your soul with the pulse of life. It's easy to believe that if you keep moving, the movement will stop time, or that you will at least not notice its passing. On the highway, you are inconsequential yet whole, and everything behind you and before you seems clear.

Yet, there is a mirage that perpetually runs one step ahead of the runner; a mirage that filters out the small, intersecting side roads that—if you tarry on them too long—can, and will, change your direction forever.

Chapter One

Arizona

Dev Summers buckled on his chaps and pulled the deerskin glove onto his riding hand, cinching it tight at the wrist. He blocked out the din of the rodeo, of everything except the sound of the announcer's baritone voice coming from the loudspeakers, smoothly playing to the audience.

"Ladies and gentlemen, our next cowboy has been riding rough stock since he was old enough to walk. Five-time Professional Rodeo Cowboy Association's World Champion, and four-time Professional Bull Rider World Champion, Dev Summers is the only man to have ever ridden the notorious Satan 101—a big, rank old bull that's been named the PBR's Bucking Bull of the Year for three consecutive years.

"Early last year in Montana, though, Old Satan got even with our cowboy and nearly ended his career. But you can't hold a good man down. Dev's back in the running, and, as luck would have it, he's drawn into another go-round with Satan."

A hush fell over the crowd as they realized this could be the ride of the night, maybe even a ride that would go down in the annuls of rodeo history. But what most of them didn't know was that Satan 101 had turned killer.

Nobody had wanted to ride him since April when Tim Roberts, a guy with whom Dev must have logged a million miles over the last twenty years, had run out of luck up at the Nampa Classic in Idaho. The bull had turned on him with the same vicious intent he'd laid out for Dev last year at the NILE Invitational in Billings, Montana. While all the cowboys had helplessly huddled in shock around Tim, the bull rider had died in Dev's arms before the Justin Sportsmedicine Team could reach him.

Tim's death had left a pall hanging over the bull riders. Every cowboy who'd drawn Satan since April had learned how to pray—and how to mean every word of it. Many had been hurt bad enough to be knocked out of the competition. Others had barely escaped injury. No one had ridden him.

The beast was at this moment trying to hook every cowboy within reach of his deadly horns, effectively sweeping them off the sides of the chute like dust from a doorframe before completing his customary exhibition and dropping to all fours, ready to fulfill the announcer's rhetoric.

Dev removed his Resistol hat to mop the sweat from his brow with his shirt sleeve. With a foot on either side of the metal chute, he eased out over the brindle's wide back, reminding himself that he could beat Satan. He'd done it once; he could do it again. All he had to do was focus and not think about what the animal was capable of doing. His entire career—maybe his entire life—would ultimately be measured by this one ride. The announcer's glowing words made him sound so indestructible, but the announcer wasn't close enough to smell his fear.

Satan felt Dev's pant legs brush his hide, and he reared again, forcing Dev to scramble to safety. Along with his other injuries, Dev had pulled his groin muscles last week, and it was there he felt the strain from his hasty retreat. He was tired of always fighting the pain, riding it out, sucking it up, swallowing it down. He was thirty-five—too old for this shit. He hurt everywhere, and he was sick of it. Damned sick of it. There was no longer a thrill to dally with death. He'd accomplished all he'd set out to do in the sport and then some. There were no more mountains to climb—except maybe to ride Satan one last time.

Walk away, man, while you still can. You've been wanting to for a long time. He heard Tim's voice in his mind, as if he were standing right there next to him. And maybe he was.

Don't worry, old buddy. Win or lose, live or die, this is going to be my last ride.

Going out in a blaze of glory, are you?

Why not? You did.

Well, they're waiting. Don't disappoint them the way I did.

Dev's eyes roamed the faces of the people lining the chutes. The bull riders were all scared for him—you could see it in their eyes and in their strained expressions. You could smell it in the air. They were all thinking of Tim and wondering if they were about to see a repeat of that tragic ride. The rodeo photographers had other concerns, mainly positioning themselves so they could get the shot that would bring the big bucks. The crowd in the stands was waiting with bated breath. In the end, a strong sense of duty, pride, a dose of revenge, and yes, even a degree of vanity held him there.

"When he comes out of the chute, he's gonna lunge to the right." Dev's dad, Jake Summers, a perpetual fixture, was passing out his usual advice from his safe perch atop the chute. "He throws that head back hard, so make sure you don't get pulled down into it or he'll break every bone in your face."

"I know what he does. I've ridden him before. Remember?"

Eyes the same sharp blue as Dev's tightened and flashed. "You've ridden him *once*. Then you let him get the best of you."

"Let him? Ah, to hell with you."

He shut his dad out completely then, letting the anger stoke the fire that needed to burn hot if he was to succeed. On the other hand, if he ended up like Tim, he could at least get some rest from the road and the bullshit about a cowboy's "try," his courage, his heart, that veneer he was supposed to wear so nothing could get through to his soul and his common sense. When he'd been young, he'd gobbled up that plateful of bullshit like a twenty-ounce sirloin, loving every bite, but somewhere along the road his taste buds had gone numb.

Wanting to get it over with, Dev tried to settle down onto the bull again, but again Satan reared, jamming Dev's right leg against the side of the chute. The metal gate rattled and clanged as the bull hit it hard. Dev rode out the fresh pain with curses through clenched teeth.

The chute men were hollering, "Watch him, Dev! Watch him! He could come over on you." His brother, Seth, was saying, "You ought to wear a face guard." Somebody else said, "Crazy bastard." And Dev didn't know if they meant him or Satan.

The announcer joined in, his tone clearly worried. "Old Satan seems to be giving our cowboy some trouble down there."

Silence filled the dead space. The audience's attention was riveted now to the commotion coming from chute eight. They, too, sensed the unusual tension.

Nobody had to tell Dev he was going to need all the help he could get to stay on this son of a bitch. Despite the announcer's declaration otherwise, Dev knew he wasn't fully recovered from last year's injuries. He wasn't sure his arm muscles would stand up to the beating 101 was bound to give. He decided his only chance to hold on was to use a suicide wrap.

He tried to tell himself that winning didn't matter, but it did. He still had enough drive that he wanted to be the only man who had ridden Satan not once, but twice. His own dad—a six-time, All-Around World Champion—had been the only one to ever ride the famed saddle bronc, Black Widow, and before Dev quit for good, he wanted to top the old man. Wanted to shut him up so he didn't have anything to lord over his head. But most of all, he didn't want Satan to walk away the victor two times running.

The bull quieted, dropped his head and set his feet, sensing his rider was tired of the foreplay. Dev slid forward again, situating himself. Heat emanated from the bull's thick hide and his muscles bunched, almost quivering with anticipation as he prepared for his leap into the arena.

With the rapid ease of an expert, Dev dropped his flat, braided bull rope down over Satan's muscled shoulders. A stock contractor employee reached under the bull's belly with a hook, snared the loose end and brought it back up, circling the bull's girth. The cowbell attached to the rigging settled directly under the bull's brisket. The bell was mandatory; its weight helped the rigging fall away when the cowboy released his grip. Another stock contractor employee was also preparing the fleece-lined strap around the bull's sensitive flank area, leaving it loose until the bull exited the chute, at which time it would be pulled tight to encourage the bull to buck harder and higher.

Earlier, Dev had put fresh rosin on the bull rope. Now, he ran his gloved hand back and forth along the rope to heat the rosin. He slid the same hand, knuckles down, around the rope.

The man assisting him pulled the slack from the rope and handed the free end to Dev who laid it across his palm. He wrapped it once behind his hand and laid it across the palm again, cinching it down as tight as he could. Then he drew the tail through two fingers and pounded it down with his free hand to make the rosin adhere to itself like glue as it cooled. The only way the wrap would come undone now was if its tail were pulled free by either himself or a bullfighter. If he came off the bull on the wrong side, or over the bull's head with his hand turned back on itself, he wouldn't be able to grab that tail, and his life would rest in the hands of the bullfighters.

His dad was still hanging over him, watching and scowling. "What in the hell do you think you're doin', boy?"

Seth, too, wore a look of concern. "Damn it, Dev. Don't use the wrap with Satan."

He ignored them both. It was more dangerous, true, but some riders used the wrap on every ride they took.

Dev settled down until his groin was pressed firmly into the fist that gripped the rope. He pulled in a deep breath, drawing strength from the familiar smells of leather, rosin, and hemp.

"Don't be stupid." His dad again. "He'll kill you and be happy to do it."

The announcer picked up where he'd left off. "Ladies and gentlemen, put your hands together for these two world champions. Coming out of chute number eight, Nevada cowboy Dev Summers on Satan 101!"

The announcer's timing was perfect. He ended his introduction just as Dev gave his nod and the gate man threw the gate wide. With incredible strength and pent-up energy, Satan whirled his massive body into the arena.

For a moment, Dev was in the zone. He was with the bull, with each lunge, each twist, each leap. He felt the power of being the victor over 2,000 pounds of brute strength. There was symmetry, grace. He matched every move of the big animal, like they were doing a Texas two-step.

Then the dance was over.

The bull surged away from Dev's hand. Centrifugal force pulled him off center. He fought gravity, grasping air with his free hand in an attempt to right himself. He tried to lean back, knowing he was dangerously too far forward.

Old 101 sensed he was slipping and exploded beneath him, but the shift in direction yanked Dev back on center. Satan came off the ground, kicking high, twisting in mid-air. He landed hard throwing Dev forward again, then he threw his massive head back, missing Dev's face by a hair's breadth. Dev heard the collective voice of the audience rise in one roar, urging him on, trying to help him keep his grip. With agility that defied an animal of his mass, Satan set into a spin. Dev felt the strength in his arm begin to weaken, and he envisioned his tendons snapping and rolling up like a window shade.

Then the eight-second buzzer blared as he began an uncontrolled spiral to earth on the wrong side of the bull, twisting his arm like a turn buckle. He made a grab for the rope's tail but missed it and was dragged alongside, held fast. The audience's roar lifted to a unified gasp, a cry of fear. A bullfighter attempted to free him from over the back of the gyrating brute. Another tried to get over him to the rope's tail to release it.

It seemed an eternity passed as he was flung and kicked, his arm twisting until the shoulder snapped with a lightning-hot jolt of pain that nearly caused him to black out. Then the rigging mercifully gave way—the bullfighter had done his job—and Dev hit the ground. The bull went over the top of him, its hooves striking his legs and lower back with sharp, deep stabs.

Satan was ready for his fall. Dev had no time to rise and run to safety, so he instinctively curled into a fetal position to protect his head and stomach just as the bull whirled and slammed its head into his backside, lifting him off the ground and flinging him toward the chutes. The last thing he heard was silence. The last thing he saw was the frightened expressions of men scattering to safety…and the bull coming at him again.

Chapter Two

It took tremendous willpower to keep snapping pictures. A cowboy was in trouble. Not just any cowboy, but Dev Summers, a man whom July Jones had called friend for over ten years.

In the end, she lowered her Nikon and ran to him, arriving as the Justin Sportsmedicine Team dropped onto their knees next to him, and the pick-up men hazed Satan 101 out of the arena.

Seth Summers stepped aside for her, allowing her to slip in between him and his dad. Her heart lurched at the sight of Dev's crumpled form and the blood flowering onto the back of his torn shirt. The medical team worked swiftly, unzipping his Kevlar vest and spreading it wide so they could check for a pulse and heartbeat. One person started an IV while another lifted his eyelids and flashed a penlight into each eye. He didn't move through the entire examination, but at least he was still alive.

"Damned stupid kid," Jake Summers muttered. "He knew better than to do that."

"Do what, Jake?" Her eyes snapped up to his.

He looked too mad to explain. "No use talking about it now."

From the way Dev had been hung up in the rigging, July suspected he'd used a suicide wrap. The oldtimers, like Jake, were against it, but, nowadays, ropes were made of new materials that supposedly kept them from getting tangled and hung up as easily as their forerunners. There were some guys who always used the wrap because they wanted the edge it gave them. Otherwise, the force of the rider's grip on the rope was the only thing that kept him on the bull. And Dev had needed the edge; she'd seen the pain in his face every time he'd ridden this year and knew his injuries still dogged him.

The Justin Sportsmedicine Team worked rapidly but carefully to confine any movement with a neck brace and head restraints. Then they moved him onto a backboard, strapped him down, and carried him from the arena to the medical center that had been set up in the building close to the arena floor. The center was equipped with a full line of sophisticated medical equipment. Onboard were an orthopedic surgeon and a well-trained medical team specializing in sports medicine and prepared for anything from scrapes to minor surgery. The team was always on hand at the PBR events, providing the care unique to the sport.

July gathered Dev's hat from the dirt, unconsciously making an attempt to brush it off as she hurried to catch up. The other contestants turned back to the rodeo, knowing they would learn the extent of Dev's injuries in due time. The announcer's voice faded into the background as he assured the audience that Dev was all right, then he launched into information about the next ride.

◆

One searing jolt of pain brought Dev back to consciousness, as if a branding iron had been pressed deep into his shoulder. He was flat on his back, floating above the ground, disembodied, or so it seemed. He managed to open his eyes but couldn't focus on the faces and the cowboy hats bobbing overhead. The background noise faded as he was ushered into the cool, white interior of the medical center; every place was different, but the basic surroundings had come to be very familiar throughout the course of his career.

He was moved from the backboard to a treatment table. While one of the Sportsmedicine team prepared to take x-rays, two others went to work on either side of him taking the liberty to finish stripping him of his dignity, exposing Hanes briefs that were filled with arena dirt. The chief physician made a quick examination of the cuts on his back and commented on the scrub job they'd have to do to get the dirt out of them, then he turned his attention to Dev's injured arm and shoulder. They were tossing around a lot of medical jargon, most of which he understood, having been on the receiving end of it too many times to count.

Seeing he was conscious, the team gave encouraging smiles

and words that covered all manner of bad news. It occurred to him that he'd accomplished his goal. He'd ridden Satan to the buzzer and gotten injured badly enough in the process that he could make his break—so to speak—once and for all, and his dad would have to accept it. On the brighter side of things, he knew he was salvageable since he could still see, hear, move his toes and fingers, and could feel pain everywhere else.

He closed his eyes again. He didn't want to talk, and he knew they wouldn't tell him much anyway. He knew the routine. He'd have to go through a barrage of x-rays and tests, sutures and injections, wraps and bandages. He hoped they wouldn't send him off to the hospital for reconstructive surgery. From the all-consuming pain in his shoulder, he knew the diagnosis wouldn't be good.

He began to drift into the pain-free world of unconsciousness when the touch of a soft hand, slipping around his, pulled him back. The subtle scent of perfume flared his nostrils. He knew who it belonged to even before he looked into worried green eyes and a beautiful face haloed by hair the color of ripened barley. It was a face he had no right to dream about, but had—more times than he would ever admit. For a moment, the pain was suspended, and he wondered if he was hallucinating because there was no good reason for July to be here except in some corner of his mind that allowed wishful thinking.

His gaze settled on her full lips. "A face that pretty must mean I died and went to heaven."

Relief softened her expression. "Not this time, cowboy. You're still with us."

"Did you get it all on film, darlin'?"

"In all its painful glory."

He smiled; it was the only movement that didn't hurt. "Did I make the buzzer, or did I imagine it?"

"You made it."

"Did I score higher than Buck?"

"You put him to shame."

His eyes closed involuntarily and the grip on her hand tightened as another sharp stab of pain ricocheted through him. He rode it out with clenched teeth. Then, "Don't go away, sweetheart.

When they let me out of here, we'll celebrate the fact that I'm still alive."

"You won't be doing any drinking, Dev," the chief physician said in his typical joking manner. "You'll be so doped up on pain killers and muscle relaxers you won't know which end is up."

"Well, as long as I'm feeling no pain... ."

With his eyes closed, he could focus on the feel of July's hand in his. Strong yet soft. Reliable yet slipping away. Always slipping away.

The doctor broke into his thoughts. "July, I'm sorry, but you'll have to leave now. Jake and Seth—you too. You're welcome to wait outside, though. Grab some cold drinks from the refrigerator on your way out."

Dev reluctantly shifted his gaze from July to his dad and brother standing near the door, hands in their back pockets. One was the replica of the other, perhaps not so much in looks—he looked more like their dad than Seth did—but in their mannerisms and in the way their minds worked in tandem like the two wheels of a bicycle. They didn't look happy, and he knew he'd hear all about it before the night was over. Well, let them boil in their own stew. He'd done what he'd done, and there wasn't a damn thing they could do about it.

July gave his hand a squeeze as she bent and pressed a kiss to his forehead. "I'll check on you later."

He had the powerful urge to lift his good arm and slip his hand up along her neck, under the loosely curled tendrils of thick hair, and draw her lips down to his. Yes, if only his arms weren't strapped down. If only she wasn't Buck's wife.

He watched her until the door closed behind her.

"That bull used you for a battering ram," the woman medical assistant bantered. "I don't know why they keep bucking that demon."

If he'd known her, he might have bantered back, even flirted a bit. He thought about responding with the usual macho cowboy rejoinder, the eternally optimistic, "Aw, shucks, ma'am, that weren't nothin'. I'll be back out in the arena tomorrow."

But he didn't say it. He didn't say anything because he had

taken his last ride as a professional bull rider, and he found a
calming peace in that knowledge.

◆

July, Jake, and Seth stood outside the room, sipping soft drinks,
listening to the buzz of the rodeo in the background, and not knowing what to do next. "It could be a couple of hours," Seth said.

"Longer if it's serious and they have to take him to the hospital." Jake was still disgusted with the turn of events. "I don't know
what in the hell got into him."

"Well, he's cooked his goose for the rest of the season."

"Yeah. Two years in a row."

Jake sat down in one of the three plastic chairs that had been
positioned in the hall next to the door of the medical unit. He
didn't look much older than his sons. He wasn't a big man. Like
Dev and Seth, he was two or three inches shy of six foot and still
lean and muscular. His thick, dark brown hair barely showed gray,
and his face had no excess flesh, only a few squint lines around
the eyes and mouth.

Pushing his hat to the back of his head, he looked up at July,
who was still standing. "Buck should be tickled, though. He'll be
a shoe-in for the title again."

July couldn't defend her husband; Jake was right. Buck and
Dev had batted the PRCA world championship back and forth for
years. Things hadn't changed when they'd both moved onto the
PBR's major league tour. Buck would have no pity for his greatest
rival; his only comment would be, "It serves the stupid bastard
right." Then he'd gloat in his victory while she prayed somebody
would topple him. Buck had been lucky; he'd never drawn Satan
101.

"Speaking of Buck, did either of you see where he went after
his ride?" she asked.

A wary look entered Jake's eyes before he quickly looked
away and tipped his Coke up to his lips again. "He's probably
found a cooler somewhere with plenty of beer in it, which doesn't
sound like a bad idea. We ought to go find one ourselves."

"Hooley always has an ample supply," Seth put in.

July had the distinct feeling they were trying to change the
subject. "Then maybe I'll start with Hooley."

"He's got his truck out on the north end of the contestants' parking lot." He looked relieved to have passed the buck onto someone else.

July started to move away. "I'll be back in a little while to see how Dev's doing."

"Aren't you going to finish working the rodeo?"

"No, it's about over and there are plenty of other photographers out there. Besides, I got the best ride."

"At least come to the dance over at the High Heel tonight."

"I might. I'll find Buck and see what he wants to do."

"You can always come without him," Jake said.

She didn't miss the suggestiveness in his eyes and voice. Jake Summers' reputation for seducing lonely women far preceded him, and he still had the looks to pull it off. A wedding ring was no barrier whatsoever. He actually preferred the married ones because with them he didn't have to worry about commitment. But she knew his type so well that she brushed him off with a laugh, and left him and Seth to their Cokes and any further conjecturing on why Dev had used a suicide wrap, and on whether she would find her wayward husband. She had a feeling that they both knew exactly where Buck was—and there was only one reason for not telling her.

Chapter Three

July wound her way across the trampled grass of the rodeo grounds and around the helter-skelter array of pickup trucks and travel trailers. She side-stepped numerous groups of people and dodged jean-clad children in oversized hats who roped imaginary steers and rode imaginary broncs. Talk of good rides and bad rides, fast times and no time drifted in and out of overheard conversations before she spotted Hooley Wilson.

On the high end of thirty, the wiry bull rider had the weathered face and graying hair of a much older man, a man who had spent his life outdoors squinting against a hot western sun. Like many rodeo cowboys, Hooley had been raised on a ranch—in his case, a ranch near Dillon, Montana—and he milked his cowboy image for all it was worth. If she'd seen him in the chaparral, she might have thought he'd traveled through time from the 1880s. Most rodeo cowboys didn't sport facial hair, but Hooley looked like Wyatt Earp with his handlebar mustache and vintage clothing, right down to the spurs he seldom removed and the faded red bandana tied loosely around his neck. But, like most of his kind, he had adjusted well enough to the twenty-first century. His favorite modern convenience was undoubtedly the plastic Wal-Mart cooler that kept his beer on ice and provided his booted feet with a resting place. He also had a good relationship with the tattered green lawn chair butted up against a two-tone brown Ford pickup that should have been compacted two decades ago.

The thing she liked the most about Hooley was that he was content with who he was and happy with his life on the road. Even when he'd had a bad ride or a losing season, his brown eyes always twinkled when he spoke, and he never complained even if he was latched onto a losing streak.

He was pleased to see her and called out in a deep Western drawl, as if she might be deaf, "Well, hell. If it ain't Miss July Jones, rodeo photographer *extraordinaire*." He started to struggle up out of the lawn chair but leaned too far to the right, tipping the chair precariously.

She reached out to stabilize it. "Whoa, cowboy. Don't get up on my account."

He landed back in the chair, grinning sheepishly. "It ain't a good sign when a man can get bucked off a damned lawn chair."

He settled down firmly into his mesh seat and offered her a drink. She said she'd have a soda, and he dug down into the cooler through the ice and came up with a Mountain Dew. While she popped the top and enjoyed a cold swallow, he glanced at the Nikon hanging from her shoulder. "I see you're still lugging that camera around."

She grinned. "What doesn't kill you makes you stronger."

The crow's feet around his eyes deepened as he cocked his head. "I still have the shot you took of me when I rode Bad News up in Cheyenne five years ago. It's hangin' on the wall right here in my camper. That was the best ride I ever took."

"It did help you win the championship that year."

"I miss those days. Course, the money's with the PBR, and if I don't do better than I've been doing, I'm not going to be one of the top forty-five." He studied her in a kind, thoughtful way. "One thing I've missed is seeing you run the barrels. You were always a pretty sight in the arena. Why, I didn't know a cowboy who wouldn't wait around to see you make your run. Maybe it was the way you sat that horse. It was just worth watching."

She laughed. "Well, thank you. Sometimes I do miss it."

He observed her hat, boots, and jeans. "No chance you'll try for a comeback?"

"No. I've gotten pretty comfortable with this camera, and the money's starting to roll in. What about you?" Her eyes sparkled as she teased. "Did you ever find that perfect wife, the one who would cook your meals and wash your socks and make love to you every night?"

He looked embarrassed. "Hell, July. I've had *two* since I saw you last. You know, once you're on a roll. I guess I wasn't meant for permanent relationships. Both of them gals were high maintenance. Sure, they wanted to make love every night, but not with me, and they needed a lot more money than this old cowboy could make. Neither one had the inclination to feed me or keep my underwear clean. Then the last one wanted me to take a job in construction with her brother. Hell."

They had a good laugh, both trying to visualize Hooley building anything short of a barbed wire fence. When the conversation lagged, July looked past him, down the narrow space between a row of horse trailers. "Speaking of old cowboys, I don't suppose you've seen mine?"

"As a matter of fact. Right after his ride. Said he was going to crash in Ricky Holladay's Airstream. He brought it along this time since he doesn't live too far away. Sophisticated piece of bullshit if you ask me." Hooley finished the can of beer and opened the cooler for another one.

"Would you know where it's parked?" She wasn't anxious for another confrontation with Buck, but she needed to get it over with so she could go back and see how Dev was doing.

Hooley pointed behind him. "Clear in the back so he'll have his privacy—he's usually got a girl or two in there. Personally, I think that's the real reason he uses it every chance he gets. You can't miss it. It's hooked to a big blue Ford diesel. Brand new. Loaded. Damned thing must have cost fifty grand."

"Thanks, Hooley. It was good to see you."

"Sure thing. You take care, and don't be a stranger."

The Airstream was right where Hooley had said it would be. All the windows and doors were closed and the blinds had been pulled against the afternoon sun. July could hear the air conditioner humming and Alan Jackson singing one of his many hits on the radio. It sounded too quiet, though, for Ricky and his usual gaggle of girlfriends. Maybe Buck truly had "crashed" and was asleep. She debated waking him; he was always testy when he was tired.

Her knuckles were poised inches away from the metal door to knock when she heard female laughter rising above the air conditioner and music. It was loud enough—and sensuous enough—to send a sick feeling plunging to the pit of her stomach. Damn it. Why had she come looking for Buck in the first place? She should have stayed with Dev when she'd seen that tell-tale look on Jake's face. It would have been less complicated to turn a blind eye to Buck's activities. They had been getting along better the last few months, mainly because they seldom saw each other, but it had been difficult at best for her to put aside ten years of lies, broken promises, and countless infidelities in order to believe his most recent vow that he would never cheat on her again. She wanted to believe he'd changed—God, how she wanted to believe—but she was no longer able to say she loved him. She was no longer able to make love *to* him.

The air conditioner clicked off. Despite the latter, someone had left a back window open about three inches, and she could hear the voices more clearly. The timbre of the man's voice was deeper than Ricky's distinctive, high-pitched twang. For the first time now, she could also detect the rhythmic, tell-tale rock of the trailer that told her without a doubt what was going on in the back room.

It could be someone else, another friend of Ricky's.

But in her heart, she didn't believe it as she walked softly to a position right under the open window and heard the voice she knew all too well. "You like it, baby? You want more?"

"You know it, Bucky."

The air conditioner clicked back on, and she lost the response, if there had been one.

July didn't know why she didn't open the door and confront him. Maybe because it came as no surprise, and maybe because anything she could have said had been said too many times before.

Instead, with no tears, no profanity, and more control than she thought herself capable, she walked away, keeping her pace steady until she reached the other trailers and vehicles again. She moved quickly now, slipping around people who slowed her escape. Tears began to pool and blur her vision while anger and pain battled for center stage. She was angry at him for cheating and lying, but she was more angry at herself for wanting to believe him and for wasting so many years of her life with a man who had no idea what real love and commitment was all about. And clearly a man who never would.

She had almost reached her rental car when she heard her name called. Not wanting to talk to anyone, she kept walking. At the car, she yanked her keys from her pocket but dropped them and saw them disappear under the door. With tears blinding her, she groped in the dirt for them, silently cursing herself for being so stupid as to cry. Buck wasn't worth it—the bastard wasn't even worth the price of a bullet.

"July, what's wrong?"

She recognized Hooley's voice. He lowered himself to his haunches next to her and reached under the car for the keys. She kept her face turned away, protected by the wide brim of her hat. He took her elbow and helped her to her feet then awkwardly put his arms around her. She welcomed the comforting embrace and buried her face in his neck while he muttered something about "that stupid son of a bitch," guessing without being told what she had found.

"Did you know he was with another woman, Hooley?"

He made a sound, as if trying to get words out of his throat, but all he managed was, "I suspected."

"He doesn't try to hide it from anybody but me. Well, he's made a laughingstock of me for the last time."

"Nobody's laughing at you. We all know he doesn't deserve you. Maybe it's none of my business—and you can tell me so— but you need to leave him, July. You're too good for him."

She wanted to tell Hooley that her tears had less to do with a broken heart and more to do with disappointment in herself for putting up with it for so long because she didn't want to admit failure and be alone. But then, hadn't she been alone all along, right from the day her parents and younger sister had died in that car crash over twenty years ago and she'd been taken in by her father's brother and his reluctant wife. The latter, along with July's two cousins, had made sure she knew she was an intrusion and a burden, taking food and money that should have been for them. The only genuine love she'd received was from her uncle and a grandmother who had died after July turned twelve.

The aloneness hadn't changed when she'd met Buck. She had concealed it by burying herself in his life and foregoing her own identity. Their relationship had always been about him, a one-way road she was so very weary of traveling.

Not until his first infidelity had she stepped out of his shadow and started to pull away, started to let go of her love for him (or had it merely been need?) little by little until there was nothing left but the financial security he provided. It wasn't easy to set out alone, not knowing where she was going and having no one waiting at the end of the journey, but now she knew she could do it because, in reality, she'd been doing it all her life.

It was several minutes before she regained her composure and stepped away, wiping her eyes. "Thanks, Hooley. It's not like it was the first time. Not a big surprise, you know."

"What'll you do now?"

She tried to laugh. "I'm not going home to cry myself to sleep, that's for sure. A few margaritas and an early start on the dancing over at the High Heel sounds much better." Her words were both flippant and bitter, but as she turned away, she realized that getting drunk might not be such a bad idea. She'd never been one to drown her problems in alcohol, but this incident warranted an exception. After all, this was the final straw; there would be no going back. The worst part was wondering why Buck had always felt compelled to seek out other women, why she had never been enough for him, yet why he had held onto her and begged her to stay with him, to forgive him, to believe him when he said he loved her and would never betray her again. Maybe he did love her in his own twisted way.

She thought about going back to see Dev, but he had enough problems without being burdened by hers. Even if she said nothing about what had happened, he would read her eyes and know something was wrong, and she would be compelled to tell him.

"I don't know if you ought to drink alone," Hooley said, as serious as a preacher. "Nobody ought to drink alone, especially when they're feeling bad."

"Can you dance?"

"Like a chicken."

It was impossible to give into pain in the face of his deadpan humor. "Are you game?"

She could see his wheels turning at a steady, serious pace. Out of habit, he rolled one end of his handlebar moustache between his thumb and forefinger. "Well, I reckon somebody ought to keep you out of trouble and be your designated driver. I doubt you'll be in any shape to drive come one o'clock in the morning. I'm a little snockered right now, but if I don't drink anymore, I'll be fine."

"You're a sweetheart, Hooley."

His lips thinned to a grim line as he opened the car door for her. "A damn fool, more likely."

Chapter Four

Dev hobbled out of the medical unit with a concussion, bruised ribs and legs, a dislocated shoulder coupled with tendon and ligament damage, stitches in his back, a bottle of painkillers in his shirt pocket, and his dad and Seth on either side of him flinging so much bullshit he thought he might suffocate. He had to get out of here and back home, get some air that wasn't tainted. As it was, he'd had to shake Seth out of a deep sleep on the hallway floor and drag his dad away from a twenty-something groupie he'd been flirting with.

And now this.

"What do you mean you're done?" Jake Summers spoke with that familiar sharp edge to his voice. "You'll have plenty of time to get healed before the next event. I can tell you one thing, that shit you pulled today on Satan damned near got you killed, and you'd better not do it again."

"I rode him."

"If you want to call that a ride."

Dev lifted his hat and wiped the sweat from his brow with his shirt sleeve. His dad's response was so typical. "I stuck to him until the buzzer sounded, and I got the top score for the night. Isn't that what you wanted, damn it?"

"And look where it got you—crippled up again. You'd have done better to let go. A man has to know when to let go."

"My point precisely."

"So that's what the suicide wrap was all about? To rub my nose in some imaginary shit you've been packin' around."

They had reached their pickup truck, a black Dodge Ram Mega Cab, hitched to a twenty-eight-foot fifth wheel travel trailer.

Dev opened the door to the trailer and made his way to the front and up the two steps to the queen bed. He threw his hat into its center and eased his body down next to it. All he wanted to do was sleep for about a week.

"I'm finished, Dad. I've taken my last ride. I figure you can have me home by tomorrow afternoon, then the two of you can hit the road again, take your time getting to Tulsa. Or better yet, stay at the ranch and fly out when the time comes."

"That isn't going to work," Seth said, as if there was room for argument. "I've got a date with that hot little number from New Mexico. She said she'd meet me at the High Heel as soon as we got away from here."

His dad tried again. "You can't quit the tour."

"Even if I had a notion to keep going—which I don't—the doctor told me he didn't want me bouncing my head around like a basketball for a few weeks at least."

"What's wrong with your head?"

"I've got a concussion. And if you'd bothered to come in and hear the prognosis instead of staking out the women, you'd know that this arm isn't in a sling just to draw female sympathy." He maneuvered himself around into a position that would be comfortable for his shoulder and arm. "As for your little honey, Seth—tell her you've had a change of plans and you'll catch her at the next rodeo."

"She won't be in Tulsa."

Jake wouldn't let it go. "So you twisted your arm. Everybody rides with injuries. If you quit now, you won't have a chance at the finals."

"To hell with the finals." Dev punched the pillow, wishing it was his dad's face.

"I don't want to hear that kind of talk. You need to buck up. You can ride with your other arm just as well. And your ribs and legs are only bruised, not broken."

"Leave me the hell alone."

"It's only eight seconds, for Christ's sake. You can stand the pain for that long. I never figured you for a quitter."

"You just said a man needs to know when to let go."

Jake's eyes narrowed to slits. "A man in your position should officially retire, at least finish out the season."

"Dad, take me home."

"If I'd had an attitude like that, I wouldn't be a six-time world champion," his father snapped. "You were out of the running last year from injuries. You can't walk away from a chance at the finals again."

Dev didn't bother to remind his dad that he was a millionaire several times over and had been since he was twenty-two. His old man still saw rodeo as it had been in his day, not as a sport that now had corporate sponsors like Ford, Wrangler, and Justin laying down millions of dollars in prize money. It was a sport that had reached prime-time television, drew huge crowds, and had turned cowboys into businessmen as well as national celebrities. The stakes were high, the competition stiff, and a professional cowboy had to be at the top of his game and in excellent physical condition. By the time a cowboy reached his mid-thirties, the years of injuries started to catch up to him. He was getting too old from a physical standpoint to compete with guys who could be more than fifteen years younger.

He could tell his dad that it wasn't just the injuries making him walk away, but the old man would never understand that riding bulls had lost its glow. He wouldn't understand that Dev knew full well he wasn't competing at capacity and, at his age, he never would again. He'd always planned to retire before he started to backslide. It was too dangerous of a sport for a man who had mentally decided to move on. He'd been fueled by a sense of duty, stubborn determination, and sheer discipline because a rodeo man didn't quit. All the while, though, he'd been waiting for the right moment to walk away. That moment had come when the luck of the draw had put him up against Satan for the third time.

His mind was set. He was going home to the ranch. Ride a sagebrush trail with Granddad; round up strays; listen to the old man's stories. Spend time together before it was too late for both of them.

His dad was still harping. "You're feeling sorry for yourself. You get bucked off, you get back on."

Dev worked his aching head into a more comfortable position in the center of a pillow. "I've been getting back on since I was five years old. This time I'm going to sit on the front porch and not do a damn thing until every bone and tendon in my body is healed. Then I'm going to help Granddad. Seth," —he turned to his brother— "be a good little brother and get me some water so I can take a couple of these painkillers. Doc said I need to start on them before the pain shot wears off."

"You're serious." Seth, still looking half asleep, gave him a fish-eye stare.

"Hell, no, he ain't serious," Jake lashed back, but there was more than angst in his eyes; there was a spark of fear. It wasn't only Dev's life being turned upside down; it was his too. "Since we've both completed our rides, Seth, I want to go home. Now, how about that water?"

Seth got a bottle from the fridge, grumbling about how Dev was being a selfish son of a bitch only thinking of himself. Dev downed the pills and didn't respond to his dad's continued attempt to change his mind. He groped around for his hat, found it, and placed it over his face. By the time Seth had the pickup in traffic, and Garth Brooks appropriately singing "I'm Much Too Young to Feel This Damn Old," Dev was sound asleep.

◆

July stood inside the bathroom stall at the High Heel, stared at the obscene graffiti with a dull mind, and decided she shouldn't have drunk those last two margaritas. Her head pounded to the beat of the music that was so loud it vibrated through the thin walls. She leaned against the stall door to get her head to stop spinning. At least Hooley had stayed sober, drinking only Coke and announcing to the rodeo crowd that he was her designated driver. She had danced with too many cowboys to count, and she'd had a good time for awhile. The drinks she'd consumed had made her a bit reckless, but now she felt depression settling in.

She reached for the toilet handle and was about to pull it when the glint of her wedding ring caught her eye. She drew her hand back and held it out in front of her.

Promises. Lies. Unfaithfulness.

They were all there in that bright and shiny chunk of rock.

Well, to hell with it. To hell with Buck.

She twisted the ring free and chucked it into the water. It hit the bottom with a dull clink. Feeling a deep sense of satisfaction, she pulled the handle and watched the ring swirl out of sight.

◆

Dev woke to darkness. The pickup was motionless. He could hear the hum of the trailer's air conditioner, and, in the distance, the blare of country music. This time it was a female singer belting out an ear-piercing message that made his head feel like it had been run over by a tank.

He removed his hat from his face and stared at the kaleidoscope of colors coming through the trailer's narrow windows and shifting across the ceiling like lights from the aurora borealis. He tried to swallow but his mouth was as dry as a sagebrush in August.

"Goddamn painkillers…make you feel like shit."

He got up on one elbow and from there to a sitting position. He drew back the curtain. The pickup was parked outside the High Heel, a bar he knew well. Neon lights the same colors as those he'd seen on the trailer's ceiling blinked in the shape of a cowboy boot.

"Christ. We could have been halfway home by now."

He swung his legs over the edge of the bed and sat up. He started down the steps but a wave of dizziness forced him to sit back down until he could gain his equilibrium. When he could stand, he positioned himself in the small bathroom, relieved himself, then stood in front of the mirror watching the faucet piddle out tepid water in spurts. Cupping it in one hand, he scrubbed his face until he began to feel human again.

He didn't feel up to changing clothes so settled for brushing the dust off his jeans and removing his sling long enough to cover his dirty, torn shirt with a thin nylon windbreaker emblazoned with rodeo emblems. The windbreaker was too hot for Arizona in the summer, but in the packed, semi-lit, air-conditioned bar he hoped everyone would be too drunk to notice. He covered his uncombed hair with his hat and, with a great deal of difficulty and discomfort, exited the trailer.

Chapter Five

Six feet inside the crowded cowboy bar, Dev found room to stand for a moment and allow his eyes to adjust to the dim, smokey interior. The noise and music made the throbbing in his head feel like a dozen jackhammers clattering all at once.

Stepping aside for a waitress balancing a tray of mixed drinks, he maneuvered toward the packed dance floor, trying to keep people from bumping his sore shoulder and the stitches in his back. Cowboys and cowgirls were belt buckle to belt buckle.

And his old man was right in the middle of it.

Through the blanket of smoke, Dev saw his dad on the dance floor doing a quick two-step with July Jones and looking way too damn cozy. She hadn't changed from earlier and still wore her jeans and white tank top. At the sight of her, his heart flipped, as it always did, and he remembered that she was going to come back to the medical unit to see how he was doing. Well, he didn't hold it against her for not showing up. There was no good reason why she would want to waste her time with a guy who could barely move when she could honky-tonk with an expert. And while it was hard enough to see her with Buck, it was a knife to the chest to see her with his own father.

He couldn't disallow the fact that his old man, at the age of fifty-six, still had the face, physique, and charm to turn a woman's head. He never had any difficulty mesmerizing females of all ages for the length of a night. And one night stands were all he ever wanted anyway.

Both he and July looked three sheets to the wind, something very uncharacteristic for her. In all the years Dev had known her, he couldn't remember her having more than a drink or two at any given time. He'd never seen her sloppy drunk. July carried herself with a natural air of dignity, a lady-like sensuality that commanded respect. Still, she had a fire about her. She didn't seem to know it, and wouldn't have believed it if you'd told her, but he doubted there was a man alive who wouldn't want to burn for awhile in the very center of that fire. Yet the no-account man she had married was too blind and self-centered to appreciate what he had. And tonight, she'd latched on to another just like him.

Dev forced his eyes away from her to search for Seth. He spotted his younger brother at a table bordering the dance floor, nuzzling the neck of a petite, very shapely brunette who was more than likely the "hot little number from New Mexico." Next to him, Dev recognized a stoic-faced, clench-jawed Hooley Wilson, staring out across the dance floor at July and Jake. Immediately Dev sensed undercurrents. He knew all too well the way his dad worked women, and it was without shame or a backward glance. July knew it too, so why was she getting mixed up with him? And what in the hell did it all have to do with Hooley Wilson?

He would never forget the first time he'd laid eyes on July. He'd been behind the chutes in Prescott over a decade ago. He'd been waiting to ride when Buck Jones had sauntered toward him, gripping July's hand and introducing her as his fiancée, showing her off like a trophy.

Dev would never forget the impact he'd felt that first time when he'd seen the sunlight shimmering across her blonde hair like white hot fire framing her flawless face. But the thing that had captivated him the most was her candid smile, unpretentious behavior, and the honesty in those eyes that were the smokey green of unripened oats.

He had been married to Mica at the time and the father of a five-year-old, and July was as good as married to Buck. Even so, his heart had stopped when she'd held out her hand and he'd taken it in his. Their eyes had met and locked, hers as startled as his—as if they recognized each other from another time, another place, a past life, or a reflection of self. It sounded like a romantic cliché, but that's how it had been.

He'd been so distracted when she'd watched him ride that he'd skidded into the dirt face first before the bull had barely cleared the gate. The only consolation was that she'd joined him behind the chutes to see how he was. She'd made small talk and smiled without guile. She'd even brushed the dirt from his cheek with her fingertips. He could still remember the bittersweet jolt he'd felt at that brief moment of contact before Buck had returned from his winning ride to lay claim to her again.

It had bothered Dev more than he had ever cared to admit when she'd married Buck. He had wanted to pull her aside and warn her about him. She had been so starry-eyed, so devoted, and Buck was such a deceiver. While Dev's own marriage had been failing from the start—and finally collapsed—Buck and July's continued, thanks to July's determination to make it work even though it swiftly turned sour. Dev had seen it firsthand plenty of times, and he'd seen the happiness in her eyes fade to haunted sadness.

The four of them had hung around together for a year or so before the rivalry between him and Buck had gotten too strong. It was Dev's divorce with Mica, however, that had ended the four-some. With Mica gone, he and July had become closer friends, sharing long conversations behind the chutes or in a café while Buck was off somewhere drawing praise and admiration from a perpetual line of teen-aged buckle bunnies. July had quit her brief pursuit at barrel racing in exchange for a career in photography and travel writing. He and Buck had moved onto to bigger things with the PBR, and he hadn't seen her very often after that.

Now, when she looked up and saw him standing there, he detected heartache and a sudden sobering as if she had come face-to-face with her conscience. He thought she was going to move away from Jake and turn to him, but Jake, sensing the cool wind that had blown in with his son, tightened his arm around her waist.

The music ended and some of the dancers returned to their seats. Dev threaded his way through the crowd to Seth's table. July and Jake joined them.

"They said you were sleeping." July tried hard to enunciate, but her words were still slurred.

"I was."

"Well, pull up a chair. Join the party. Hooley's staying sober so he can drive. He's such a sweetheart."

Hooley had a determined set to his jaw. "I said I would keep you out of trouble, July, and I meant it." But the look he cast at Jake suggested he knew he was in over his head.

Dev squinted through the thick veil of cigarette smoke. "Where's Buck?"

Anger flashed across July's face as she gathered her drink and downed it in one long swallow. Her tone was indifferent, but her pain was palpable. "The last time I saw the little bastard he was screwing some woman in Ricky Holladay's trailer. So I thought, hey, what the hell, I might as well have a little fun too. After all, that's the cowboy way. Right?"

Maybe she was lashing out in anger, but Dev feared that her liquor-glazed plan to "have a little fun" could take her to a place she would regret tomorrow.

And so could a rounder like his dad.

If he didn't hurt from head to toe, he might have been inclined to stick around and help Hooley keep her out of his dad's clutches, but he wanted to go home, and the mild-mannered Montana bull rider would be no match for the smooth-talking Jake Summers. So he gently took July by the arm and drew her to her feet, knowing, even as he did, that he was opening the door to a whirlwind of shit. His dad would hold onto his manners until they were outside, though, because one good thing about Jake Summers—maybe the only good thing—was that he didn't air his dirty laundry in public.

"Come on, July. I think it's time to call it a night." Dev met his dad's scowl with one of equal force before turning to address Hooley. "I'll see she gets to her hotel room."

Hooley seemed relieved to be taken off duty and didn't object. "She drove a rental car. Want me to follow?"

"Would you?"

"No problem."

Jake stood up, gyring like a top that's about to run out of momentum. He was still holding his liquor better than July. "What gives you the right, boy, to come waltzin' in here, bustin' things up and ruinin' people's fun?"

The band kicked into another song, a fast line dance, forcing them to raise their voices above the hoots and hollers, the pounding beat, and the cowboy boots clomping on the hardwood floor. The room literally vibrated with sound and motion.

"I'm taking July out of here, Dad, before she does something she'll regret tomorrow."

"What she does is her business." Jake tried to reach for her again but some dancers bumped into him, throwing him off balance and forcing him to grab the back of a chair.

"Can't go, Dev," July inserted. "Can't ever go back."

She was unsteady on her feet, leaning into Dev for support. Even though her weight hurt his arm like holy hell, her nearness pulled his mind to a different sort of pain. Her breath tickled his neck; her full breasts were soft and warm against his chest; her flat stomach brushed his loins.

Damn. She was trouble. Pure, sweet trouble. Yet he was compelled to get her out of this place and save her from further heartache.

"What made her go off the deep end anyway? It's not like this is the first time Buck's cheated on her."

His dad shrugged. "Maybe this time was the last straw. What difference does it make? She needs consolation, and she's got a right to have it with whoever she pleases."

"She'll need more than consolation when she rolls over and sees your sorry face on the pillow come morning. Now get her purse and anything else she brought. Seth, you too. Help me get her to the truck. We'll drive her to her hotel."

"Screw you. I'm not ready to leave."

"You can do anything you want after I get her to the truck."

"You can't leave without me. I have the keys. Besides, you're in no condition to drive."

"Neither are you. As for keys, if you won't cooperate, I'll take the spare set from under the hood."

Dev put his good arm around July's waist and steered her across the crowded dance floor. She could barely stand, let alone walk. What she needed was a pot of black coffee — or twelve hours of uninterrupted sleep.

The others followed, not having much choice. Seth's keys weren't going to do him any good without the wheels to go with them, and he was lucid enough to realize that. His girlfriend wasn't happy, but he left with promises to keep.

Jake had gathered July's large leather bag from under the table and was carrying it by the handle. He looked silly as hell, but he was too drunk and preoccupied to notice the amused smiles of those who cleared a path for them. He kept clipping Dev's heels, trying to grab his shoulder, but Dev stayed just beyond reach. He was supporting most of July's weight now as the alcohol took its toll on her. The effort sent searing pain throughout his body.

"I need my drink, Dev. I left it—" She waved toward the table they'd vacated.

"We'll do this again someday, July. I promise."

"Yeah, well...promises suck."

Outside, Jake got a grip on Dev's collar and brought him to a halt. "You quit interfering with my life, boy. It's none of your business what that woman does. You can't stand to think she might be attracted to me."

"If you think she is, then you're hallucinating." Dev gripped July tighter around the waist. She was getting heavier by the second. Her head flopped around on her neck like a Slinky and bounced against his shoulder several times. He thought that last drink must have been the one to send her over the edge. "Christ, Dad, you're an old friend, like Hooley, somebody she ought to be safe with, but here you are taking advantage of her condition and state of mind. Hell, she's young enough to be your daughter. Would you want some guy your age hitting on your daughter?"

Jake managed to look hurt and defiant all at once. "I don't have a daughter."

"Well, I do, and I sure as hell wouldn't want some old man like you taking advantage of a vulnerable moment."

"I'm not an old man, damn it."

"Whatever. If July takes the notion to warm up to you when she's sober—and I doubt it—then I won't stand in her way. Until then, this is the position I'm taking." Dev bent his head to July's. "What hotel are you staying at, darlin'?"

Her brow wrinkled as she thought about it. "I don't think I have one."

"All right. We'll get you one. You can go home tomorrow."

"No." She shook her head. "Can't go home."

He doubted he could have been as patient with anyone else. "Then where will you go?"

She looked up at him with those eyes that, at the moment, reminded him of a lost child. "I could go with you."

His heart melted. "Do you mean to the ranch? Because that's where I'm headed."

"Why not? I like your ranch. The horses...the cows... Baxter...." Her eyes rounded as if a new thought had made its way past the liquor in her brain. She started to look around the parking lot, searching for something. "I think I brought a car." Then she giggled, covering her mouth with her hand. "So I guess I...can't go with you."

"Your car is right over here," Hooley explained. "It's a rental, remember? We'll get your stuff out of it, and I'll return it to the airport for you."

"Well, now...there's a solution." She patted him on the cheek. "You're so smart. Such a sweetie too." She seemed to be getting drunker by the second, if that was possible.

Hooley showed them the way to the rental. He had seen her put the key in the front compartment of her bag. While Jake held it up, he dug into the pouch until he found it. Hooley drove it next to the pickup truck. Between all of them, they transferred her bags and belongings to the travel trailer. She didn't want them to smash her Stetson so she put it on her head—backwards. Dev didn't bother to right it.

With his body aching from carrying too much of her weight, he propped her against the hood of the truck while he shook Hooley's hand and thanked him for looking after her.

"I won't be seeing you in Tulsa, so good luck."

Hooley grinned. "I might have a fighting chance now that you're out of the running." Then he leaned close to Dev's ear. Lowering his voice, he said, "Now that she's made the break with Buck, don't let her change her mind."

"That might be tough, Hooley, but I'll do my best."

A peculiar look suddenly crossed July's face, her eyes went blank, and she started a spiral toward the pavement. Hooley made a lunge for her. Dev tried to hold onto her with his good arm, but it was Jake who kept her limp body from hitting the parking lot concrete. He gathered her up, re-staking his claim.

"She won't be good for nothin' now," he grumbled.

Dev shook his head in disgust as he scooped July's Stetson from the ground. There was nothing more maddening than dealing with drunks.

His dad headed to the trailer with July, but Dev caught his arm. "Oh, no, you don't. She's riding in the truck with me. You and Seth get in the trailer and sleep until you're sober."

Despite more grumbling, they relented. Seth handed over the keys and flopped onto the sofa; Jake deposited July in the back seat of the quad cab then staggered back to the trailer and up the steps to the bed. They were both out cold as soon as their heads hit their respective pillows. At least Dev wouldn't have to listen to them on the long road home, and that was about as good as his life got.

Chapter Six

Northeastern Nevada

Baxter Summers ground the unfiltered butt of his cigarette into the dirt with his boot toe until there was nothing left of it. The cattle had cropped the grass short next to the barbed wire fence, but it was still tall enough for a spark to set it off. It was another dry year—the third in a row. It hadn't rained for six weeks, and there hadn't been much snow the previous winter. Even if the rains came at the end of July or early August, as they normally did, it would still be too little too late to revive the stunted grass.

He reseated his sweat-stained hat, squinting under the battered brim at the distant looming mountains of the Jarbidge Wilderness and those closer, clothed with aspens and pines and cut through by rivers—the Jarbidge, Bruneau, Mary's, Owyhee, Bull Run, and the North Fork of the Humboldt. Wildflowers dressed mountain meadows and rocky knolls, while creeks—many of them dry this year—crisscrossed sagebrush valleys and rolling grasslands where cattle, sheep, and wildlife grazed in the sun.

He took a deep breath of the clean mountain air as he gazed up at the ever-changing sky. He thought of the cycles of wet and dry, the good years and bad. He'd been on this range his whole life—nearly eighty years now—and he'd learned to take this country in stride. If a man didn't, it would break him. A man had to cut his losses and keep going; and he had to keep enough notches in his belt to tighten it up when times got hard.

If truth be known, there had been more bad years than good, but he'd never considered leaving or doing anything else. He'd been born on this land; he didn't know how to leave it. If he had his way, he'd die on it while fixing fence or rounding up cattle on his little buckskin gelding, Dinky.

It was a hell of an undignified name for such a smart pony, but the horse was only fourteen hands. A bigger man would have looked silly on him, but Baxter was a wiry five-foot-nine and didn't weigh more than a hundred and fifty. The horse was Baxter's favorite; a true cow pony with spirit, speed, and endurance. And he never tried to buck, which was what Baxter liked the most because he was too darned old to be taking tumbles off a horse. He wouldn't admit that to anyone, but it was true.

He'd had adversaries of course—Uncle Sam, Mother Nature, and livestock prices that hadn't increased much in sixty years—but, all in all, he felt fortunate. He'd had a good wife and good health. The only real disappointment was his son.

He'd wanted to work alongside Jake, have him take an interest in the ranch. He'd put so much of his blood and sweat into this land, and yes, even an occasional tear when nobody was looking. He hated to see it slip back into the wilderness it had been when his great-grandfather had homesteaded it over a century ago. Or worse, see it go to housing developments. But already he could see all that coming as ridiculous labor laws, escalating operating expenses, and his age forced him to cut back on his operation to the bare bones and try to get by with two hired men for the daily ranch work and temporaries for the farming. At least when it came time for branding and roundups, Baxter and several of the neighboring ranchers got together with their families and full-time cowhands to help each other out.

He'd been lucky to find the Forrest family a few years ago: Ern and Sarah, and their son and daughter-in-law, Kurt and Babs. Before that, he'd had trouble finding and keeping good help. Plenty of people wanted to be a cowboy, but they didn't want to do the work that went along with it. They wanted city wages and couldn't seem to abide blisters and their own company.

As times changed and chipped away at all the old traditions and ways of life, Baxter drew strength from the accomplishments that had taken place in the past one hundred years as three generations of Summers men had made a living off this land. He didn't want to be the one to sell out.

He squatted at the creek and stuck his hand into the cold water and fished out his canteen. He took a long, unhurried swallow, knowing he shouldn't dwell on the past, but it was hard not to when all the future held was more loneliness and deteriorating health. Those had been good times, and he sorely missed them. Sorely missed his late wife, Cecilia, too.

After drinking his fill, he recapped the canteen and looped the strap around the saddle horn. He stood for a moment next to Dinky and gazed down the length of the fence that disappeared into the horizon. There was plenty of daylight left, but he was tired and decided to call it a day. There would always be repairs to be made somewhere on the miles and miles of barbed wire fences that encircled the ranch; there was no reason to get in a hurry. All he ever had these days was time. Besides, he didn't mind fencing. It was peaceful, steady work, and it served a purpose. Still, when he thought about passing on, he hoped there would be no fences in heaven, just open range and good horses on which to ride it.

"Well, let's go home, Cappy," he said to his blue heeler dog that had fallen asleep under a sagebrush. Hearing Baxter's voice, the dog woke with a start and leaped to his short legs. He was getting old, too, and wasn't quite as limber and energetic as he used to be, but on occasion, like Baxter, he forgot his age and tried to act young again.

Baxter shucked his fencing pliers, hammer, and staples in his saddle bags. Gathering his leather reins, he swung into the saddle. He had only to lean forward and Dinky pivoted on his back feet and moved out on a long, ground-eating walk, his small ears pointed forward with eagerness.

They followed the fence line for a while, then took the short-cut through the sagebrush to the old summer cabin. He would leave Dinky there in the pasture with the other horses and drive back to ranch headquarters down in the foothills.

Baxter found himself thinking that a sirloin steak at Joe's Crossroads Café would taste darn good. They served it with mashed potatoes, brown gravy, and hot yeast rolls smothered with real butter and homemade jam. Sometimes they had vegetables and fruit in season. His favorites were sweet peas and pears. He thought he would order a lemon meringue pie, too, and have them box it up so he could bring it home. A big slice would taste good tonight while he watched the ten o'clock news. They made pies almost as good as Cecilia used to do.

It wasn't just the food, though. Almost always he'd run into a neighbor or two, and they'd sit and talk about ranching, the weather, cattle prices, local gossip, the old times, or the way the world was speeding past them. If he happened to be there alone, the waitresses always carried on with him, joking and sometimes even sitting down and talking if they weren't too busy. He knew they only doted over him because he was an old man and they felt safe with him—or sorry for him—but it was all okay because it was the only female attention he got these days. It would be nice to have more than the one-sided conversations he'd been having with Cappy and Dinky. Besides, he'd gotten a week's worth of dishes and pots and pans washed up last night, and he sure didn't want to start over with it tonight.

He'd tried—God knows he'd tried—to get first Jake and then his grandsons to settle down and take over the ranch. For twenty years now he'd been living alone while they gallivanted all over kingdom come, chasing gold buckles. He wasn't going to live forever even if they seemed to think he was. He wished they'd give up that nonsense and come home.

Jake, for one, had never been prone to sweat in the sun, although he had gladly worn his sorry ass down to the bone chasing glory. When Jake hadn't been able to ride the bulls anymore, he'd sent Dev and Seth out to tangle with them while he hollered out advice and criticism. Baxter figured, knowing Jake, it was more of the latter he dished out than the former. Baxter hated to say it, but he and Jake, his only child, had never gotten on worth a tinker's damn.

Now, maybe it was because he was tired, or because he had his mind on that damned Jake who wouldn't grow up and refused to settle down, but when that sage hen flew up out of the brush and right into Dinky's face, the little gelding hit the air going sideways. And Baxter wasn't ready at all.

Chapter Seven

July regained consciousness on a long strand of Nevada highway running north. Groaning and clutching her throbbing head, she swung her feet off the seat and sat up. Morning sunlight reflected off the highway's patched, gray surface, forcing her to shield her eyes against the stabbing brilliance. "Oh, my God...my head."

She flopped back down and, for the first time, became aware of the man in the front seat of the pickup. Afraid of who she'd find beneath that cowboy hat—for vague memories of last night flickered through the pain—she sat up again, peered around at his face, and found herself looking at Dev Summers with his left arm confined in a blue sling. He saw her in the rearview mirror and smiled. "You're awake."

"Thank God for familiar faces. Where am I, and how did I get here?"

"You don't remember?"

"I remember a lot of margaritas and....I didn't do something really stupid, did I?"

He chuckled, glancing over his shoulder at her. "No. You were rescued in the nick of time by a knight in shining armor."

"Ah, my memory returns." She rubbed her temples. "Damn that son of a bitch."

"And here I thought I was doing you a favor."

His sunglasses blocked the teasing glint in his eyes, but she heard it in his voice and saw it in that lopsided grin. "Not you, Sir Lancelot. I was referring to Buck. If it hadn't been for him, I wouldn't have made a fool out of—" Suddenly she clutched her stomach. "Oh, God. I'm going to be sick."

"Hold on. I'm pullin' over."

In a matter of seconds, he brought the pickup and trailer to a shuddering halt. She yanked open the door, nearly falling out. Stumbling, she barely made it to the borrow pit before expelling last night's drinks onto the gravel between her cowboy boots. Two cars whizzed by, but she was too sick to care.

Dev waited behind the wheel, wishing he could do something to ease her pain, like beat the crap out of Buck Jones. Unfortunately, in his present condition, revenge was no more than a distant dream.

After July had recovered, he put on the emergency brake so he could leave the engine running, then he maneuvered out from behind the wheel and limped to the trailer. The hours driving had added insult to injury. At least the medication was keeping the pain at bay. He'd been struggling with drowsiness, too, so it was a relief to have a break. Maybe he'd turn the wheel over to July in an hour or so.

As quietly as possible he opened the trailer door, hoping the sudden stop hadn't brought his dad and Seth to consciousness. The longer he didn't have to listen to those two, the better. To his relief, they were still sleeping soundly. He retrieved a couple of Diet Cokes from the refrigerator and pressed the trailer door closed with a faint click.

July had returned to the edge of the pavement and was sitting on the ground with her back against the front tire, daintily trying to wipe her mouth with the only thing she had available— the cuff of the jacket he'd lain over her while she'd been sleeping.

She looked up at him sheepishly. "You weren't supposed to see that."

"What some people won't do to get a new jacket." He handed her one of the Cokes then reached into the glove box to produce a roll of smashed and tattered toilet paper. "This is about as close as a cowboy gets to Kleenex."

July accepted the tissue, finding herself captured once again by the face she knew so well, the face that grew more handsome and honed with each year. It was easy to understand why every unmarried female who followed the rodeo wanted to win his heart. Even the married ones had their daydreams of being in his arms. What she didn't understand is why he had closed himself off to everybody after his divorce from Mica. Rumor was they'd only gotten married in the first place because they'd had to. It was one of those teenage romances that had been all wrong.

After tearing off a length of tissue, she turned her head to dab at her lips, ashamed that he had to witness her disgrace. Then she took a long swallow of the Coke, appreciating the way it burned the bad taste from her mouth. When she drew the can away from her lips, she said, "Thank you. I don't know what I would have done without you."

He presented that crooked grin again. "Something you'd have regretted more than likely. And with my old man to boot."

She leaned her head against the tire, assured by his smile that everything would be all right. "I feel like such a fool. Believe me, your dad is a handsome guy and has a nice shoulder to cry on, but that's as far as it would have gone."

"Don't take it personal. Dad can bring out the worst in the best of us."

"He *can* turn on the charm."

"At least you didn't sell your soul for a dance and a two-dollar drink."

"Words of wisdom from a voice of experience?"

He shifted his weight to the other leg. For a moment, he seemed lost in the follies of his past as he gazed across the wide sagebrush basin that sprawled peacefully between north-south bands of stark, inhospitable ranges of mountains. She thought she saw the emptiness of the land reflected in those eyes as blue as the Nevada sky.

"I've done it a time or two," he replied. "It's not something you walk away from with a sense of pride." Then he painstakingly lowered himself to his haunches next to her, removed his sunglasses from his pocket and handed them to her. "Here. They'll cut the glare. Maybe help the headache. If that doesn't work, I've got an arsenal of painkillers."

"Don't you need them—the sunglasses?" She asked as she put them on.

"I have another pair in the glove box."

Loneliness and despair seized her. She was glad he couldn't see the moisture pooling in her eyes. "I'll catch a bus at the next town, Dev. I'm sorry about this. Sorry about the inconvenience."

"Inconvenience? Helping each other is what friends are for. Last night you wanted to come to the ranch. There's no need to change your mind now. It'll clear your head and put everything into perspective; I guarantee it. And you can stay as long as you want."

"I couldn't impose."

"You won't be. We'll put you to work." He grinned. "I can guarantee that too."

She jerked upright. "Oh, my God, my bag! My camera was in there. And my journal. If anybody reads it—"

She tried to get to her feet, but Dev placed a restraining hand on her shoulder. "We got it, July. We got everything you had with you in the car."

She slumped back against the tire and closed her eyes against another sharp pain in her head. "You really are a saint."

His brows came together in a concerned knot. He placed a hand on her forehead. "Mmm, as I expected."

"What?" She looked worried.

"If you think I'm a saint, then you're definitely delusional. But you're real pretty when you smile."

"Talk about a sweet-talker."

"Hey, I learned from the best. So are you coming with us or not? If you want to go home, we'd better take you back to Vegas so you can catch a plane."

"Where are we anyway?"

"A considerable distance from a bus stop."

His playful tone shifted her smile to a derisive slant. "I was beginning to suspect as much. All the while we've been on the side of the road, only two cars have passed."

"They were probably lost."

He made her laugh. She loved him for that. Loved him for being here when she needed him most. She wanted to pull him into her arms and hold onto him until she felt strong enough to stand alone. But being in Dev's arms. . .oh, that would be playing with fire, a fire she might not be able to put out.

But the sanctuary he offered sounded tempting. Maybe it *was* what she needed. A place where Buck would never think of looking. Yesterday she'd been so confident about walking away and never looking back, but now that she was faced with doing it, the apprehensions began to settle in. She had never been strong where Buck was concerned. All he'd ever had to do was flash that boyish grin, say he was sorry, beg forgiveness, profess his love, then promise to never step over the line again. And she would go back. She always went back out of obligation to her marriage vows. She didn't want to do it this time. She wouldn't.

"I left a rental car at the High Heel."

"Hooley's returning it today."

"You're making this too easy, Dev."

"Then maybe it's the right thing to do."

She not only regretted her actions last night, but regretted the road she'd taken all those years ago that had landed her in this emotional wasteland. Maybe it wasn't too late to straighten the road, to take control of her future in a wiser way than she had when she'd been that naive, lonely young woman who had hitched her wagon to Buck Jones's star.

"The ranch sounds good, Dev. And I *would* like to see your grandfather again, but I will only stay if you let me earn my keep. I can cook and help out around the place. I'm not too shabby on a horse either."

Dev took her by the elbow and helped her to her feet. "Granddad would be happy to hear that, especially the part about the cooking."

July allowed him to help her into the front seat with him, although, from the stiff way he was moving, it should have been her helping him. She offered to drive, but he said he'd give her an hour to see if her headache went away.

She settled near the passenger window in the front seat, thinking again of how fortunate she'd been that he had come along when he had. Unlike Buck, nothing was conditional with Dev. He had always accepted her for what she was. He'd always been a true friend, one she could trust with her life. From the very beginning there had been a kinship between them that had made both Mica and Buck jealous. Over the years she had wondered what would have happened if they had met first. Still, that was a place she wouldn't go. Getting romantically involved with someone she considered a good friend was out of the question.

She studied the chiseled line of his jaw. The introspective look had settled on his face again as he looked down the long road home. What was he thinking? He had regrets, that much was certain. Like her, he had changed over the years. At twenty-something, he'd had the world by the horns. Now he looked like a man who was more than ready to hand it over to somebody else.

A significant change in him had taken place after his divorce and after he had fought for, and lost, custody of Dusty, his daughter. July remembered well the little dark-haired dynamo who had been her father's spitting image and who was usually seen riding high on his broad shoulders. When she had gotten too big for that, she was by his side, like glue, with her small hand in his, her tiny booted feet trying to keep up to his longer strides. They'd been inseparable, which was fine with Mica because she'd always had her own agenda.

July would have loved to have had a child.

Like a free-fall, her mood plummeted even more, hitting rock bottom with a jolt. She looked at the Great Basin vastness from over the top of the roll of toilet paper that was pressed between the windshield and the dashboard, reminding her just how long a Nevada highway could be. Without warning, she wanted to cry.

"Are you going to be all right?"

She felt Dev's eyes on her and knew he wasn't referring to the hangover. How could he be so intuitive to her every mood?

It was a moment before she could swallow the lump in her throat. "I can't believe I left. Just like that. No planning, nothing."

"Sometimes that bend in the road takes us by surprise."

"And when it does, there's no turning back, is there?"

"I'll stop anytime you tell me to, July."

"No. Keep going. Just keep going."

They talked awhile and got caught up on what had happened since the last time they'd seen each other. She teased him about being a millionaire and still driving his truck to rodeos instead of flying. He confessed that he had to watch his dad and Seth or they'd go through that money quicker than a Mississippi gambler. He explained that they normally didn't take the trailer, but they'd brought it this time because the event hadn't been far from home and they'd had plenty of time before the next rodeo.

"Besides," he confided. "I don't like to fly when it isn't necessary."

"You'll ride killer bulls but you're afraid to fly?"

"Hey," he defended. "It's not nearly as far to fall."

They reminisced about the good times, which drifted into reminders of times they preferred not to remember nor discuss. In an introspective lull, Dev turned on the radio and fiddled with it until he found a station playing classic country music. July removed her journal from her bag and began to write:

> *I shield my eyes against the piercing radiance of the afternoon sun. Intense heat shimmers up from the pavement, forming one mirage after another. I close my eyes for a moment and try to see the images of what I left behind—Buck, the house, the city—just to see if my heart might ache with regret. But the images are swallowed by the pungent reality of the ubiquitous sage, and by the vast emptiness that diminishes human existence to the importance of an ant hill.*
>
> *Nevada makes me feel even more obscure than Buck did, like a stink bug trying to cross the highway before being flattened by somebody's tires. But that's okay—about Nevada making me feel the way it does—because I don't want to be seen or found or risk losing this unexpected, newfound freedom. For the first time in my life, I want to be invisible.*
>
> *A family of my own was all I ever wanted. The need was always buried in the root of everything I did. Yet, here I am, alone, running hard and fast and long. I wonder if in a day or two, or a decade or two, I'll regret my flight and find that I have merely exchanged one desperation for another. Still, there was no substance to anything I left behind. I was little more than a shadow in that existence, and I am no longer honor bound to emptiness.*
>
> *When I look back, I see nothing but pavement, and daylight will run out long before the highway ever does. Then I will be safe in the darkness, enclosed in a protective cocoon where the delusions will no longer control me. Where the shadow will find solidarity with the night. Where newfound pieces of life will make me whole once again.*

Chapter Eight

The first thing Baxter became aware of was the heavy, pungent scent of sagebrush and the stems of dry grass beneath his cheek. He felt no pain in those initial moments, just a sense of bewilderment. How could he have been caught so completely off-guard? Hell, he hadn't fallen off a horse—or been bucked off—for over twenty years. Even then he'd been young enough to go asking for it and had been agile enough to hit the ground rolling, not like a damned sack of bricks.

He hauled himself to his feet and decided nothing was broken, but his pride was bruised along with his shoulder and wrist that had taken the brunt of the fall. A spot on his cheek was tingling, and when he touched it, his fingers came away bloody.

Dinky nudged him in the back and seemed relieved to see him on his feet. Baxter turned to him and took up the reins. "Why'd you go and let a sage hen spook you like that? A few years ago you'd have known it was there long before it flew up in your face. You might not be getting too old for this shit, but I am. And you, Cappy, why weren't you out there flushing it out?"

Cappy's ears drooped. He whined and looked sufficiently reprimanded.

Baxter looped the reins around Dinky's neck and hauled himself into the saddle, still shaken and thinking it was a good thing he hadn't broken a leg or his back—or his neck. Had he, he would have lain out here in the sagebrush until he died because nobody would have missed him for days, maybe even weeks. By the time they would have found him, if they did, there would have been nothing left but what the coyotes and buzzards hadn't carried away.

The thing that upset him the most, though, wasn't the fact that he might have died out here, it was the humiliation that it would have come from falling off his horse. That stung his pride. Why just a month ago, Jake had told him he was getting too old to be riding horses and shouldn't go out alone. The last few years, Jake had taken every opportunity to make mention of Baxter's degenerating condition and his escalating age. Well, damn it, Baxter didn't need to be reminded that the best years of his life were behind him, so he had lashed out. "If you think you're going to keep me off my horses, Jake, then you'd better think again. The day comes I can't straddle a horse, then I might as well be dead. As for going out alone, I don't have much choice—do I?—since you won't stay home longer than it takes to get a fresh set of clothes."

Baxter pointed Dinky down the trail again, feeling soreness settling into every bone and muscle in his body. His knees were quaking, too, as he tried to grip the sides of the horse. That tumble had shaken him up more than he cared to admit.

All in all, he figured he'd messed things up worse than a chicken scratching in a pile of cow dung. He had a dilemma, and he saw only one solution to it. By the time he got back to the cabin and turned Dinky loose in the pasture, his mind was set. He wasn't going to tell the boys anything. The scrape on his face would be healed by the time they got home, and if it wasn't, he'd say he had caught himself with a piece of barbed wire. They wouldn't question that.

◆

An hour later, Baxter drove his flatbed Ford over the top of a tumbleweed that had snagged on something in the middle of the gravel road. His aches had settled even deeper, and he thought that soaking in a tub of hot water with a cup of vinegar in it might be a good remedy to pull the soreness out. He'd have to do something about his cheek too. At the cabin, he'd cleaned off the dried blood and put an antiseptic on it, but it throbbed now and his whole cheekbone had turned purple.

The cut needed stitches, but he had no intention of going to the emergency room. He was too tired. Besides, they'd charge him several hundred dollars if they charged him a dime. Some time back, one of the boys had ended up with a bunch of steri-strips from some mishap. He would use a few of those and that would be good enough. At his age, it didn't matter if he ended up with a scar.

The Ford nearly stalled as he took his foot off the gas, reminding him that he needed to fix the carburetor or he was going to be left high and dry one of these days. If it would just hold out until Dev got home, then maybe he could get the kid to take a look at it before he hit the road again. He seemed to enjoy tinkering with the damn thing, whereas Baxter didn't have the patience or the eyesight for it anymore.

As he turned down the gravel road leading to the main house, he shifted gears and felt the sharp pain in his shoulder again. A few minutes later, he pulled up in front of the two-story, white frame farmhouse. When the dust cleared, he opened the door and stuck his foot out, only to draw it right back inside and sit there gripping the steering wheel.

The house, with its second-story dormers and wraparound porch, sat in its wide valley as peaceful as it had been for as long as he could remember, overlooking Mustang Creek and its broad, grassy meadows. From behind, it was protected by the gentle rise of rolling hills and the upthrust of the Jarbidge Mountains that curved over its shoulders like a giant's arm. The once-painted picket fence was still on the verge of falling down where it ran between the two old silver-leaf poplars. Everything was as Baxter had left it. Everything, that is, except the black Dodge pickup parked in the driveway.

Dread shallowed Baxter's lungs making it hard to draw air. He hadn't figured anybody would be around to see the shape he was in, but now he'd have to put that story of his into play. He toyed with the notion of high-tailing it back to the mountains, but it was too late, thanks to Cappy who was already off the flatbed and running to the house, carrying out his duties by barking at the pickup in the driveway.

"You won't keep me off my horse, Jake Summers," he muttered. "You just try."

He got out of the Ford, mentally rolling up his pant legs, because a smart man did that before stepping out into deep shit.

By the time Baxter's foot reached the first porch step, he was angry. Angry that Jake had put him in this position in the first place. Angry that he had proved Jake right by falling off his horse. Angry that he was old. Angry that he was forced to be on the defensive all the time and skirt issues to keep peace between him and Jake. Hell, he'd even had to start hiding everything from candy bars to conversations to keep Jake off his back. If his son had his way, he'd put him in an old folks' home so he wouldn't have to deal with him. Maybe Baxter *was* too old to be riding horses, but he'd go hang himself out in the barn before he'd let Jake hog-tie him.

He heaved a heavy sigh and stepped inside.

Voices led him to the living room. By the time he looked into the room, he'd taken a battle stance, ready to defend himself, but he was thrown off guard by the woman sitting in his recliner. He hadn't seen her for years, yet July Jones hadn't changed. He knew something was off kilter, though, when there was no sign of Buck. He didn't like the boys bringing women to the house unless they planned to marry them—something he'd given up on in this life-time—but for whatever reason she was here, July's presence was going to change the complexion of things. Men couldn't have an all-out fight in the presence of a woman, so he wasn't going to look a gift horse in the mouth.

Jake took one look at his face and said, "Hell, Dad. What happened? You didn't get bucked off your horse, did you?"

Baxter rankled. "No, I didn't get bucked off my horse, but I imagine you'd like to hear that I did so you could say 'I told you so'."

"Then what *did* happen?"

"I had a run-in with a rotten fence post and some barbed wire. I went to pull a staple and the post let loose and hit me in the face. Now, enough said." Silencing Jake, he softened his eyes and his voice as he gave his attention to July. "Well, young lady, it's been a good many years since I saw you."

July rose from the chair, offering her hand and a smile. The gentleness that surrounded her was like an aura of golden light, so in contrast to the hardness of the Summers men. It caused Baxter to forget his anger and loneliness, his frustration at getting old, even his need for a smoke. It had been that way when Cecilia had been alive, and he felt the pang of his wife's death more than ever.

"It's good to see you again, Baxter. It's been too long."

"That it has," he replied. "Now, tell me, how did you get hooked up with this bunch? I hope it wasn't by choice."

She laughed. "A little by choice, a little by accident."

Before she could say more, Seth chimed in. "She caught Buck cheatin' on her and we found her at the High Heel, three sheets to the wind. She didn't want to go home, so here she is."

July looked as if she would have crawled into a hole if one had materialized. "I don't usually drink. I was just feeling sorry for myself for awhile."

Baxter threw Seth a warning glare. Wasn't it just like that kid to have no tact? "It's all right, July. Every one of us has overindulged at one time or another—and for less reason. Isn't that right, Seth?"

"Sure, Grandad. Sure."

Baxter saw a shadow pass over July's eyes. He'd heard about Buck's unfaithfulness. There was a weakness in the man's character that Baxter always figured would come to no good in the end. He was all hot air, no substance, a bandy rooster strutting around as if he were the best thing to ever grace the earth.

Baxter said, "I'm glad you came to visit, July. Now, you all just continue what you were doing. I'm going to see if I can find something to eat before my big gut eats my little gut."

Dev quickly rose from the sofa. "We could all use something to eat. I'll help you."

July offered to help, too, but Baxter said she'd be much more useful if she'd stay in the living room and keep Jake and Seth out from under foot.

When Baxter and Dev were alone in the kitchen, Baxter got a good look at his oldest grandson, and he didn't like what he saw. "Well, son, you look like you've been dragged for a mile through the sagebrush at the end of a short rope."

Dev ran a weary hand through his hair. The injuries and the long hours behind the wheel had taken their toll. "I've been better, Granddad."

"Maybe a good meal will help. I was going to go over to Joe's but, well, that's a long story."

Dev knew if his grandfather wanted to disclose the facts about his injury, he would. If he didn't, there was no sense trying to pry it from him. "What can I do to help?"

"Pull a stool up to the sink, and I'll bring the spuds for you to wash. Looks like that's about all you're up to."

Dev performed the task one-handed. While Baxter peeled and sliced the potatoes into long, thin slices—and muttered that he was sure getting damned tired of doing his own cooking— Dev removed several packages of sirloin steak from the freezer and placed them in the microwave to defrost. From the living room, they heard Jake offer to get some aspirins for July's headache but then he told Seth to run and fetch them.

Baxter glanced in the direction of the living room and lowered his voice. "That damned fool is four years shy of sixty, and he's falling all over that woman like a sixteen-year-old kid. What in the hell's the matter with him?"

Dev shrugged. "You know Dad. He'll be chasing women til the day he dies."

Baxter shook his head. "I went wrong somewhere with him, but it's too late to rectify it, I suppose."

"You can't blame yourself, Granddad. Sooner or later a man has to take responsibility for himself."

"If that's the case, we're in for a long wait. Now, are you going to tell me what happened to you?"

Dev went through the unpleasant details of his ride on Satan 101 that had led to rescuing July from his dad's clutches. "She said she'd only stay if we let her cook and help around."

Baxter's eyes lit up. "Well, this day is turning out pretty good after all. I wouldn't object at all to having a *decent* woman around this place again. One who can do something besides entertain Jake and Seth. She isn't sweet on one of them, is she?"

Dev noticed how the old man's grumpiness returned at the mention of that possibility. Most of the women his dad brought home didn't have enough class to fill a snuff can. They wouldn't have waited until supper was cold on the plates before wandering out to the bunkhouse with him to "see the ranch." Granddad never allowed their shenanigans under his roof.

"No, she's just on the run right now," Dev finally replied.

"Well, I hope she has better sense than to take up with either of them. Of course, she wasn't smart enough to cut a swath around Buck. I suppose some women just have a knack for picking the wrong men."

"Maybe she won't make the same mistake twice."

While Dev put the sirloins on the gas grill outside, Baxter filled him in about how the cattle were doing on the summer range and how the brothers doing the custom farming were reliable but still weren't getting the hay up as quick as Baxter would have liked.

"Like everybody else nowadays, they've got too damn many irons in the fire."

Baxter dropped the sliced potatoes in some oil to deep-fry them. While they cooked, Dev opened two cans of green beans to heat in the microwave. All the while he tried to listen to the conversation in the living room but couldn't hear more than a few scattered words and some laughter now and then. He told himself not to be jealous that July might be enjoying his dad's practiced charm, or Seth's sweet talk and suggestive one-liners that always worked well on the buckle bunnies. It didn't matter. She would go back to Buck; she always did.

When the food was ready, Dev told the three of them to come and eat. Seth and Jake sauntered in on either side of July as if they thought she still wasn't capable of walking a straight line. They seated her at the table between them. It was pathetic to see them not only trying to gain her favor, but competing with each other to do it. It was a sure sign, at least to Dev, that neither of them had any true feelings for her. They were just looking for another one-night stand and would take it where they could get it.

For most of the meal, his dad and Seth relayed to him the tidbits they'd pried out of July while they'd been in the living room with her. How she'd been having a good time traveling all over the West taking pictures on assignment for various magazines.

"She's like the guy who used to be on that television show who went across the country on his motorcycle, just wandering and being free. You know the one." Jake was more animated than usual as he included everyone in his comment.

"I think that was before our time," Dev said.

Jake turned to Baxter, still trying to get a spark of acknowledgment from somebody. "Dad, you remember the show. They had this great theme song about 'goin' down a long, lonesome highway'."

"Oh, yeah," Baxter finally recollected. "The guy never had a purpose that I could see except getting in the middle of other people's affairs then riding off into the sunset when he got them all ironed out. Had a different woman in every episode."

"Sounds like a man you can truly relate to, Dad," Dev remarked dryly.

Jake shot a warning scowl at Dev, who pretended he didn't notice as he tried to cut his steak without success. With the knife in his right hand, he tried to hold the meat on his plate with his left that was restricted by the sling. Pain streaked through his shoulder. Inhaling sharply, he dropped both utensils and grabbed his shoulder.

July frowned with concern. "Are you all right?"

He nodded, slowing releasing his breath.

"Here, let me help you with that."

She left her chair and bent next to him, cutting the steak in neat, bite-size pieces. He could smell the soft scent of her perfume and wondered again what he'd been thinking when he'd asked her to come here. To have her so close and not be able to touch her was going to be more torturous than all his injuries.

"Jake says you've got a good shot at the championship this year," she commented. "Maybe even that million-dollar jackpot again. But I wonder if you should be pushing it."

Dev took another deep breath, this time to tamp down the rising anger. Why couldn't the old bastard ever keep his mouth shut and quit living vicariously through him and Seth? Dev couldn't fault July for not knowing about his plans to retire, or, for that matter, that his injuries were too serious to get back into the running, even if he'd wanted to. He hadn't mentioned any of it to her on the drive up here. Except for an hour or so when she'd been writing in her journal, they'd made small talk, then he'd turned the wheel over to her while he slept.

"I've made the decision to retire and stay here on the ranch to help Granddad," he explained. "Dad knows that."

Seth winked at July. "Now that July's here, maybe I'll stick around too. God knows she'll need someone to liven this place up with only Dev and Granddad for entertainment."

Jake's eyes shone with a suggestive glimmer. "That's not such a bad idea."

Baxter shot him a look that had the punch of a mule's two-footed kick. "You boys keep it up, you'll have her standing on the road trying to hitch a ride out of here."

"As for Dev and the championship," Jake went on as if he hadn't heard his dad's warning, "he wants it no matter what he tells you. He'll be back."

"Oh, I don't think so," Seth quipped. "Since Tim got killed, Dev's developed a streak of something right up the middle of his back, and I don't think it's blood poisoning."

Dev's appetite, or what there was of it, vanished. He set his utensils aside and slid his chair back. "If you'll excuse me, July, I need to take a handful of painkillers and go to bed. I'm not sure what hurts worse, my throbbing arm, or my aching ass." He gave Seth a hard look of contempt then left the room.

He hauled himself up one stair after another and down the hall to his bedroom. It was another slow effort to get out of his clothes and crawl between the sheets. He thought of Tim dying in his arms, and the others who had died before him. He thought of the pain and the "try" and the emptiness of defeat; of the fragile, fleeting moments of fame and glory. He thought of the years, the miles, the women, the towns, and how it had all eventually converged into one big blur.

Hell, he was just tired. Things would look better tomorrow.

He closed his eyes, but they kept popping open and staring at the ceiling. He started to think that if only his eyes had been wide open fifteen years sooner, maybe he wouldn't be here now, broken and alone.

Chapter Nine

"That wasn't called for," Baxter snapped. "Tim was a good friend of Dev's. A damn good friend."

"Oh, hell, Granddad, it was only a joke."

"Then it was a bad one." A further lashing was poised on Baxter's tongue, but he opted to swallow it for July's sake. His chair scraped across the vinyl floor as he pushed it back from the table. "I'm going to shower and then watch the weather report. You boys clean up this mess." He turned to July; his tone softened. "They can handle the cleanup. You just take it easy."

"I don't mind helping. Really."

"Well, that's up to you, but watch these two that they don't stand by and let you do it all." After Jake and Seth's good-natured objections that they would never dream of doing such a thing, Baxter went right on as if he hadn't heard them. "They'll sure enough take advantage of your good nature if you let them."

Smiling, she said, "I'll keep that in mind."

Jake waited until Baxter had left the room, then he turned to July with flirtatious eyes. "What do you say we head on into town...finish what we started down in Arizona."

July laughed as she carried a stack of dishes to the sink. "I wasn't thinking with a clear head in Arizona."

He set two coffee cups on the counter, sidled up next to her and bent close to her ear. "I can show a lady a good time."

"So I've heard." She eased away and returned to the table for more dishes.

"Hey, don't listen to him, Firecracker." Seth leaned against the counter and folded his arms across his chest. "If you want a good time, you'd be wise to stick with me."

July was amused by his nickname for her; he had started calling her that years ago when he'd found out she was born on the Fourth of July. It rolled off his tongue, though, with a hint of sexual connotation.

"What about the girl you were with at the High Heel?"

He grinned devilishly. "Out of sight, out of mind."

"I might have known." With the moves of an experienced waitress, which she had once been, July worked her way to the sink between the two of them, started the water running, and squeezed a healthy stream of dish soap into it. "Nobody could ever accuse you boys of not trying. All I can say is that it was fortunate Dev came along when he did. I've got to get my head straight about Buck and decide what I'm going to do."

"What's to think about?" Seth lifted his shoulders in a half-shrug. "Divorce him and marry me."

She patted his cheek and placed a dish towel in his hand. "Dry the dishes, sweet thing. You'll be better at it than making marriage proposals you can't possibly follow through on."

"You break my heart, July. A woman like you just might be the one to make an honest man of me."

"Ah, the key word there is 'might.' In case you hadn't noticed, I'm not one of your naive buckle bunnies."

"Mmmm, a mature woman," Jake put in. "Now, there's an interesting switch. A challenge I'm game to try."

July clicked her tongue revealing her impatience with both of them, but there was a smile in her eyes as she held onto her good humor. "You'd better hurry and finish here if you want to get to town before the action starts without you. As for me, I'm going to pass a few hours with Baxter."

"Now, isn't that the luck," Seth quipped. "We lose to an eighty-year-old man. He always did have a way with women. You ought to see how those gals down at Joe's make all over him."

"Maybe you two should take some serious lessons from him then." She took him by the arm and about-faced him toward the foyer. "Just go. I'll finish."

Being good sports about it, and not wanting to do any more dishes anyway, they admitted defeat and gathered their hats, but not without one last invitation from Jake. "If you change your mind, we'll be at the Red Pony in Wells."

The town was a good hour away, but distances were part of daily life in Nevada, and people in remote areas—especially rodeo people who spent their lives on the road—thought nothing of traveling several hours to do something as simple as go to the grocery store, see a movie, or have lunch with a friend.

Relieved that they were gone, July spent a few minutes wiping counters and the table then joined Baxter in the living room. He was sitting in his well-worn leather recliner, trying to find something to watch on an older model Zenith television. He had taken his shower, changed to clean clothes, and pressed steri-strips across the cut on his face. The bruise was now showing its full colors.

As July settled onto the sofa, she took in the room that hadn't changed much since the last time she'd been here. The dominate feature was a large stone fireplace with a unique mantel made of bristlecone pine whose historic life atop a mountain somewhere was written in its knotty grain and twisted form. An antique black pot with lid and handle graced the hearth, and above the mantle hung a new oak-framed Oleg Stavrowsky print, portraying a cowboy parting ways with his bronc.

Also new was the forest green plaid sofa and chair. A matching rug at the foot of Baxter's recliner protected the hardwood floor from his boots. Everything else remained as she remembered: the oak curio cabinet with its knick-knacks; the simple decorations and framed pictures on the walls denoting ranch scenes from both past and present; and the old upright, black walnut piano providing a shelf for family photographs.

Settling deeper into the corner of the sofa and hugging a corduroy throw pillow to her bosom, she realized that while people came and went, this room, this house, this ranch—even the wide Nevada spaces—provided a calm constancy which she desperately needed.

"I'll be glad when Seth and Jake are back on the road," she joked. "I'm exhausted from trying to outmaneuver them. Or maybe I'm just exhausted from the last twenty-four hours I've spent turning my life upside down."

Baxter, matter-of-fact as always, glanced at her before return-ing his attention to the TV. "At least you had the good sense to turn a deaf ear to the two of them."

"I don't know what I might have done if Dev hadn't come along. I haven't been that stupid since I was seventeen."

"Don't beat yourself up over it. You didn't do anything but have a few too many drinks, so that's all that counts."

A moment of silence passed between them as Baxter contin-ued his quest for something to watch. She didn't know how he would take it, but she felt compelled to explain her situation, to somehow apologize for ending up on his doorstep.

"I guess you've heard about my trouble with Buck."

"Some of it," he acknowledged, still seemingly intent on the TV. "That boy never did have good sense."

"I'm going to file for divorce this time, but I can't be around him right now. I need some time and distance, and then I'll go back to Albuquerque and see a lawyer."

Baxter's finger paused on the remote; his eyes were sympa-thetic yet dead serious. "Sometimes time and distance aren't the best things, July. They dull the senses and make you forget. The air clears, and with it comes false hope. You need to act while the iron's hot. He won't change."

It was heartbreaking to hear the truth so point blank. Baxter's words finalized the end of her marriage in a way they never had when she'd said them to herself. She'd married with the idealistic ideas of youth and love. Buck had been her first love, the only man she'd ever given herself to. In the beginning, she had be-lieved she was the only woman in his heart too, but now all she wanted was to be free of the constant pain and turmoil, decep-tion, lies, and fighting. Everything had been about him, for him. He was selfish and immature. Spoiled. She had always had to do the bending to make the marriage work.

She knew she would never be able to resurrect the feelings she'd had for him in the beginning. They were gone, wasted, as were so many years of her life. Still, she was only thirty. It wasn't too late to start over and find a man who would love her the way she had always dreamed of being loved; a man who would give her children before she was too old.

"Are you sure you don't mind me being here for a few days?"

Baxter's mood brightened. "July, you can stay as long as you can tolerate us."

She caught his teasing mood. "Oh, you Summers men aren't such a bad lot."

"You're optimistic, especially after that game of dodge you just played with Jake and Seth. If those two weren't grown men, I'd tan their hides."

July laughed, visualizing the no-nonsense Baxter taking them to the wood shed like recalcitrant children kicking and screaming the entire way. Not only was he brutally honest, he was also short of patience for foolishness.

"And don't ever hang your star on one of them," he added.

Her brow lifted quizzically. "Does that include Dev?"

"I'm sure that boy has had his share of women—hell, he's been divorced for ten years—but he's the settling kind at heart. That's why he and Mica were such a mis-match. I tried to warn him about her. They were both nineteen, but he was feeling his oats and she'd been around the block a few times. Sometimes people just have to learn things the hard way."

"Does she come here anymore?" July didn't want to see Mica now or ever, and if the woman made a habit of visiting the ranch, it might change the complexion of things.

Baxter snorted. "Only when she wants something. Or when she's dropping Dusty off for a visit. She never liked this place. Too far from a watering hole." He resumed pushing buttons, muttering that for as many TV stations as he had with his satellite dish he still couldn't find a damn thing to watch.

July breathed a sigh of relief. She and Mica had never been close. Mica was too competitive. And there had been that rumor years ago that Mica and Buck had had an affair. They'd denied it, but shortly afterward Dev had filed for divorce. July had pushed aside the niggling doubts, convincing herself that the breakup had had nothing to do with the rumor. She hadn't known then that Buck could lie with such a straight face.

"I'll try not to wear out my welcome."

"Like I said, Dev and I won't mind, and Jake and Seth will be hitting the road soon so don't let them chase you off. Besides, if you're willing to help around here, we'll let you have room and board forever." He gave her a lopsided grin that reminded her of Dev. "Hell, I'll even pay you."

She was amused by the offer but had no intention of taking money from him. "You've never considered hiring a housekeeper since your wife died?"

"Oh, sure. I've had a few, but most of them tried to run *me* instead of the other way around. One was so lazy it hurt. One was a drunk. One wanted to marry me. And one was a real looker with a loose hinge; offered to sleep with me if I'd cut her husband in on the ranch. Hell, he wasn't even a good hand."

They laughed over that, but July thought about how lonely he must get, and she understood because she'd been in that place most of her life. She had known from the beginning that her aunt had only tolerated her out of a sense of obligation, so she had thrown herself into school work and taken on menial jobs to have her own money and spend as much time out of the woman's house as possible. At sixteen, she had worked at Burger King; at seventeen, she took a hostess job at a family restaurant, which had worked into a part-time waitress job and good enough tips that she had been able to force herself to smile past rude comments, groping hands, and wandering eyes. She'd studied hard to maintain a 4.0 GPA in high school, and she'd been able to land a full-ride scholarship to the University of New Mexico in Albuquerque. At nineteen, she'd started another waitress job in a classy restaurant where the food was expensive and the clientele rich enough to toss out twenty-dollar tips. She had just turned twenty when Buck Jones walked in after a rodeo; by the time he walked out, he had her heart.

Now, ten years later, she studied Baxter Summers while he channel-surfed. He hadn't aged much, and he still seemed comfortable having her around, as if she were his own granddaughter. There had always been a kinship between them, like old souls that have known each other in past lives. He reminded her a lot of an older version of Dev, which was why she probably got along so well with both of them.

"You can use Cecilia's room," he said. "Although I can't guarantee the condition it's in. We'll have to get some clean bedding from the linen closet." With that thought in mind, and having given up on TV, he rose from his chair. "I'll help you carry your bags."

"You don't have to do that, Baxter. I only have my laptop and camera case and two other bags that aren't very heavy."

He wouldn't be deterred. He went into the foyer where she'd left them and picked up one in each hand while she took the laptop and camera case. She led the way to Cecilia's room, the only bedroom on the ground floor. After he placed the bags inside the door, he glanced around the room with the look of someone catching a glimpse into the past. Then, as if the memories were too vivid, he stepped back into the hall.

"Go ahead and fix things up the way you want them. Besides sheets and pillowcases, you'll find towels and soap and toilet paper in the linen closet. Now, I'm going to get a bowl of ice cream. Want some?"

"That sounds good."

"Chocolate sauce on it?"

"Even better."

"I'll dish it up."

While he served up the evening treat, July found the linen closet and selected the items she thought she would need. She had never known Cecilia, who had died before July had become acquainted with the Summers family, but somewhere over the years, the room had acquired her name. The story went that Baxter hadn't been able to bear sleeping in the room without his wife, so he'd moved upstairs into one of the smaller rooms. He'd asked Mica to box up all of Cecilia's clothing and give them to goodwill. Then he had closed the door to the room and never gone inside it again. He'd left the cleaning and upkeep to others. July couldn't help but wonder what it would be like to have that kind of love and devotion from a man. Cecilia must have been a very special woman, or Baxter was a very special man.

Nothing had changed about the room since the last time July had been here. She was pleased to be granted the right to stay in it. It was in contrast to the rest of the house that was simple and unadorned. Cecilia's room was a step back into the graceful Victorian era of dark cherry wood and antique lace. It was as if the room had been the one place on the ranch that she had been able to call her own and to decorate as she pleased; a haven where she could be alone to relax, read, or sew without worry of the rough and rugged men in her family marring it with dirty boots and jeans, dusty hats, and ranch paraphernalia.

Rich dark hardwood covered the floor and was topped with a large, plush rug in shades of rose and pale green on a cream background. A delicate, ecru crocheted bed cover gave the room a nostalgic, romantic look. Lacy curtains hung at the room's one large window; a heavier drape stretched across the French doors that opened onto the veranda. A Queen Anne chair and ottoman, in tapestry upholstery, waited next to the bed for a weary occupant. Gracing the chair was a round side table covered with a dainty hand-crocheted doily, a hurricane lamp, and a stack of leather-bound classics. A night stand with three drawers stood on the far side of the bed. Nearly all the knick-knacks and furniture were genuine antiques: a China flower vase filled with silk, peach-colored roses; several framed wall prints of Victorian scenes; a porcelain bisque wash bowl and pitcher; a mirrored corner curio cabinet replete with trinkets. There were, of course, the modern amenities of electric lamps, a radio alarm clock, a walk-in closet, and an adjoining master bathroom with a shower installed over a claw-foot tub.

Other than needing dusting, the room was spotlessly clean and radiated serenity. Feeling oddly as if she had come home, July set the linens on the bed. When she returned to the living room, Baxter had set a bowl of ice cream for her on the coffee table with a squeeze bottle of chocolate sauce next to it. She took up the bowl, swirled sauce on it, and reclaimed her seat in the corner of the sofa.

"This is wonderful, Baxter. Thank you."

"It hits the spot. And numbs my throbbing head."

"How did you say the accident happened?"

After a spoonful of ice cream, he said, "Barbed wire and a fence post."

She detected something in his tone and in the way he avoided eye contact that made her question the explanation, but she kept her thoughts to herself.

After a moment, he blurted, "Hell, that isn't the truth and you know it."

"I didn't say a word."

"That's how I know you know. Cecilia was the same way. She would just give me that look and not say a word."

"Then it *was* a horse accident."

"Yes, but I don't want Jake to know." His eyes, the same sky blue as Dev's, lit with fire as they usually did when Jake became the topic of discussion.

"Why? What would he do?"

"If he thinks I'm getting dangerous to myself, he'll take away all my horses and my wheels and even the key to this house and put me in one of those old folks' homes."

"Has he said as much?"

"He's piped up with stuff like that."

"Maybe he's just worried about you."

Baxter continued to work on the ice cream, determined to enjoy it no matter what. "I don't know, but I do know that I've gone to those places to visit friends, and I don't like what I see. Now, granted, if I get to where I can't take care of myself, then I'll accept that as necessary. But I'm afraid Jake will put me in one of those places just so he won't have to deal with me. He doesn't like anything cramping his style. He's always looking down the road to the next town, but he never sees what's coming over the rise. Never sees that one day he's going to wake up and be an old man like me and not have a dollar in his pocket. I think he figures that when I die, he'll sell this place for a few million. Milk it for what it's worth and blow the money on women and booze. He's even got his eyes on the money Dev's put away, thinking somehow he's got a claim to it, or that Dev will feel sorry for him and take care of him in his old age—which, of course, Dev will.

"No, Jake's always been the sort to run something right into the ground," he continued. "Then, instead of trying to fix it, he'll walk away to something else he can bleed dry. My only hope for this place lies in Dev. Seth might come around, but he won't as long as Jake's got an influence on him.

"I haven't said that to Dev though. I didn't want him to quit the rodeo until he was good and ready. He's a famous man. His picture is in that cowboy magazine every month. Of course, you know that. You probably took most of those pictures yourself."

July smiled. "I can take credit for a few of them."

"He's doing all those endorsements for every company from hats to saddles to pickup trucks," Baxter continued. "I couldn't ask him to give that up. He won't make that kind of money ranching."

"But he's back now for good," she assured, "and with a big enough nest egg that he'll invest it wisely and do okay. They'll keep after him for endorsements and probably even rodeo commentary for awhile. If he wanted to, he could even take an active role on the PBR Board of Directors."

Baxter was silent, finishing the last few bites of ice cream. Then his lips thinned to a straight line. "How do I know you can keep a secret and not tell Jake?"

"Because I wouldn't want to see you in an old folks' home."

He shifted in his recliner. His expression relaxed, and he proceeded to tell her about Dinky and the sage hen.

◆

Later, alone in her room, July knew that with everything bouncing through her mind—from Baxter and his accident, to an unfamiliar female voice calling out Buck's name—she would have a hard time sleeping. After she and Baxter had run out of events to exchange, they had tried to watch an old western movie, but he'd fallen asleep ten minutes into it. It had been a long day for both of them. Not interested in watching the movie, she had left the TV running, turning it down low, and slipped quietly into Cecilia's room.

Even though it was nearly midnight now, she decided to take a hot shower. After gathering towels, soap, and shower cap, she stepped under the water, hoping she wouldn't disturb Baxter, or Dev, whose room was directly overhead on the second floor.

As she had hoped, the pulsing water acted as a massage for her tired body and overworked brain. She thought of Baxter's story and how he had made it sound so funny. He'd had them both in stitches by the time he'd picked himself up from the clump of sagebrush. Tougher than nails, he hadn't whined, hadn't moaned about the injuries, hadn't asked for pity or sympathy, and he hadn't given himself any either.

Still, she was unsettled by the thought of what could have happened to him out there alone. She had half a notion to give Jake Summers a piece of her mind for neglecting his father the way he had, to shake some sense into him and tell him how lucky he was to *have* a father, that he could lose him any day, that he should come home and look out after him. But she had promised not to say a word about the incident, and she wouldn't.

Now, with the hot water running over her back and shoulders, she felt the tension leave her muscles. She felt calm for the first time in a long while, and the world around her felt calm. As she watched the water run down her legs, over her toes, and down the drain—exactly where her entire existence seemed to have gone—she kept thinking of her wedding ring at the bottom of that sewer in Arizona. But she felt no regret, no remorse.

You didn't think I would ever do it, did you, Buck?

Well, I didn't think I ever would either.

Sleep had barely settled over Dev's troubled mind when the urgent ring of the telephone jerked him back to consciousness. He squinted through the darkness at the clock: one a.m.

"Jesus Christ," he muttered. "Who's calling this time of the night?" He grabbed the phone off the hook and barked into the receiver. "What?"

"Is that you, Dev?"

"Yeah. Who wants to know?"

"Buck Jones."

Dev came fully awake, speechless.

"You still there, Summers?"

"What in the hell do you want, Jones?"

"You know why I'm calling."

"No, I'm afraid I don't."

"I want to talk to July. She's there with you, isn't she?"

Dev rolled to his back, gingerly settling his injured shoulder onto the mattress's support. He stared at the darkness, deducing that somebody must have told Buck about seeing them together at the High Heel. There was only one thing he could do.

"Christ, Jones. Is this some kind of joke? The last I saw of July was in Arizona. She had decided to shit-can you, and we were helping her celebrate."

There was a long silence on the other end of the line.

"Why?" Dev prodded, feeling both guilty and smug to be putting Buck's shorts in a knot. "Is something wrong?"

"Do you know what hotel she was staying at?"

If Dev wasn't mistaken, Buck sounded more irritated than worried. Damn the little bastard for treating July the way he had and then thinking a lame apology would bring her back. It was all the more reason to hold back the truth.

"Hell, Buck. I don't have a clue."

"You're a lyin' sack of shit, Summers. I'd bet a month's earnings she's there with you right now."

"Then you'd lose your ass."

"If I find out she's there, you'll both regret it."

"I'm shaking in my boots."

The only response was a mumbled curse and the sound of the receiver clicking in his ear.

"You blazing asshole," Dev muttered as he fumbled in the dark trying to return the phone to the cradle. He felt the return of the pain along with the guilt for lying. It wasn't any of his business. He had no right interfering in July's marital problems. He had no right helping her down the road to divorce.

"Shit." He tossed the covers back and reached for his Levi's on the nearby chair. This was one time he wished he was more like his old man—born without a conscience.

Taking the stairs barefooted, and with considerable pain in every movement, he reached the downstairs bedroom. From the living room, he heard Granddad's deep snores. He poised his hand to knock. Should he wake her or tell her in the morning? Then he saw the narrow band of light under the door. There was a telephone in her room; the call had probably woke her too. At last he tapped softly and spoke so as not to wake Granddad.

"July, it's me—Dev."

A moment later when the door opened, she stood before him wearing silk shortie pajamas in pale lavender with her long legs fully exposed and beautiful. The fabric draped softly and seductively over her slender body. Her golden hair, tumbling around her shoulders, completed the picture, awakening a sexual need he hadn't been bothered with for God-knows-how-long. A fine time for it to return, too, when he was trussed up like a Thanksgiving turkey.

He forced his eyes to hold onto hers, lest they wander. "I guess you probably heard the phone ring."

She didn't seem annoyed at all by his middle-of-the-night intrusion. She laughed softly and said, "Yes, but it didn't wake me up. I was writing in my journal." A look of concern crossed her face. "Has something happened to Seth or your father?"

Dev swallowed hard, feeling like a fool now to have to explain away his lies. "No. It wasn't Dad and Seth. It was Buck. He's looking for you."

Chapter Ten

July turned back to her room. "I don't want to talk to him."

Dev followed her inside. "He isn't on the phone. I told him you weren't here."

She sank down on the edge of the bed, releasing a sigh of relief. "You really are my knight in shining armor."

He saw her journal in the center of the bed and wondered if she wrote words of regret for leaving her sorry excuse of a husband. "Looks like you've been burning the midnight oil."

"I couldn't sleep so I started writing and lost track of time."

"Buck should have waited until morning to call."

"The rules never apply to Buck," she said bitterly. "I'm sorry he woke you. He probably woke Baxter too."

"No. Granddad's still sound asleep in the living room."

Her shoulders sagged. "I'm causing you a lot of grief by being here."

"Wrong again."

Her gaze lifted, wrought with concern. "I should go back and settle things with him, once and for all, but it's going to be an ugly scene. I never thought he'd find me here."

He sat down next to her. The mattress sank; their shoulders touched. He caught the scent of soap lingering on her skin just as her journal slid against his back and she moved it to the center of a pillow. She struggled to contain tears. He felt renewed anguish at his own failed attempt at love and marriage. With guilt and regret that never completely went away, he remembered the day he'd given up custody of Dusty in exchange for freedom from her mother. Now July faced a similar battle that might be the most difficult of her life.

"Are you certain you never want to go back to him?"

She stared at her hands in her lap for a long time before giving a small nod, as if she weren't quite sure.

"If you're afraid to face him, I'll go with you. We all will. If he gives you trouble, we'll beat the shit out of him."

She smiled at his magnanimous gesture. "And what would Jake and Seth think about you volunteering their muscle?"

"Hell, they'd jump at the chance to put Buck in his place."

"I'll keep it in mind."

"Keep something else in mind: life is too short to spend it with someone who treats you the way he does."

Dev found it too easy to offer advice because he didn't give a good goddamn about Buck Jones, and he didn't want to talk about him anymore. What he cared about was July. She might not be ready to turn to another man for love—and she may never turn to him—but he needed her this very moment like a dying man needs a prayer. His skin absorbed her heat; his nostrils inhaled her scent. His fingertips yearned to stroke her skin. He should move away from her, break contact. She might legally be Buck Jones's wife, but he wanted to lay her back against the pillows and make love to her until he collapsed, or died. Until the harsh realities of the world went spinning away forever. He wanted to end the protocol that kept them apart.

But he'd made enough stupid mistakes in his life.

She left his side and went into the bathroom. He listened while she blew her nose. When she came out, she tried to make light of it. "I'm going to owe you big time for covering for me. You don't know how much I appreciate it."

She stood too close, challenging his willpower. Did she have any idea what her nearness did to him? He felt himself hardening in his painful need for her.

It was time to leave. Definitely time to leave.

At the door's threshold, he said, "If he calls again, what should I tell him?"

"That I'm still not here."

He hoped to see something in her eyes that would assure him she was truly done with Buck, but all he saw in the green depths was sadness and indecision.

"Follow your instincts, July. They won't lead you astray."

He closed the door and went into the living room, deciding he was going to have to stay clear of her from here on out or he'd do something foolish for sure. His feelings for her were too strong. It didn't help that he hadn't been with a woman for God knows how long.

When he turned off the TV, Granddad came awake with a start.

"It's half past one, Granddad."

"Hell."

The old man struggled up from his chair, and Dev followed him up the stairs. In the darkness of his own room, Dev removed his Levi's and crawled back in bed. An hour later, he was still wide awake and cussing Buck Jones for his sleeplessness. Deep in his heart, though, he knew it was the man's wife who was to blame.

◆

Jake and Seth normally couldn't wait to beat tracks to the next rodeo. They would spend a night at the ranch and leave with nothing but a fresh hangover and not so much as a strip of bacon in hand, but July's presence had, in Dev's opinion, turned their brains to the consistency of oatmeal. For the first time ever, they were in no hurry to leave, deciding to wait until the last minute and fly out to Tulsa. They didn't give July enough space to take a breath. So, being a woman with a creative nature, she did the only thing she could do: she took advantage of it.

With Baxter's approval, and under her supervision, she assigned them the task of fixing the downed picket fence while she cleaned out the flower beds nearby. With equal shares of complaining, joking around, and flirting with her, they not only got the fence standing again, but dressed it up with a fresh coat of white paint. Then they hauled stacks of weeds away in wheelbarrows and pruned the old yellow rose bushes that had been Cecilia's pride and joy.

Baxter was impressed. He'd never gotten that much work out of them willingly in their lives, so he stayed out of the way and kept his mouth shut.

Dev spent most of the time sleeping, allowing his body to heal, or sitting in the porch swing watching the manifestation of a side to his father and brother he hadn't known existed. July had to show them how to use the pruning shears, but they caught on fast enough. Maybe there was some truth to the adage that with women came civilization.

It didn't get either Jake and Seth any closer to her bed, though. At the end of every day, they'd spruce themselves up and try to persuade her to go into town and go dancing.

A week went by, and tonight was the same as all the others.

"No reason to hang around here," Seth said. "It'll be pretty dull watching TV with Granddad and Dev."

"You go without me. I'm working on some articles."

Seth wouldn't give up. He eased her up against the sink and held her there with an arm on either side and his hands pressed against the counter top. "All right. Dad can go alone. I'll stay here, and we'll go for a walk down by the creek. It's a beautiful evening."

With a restraining hand on his chest, she flashed a tolerant smile. "That's not going to happen, sweet thing."

"Come on, July. You can't close yourself off in your room every night because of Buck. You can bet your boots he's not."

"Buck has nothing to do with my decision. I have to keep my career going; I can't just quit or I really would be homeless. I have commitments, contracted articles."

Dev had stayed in pretty good humor through it all, but watching his brother's advances mad him angry and jealous. "For Christ's sake, Seth, leave her alone. She doesn't want to go with you. What part of no don't you understand?"

Angry to be reprimanded like a child, Seth stalked out of the room. He grabbed his Stetson and left the house but not before brushing past Dev and muttering, "It's a damn good thing your arm's in a sling."

July breathed a sigh of relief when the door closed behind him. She watched from the window as he joined Jake in the pickup. "Thank you. I was beginning to feel like Tweety with Sylvester at my cage door."

"He ought to have the sense to know when a woman doesn't want anything to do with him. You don't, do you?"

"I'm afraid he's worse than Buck. No direction whatsoever,

unless he's being led to bed by a buckle bunny. But he's got a good heart. So does your dad. They're just free spirits. I can't be mean to them."

"They may have good hearts, but they don't have good intentions." He raked a hand through his hair. "Hell, that doesn't even make sense to me."

July laughed, looking up at him with those wide, luminous green eyes that made his heart flip and brought that familiar tightening to his loins again. She said, "You know, that idea about taking a walk sounds good. Are you up to coming along?"

He should take another dally on his lonely heart—and maybe a cold shower—or tell her he was tired and in way too much pain. Instead, he said, "It would probably do me good."

"Then come on, you poor old crippled cowboy. I'll try to hold you upright." She slipped her arm through his as if being so familiar with him was as easy as taking her next breath. And he leaned into her with the same carefree attitude while pretending to be at least a hundred years old, which wasn't hard in his present condition.

"Well, now, dearie," he affected a voice as weak and wavery as that of a centenarian. "Maybe we ought to get my wheelchair. I wouldn't want to have a heart attack. Unless you know CPR." He smiled slyly and affected a lecherous chuckle.

Laughing, they made it to the door before ending the charade. Outside, she kept her arm playfully linked with his as they walked across the yard. He wondered if she was aware of each point where their bodies touched, or if she just considered the two of them nothing more than good friends, the way she did his dad and brother.

The ranch headquarters stretched out along either side of Mustang Creek, spreading out below the house that sat back by itself on a rise. They took the well-beaten path past corrals, the barn, a riding arena, and several large hay sheds to a metal equipment building large enough to house everything from tractors to the small motor boat they used for the occasional fishing trip to Wild Horse Reservoir.

Adjoining the equipment shed was a repair shop where Dev admitted that he enjoyed working on the machinery.

"So you're a mechanic too?"

He shrugged. "I like working with my hands. It's a way to relax after being on a high run all the time."

They wandered into the livestock barn where the gas, diesel, and oil smells of the equipment building and shop were replaced by the earthy scents of hay and straw, leather, wood, medicines, and even horses, although they were all out in the pasture enjoying the summer warmth.

The building was constructed of heavy wooden beams, poles, and rough lumber, and designed with stalls on either side of a center alley. Near the door, a small room contained pitchforks, two wheelbarrows, and an old refrigerator containing medicines. A cabinet held other vet supplies and useful aids: switches for sorting animals, dehorners, branding irons, electric shears, ear-tagging pliers, and a calf puller. The latter was an ungainly mechanism used to assist pregnant cows who were having difficulty giving birth.

July found the tack room more interesting than the vet room and lingered to observe Baxter's many saddles, saddle blankets, bridles, halters, and ropes neatly arranged on saddle trees or hooks on the walls. There were harnesses dating back a hundred years that had belonged to the first Summers men who had lived on the land and who had used teams of Shires for everything from farming to bringing logs and firewood down from the mountains. Baxter had even kept an old buggy, sleigh, and a lady's sidesaddle tucked back in one corner of the large building.

Fascinated, July went right to the sidesaddle. "How wonderful, and it's still in good condition. I always wanted to ride one of these. Did your grandmother use it?"

"Not that I remember. It belonged to my great-grandmother. But if you want to use it, all we need to do is put on a new cinch, clean it, and oil the leather."

"Oh, I'd love to. And the buggy and sleigh, did they also belong to her and your great-grandfather?"

"Yes. Apparently she was quite a character. Of course, living clear out here, they didn't get to town too often back in those days. But when she went, she would take her buggy down to the race track and find someone to race against. There was even betting, and she made enough money to pay for whatever she bought that day in town."

"Racing a buggy sounds like a wild ride. Now I can see where you boys get your reckless nature."

"Reckless?"

She grinned. "Sure, it takes a little of that to be a bull rider, don't you think?"

By the time they reached the pasture, Dev was hurting in every fiber of his body, but he suffered in silence to prolong the moments with her, which, he deduced, put him on the same level as his dad and Seth.

The sun moved through an evening calm, sinking into strands of cirrus clouds. From those distant places where shadows had deepened, mourning doves released their haunting, melancholy *coo-ah, coo, coo, coo*. Up ahead, Cappy trotted into a peaceful pastoral scene where horses grazed in golden light and in their own shadows that lengthened across lush, green irrigated grass.

The animals were happy to see them, thinking, no doubt, that they might be offered a handful of oats. Dev opened the gate and they walked in among them. July was thrilled that the horses came right up to her even though they didn't know her. She took turns stroking their noses, straightening their forelocks, rubbing their necks, and speaking sweet nothings to them.

"How do you get them to be so friendly? The registered horses that Buck's parents raise are the most ill-tempered creatures I've ever seen."

Dev draped an arm over the back of an Appaloosa gelding named Stripe. "Granddad likes spirit, stamina, and endurance, but he sells anything with a mean or unruly disposition. He doesn't procreate it. He's very good with horses. He lets them know he's the boss but gains their trust by never abusing them or making them do something that could hurt them. In turn, they'll do anything he asks."

"I haven't ridden for a long time. Would your granddad mind if I rode one of them right now, just bareback?"

"Not at all."

She was thrilled. "I'll run back to the barn and get a bridle. You stay here."

She sprinted off. Without her administrations, the horses lowered their heads and resumed grazing, but Stripe stayed with Dev until July came back. They determined the bridle would fit him the best so July slipped it on him, made a few adjustments to the headstall, and, to Dev's surprise, grabbed a handful of mane and swung effortlessly onto the horse's back.

"I haven't done that for years. I'm surprised I made it." She scooted up close to the horse's withers. "Can you ride?"

"Probably, but I'm not going to be able to swing this battered body up there the way you did."

"Well, I want to ride down along the creek, and I want you to come with me." Her wheels were rolling as she looked around the pasture, spotting a dry wash that was a remnant from another water course. It was worn down in the middle where Baxter had driven through it with his trucks and farming equipment. "That wash isn't far away. If you can walk there, I think we can get you up behind me."

Stripe stepped into the dry wash and stood patiently while Dev climbed the bank and half-stepped, half-slid over onto the horse's back. Dev put a few inches between him and July, but by the time they'd backed out of the wash and emerged into the field, their bodies had slid together. His inner thighs fit snugly against her denim-clad backside; her straight back heated the wall of his chest even though his slinged arm was wedged between them. Her long hair occasionally blew back to tickle his face, and he gently moved it aside. Desire stirred deep in his core; it took all his willpower to lasso his wayward thoughts.

"Are you all right?" She asked from over her shoulder.

"I'm fine," he lied. "I nearly forgot what it's like to ride something that isn't trying to kill me."

She took a leisurely pace to the creek that flowed through the top end of the pasture. By the time they got there, the sun had vanished behind the western cordillera, painting the sky and clouds vivid shades of lavender blue and rose pink.

She allowed Stripe to drink from the cool stream. With his head lowered, she swung her right leg over his neck and slid off the left side. Dev did the same, figuring he would worry later about how he was going to get back on.

Acting on impulse, she handed the reins to him, sat down on the creek bank and pulled off her boots. She rolled her pant legs up as far as she could and, with arms extended for balance, stepped into the cool water.

"Oh, that feels good. You ought to come in."

The horse had finished its drink and was watching her, ears perked forward, as if he had never seen such a mesmerizing creature. Dev felt the same way as he dropped the reins, knowing Stripe would stay as he'd been trained to do. He managed to get his boots off but didn't try to roll up his pant legs. Wincing at the rocks gouging into the tender flesh of his feet, he stepped into the creek.

"I haven't done this sort of thing since I was a kid," July said. Then, with no warning, she scooped up a handful of water and doused him. He let out a yowl of shock, then laughter, followed by instant retaliation. In seconds, they were both wet to the skin, although neither was about to be the first to cry uncle. Cappy started barking and dove into the water, deciding to get in on the fun. He somehow got between Dev's legs and the next thing Dev knew he was falling forward into July. She tried to catch him, but her feet went out from under her and they fell together, in slow motion it seemed, trying in vain to stop their descent onto the grassy bank.

They lay there for a moment, laughter fading to smiles as their gazes collided and held. The only sound was Cappy's barking. Even that grew distant as stillness settled over them, along with an acute awareness of their bodies intimately entangled. The fading light of sunset had, in the few moments of their childish play, deepened to dusk. The moon had not yet started its climb over the eastern mountains, but it's glow was at the ridgeline.

Dev heard crickets now and the mourning dove calling out again, answered this time by another dove, perhaps its mate. The loudest noise was the thumping of his heart against the softness of July's breasts. Could she feel it too? His free hand had gotten tangled in the mass of her hair that lay in disarray. His focus shifted to her lips and the drops of water beaded there. He nearly forgot himself, nearly bent to lift away those beads of water with the tip of his tongue. Then Cappy began tugging at his pant leg.

Rescued from his own foolishness, Dev rolled onto his back into the grass. Laughing, he tried to disengage the dog. The harder he shook his leg, the more fiercely Cappy hung on.

July sat up, amused by his predicament. The sweet, husky music of her laughter crumbled the walls around Dev's heart the way a bluebird's trill at daybreak pulls back the cover of darkness.

"How about getting this killer dog to let go."

With eyes twinkling, she called, "Cappy, come here! Stop being so mean to Dev."

The dog released Dev's pant leg and moved next to July in a protective stance.

"His loyalty shifted in a hurry." Dev accepted the hand that July extended to him.

"Forgive me?"

"For what?"

"For taking advantage of an injured man."

"I think I defended myself pretty good."

She looked toward the mountains and the moon lifting its head above the peaks, casting its golden light onto the darkening land.

"Do you want to ride up to the hollow?" he asked, realizing it was a delay tactic to keep her with him a little longer. So much for his vow to stay clear of her.

"Where is it?"

"Not far. It's a place where we used to play when we were kids, where we'd camp in summer and sled in the winter."

"Are you doing okay?" She indicated his arm.

"I'm fine," he lied again. "I'll be all right."

She led the way out of the creek and up the bank, extending a hand to help him. Dripping wet, they remounted Stripe as they had done before. They held their boots in front of them and rode up the field to the hollow where willows and cottonwood trees grew and where the stillness was pure and sweet. July stopped the Appaloosa, and they sat silently absorbing the tranquility of the empty land.

"It's so beautiful here," she murmured. "So peaceful."

She shivered; he whispered close to her ear, "Cold?"

"A little."

"It doesn't take long when the sun goes down." He put his free arm around her to give her some of his body warmth, and she nestled against him, grateful for it. He would have drawn her inside him if he could have. He could almost imagine that there were no barriers between them.

"We should go back."

Something in her voice said she was no more eager for it to end than he was. Were they getting too close to the line that separates a single man from a married woman? The line that separates friends from lovers? Did she want to step over it as badly as he did?

She reined Stripe back down the moonlit trail. They rode in silence, saying little more until their good-nights in the hallway outside her room.

After her door closed behind her, Dev stood for a moment at the foot of the stairs, inhaling the lingering scent of her perfume and wondering what kind of fool he'd been to bring her here.

Chapter Eleven

Dev struggled to pull himself out of his drug-induced sleep, drawn to consciousness by an incessant hammering that, at first, was buried in a strange dream. A dream wherein he and Tim Roberts had been hammering boards onto an arena fence dismantled by Satan 101 during one of his infamous rages.

When Dev's eyes did open, his head cleared but the hammering persisted in a sporadic yet rhythmic way that he could almost keep time to. Pound, pound, pound. Silence. Pound, pound, pound. Silence.

The sunlight sneaking through the slats in the wooden window blinds indicated it was around eight a.m. He moaned, realizing he'd slept through breakfast.

He focused on the sunlight while his mind brought him up to date, rolling back to last night and the moonlight ride. He wouldn't have traded that ride for the world, but he'd paid for it with pain and had needed a double dose of painkillers to go to sleep.

He threw back the covers, sat up, and dropped his feet to the rug. He wanted to lie back down, but if he ever expected to get better he had to keep going. He wanted to fix the carburetor on the Ford today. First, though, he was going to see what in the hell the pounding was all about.

It was hard to get his Levi's on with one hand and it was way too much effort to grapple with the top button. He removed his sling long enough to pull on a shirt but went downstairs with it unbuttoned and the shirttails hanging.

The house was empty so he went onto the veranda. The wooden planks, painted many times over the years, held the warmth of the day and were almost hot beneath his bare feet. He had a lot of memories of moments spent on this porch: memories of a boy playing with Seth; helping his grandmother shell peas and snap green beans fresh from the garden; listening to Granddad recount the exciting times he'd had as a young man; sitting in the porch swing, holding Dusty as a baby while she squealed with delight; and even memories of stealing his first kiss at the age of sixteen with a girl he'd dated for awhile.

He followed the pounding to the west side of the house. There he saw Granddad down on his bony old knees, hammer in hand, slamming nails into the wood with an arm more powerful than it looked.

"What are you doing, Granddad?"

The old man looked up, hammer poised for the next swing. "I didn't hear you."

"Well, I didn't put on my boots."

Granddad frowned at his bare feet. It had always been a cardinal sin to go barefoot around the ranch. He'd done it a lot when he was a kid, but somewhere around the age of twelve he'd finally learned the wisdom of wearing boots after he'd cut his feet too many times to count; stepped on nails and suffered tetanus shots; got stung by bees pilfering pollen from the clover in the grass; having Granddad dig slivers the size of toothpicks from his toes—the list went on and on.

"Seems nobody wears shoes anymore," Granddad muttered. "Or if they do, it's those stupid damned sandals."

Dev was amused by the old man. "I don't own a pair."

"Neither do I, and you'll catch me dead before you do."

Granddad started hammering again as if he was gleaning a lot of satisfaction from the job. He was finding all the nails that had worked their way out of the wood and were sticking up. Dev didn't ask him what had gotten into him. Granddad seemed to think he owed him an explanation for his productivity.

"I don't want that girl getting her toes caught on one of these nails," he tried to sound gruff. "She likes to come out here in the morning—barefoot, of course—with her cup of tea. You'd think every dang one of you kids nowadays had been raised in town with all that cement. Some of those poor kids don't even know what dirt is."

Dev suppressed a smile. "Where is she anyway?"

Granddad jerked his head to the left. "Out back, pulling up weeds. Cecilia would be tickled to know somebody's taking care of things again. Hell, I wouldn't know a flower from a weed or I'd have done it myself."

Dev could have argued with that; the old man knew every wildflower that grew in the mountains. But he settled back against the porch railing and watched him zero in on more protruding nails.

"The girl's got ambition," Granddad continued, "and she's too proud to accept charity. Maybe working just keeps her mind off Buck, but she meant every word about earning her keep."

It was true. July had not only tackled the yard, but she was up every morning fixing breakfast and seemed perfectly content with her self-appointed domestic role. Dev helped her as much as he could with one arm in a sling. She was, after all, their guest, not their housekeeper. Even granddad took up the broom, pushed the vacuum cleaner around, and hauled out the garbage.

"Has she let Buck know she's here?" Granddad asked.

"Not that I know of."

"He'll find out when she uses a credit card or the ATM."

"She has money coming from her freelancing, but I never thought she'd stay more than a couple of days," Dev admitted.

"Well, neither of us ought to get too comfortable having her here. She'll be moving on sooner or later."

Dev pushed away from the porch railing, thinking again of their bareback ride last night and convincing himself it would be better if she left sooner than later. The door to his heart was opening, and he wasn't keen on going through all that angst to have it slammed shut in his face. It wasn't that he didn't want to love again, but he wanted it to be with someone who was free to make a future with him.

"Are you still going to town this afternoon?" he asked.

"I was planning on it. I need to go to the Farm and Ranch Supply, but I'll see if July will drive. You know how I hate driving in town."

Yes, Dev knew. Granddad no longer trusted his driving skills on anything but a back road. The world had gotten too fast for him with the interstates and on-and-off ramps, big truck plazas and shopping malls. He would drive into Wells, but that was about the extent of his off-ranch driving.

"She's probably working on those articles she said she needs to get done. I can drive, but give me a chance to take a look at the Ford in case we need to buy some parts."

Granddad gave him a disapproving look. He might not trust his eyes and his reflexes anymore, but his insight was still keen. "We at least ought to ask her to go. We didn't take her with us last week when you went to the doctor. We don't want her to think she's wearing out her welcome."

Dev decided his granddad would do about anything to keep July around. Why, if the old man was forty years younger, he'd probably go courting. Dev, on the other hand, was torn between being with her and knowing every second in her presence was mounting to a temptation too hard to control.

"Okay, I'll ask her."

"And, Dev—"

He turned back.

"Do up your pants and tuck in your shirt before you go talk to her."

"Nothing's showing."

"Damned near."

Dev chuckled. "Yes, Granddad."

Baxter scowled. "Sometimes dignity is all a man has in this life, son. You remember that."

Dev started tucking in his shirt with one hand.

Satisfied, the old man let loose on another nail.

◆

"It's not for me to give you that information." July stood by the French doors in Cecilia's room where the signal was the strongest for her cell phone. She'd finished weeding and had come inside to wash and change clothes and make the phone call.

The voice of Eric Lancaster, managing editor of *Heart of the West Magazine*, was now coming through loud and clear. "Then tell me off the record—is Dev Summers coming back to compete for the million dollar jackpot? Hell, he walked away from the last rodeo without saying a word to anybody, and now he's holed up in the middle of nowhere and nobody knows anything."

"It's not the middle of nowhere. It's his home."

Eric didn't seem to hear, but went right on without taking a breath. "Then you call up and say you're there with him. I can't let an opportunity like this pass. I'll make it more than worth your time to give me an article on his condition and what his plans are. I'll even add a couple of pages to the feature we're running on you and your photography in the February issue."

"I don't work well to bribery, Eric."

"Think of it as incentive. If you would do a piece on Summers for our rodeo section, I'd make it right for you. A piece on all the Summers men would be really unique. Jake, Dev. Even his brother Seth. A rodeo family. With your pictures, we'd have a winner. Summers hasn't given interviews for years. This would be great."

July could imagine him almost salivating. "His grandfather is a very interesting character too."

"Ex-rodeo?"

"No. Honest-to-goodness cowboy. A rancher."

"Last of a breed." Eric's wheels were turning at yet another angle, and he liked it all. "Then throw something in on him for good measure. This would be great, July. Just great. You've got to do it."

Through the window, July saw Dev on the veranda talking to Baxter. He'd thrown on a shirt but hadn't buttoned it. Dark brown hair swirled across his chest and narrowed down the center of his flat belly until it disappeared below the waistband of faded Levi's that molded perfectly to his narrow hips. The Levi's top button gaped open too, elevating her awareness of him to a higher degree and reminding her of how warm and solid he had felt pressed against her on their moonlight ride. She hadn't felt such desire for years, wherein lay the danger. She was too vulnerable right now, and perhaps he was too. She'd felt it in him, seen it in his eyes when he'd nearly kissed her. If left together too long, they might succumb to that need and do something they would regret.

Eric's voice interrupted her thoughts. "Is he interested in trying for the jackpot? Is he up to it? Everybody's been looking all season for him and Buck to be the main contenders."

"I don't know, Eric. He hasn't said."

"Come on, July. In two weeks he hasn't talked to you about

riding for the jackpot? Hasn't said a word about what he plans to do?"

"No. I haven't seen much of him. He's been doing a lot of sleeping and recuperating. Besides, he won it a couple of years ago. The man's already a millionaire several times over. I think money is the last thing on his mind right now." She knew Dev planned to retire, but she wouldn't say as much, even off record. It was Dev's place to make such an announcement, not hers.

"Then what in the hell *do* you talk about? What have you been doing out there? Taking a lot of pictures, I hope."

"I've just been living."

"That sounds exciting as hell."

"Actually, it's been pretty nice."

"Shit, I don't believe this." His tone changed. "You're estranged from Buck Jones and staying with Dev Summers on his ranch. Is there something I should know, July?"

"We're not having an affair if that's what you're insinuating. I've known Dev and his family for years. Now let it lie, or you definitely won't get that piece you want."

"Doth the lady protest too much?"

"Eric, give it a break. You're not working for one of those tawdry tabloids, remember?"

"Okay, okay. I don't want to chase my best contributor to the competition. How long will you be there?"

"Dev said I could stay as long as I want." *But I should be leaving.* An ache caught in her heart even as she made the admission to herself.

She moved away from the window; it was too hard to think straight while her eyes and her mind were on Dev. She could run away again. She could run for the rest of her life, away from anybody that stirred her need for love and a warm embrace in the night. Yet, when she thought of stepping out onto the hot Nevada highway to walk away, all she could see was Dev's eyes looking into the center of her soul and knowing what was in her heart. He held onto her without touching her, and she couldn't let go.

Every day since she'd been here she had asked herself if she was ready to file for divorce and go through the nasty court battle that was bound to ensue. Buck and his family would make sure she walked away with nothing but her personal belongings. Without a doubt, she had reached the bend in the road where she could not go forward until she closed the door to the past. Even though she knew what she must do, she needed strength besides what she could conjure inside herself, and the only source she had was from her surrogate family: the Summers men.

"Give me an answer in a couple of days," Eric was saying. "I need this piece, July. I really need it."

"And I need the advance on that feature I just submitted."

"It's in the mail, sweetheart."

"As of—?"

"I'll make sure it goes out no later than tomorrow."

"Don't forget to send it here."

"Sure, sure."

"Thanks, Eric. I'll be in touch."

She ended the call and set the phone on the night stand. A story about the Summers men would make a wonderful human-interest piece if she could do it right, and if the four of them would all consent. She couldn't help but feel sleazy for mentioning it, though. It was as if she would be using their generosity for her own gain. They had accepted her like one of their own, and she had made them the anchor she so desperately needed. She didn't want to do anything to lose their respect.

The proposed article was indeed a story worth telling. She could even envision enough content to fill a book. A project of that magnitude was intimidating, but she already had a major publishing house considering a book about the rodeo life told through her photographs. She could pitch the idea of a biography to her agent about World Champion rodeo cowboys Dev and Jake Summers and see where it took her. If the idea took root, she would have a valid reason to stay. And she wanted to stay.

First, she could no longer put off the call that would start the battle with Buck; the call to her lawyer in Albuquerque.

◆

Dev stepped out of the shower, wrapped a towel around his waist, and walked across the hall to his room only to find that Jake and Seth had plunked themselves down at the foot of the four-poster bed. His dad was nursing his mid-morning Coors between gripes.

"Damn, when that woman sobers up, she really sobers up. No wonder old Buck took to wandering. She's turned into a regular Suzy Homemaker."

"Granddad thinks it's fine," Seth put in.

"He would. He thinks a woman's place is in the home, baking Toll House cookies."

"He's going to be lost when she leaves."

"He's not the only one. Isn't that right, Dev?"

Dev didn't care to be drawn into the conversation, and he didn't want to talk about how July's leaving would affect him. It was none of their damn business. How could they know how he felt about her anyway? Instead of responding, he announced he had to take a piss and went back into the bathroom. He took his good time about it, hoping they'd leave, but when he returned they were still on the bed and wouldn't let the question die.

"She's sure been doting over you," Seth said with a knowing gleam in his eyes.

Dev was testy. It wasn't the way he'd hoped to start the day. "Don't make something out of nothing. She's here until she gets her head straight about Buck."

Jake's eyes burrowed into Dev, as if he knew all about Dev's secret passion for July. At least he didn't say any more, just stood up and pulled his hat down tight onto his forehead—the signal to leave.

"Seth needs to get to Tulsa so we'll be hitting the road, but we'll swing by here in a couple of weeks and see how you're doing."

The real reason for leaving, of course, was not so Seth wouldn't miss any rodeos but because Jake Summers's feet got restless after a few days. He had to have that highway before him and the miles slipping away behind him. It was as much an addiction as the beer in his hand. Besides, if he hung around the ranch too long, Granddad—or July—would find more work for him to do.

"Sure you won't change your mind and come along?"

Dev moved to the closet to see if he had a clean shirt and Levi's to wear to town. "I'm sure."

"I wouldn't want to leave either if I had July Jones waiting on me hand and foot," Seth quipped.

"She isn't waiting on me hand and foot."

They laughed as they moved to the door; Jake paused on the threshold. "Don't let her get under your skin, boy. She hasn't seen the last of Buck."

Chapter Twelve

Things were peaceful with Jake and Seth gone, but they didn't stay gone long enough to suit Dev. On the day they returned, he'd been working on the Ford all day while Granddad and July planned a barbecue for the evening. When he saw the Ram drive into the yard, it was all the more reason to wait until the aroma of steaks sizzling on the grill summoned him to quit. As he figured, the two of them halted him on the veranda before he could get inside to shower off the grime and join July and Granddad in the back yard.

The moment they'd arrived, they'd settled there with a cooler of beer. They were already too drunk to carry on a sensible conversation, but it didn't stop them from trying.

"That arm must be better," his dad remarked. "Granddad says you've been fixing the Ford."

"Trying." Dev suspected where his dad was going with the comment and wanted to side-step it, but if he didn't get it over with now, they'd bring it up later, probably in front of July. He stood with a hand on the screen door handle.

He didn't have long to wait.

Jake's eyes darted over the panoramic view of the valley, mountains, and sky stretching to infinity. "A man can only take so much of this peaceful bullshit before he loses his mind. We figured you'd be ready to get the hell out of here by now, so we came to rescue you."

"You needn't have. I'm loving every minute of it."

Jake tried another tactic. "The old man hasn't turned you into a hired hand yet—or a slave?"

"If you mean Granddad, no."

Jake's top lip curled. "The old fool's following July around like a lost puppy. Last we heard, he was going to find a red plaid tablecloth to put over the picnic table."

"There's nothing wrong with him wanting to help her. And nothing wrong with her trying to civilize the bunch of us with a tablecloth."

"She's mighty sweet to him," Seth put in. "Makes me wonder if she's one of those women who take up with old men to get their money."

The last thing Dev wanted was to listen to such an asinine notion, but he was afraid if he continued to the back yard, the conversation would be overheard by July or Granddad. "You're on your ass, Seth. They have a grandfather/granddaughter relationship—and they also happen to like each other. There's nothing more to it than that."

"Believe what you want, but I think she's taking advantage of his generosity." Seth seemed to think the idea was a clever one to chew on. "Why else would she want to stay here? It can't be because she enjoys being a housekeeper for free, or that she finds you interesting."

Dev shook his head in disgust. "I might of known you were leading up to something. I don't care what you think of me, but don't try to tarnish July's image because you're jealous that she's showing Granddad attention and not giving you what you want."

"You're so full of shit," Seth said. "You criticize me, but you've probably already had her in bed."

"Christ, Seth, is sex all you think about?"

Seth slugged down the remainder of his beer. "Yeah, when I'm not doing my eight seconds somewhere else."

"That's not something I'd be bragging about."

Losing patience with their senseless squabble, Jake shouldered Seth aside. "July isn't what we came home for, Dev. Willing women are a dime a dozen; we can have one any time we want one."

"Oh, that's right. You came back to rescue me."

"I know you said some things you didn't mean after that last ride. I know you've got to be having second thoughts about giving it up now that you're healed. Rodeo is in your blood, boy. You couldn't give it up any more than you could give up breathing."

"I always suspected you didn't know me from horse shit. And I'm not healed."

Seth's eyes were liquor-glazed. "You're serious, aren't you?"

"A state of mind you've never experienced, I'm sure."

"Goddamn it, you two," Jake barked. "I swear, you're driving me to drink."

There was no slack in the scrutiny Dev gave his father as the latter lifted the Coors to his lips again. "Since when did you need an excuse, Dad?"

Jake ran the back of his hand over his bottom lip where some of the beer had dribbled. For once, he didn't have a rejoinder.

"I'm still riding, damn it." Seth pointed out. "We don't need Dev."

Too much liquor consumption was making Jake more insensitive than usual. "You're too damned busy chasing tail to get down and dirty on the back of a bull. You couldn't even stay on the corral fence over in Tulsa. If I wasn't fifty-six, I'd settle down on those bulls myself and show you how it's done."

Seth tried to defend himself. "If those judges would look at my riding instead of always comparing me to Dev. Nobody takes me seriously. Least of all you."

Jake shook his head. "The judges aren't biased. When are you going to learn that it's not just a ride. It's a show. People come to the rodeo to see a show. You have to have a style, a certain way about you that will turn people's heads. That's what I've been trying to hammer into you boys' heads for twenty-five years."

"Then I'd say you must be as sick of it as we are." Dev headed across the yard, giving up on getting to the food but hoping to rid himself of these two nematodes. They scrambled after him like little boys afraid of being left behind. God, he hated it when they were drunk, which was most of the time.

"Christ, man," Jake continued. "Seth is moments away from being dropped from the top forty-five contenders, and here you are in the position to be number one. All you have to do is outride Buck. You could walk away with another million dollars in your pocket. How can you let that go?"

Dev whirled so fast his dad collided with him. "Look, damn you. My riding arm is worthless." He tried to shove it in his dad's face but the damaged ligaments and tendons wouldn't allow it. "I couldn't hold onto a bull rigging if I wanted to. And I'm tired. Goddamn tired. I don't care. Do you hear me—*I don't care!*"

"How can you not? It's your life. Our life."

"It's not my life anymore, and if you two would get over your damn rodeo fever, you would put it behind you, too. You could stay here and help me run this place the way it's supposed to be run. We could make a living here."

"A living?" Jake sneered. "Compared with what you make now, the amount you'll get off this land will be nothing but chicken feed."

"It doesn't have to be that way with proper management, good investments, and hard work. But I suppose that scares the shit out of you, doesn't it?"

"You're making a big mistake, boy. The world's changing. We're in the twenty-first century, not the nineteenth, and there isn't a place for ranchers. They're getting squeezed out of business every day. Your granddad's the last of the breed."

"Every rodeo cowboy has to retire sooner or later unless he dies in the arena. Is that what you want for me and Seth?"

"No. I'm saying you should stick it out for the rest of the year. You could even go two more."

"One, two? What's the difference?"

"A goddamn lot of money. Money you'll need to keep this place going."

"I suppose it never occurred to you that we shouldn't be leaving Granddad here alone. He'll be eighty in a few months. He could get sick or hurt bad."

"He's got hired help. He wouldn't want us hanging around getting in his way and doting over him."

"Nobody said anything about doting."

"You've got to think of your future, Dev. Once you quit for a year, there won't be any going back at your age."

"That's my whole point, Dad. I'm already too old, and Seth soon will be. It's getting harder every year to compete with those kids. You had to quit it yourself—"

"Yes, but I was forty years old when I did. You boys were getting into the spotlight by then. I wasn't going to compete against the two of you."

"Don't feed us bullshit, Dad. You quit because you were too old. You were losing. Admit it. And now you don't want me to quit because if I do, then you won't be able to live your freewheeling lifestyle anymore, the life you're as much addicted to as you are that can of beer."

Jake shrugged. "I always thought you drove yourself as hard as you did so you could top me, but if you're happy to come in second, then so be it."

"Jesus. You don't give up, do you?"

"No, because I don't want you to give up."

Dev took a new grip on his temper. "Listen, Dad, and listen real good, because I won't explain this to you again. I have all the titles I want. I have all the gold buckles I want. I didn't retire to turn your life, or Seth's, upside down. You can keep following rodeos for as long as you want, but you need to face a couple of truths. You can't eat those gold buckles, and they won't keep you warm at night. You can't ride forever on six world championships you got three decades ago."

"How would you know anything of how I feel or who I am?"

"Maybe I don't, but I do know this ranch is something to hold onto, and there's room for all of us here."

Jake fixed his jaw hard. "You know damn good and well why I don't want to stay on this godforsaken chunk of land."

"Yes, and you have only yourself to blame for that too."

"Think what you want, but before you sink a lot of time and energy into this place, you'd better make sure your grandfather has intentions of passing it down to you."

"I don't expect him to give it to me. I'm willing to pay for it; that's why I've ridden my guts out since I was a kid so I could have the money to keep this place from going out of the family. Granddad would have given it to you already if he'd thought for a second that you wouldn't turn around and sell it to the highest bidder."

"If I'd wanted it bad enough to take it, he would have stood over me, breathing down my neck, pushing me to do things his way. Pushing like he's always done."

"That sounds familiar."

"Don't get smart with me, damn it."

"Is that why you and Mom bought the ranch in Clover Valley? Because you and Granddad couldn't get along?"

Jake looked away; it was a subject he clearly didn't want to broach. "So what."

"Then you drove off and left *her* to take care of it. That was a cheap shot, Dad."

Jake wouldn't admit to having done anything wrong or selfish. "It was her dream, not mine. I wanted to rodeo, and I had a talent for it. I would have been stupid to throw that away. Your mother could have hired people to run the ranch for her if she had wanted to keep it bad enough."

"As if she had the money to pay wages with you blowing it over both shoulders and out your ass."

His dad took a step toward him with fists clenched. "I ought to beat the crap out of you, you insolent little bastard."

"Go ahead and try."

His dad made no move, just glared at him. Dev, seeing there would be no physical altercation, turned back to the house. When he had reached the front door, Seth called after him. "What are we going to tell everybody? You can't just disappear, Dev. You owe your fans an explanation. Hell, there's even a rumor that Satan killed you."

Dev paused with one foot inside the house. "Then I'll make an official announcement of my retirement."

Jake swore and pulled his cowboy hat down tight onto his forehead. "I've had my fill of this shit. I'm going to town." He headed for the pickup with Seth keeping stride next to him. In a moment, the Dodge leaped into gear, spewing gravel all the way to the main road. The drunks at the Red Pony were going to get the honor of rubbing elbows again tonight with a world champion bull rider—six times over. And his wannabe son.

"Dev?"

He turned to the sound of July's voice and the touch of her hand on his shoulder like a soothing balm.

"Is everything all right?"

"It is now."

She followed his gaze to the truck leaving the ranch. "Why did they leave? We're about ready to eat."

"I think it was something I said."

"Another argument?"

"No, the same one."

Her hand slid off his shoulder. "Then maybe it's better they're gone."

"I'm sorry about the barbecue. I know you've been cooking all day, but don't worry, I'm hungry enough to eat a cow."

"You'd better be. Baxter nearly cooked one."

"Give me a few minutes to clean up."

He joined her and Granddad fifteen minutes later, wearing a clean shirt and jeans and with his hair still wet from the shower. The three of them spent the rest of the evening in easy companionship playing horse shoes, and then cards on the veranda.

By midnight, he'd slipped into a pleasant dream of walking with July by a wide but gentle river beneath the soft golden light of early morning. In the dream he had pulled her into his arms and was bending his head to kiss her when the all-too-familiar whiskey voice shattered the dreamland and plunged him into dark reality.

"Wake up, boy. I need to talk to you. It's...Seth."

Chapter Thirteen

His dad had turned on the hall light and left the bedroom door wide open. The light reflected off the dresser mirror and right into Dev's eyes. He lifted his arm as a shield but was hit with a wave of searing pain. He brought the arm back close to his chest, riding out the pain with gritted teeth. When it had subsided enough to breath, he said, "So what's happened to Seth? Is he in jail or something?"

His old man's breath reeked of whiskey, forcing Dev to turn his head away. "No, passed out...in the trail-l-er. Couldn't make it to the...house."

"You woke me up to tell me that?" At least Seth hadn't gotten himself killed.

The pain in his shoulder settled to fierce throbbing. With the hall light still reflecting in his eyes, he groped toward the night stand and pawed around until he felt the scattered pills and glass of water next to them. He lifted himself up enough to swallow two of them, but his aim wasn't good and the water spilled down either side of his face and ran off onto the pillow. He cursed as he wiped the wetness away with the back of his hand.

Jake started to whine. "No. I needed to talk to you...without him. He can't cut it...he can't win s-s-shit."

Dev rolled the spare pillow onto his chest and rested his aching arm across it. "What a goddamn news flash, Dad."

"You've got to com-m-m-e with us, Dev. Finish the...season. You quit and those...deals quit...all those...en-dorse...ments. Those oppor-r-r-tun-ities..."

"I told you I wasn't going to talk about this again."

"Okay, okay. Then just loan us a few thousand." He sounded

pathetic now as, even in his drunken state, he could see his way of life slipping through his fingers.

Dev was tempted to give them whatever they wanted just to get them the hell out of his life, but no matter how much he gave his dad now, he would be back for more later. "Dad, you and Seth need to start making your own way. Seth's got money. He couldn't have spent it all."

"Then you won't loan me any money?"

"No."

The bed lifted, relieved of Jake's weight as he stood up and staggered from the room, muttering, "Thought I raised you better than to…turn your back on your…own dad."

"Hey, turn off the goddamn light and close the door!"

Jake didn't hear, or if he did, he ignored him, as he went into his own room, forcing Dev to get out of bed to douse the light. By God, he wasn't going to let his dad's demands and pleas make him feel guilty for the decision he'd made. His dad should have made preparations of his own. He should have seen the end coming a long time ago and readied himself financially. Dev shouldn't be forced to carry the burden for someone else's lack of foresight. If he kept giving his dad money, the old bastard would never stand on his own two feet.

He tried to go back to sleep, but the minutes ticked by, and then the hours, leaving him wide awake and embroiled in pain that no pills could erase. Just before dawn, he hauled himself from bed, pulled on Levi's and a shirt and went downstairs to the porch swing, hoping daylight would chase away the ghosts and clear the darkness from his mind.

◆

The sun brought July from the house, dressed in a robe, and carrying a cup of coffee in one hand and tea in the other. Dev had been lost in thought, staring out across the expanse of land and sky. It was a scene that had provided stabilizing strength during those times when the winds of life had threatened to blow him away.

"You look like a man who could use some caffeine," she said, smiling as she handed him the coffee.

He graciously accepted the steaming brew. "You're timing is perfect, as always."

She shrugged. "I saw you out the kitchen window. You look like you've been hammered on all night."

"I feel like it."

He watched her settle on the top step; he would have gladly made room for her in the swing if she'd wanted to join him.

She curled her hands around her mug of Earl Grey and looked at him curiously. "I heard your dad and Seth come home last night. I'm sorry, but with your room right over mine, I heard you talking. I couldn't understand what was said, but I gathered from the tone that it wasn't a pleasant father/son discussion."

"They never are with Dad. The second he enters the scene it's like having a black cloud roll over and dump ten inches of rain. It was the same old crap. He was trying to convince me again that I was making the worst mistake of his life by not going back on the tour."

"The important thing is how you feel. Are you happy to be home?"

"Hell, yes."

"Then he'll get over it if you stand your ground."

It was amazing how her presence was all it took to lift his spirits. They sat quietly for a few minutes sipping their respective brews. The sun was bursting above the horizon, and they watched it until it cleared the mountaintops.

"Mornings are my favorite time," she offered, sounding very content. "You're lucky to have such a view so you can truly enjoy them."

"I never used to be able to. I've spent my life waitin' on sundown so I could get to the next rodeo, the next dollar. Mornings meant that I was tired, or in a hurry, or—" He grinned, "driving with a hangover."

"I was just the opposite. The end of the day meant wondering where Buck was—and with whom. Now I can honestly say I don't care what he's doing." She looked over her shoulder at him with sincerity in her eyes. "I'm so glad you let me come here, Dev. There's something about this place that soothes the soul. I needed it, and all of you, to help me through the haze."

"I don't know how you could have needed my old man," he said sardonically, "but this ranch *is* a good place to hide when you can't run from yourself anymore. I don't mean you specifically."

She smiled. "If the shoe fits."

"And as long as I'm apologizing, I want to say too that I'm sorry for not being the best company since you've been here. It's just all this baggage I haven't quite unloaded."

"I've dumped all of mine onto you so turnabout is fair play."

He had more baggage than she could ever suspect, but he wouldn't tell her how old and disillusioned he felt, and it wasn't just from lack of sleep and recent events. It was a condition that began about the time he gave up custody of Dusty. He had buried himself up to his neck in rodeo then, even more so than before, thinking he could fill all the voids by keeping busy, winning, and rising to fame. Being among the top rodeo personalities in the world was a success he'd needed to hold onto for all it was worth to keep from falling into self-destruction the way his dad had when their mother had left. But the truth was, his life was empty, and he needed to fill it with something besides fame, glory, and money.

She leaned against the step railing, still sipping the tea. "You did the right thing, Dev. I know it's hard, but don't let your dad and Seth make you doubt it."

As if her words had summoned the latter, the trailer door flew open and Seth, more than unsteady, half-stepped, half-fell out onto the ground about the time Dev uttered a profanity.

"So much for a peaceful moment."

July grinned at him from over her shoulder. "Humor him. He's your little brother and totally harmless."

"Don't you believe it." Dev couldn't be consoled. He felt like an old rattler who'd been sunning on his favorite rock only to have a predator decide he'd make a good meal. Instinctively, he tightened every muscle and raised his coils.

Seth, of course, was oblivious. He righted himself and staggered to the porch, not even seeing Dev and July until he was almost upon them. His gaze followed the length of July from her toes to the top of her head, and didn't miss her subtle movement to draw her robe over her bare legs. A slow smile opened his features and made him look too handsome for his own good. "Don't cover up on my account, Firecracker."

Dev tensed, knowing what was coming next and knowing he couldn't do a damn thing to stop it.

Seth, in a leonine way, settled down onto the step below July and leaned next to her on one elbow. With that disarming smile in place, he reached up and fondled a lock of hair resting on her breast, as if it was the most natural thing in the world to do. "I don't believe I've ever laid eyes on a prettier sight so early in the morning."

To Dev's disgruntlement, July was friendly and polite. "And I don't remember the last time I received such a gracious compliment."

"Oh, come on, sweetheart. I can't believe that husband of yours didn't make all over you. Or even Dev here. What's big brother been doing all this time? Lickin' his wounds?"

Dev glowered, wanting to throw Seth on the ground and beat the shit out of him. He might have done it, too, if he'd had two good arms.

July laughed. "Buck is no good with compliments unless he's receiving them, and Dev's been minding his own business."

"Isn't that typical?" Seth edged closer until his shoulder was pressed against her thigh. "You know, this is too beautiful of a day to waste it indoors. What would you think of going to the cabin after breakfast and riding around up there for awhile?"

"Do you remember how to get there?" Dev quipped.

While July found the facetious remark amusing, Seth ignored it. "I have to hit the road again tomorrow so what do you say?"

Dev bristled. "July has things to do."

"I'm just trying to show the lady a good time."

July stood up, moving to the front door and stepping out of the middle of their sibling rivalry. "I'm going to fix breakfast. Baxter will be up soon."

Seth leaped up right on her heels and blocked her escape. "Hey, don't let Old Hard-Ass here upset you. He didn't hire you so he sure as hell can't fire you. It's a beautiful day. You could bring your camera."

July considered it. "All right. How about ten o'clock?"

Seth leaned closer. "I'll be counting the minutes."

July placed a hand on his chest to keep him at arm's length

and, at the same time, leaned around him toward Dev, who was still scowling into his coffee. "Come with us?"

Dev had no hankering to share her with Seth or compete with his brother to win her attention. No hankering to watch Seth stumble all over himself trying to get to her. No hankering to hear Seth call her darlin' or Firecracker or sweetheart. No hankering to see her fall for his kid brother.

"No, thanks, July. I'll gladly let you baby-sit today. I could use a break."

Seth glowered at Dev, but, if he wasn't mistaken, July looked disappointed. She went inside to start breakfast, and he felt ashamed for turning her down.

When the door closed behind her, Seth attacked him. "You always have to belittle me, don't you?"

Dev fingered his cup, glancing at the open window and lowering his voice so she wouldn't hear him. "Leave her alone. She's not your type."

Seth, too, realized their voices would carry and toned his down to an attacking growl. "And you think she's yours? Ha! A fun-loving woman like her wouldn't want to be shackled to a man caught in his own loop. She's on the rebound. She won't mind a romp in the hay. She's no different than the rest. She'd welcome some action with no strings attached."

"She's not interested in you, or any of us. She has her own agenda."

"How do you know?"

"Because I do. She's had enough trouble with Buck. She isn't looking for more of the same."

"I guarantee there's a woman's fire inside her just waitin' to be stoked. You've had your chances with her. If you blew it, it's not my fault."

Dev knew why his brother looked at every woman as nothing more than a potential romp in the sack; the poor bastard had learned it from tagging along with their dad too long. Regardless, he held onto hope that maybe one day Seth, too, would wake up and see he was heading down a dead-end road destined for loneliness.

"Maybe you *should* stay here and take her out on some real

honest-to-goodness dates, Seth. Dinner with candlelight and flowers. Let her know how much she means to you." He knew what Seth's response would be, and he wasn't disappointed.

"For Christ's sake. We're not talking marriage here."

"Oh, I get it. We're talking one-night stand. Sorry I mistook your intentions, little brother."

"Forget about her. What's really in your craw is that you don't want me to win—at anything. You see me going out there and riding and having my pick of the women, and you're sitting here starting to resent it. If you think you can convince me and Dad to quit so your misery can have company, then you're on your ass. I'm looking forward to the look on your face when I bring home that world championship. You're like everybody else. You've always assumed I couldn't do it."

"It *is* getting a little late in the day. What are you now? Thirty-three?"

Seth shut him off and went inside where he announced his and July's plans to Granddad who had just come downstairs. The old man's voice carried through the open window to the porch. "As long as you're going to be out there, make yourself useful and check the salt licks. You can load up those ten blocks I have out in the shed."

Dev could almost hear Seth groan.

He stayed in the porch swing until the sun was another thirty minutes in the sky and until July called out through the kitchen window that breakfast was ready. At ten, he stood at the same window and watched her ride away in the pickup truck with his brother, and kicked himself in the ass for being so stupid.

Chapter Fourteen

In his whirlwind life of women and bulls, of booze and high-ways, Seth Summers dangles like a hanged man, twisting one way and then the other, swayed by an invisible breeze, seeking a straight course and finding only air beneath his feet and his hands tied behind his back. The space all around him is not loneliness but emptiness, and the pain in his chest is caused from a hard fall, not a heartache. That's what he'll tell you. That's what he might even tell himself.

He has nothing, and in his heart he knows it, but he drinks and laughs and makes love and tries to convince himself that his life is just as he would have it. The darkness surrounds him, closing in on his delusions. He knows if he closes his eyes for one second too long, the truth will strangle his objections and the darkness will swallow him whole, just as his shadow is swallowed by those who have gone before.

Sometimes he feels as if he has never been and never will be, and if there is anything he believes in, he'll pretend he doesn't.

July put down her pen and reflected on her ride with Seth. Like the silver-tongued devil, he had tried to tempt her with a beguiling smile and promises he had no intention of keeping.

He had stretched full length on the blanket that covered a thumbnail of land on Summers land and asked her to make love, as easy as that. Even now, hours later, July could still feel the blazing sun on her back where she'd sat, knees drawn up encircled by her arms. She could still hear the insects buzzing and the birds singing....

◆

Their horses grazed nearby, picking at the grass beneath the twisted branches of sagebrush and sniffing curiously at a potato chip bag that had blown between their hooves.

Seth had worked his horse pretty hard earlier, roping a calf that had gotten on the wrong side of a fence and was separated from its mother. He could handle a rope as well as the men who competed at the rodeos. When she'd complimented his prowess, he'd shrugged it off. "Hell, what's to throwing a loop? It's the most natural thing I've ever done."

Reflecting on his talent, she filled two tin mugs from the coffee thermos. "There's cream and sugar in the saddlebags."

"I take mine black and strong, sweetheart."

"You probably don't eat quiche either."

"It's not like anybody would know. Least of all Buck."

Her brow furrowed with puzzlement. "Know what? That you don't eat quiche?"

"No. If we were to make love," he said in a voice that had gone Black Velvet smooth, and his eyes, the same color as the coffee, glittered seductively as they attempted to hypnotize her into believing that caution and reason had no place in this universe he had created for himself. He held out his hand to her. "Let's not pass up a moment that might never come again."

She wanted to be held, desperately, but not by Seth. It was the image of his brother that came to mind and stirred her desire. If only Dev had come with them! She had expected Seth to continue his flirtations and had been prepared to deal with him. What had surprised her was that he had been on his best behavior up to this point and hadn't made any sexual overtures at all. Now, he'd slipped back into his playboy role, and she wasn't going to let it go any farther. She stood up and went to the horses to tighten the cinch on her saddle.

"Hey, I didn't mean to chase you off. Come on back."

"I know you're seeing how far you can get, Seth, but I wish you wouldn't."

"Buck isn't holding out for you, so why hold out for him?"

"I'm not holding out for him because I'm never going back to him. But I need space and time. Would you just be a friend?"

He shrugged. "A guy's gotta try. Hell, I've never had a woman for a friend, but if that's the way it has to be—" He patted the spot where she'd sat on the blanket. "Come on. We'll talk. I'd forgotten how nice it was to be out here, away from it all. I'm not ready to go back."

She saw something shift in his eyes that made her believe he could let it go that easily, verifying her suspicions that he had no special feelings for her. She was just another woman to conquer. She was relieved because she had no special feelings for him either.

She loosened the cinch and returned to the blanket, taking up her coffee and opening a bag of Oreo cookies.

"I don't understand you, July. The women I meet seem to want it—anytime with anyone. You were doing a pretty good job of giving that impression at the High Heel, but now your whole attitude's changed."

She took a bite of cookie and followed it with a sip of coffee, keeping her eyes on the distance to avoid his waiting gaze. "I'm sober now, and I've had a month to separate myself from it. Besides, you can't right a wrong with another wrong."

"Maybe not, but finding consolation in another man's arms won't do any harm, especially if you have no intention of going back to Buck."

"It might do more harm than you think, and it definitely won't do any good. Be honest. Do you truly find satisfaction in having sex with women you don't love? Doesn't it leave you feeling empty when it's over?"

He tipped his head so the brim of his hat covered his eyes. "I wouldn't know. I've never been in love."

"You say that with such nonchalance, almost pride, but I find it hard to believe. There had to be someone at some time in your life. Your heart isn't made of stone."

He clearly didn't like being put in a spot where he might have to examine his actions, or his heart. "I guess I've met one or two that were special, but it never worked out. Oh hell, let's change the subject."

He helped himself to an Oreo with an air of indifference, but July sensed it was a mask to cover the pain that hid like a starving fugitive in his heart.

"Okay, how about the real reason why none of your relationships have worked: your dad."

He rolled his eyes. "Oh, that's a fine subject. Can't you come up with anything better?"

"No, I think it's a pretty good one. What happened last night that made you get so drunk you passed out in the trailer?"

"Nothing."

"Are you afraid of the truth?"

"Shit, no. Well, okay, so something happened. Dad made a fool of me in front of a bunch of people at the Red Pony. He said he had to figure a way to get Dev back to the rodeo because I sure as hell wasn't cowboy enough to bring home the money. He never considers how his crass remarks make me feel. Dev might be tired, but he doesn't know what tired is. He doesn't know about the continual failure to reach the top, the continual reminders by the announcers that always come right when you settle down on a bull or a bronc, and they launch into telling your life story to the audience, about how you're the son of a six-time world champion and the brother of a five-time world champion, but they never talk about *you*, only who you're related to and all *their* successes. When they're done, they've convinced you that you're a loser before the gate even opens, and you wonder if they've convinced the judges too. Then it becomes a vicious circle. You spend your life so far down the ladder that you don't even count in the big scheme of things.

"But I'm not going to quit. I'm going to show the sonsabitches. All of them, especially Dev and Dad. I won't quit until I win the PBR World Championship, or I die trying."

"Don't let it kill you, Seth. It's not worth it." She wanted to lay a comforting hand on his shoulder but feared he would misinterpret the act of sympathy and compassion as something more.

"What is worth it then?" His brown eyes had lost their cocky, arrogant gleam as they trained on her, point blank, and demanded an answer he had never found for himself.

"For me, the answer to that question would be a family that loves me, and knowing I did the best I could. Haven't you ever wanted a wife and children? People who believe you're a champion even without the title? Something to round out your life so you don't have more than an endless highway stretched out before you?"

He blew it off. "Hell, women might play with a poor boy, sweetheart, but they want to marry a rich man."

"Not all women."

"Yeah, right. Look at you. You went for the guy who had the handle on the world and who could carry you along with him."

"Buck knew what he wanted, but he didn't have it when I met him."

"He didn't have to have it. His folks had enough to go around. As for success, some people fall into it like the rest of us fall into shit."

She started to get up again, but he caught her arm and held her there. His eyes were almost beseeching. "Hey, I'm sorry."

"Then don't blame what you perceive as your failure on Dev or your dad, or anyone else. And don't hold it against Dev for wanting to retire. You've got to ride your own bull, Seth. If you can't make it, then do something else."

He held up his hands as if fending off bullets. "Okay, okay. Don't rip into me, but bear in mind that all I know is riding bulls. Sure, I'm in the top forty-five, but I'm at the bottom of that rung. And now Dev pulls this retirement shit, knowing it's going to be damn tough to stay on the road without him. You can't blame me for being upset."

She took a steadying breath; he was making her very angry. "You may think you can't make it without him, but you can. You have knowledge and experience you can use. Dev's retirement isn't the end of your career. It could be the beginning of new opportunities for you. If you have something to prove, then put that rope to use. You could go into that arena tomorrow and be a winner."

He hid his eyes beneath the brim of his Stetson. "Maybe so, but Dev's sure throwing away another shot at the championship, not to mention all the bonus money cropping up for the leading contenders. What I'd give to trade places with him."

She could see it was easier for him to cling to failure than attempt success. "Be careful what you wish for, Seth. Maybe where he's at right now isn't the greatest place to be either. It can't be easy for him to have come to this decision when the money in rodeo is bigger than ever, and he's turning it over to the younger guys who've been trying to beat him for years."

"No, there's something else going on in his head, July. I've never seen him this bummed out. It's like he's turned a corner where the rest of us can't follow. He's pulling away from all of us, pulling inside himself."

July understood what Seth didn't; she had rounded that corner herself and felt the need to focus inward for awhile. "People expect certain things out of us," she said, "but sometimes we have to do what's right for us."

Seth reached for another cookie, but he rolled it between his fingers, having no appetite for it. His eyes grew distant. "Dev tried to make me run away once. It was right after our mother left. I've often wondered where we'd be now if I hadn't stopped him. If things would have all been different. Dad was on a drunk because he knew he'd finally pushed Mom over the edge, but he still had the gall to be surprised when she left. Being kids, Dev and I had hope that she would come back."

As he watched an eagle circling the valley, he fell deeper into the memory. "Dev and I had been out checking cows on the range. When we walked into that five-room clapboard in Clover Valley, Dad was passed out on his bed like he'd been for the better part of two weeks. Dev stood there for a minute and stared at him, and I could feel his rage. All of a sudden he reached over and grabbed Dad by the shirt front and jerked him up—hard. He shook him enough to rattle his teeth...."

◆

"Damn you, old man. You had to keep on until you drove her away, didn't you? You weren't thinking of anybody but yourself, least of all, me and Seth."

Jake Summers stared unemotionally at his oldest offspring. Spit trickled from his mouth and he lifted a limp hand to wipe it away. There was a scraping sound in the quiet room as his uncut fingernails made contact with the stubble on his face. "Ah, go to hell, both of you. You ain't caused me nothin' but grief and trouble. Same as her." He had to stop to catch his breath, for talking was even an effort. "She could never accept what I did for a living. So she walked away, left this ranch, this home I bought for her. Left me for another man."

"That isn't true, and you know it. All she ever wanted was

for all of us to be here with her."

"She should have come with us. It was how I made a living."

"You could have met her halfway, you stupid bastard." Dev flung him back against the headboard and watched his body slump before it fell sideways onto the pillows. Jake relaxed into his drunken stupor.

Dev stalked into the living room. Seth followed him, fearful of what he would do. He watched as Dev's eyes took in the old Winchester rifle over the fireplace, larger than life, more powerful than their father who even now held the upper hand and controlled every facet of their lives.

"I could kill him for a buck. A measly buck," Dev said. "But the way he's headed, he'll end up dead sooner than later."

"What are we gonna do?" Seth stood in the middle of the room, tears stinging his eyes while he watched the scene that had been played out too many times in the past weeks. Hope floated away like an irretrievable leaf in a stream.

Dev took a deep breath and wiped his hands on his faded Levi's, as though wiping away any connection between him and the man who had fathered him. Then he went outside where the air didn't smell like whiskey and two-week-old sweat. Seth sprinted after him, frantically propelling his gangly legs to keep up with his brother's because he was afraid Dev would leave too.

Dev searched the austere Ruby Mountains with eyes hard and mature beyond his years. "We'll keep rodeoing. I'll take care of you."

Seth wiped his tears away and saw the stubborn set to Dev's jaw and the emotions playing across his face. He wanted Dev's assurance that everything was going to be all right, but his brother was only making him more scared. He didn't want to leave home. Maybe they *had* been rodeoing with their dad, but they always did so with the knowledge that they had a place to return to when they got tired or when the money ran out.

"Maybe we ought to see if we can find Mom."

Dev whirled on him. "Why should we? She didn't want us either or she wouldn't have left."

"She left Dad, not us."

"She left us, too, you stupid shit."

Seth almost didn't dare speak again, but he didn't want to

run away. Sure, Dev might feel that way now, but he was sixteen, old enough to take care of himself. Seth wasn't, and he...he just wanted someone to turn to. In a small voice, he said, "We could see if Granddad would take us in."

The rage dissipated; it was too much of an effort to hold onto it. Dev released a heavy sigh. "I guess you're right. Granddad won't turn us away."

◆

Seth brought himself back to the present with considerable difficulty. "For years, I kept hoping she'd come back. She wrote letters at first, apologizing for leaving us and trying to justify it, asking us to come and live with her. Then she re-married, and we grew up and none of it mattered anymore."

"Have you seen her again?"

He sipped at his coffee, found it to be cold, and tossed what was left of it into the grass. "She's come to some of our rodeos. Dev and I visit her in California when we're out that way. She's always glad to see us, but there are all those miles and years between us, and none of us can seem to build a bridge."

"How did your dad ever get over her leaving?"

"I don't think he did, but he sobered up long enough to realize we'd left him too. He got himself straightened out with Granddad's help, then he hit the circuit again, more determined than ever. He was still his freewheeling self to people's faces, but her leaving left its mark in a place where nobody could see. There was resentment under the surface that ate its way deeper in all directions until it started showing through in everything he did and said. We went with him because he was our dad, or maybe because we caught the rodeo fever, I don't know. We were all just trying to make some sense of our existence, trying to fill the hole she left behind."

Now that he was on a roll, he continued to purge his soul. "I became more dependent on Dad. I was afraid he'd vanish like Mom had. I wanted him to see me, to care about me enough that he would never think of leaving. But all he saw was Dev, and only because Dev was a natural on a bull's back. There never was any real father/son connection between the two of them. I don't know that Dad had any more feeling for us than he did some Joe Blow on the street. We were people he could use to get what he wanted."

Seth's eyes were pinned on the distance, as if the past existed in a dimension so accessible he could touch it, smell it, taste it. "There was a windmill on our Clover Valley ranch, in the yard next to the house. After we left that day, and in the months to follow, Dev and I went back there a couple of times before the place got sold, but that windmill never pumped water again, even when the wind blew. It just stood there, no longer having a purpose or being part of a whole. For years, I felt like that windmill. Sometimes I still do."

As Seth pondered the past, he seemed to have forgotten July was there. Then he put it all behind him and flashed his old cocky smile. "Well, hell, Firecracker. That was a dismal little story. I should have kept it to myself."

"No, Seth, I'm glad you shared it. The road can be a real empty place sometimes."

He avoided her sympathetic eyes. "Well, this sun has me drowsy, and I'm plumb drained from spilling my guts so I'm going to close my eyes and grab a few winks. You won't mind, will you?"

"No, I'll wander around and take some pictures."

He lays back on the blanket, puts his hat over his face and feigns sleep. He has to do that before I see the painful way the darkness has swallowed him.

I pick up my camera and exhaust the scenery, then I turn to snap close-ups of his Tony Lama boots, his silver-plated belt buckle, his Stetson, his tanned hand resting on his broad chest, his blue chambray shirt collar pressing against his hard jaw, the frayed hem of his worn Wrangler jeans.

The intimate details of a cowboy lost.

July set her pen aside and closed her journal. She turned out the lamp by the bed and hid in the darkness with her doubts and a rising anxiety. Maybe she should leave tomorrow, first thing. Eric wouldn't be happy if she did. He wanted that story about the Summers men; he wanted it bad. But how in the world could she ever be objective enough to write it, now that she had seen all the scars on their hearts.

Chapter Fifteen

Dev sat in the porch swing and savored the sight of the pickup spewing dust all the way to the main road. With his dad and Seth gone again, it was a yoke lifted from his shoulders.

Baxter came out of the house picking bacon from his teeth with a toothpick. He stood next to Dev and watched the dissipating dust with a peevish eye. "Riding goddamn rainbows again. I hope you didn't give them too much incentive."

Dev sensed the disappointment in his grandfather even if he covered it with irritation. "Only a thousand. I wasn't going to, but then I decided it might keep them away for awhile."

"Seth will try harder if he knows there's no more."

"He might do fine, Granddad."

"Yes, sir, and if frogs had wings they wouldn't bump their asses so often. *And* if he didn't have Jake drinking his good intentions."

"Seth isn't exactly a slacker in that department himself."

Baxter heaved a sigh. "I figured July could keep them around, if anybody could."

"Only if she was giving them what they wanted."

Baxter nodded in silent acknowledgment. "I'll hate to see that girl leave. She's made this old house feel like a home again and not merely a place to camp. She reminds me a lot of Cecilia when she was that age."

"She seems a little partial to you too."

Baxter tried to cover his satisfaction. "Ah, hell, she dotes on me because I'm old and gettin' feeble. That's all."

"But you like it."

"A man never gets too old for female attention."

"You'd better watch her," Dev goaded with twinkling eyes. Then using Seth's crazy notion, he said, "I've heard about women who look for elderly men to marry and then wait for them to die, or help them along with a little arsenic in their oatmeal. This ranch would make a pretty penny if a body had the mind to sell it for subdivisions or turn it into a dude ranch with log cabins dotting the hillsides."

Baxter snorted. "There's a difference between me and your run-of-the-mill doddering old man who would fall for such a ploy in the first place."

"I didn't say you were doddering, Granddad."

Baxter's eyes sparkled as he egged Dev on, making it clear that he was getting a kick out of their bantering. But when he didn't say anything, Dev prodded. "And what's the difference?"

"Vanity. I'm not vain enough to think a pretty young woman would be interested in anything *but* my money. All I have is a ranch that keeps me running nonstop, and right now I need to check the range for sick cattle."

"What about Ern and Kurt? Can't they do it?"

"Oh, hell, they're busy building that fence. Besides, I might be old, but I can still ride out and check the cows."

Dev pushed himself out of the porch swing. "I'll go with you. It's been a long time since I was in the mountains."

Baxter kicked at a nail he'd missed during his earlier repair mission. "Well, now, I don't think that would be a good idea what with your shoulder still bound up."

"It's no big deal. It's on the mend."

"Yes, and for that very reason you don't want to do something to damage it all over again."

Dev wanted to go with him, like he had when he'd been a kid. He would suffer a little discomfort. He needed to be out in the mountains winding along a sagebrush trail under a hot sun where the only sounds were insects in the brush, birds overhead, and the occasional distant whine of a jet heading for Reno or Vegas. He needed to get back in touch with the land and with who he was.

"I can ride Stripe or Dinky," he insisted. "Dinky won't buck or give me any trouble."

Baxter shifted the toothpick to the other side of his mouth, thinking that wasn't entirely true, but to mention the incident with the sage hen would mean giving away his secret. By the same token, he knew if Dev had been on Dinky, he'd have been alert enough and agile enough not to be left clawing air. Hell, the kid could stay in the saddle with his hands tied behind his back.

There was more than that behind his hesitation to take Dev with him. He had an ulterior motive—a plan—and he'd been working on it for a couple of days now. He had to be coy though; he didn't want Dev to see right through it.

"Actually, I'd like you to take July into town and help her get groceries. I think she had some pictures to develop. If we keep avoiding her company, she'll leave."

"I recall you mentioning that before."

"Well, it's true. A woman with her talents has bigger fish to fry than what this old pond can grow. She needs incentive to stay. You sure haven't been giving her any—you stay holed up in the shop tinkering with that damn truck—and I think that makes her feel bad."

"Did she say so?"

"No, but she went riding with Seth when she'd rather have gone with you."

"How do you know that?"

"Because I do."

Dev didn't want to tell his grandfather the truth, which was that he avoided situations where he was alone with July because she was too much of a temptation. So far, it hadn't been hard staying away from her, what with his dad and Seth hanging all over her like she was cotton candy. But he knew that if he stepped over the line, and she didn't reciprocate, it would destroy their friendship forever.

Damn it, he didn't need more complications in his life just when he'd set his mind to do some heavy-duty culling. On the other hand, whose fault was it that she was here in the first place? He'd asked for every bit of it, and more.

"We're out of milk and coffee, and I'm almost out of cigarettes," Baxter continued. "And see she buys the things we like to eat. I don't want her trying a bunch of newfangled concoctions on us and coming home with a bunch of greens and tofu—whatever the hell tofu is."

"Give her a list, Granddad. I'm sure she's an old pro at buying groceries. And I'm sure she's capable of driving your pickup. I don't need to go."

"Like I said before, she might like company."

"Are you asking or insisting?"

"Don't worry, son. Familiarity breeds contempt. If you try hard enough, you'll find something about her to dislike, the way you have all the other women you've met over the past decade."

"I haven't done that."

Baxter found that entertaining. "You've been, by my calculations, running from commitment ever since your divorce. Don't let what happened with Mica sour you on all women. She's the exception more than the rule."

"Don't be so sure. You've been on this ranch so long you don't know what's out there. Women nowadays aren't like they were when you were young. They don't need men, and they don't mind letting us know it. Hell, some of them don't even need us for sex anymore."

"That's hogwash. You've been watching too much TV."

"So, what's this all got to do with July?"

Baxter shrugged. "Nothing. Unless you fall in love with her on the way to the grocery store."

The conversation was not only backing Dev into a corner but making him cranky as hell.

Baxter's eyes narrowed a bit too knowingly. "What are you so damned afraid of anyway?"

"Quit trying to hitch us to the same wagon, Granddad. It won't work. I like July, a lot, but she's still married, and before it's over with, we all know she'll go back to Buck."

"Then make sure she doesn't."

"I can't *make* her do anything."

"If you don't know how to make her see she'd be a fool to leave you, then I'm sorely disappointed. All this time I was under the impression you had the knack to turn a woman's head."

"Maybe there's too much at stake here, Granddad. I'm too damned old for getting my heart broke, okay?"

The old man's eyes bored into him with that look that said he'd run out of patience.

Dev held up his hand in defeat. "Okay. I'll take her, but you be careful out in the mountains by yourself. Be back by sundown or I'll have a search and rescue party after you."

Dev knew that would get the old man's goat. His eyes snapped, but there was still good humor in his voice. "I've been gettin' along just fine for years out here by myself so don't you go making a fool out of me. If I'm not back by dark, you come looking for me yourself."

Dev grinned. "You just said you didn't want me to ride."

"I'll make a goddamned exception. Now git!"

Laughing, Dev went inside, but Baxter remained on the porch for a moment longer, chewing the toothpick and wondering why he'd pushed the boy into a corner. If he wasn't careful, he'd push him right back out into the rodeo arena.

"Ah, what the hell." He tossed the toothpick into the grass. It would all work out in the end. Things always did.

◆

Dev figured if he could walk, he could drive, and at least his legs weren't hurting anymore. When he folded himself behind the steering wheel of Granddad's Chevy Silverado, though, he twisted his shoulder the wrong way and the pain grabbed him.

"Are you sure you can drive?" July asked, sliding in on the passenger side.

When he could breath again, he said, "No, but a man has to retain his pride."

"At any price?"

"Uh-huh."

"You could have gone with Baxter. No sense in both of us poking cantaloupes and squeezing tomatoes."

"Granddad was scared to death you were going to buy tofu and strange vegetables."

July laughed. "What is tofu anyway?"

"Sweetheart, your guess is as good as mine."

"Well, no offense, but I'd rather be horseback riding than buying groceries." She looked longingly toward the Ford where Baxter was loading his necessities for the day. The sunlight reflected in her green eyes and danced through her hair, making it look like spun gold.

"That makes two of us," he said, "but I guess somebody has to do the dirty work."

She reached across the seat and patted his hand with mock consolation. "We'll just have to make the most of it."

He put the truck in gear and pointed it down the gravel driveway. Dust spiraled out behind them like a long, gray scarf twisting in the wind. They reached the county road, and although it was also gravel, it was graded good and he was able to pick up speed. Shielding her eyes with new sunglasses, July settled back for the long ride to Elko. Oftentimes, they were able to do all their business in Wells, but the photo shop that did the best job on her prints was in Elko.

Dev glanced at the tote bag on the seat that held several rolls of 35mm film and a couple of digital memory cards as well. "You must have taken a lot of pictures on your ride with Seth."

"I did, and I got some great shots too."

"Did little brother mind his manners?"

"You know Seth. He tried to be bad."

"That's what I was afraid of."

"Don't worry. I kept him in his place."

Dev feigned indifference. "You're a big girl, Firecracker. You can do whatever you want, with whomever you want."

Her mood turned on a dime and her eyes snapped indignantly. "Your brother can call me Firecracker. Your father can call me Firecracker. But *you*, Dev Summers, will *not* call me Firecracker."

"Well, hell, July. I didn't know I was a special case."

"And while we're on the subject—" She ignored his droll smile, "you didn't seem to have that particular philosophy back in Arizona."

"What philosophy is that?"

Her eyes teased. "If I recall, you were out to be my knight in shining armor, convinced that I couldn't take care of myself. Now you don't seem to care *what* I do or who I do it with."

"Yes, and you were drunk—if I recall. I was only protecting you from two idiots who would have taken advantage of your condition and state of mind. Now you're sober and capable of making your own decisions, so I won't interfere. Just stay ahead of Seth and Dad."

She leaned her head against the headrest, rolling it to the side to study his face shadowed by the brim of a white, straw Stetson pulled low over his eyes. The masculine contours held no trace of softness. There was something about him that was inherently different from his father and his brother, even though the same blood ran through their veins. At first glance, he looked like a wild young man, cocky enough and game enough to tear up the town. If she looked deeper, he reminded her too much of herself, a person stewing in a cauldron of disappointments, searching for a fragment of life's meaning, hoping to find it in the white lines of the highway perhaps, or in the lonely terrain that stretched forever into the sea of never-ending sagebrush.

They were empty. Disillusioned. Both of them. *All* of them. Cheated by the foolish decisions that had altered the course of their lives forever. But when you're eighteen, life stretches out before you, long and sweet and full of promise, and you do things without fear nor judgment. Then one day you wake up, thirty-something, and the sweet promise has turned to a shit hole eight feet deep, and you're floundering in it with no life line in sight.

He looked over at her, rubbing a hand across his cheek. "Did I leave breakfast on my face or something?"

She had the overpowering urge to run a hand across his strong shoulders or a finger along his cheek. A touch, just a simple touch to somehow tell him she understood him better than she had any man. Instead she continued the playful banter. "Oh, I wasn't going to tell you. I thought I'd let you walk around all day that way."

He glanced in the mirror to see if she was telling the truth. She wasn't, and he gave her a look that made her laugh.

"By the way, do you always drive as if you have flood waters at your heels?"

He pulled his foot off the gas. "Sorry. I guess I'm still trying to make the next rodeo. Old habits die hard."

"Will you miss it, Dev? The rodeo?"

He shrugged. "I haven't so far, but someday, probably."

Dev sensed her eyes penetrating his soul as if she could see the thoughts tumbling through his head. Was she intuitive enough to know that he wanted to pull over to the side of the road, bury his hands in that mane of hair, and make love to her right here and now?

Damn it. The next time the cupboards were bare, his granddad could damn well drive her to the grocery store himself.

"At least you have something to show for your effort," she said. "All I have are photographs of moments from other people's lives, and a house filled with Buck's memorabilia—his trophies and titles I worked as hard for as he did. I hate to think of the lost years, the lost effort."

"At least you gave it your best shot."

"I did try, maybe for a lot longer than I should have. Even to the point of making a fool of myself." With a sigh, she removed her sunglasses and, closing her eyes, leaned her head against the headrest. "I'm sorry, Dev. I didn't intend to go off on that back road."

At the moment, she looked small and tired, almost like a child who's been running all day and who finally collapses on the floor in a state of exhaustion. He reached across the distance and touched his hand to her cheek. Surprised by the comforting gesture, she opened her eyes to his.

He started to draw his hand away, but she brought hers up to cover it. Turning her face into it, she brushed his palm with her lips as if she did it everyday. Then she released him and closed her eyes once more.

He put his hand back on the steering wheel, but his flesh retained the memory of her kiss as he focused on a distant mirage forever dancing one step ahead.

Chapter Sixteen

Dev found the photo shop, but they had to settle for a parking spot a block away. They jaywalked across the busy street, passing numerous casinos where darkened interiors were occupied even at the noon hour. The small town whose roots had been cattle, sheep, and mining now hummed with new-age prosperity and the energy of gambling.

"Hey, Dev Summers!"

They both turned at the shouted greeting. A man, wearing a bartender's apron, and who had been leaning in the doorframe of the Bull Horn Saloon & Dance Hall, now stood in the street, grinning from ear to ear.

"I thought that was you crossing the street."

"Winston." Dev was delighted to see him. "I figured some bull had stomped your head in a long time ago." He walked back toward the man, steering July with a hand on the small of her back. As soon as they were close enough, the men shook hands in greeting, but Winston's gaze shifted to July.

"Are we team ropin' now, Summers?"

Dev introduced the two, and Winston's hand slid from Dev's to engulf July's. "My pleasure, ma'am." He slid perusing eyes over her. "Pardon me for staring, but I swear I've seen you before. Are you a movie star or something?"

July laughed. "Not hardly, but thank you for the compliment." She had seen Sinclair plenty of times in action, even had photographs of him, but she preferred not to mention it, knowing that the subject would lead to another, and another, and end up on Buck.

Sinclair's eyes suggested he was still trying to place her, but he let it go and motioned toward the door. "Come on inside out of the heat. I'll buy you a beer, and Dev can tell me what brings him to Elko on the arm of such a lovely lady."

He gave them no choice. Taking each by an elbow, he hustled them inside through the saloon-style doors and then through interior doors that stayed closed to contain the air-conditioning. He sat them at a small table on the edge of the dance floor. The dance hall, a dim cavern, echoed its emptiness. The bar flies, four of them, twisted on their stools to gawk at the new arrivals. A man who was shoving quarters into the slot machine by the door stopped long enough to assess them through indiscernible, whiskey-pickled eyes.

Winston brought two cold beers, lifted the caps, and settled himself on a chair next to July. "Dev and I go back a long way," he said. "I was a rodeo clown. I got his ass out of a sling more than once." He spared Dev a glance. "It looks like he could have used a good bullfighter on his last go-round."

Dev downed a third of the icy brew. "I had a good bullfighter *and* good advice—" He returned the bottle to the polished wooden table, "but I didn't listen to the latter so there wasn't much the former could do, although I still credit him with saving my neck."

"What in the hell did you do anyway?"

Dev fingered the bottle, not overly anxious to tell Winston. If anybody would understand, though, it would be him. "To start off, I drew Satan 101—"

"*Again?*"

"Yeah. Then I took a suicide wrap."

Winston sat back in his chair and stared at Dev as if he thought he'd been banging his head on a post. "Christ Almighty, Summers. Why did you feel compelled to do that, with old Satan no less. He'd just as soon kill you as look at you."

Dev downed another third of the beer. He felt July's eyes on him as curious as Winston's. He pushed his hat to the back of his head. "I don't know. I got a wild hair. The old man had been hounding me. I was sick and tired, ready to quit. My arm hadn't recovered from last year's pounding. Take your pick or choose all of the above."

Winston's expression softened with understanding. "I know

the feeling. Sometimes a man has to let go, and in rodeo, it's sooner than later. It's a sport for young men. I had to face the fact that I couldn't out-maneuver and out-run those old bulls anymore, and I sure as hell wasn't getting rich. It took me two wives, dozens of girlfriends, more broken bones than I can remember, and twenty years before I found the nerve to turn the page to the next chapter in my life. But damn, I did have fun while it lasted."

Dev finished his beer and set the bottle on the table. "That's the realization button—when it ceases to be fun."

"Ain't that the truth? I got to where I'd wake up in a cold sweat, dreaming of some big, bad-assed bull cleaning my plow. That's when I took my savings and bought this bar."

Dev looked around the place with renewed interest. "I didn't know you'd done that. We used to have some good times stomping around on that dance floor, didn't we? It was the best one in Nevada. Hell, maybe the whole West."

Winston looked around the place with pride of ownership. "It still is, but it's kinda dead at the moment. Come sundown, though, it'll pick up."

Two ranchers about Baxter's age sauntered through the door. Winston stood up. "I'd better go wait on the customers. Those two old boys come in here about once a week to talk cattle. For some reason they like to get my input, as if I know a damn thing on the subject. Anyhow, you two enjoy yourselves. Play the jukebox, if you want. I've got a lot of the old tunes I know you'll like." He turned to July, his smile softening. "It was my pleasure to meet you, ma'am. My only regret is that I didn't see you first. But I guess you could do a hell of a lot worse than this old cowboy right here." He gave Dev a friendly slap on the back, assuming there was more to his and July's relationship than what there was.

July smiled. "It was a pleasure to meet you too."

After Winston was gone, Dev fingered his empty beer bottle. "Well, let's go get your film developed."

But July was looking around the place, taking it all in, particularly the many historical photographs of the region, which were arranged on the rustic board-and-batten walls between pieces of cow town memorabilia from the late 1800s and early 1900s. "I love this atmosphere. If these walls could talk—the stories they could tell. And those old men—what wonderful subjects. I should get my camera and take some pictures of them."

"If it's a picture of a drunk you want, wait until Dad gets home."

"You're too hard on him, Dev. Maybe you should try to encourage him to get on with his life."

"Hell, he'd die if he couldn't be around a rodeo."

"Then he should get into something rodeo-related, like stock contracting or team roping."

"Team roping? Jake Summers? He thinks ropers are at the bottom of the gene pool. He's a rough-stock rider, remember? The best there ever was." His statement bled with sarcasm.

"Roping takes as much talent as bull riding."

"Try to convince him of that."

"Maybe I will," she said with good-natured determination, then left him sitting at the table while she went to the walls to study the old black and white photographs and spend a few minutes with Win and the two ranchers who told her who some of the people were and their contributions to history. From his seat, Dev watched the emotions change on her face as she thrilled to the stories behind the pictures, and then studied the various photographers' techniques.

When she returned to the table, her eyes were aglow, and she went on for a while about the photographs and how she'd like to shoot some real ranch scenes if Baxter would let her. Then she said, "So, this is the best dance floor in Nevada?" A slender eyebrow lifted as a look of mischievousness appeared on her face.

"Bar none."

"Then I'd be foolish to come this far and not scuff it up a bit. Are you up to a dance?"

In the first years after his divorce from Mica, Dev spent many a lonely hour holding beautiful women in his arms. Now he was older and wiser and more cautious. He was also lonelier than he'd ever been, and July was, as always, messing with his heart and his head. But temptation was stronger than good judgment on this go-round.

He stood up and held out his hand. "Never suggest to a cowboy that he might not be capable of doing something. He'll prove you wrong even if it kills him."

With a hand on her lower back, he walked her to the old-fashioned jukebox updated to play CDs, and they surveyed the illuminated offerings under glass. Winston had a good mix of classic and current, the best of the best. July knew what she wanted to hear: Deanna Carter's "Strawberry Wine," and a couple of songs by George Strait, her favorite country singer. "He's just the cutest thing alive. Sort of reminds me of you, Dev. I'll bet you've heard that before, though, haven't you?"

"Oh, yeah, I hear it all the time." Dev humored her as he fished a bunch of quarters from his pocket and dropped them into the machine.

July made the selections.

He took her hand. "Come on then. Pretend I'm old George."

He led her to the middle of the dance floor. The ranchers and bar flies swiveled on their stools to watch. The one playing the slots by the door paused to see what they were doing.

The beat of "A Fire I Can't Put Out" filled the empty room and resounded on its perfect acoustics. Dev released July's hand long enough to remove his sling and toss it across the floor. It hit the table leg and stopped.

"Isn't your shoulder going to hurt without the sling? Maybe we shouldn't...."

He once again offered his hand. "It'll be all right if you don't get too wild with me."

As they faced each other with gazes locked, he felt the invisible band of sexual tension strung between them as taut as a tightrope. He knew too well where this intimacy could lead if they allowed it, and from the half-shuttered glimpse of need he saw in her eyes, he knew she felt it too. Still, she took his outstretched hand, and with heightened senses he curved his arm around her slender waist and drew her toward him. When she slid her left hand up his arm to his shoulder and then around to his shoulder blade, something sank and rose inside him like a thousand butterflies trying to escape. For a moment, the strength drained from his legs and he felt wobbly and drunk. God, had she intended the movement to be so slow and sensuous?

Her breasts made heart-stopping contact with his chest. His belt buckle brushed against her flat tummy, and his blood began to pulse so loud he could hear it in his own ears. But with his growing need came strength. Throwing fear and caution aside, he molded her curves to his length, vividly aware of how right she felt in his arms. An unconvincing voice told him he should run while he could. Instead, he found the beat of the music and apologized for being a little rusty.

"I'm not complaining." Her whisper brushed his throat with arousing warmth. "But I wish those guys would quit watching us."

He looked down at her, and she tilted her chin upward to meet his gaze. "We're the only entertainment in here, darlin'. Besides, they're too drunk to be critical."

She was like fire sucking the oxygen from his lungs. Her skin burned his hand through her cotton top and scorched the length of his body. He closed his eyes and sank into the flames. Agony had never been so sweet.

His lips, seemingly of their own volition, dropped a feather-light kiss to the top of her head while his mind memorized the soft texture and scent of her hair. By degree, the tension drifted from her body, and she relaxed against him. He held her tighter, not wanting to think about when the moment would end. For the first time ever he had her in his arms, and they were making love simply by the way he held her hand, the way she pressed her cheek against his, the way her fingers caressed his back, the way their legs touched and intertwined as they moved to the rhythm of the song. It had been so long since making love had been about love. So long since it had even been about desire. It had been about convenience and opportunity, disappointment, emptiness, and need.

And God, how he needed July, but in a way so different from all the others.

The songs they'd paid for played one after another and when those ended, more followed. Dev noticed the guy at the slot machine had started shoving his quarters into the jukebox instead. He was at the bar now, nursing a beer, and watching them with a sad look of longing in his eyes.

An hour later, Dev knew there was no getting his heart back. He didn't know the exact moment he'd lost his tenuous grip on it, but he did know that holding July in his arms felt more right than anything he'd ever done. He'd had a little of her; now he wanted all of her.

If it hadn't been for the lightning bolt and subsequent power outage, they might have danced all afternoon, maybe all night. The lights blinked out and the jukebox wound down to a stop. They were a beat or two behind it and came to a swaying halt like two sots lifting their heads from a stupor, remembering that they weren't a world unto themselves.

"Goddamn storm comin'," the jukebox drunk slurred. He looked at the two of them as if he was as disappointed at the timing as they were.

Dev was reluctant to let July go, knowing when he did that the chance to hold her again might never return.

The gray light from outside filtered in through the windows, and he saw his regret reflected in her eyes. "I guess it was time to go anyway," she murmured.

Keeping her hand in his, he led the way from the dance floor, scooping up his sling and saying farewell to Winston and the others who acted like they were old friends now.

They made it to the pickup just as the sky released its rain. Dev fumbled in his pocket for his keys while July, laughing, moved to the center of the street that had gone empty, held out her arms with her face lifted to the rain. She started to turn in circles, oblivious to the world. The harder the rain came, the harder she laughed, not noticing the way it was soaking her cotton top, outlining every intricacy of her breasts and scanty bra. Not noticing the people watching from windows and doorways along the street as they took shelter from the storm, some smiling, some scowling, perhaps in approval or disapproval of her, the rain, or both.

At last she stood motionless, face lifted to the clouds, eyes closed, lips full and inviting and slightly parted to the sweet taste of the sky's nectar. The moisture clung to her lashes and slid off her face. Her arms fell to her sides, and she stood stock still for a moment, allowing the rain to wash over her and into her being.

As he watched, Dev wondered if he dared take the next step and travel to the center of her soul, to surrender his heart to her. If he did, would it be a journey of no return?

Then a car turned onto the street, and she ran back to him. Her happy smile finished melting his heart until it was nothing but another puddle in the street. "Thank you for wonderful time, Dev."

With the pickup pressing into his spine, he reached for her and pulled her into his arms; it now seemed a natural place for her to be. "Don't forget to thank me for the rain. That was no easy feat."

She opened her eyes halfway against the downpour. He turned his head so his hat acted as a shield. The rain shimmered off her lips. He wanted to taste her pure sweetness. He had always wanted to taste her since the first time he'd laid eyes on her all those years ago. Desire and need rose to such a crescendo inside him that he could have taken her right then and there.

She stepped away, slipped from his arms, and ran for the passenger door. "It's locked! Hurry! We're getting drenched."

He laughed. "We're already drenched!"

He hurried to the passenger side to open the door. She dove into the interior and reached for the jacket behind the seat.

Whatever had happened between them was over.

By the time he had maneuvered himself under the steering wheel, the rain was pouring off the brim of his Stetson, soaking his crotch.

She grinned as they both took note of the wet bulge. "Isn't it just like a cowboy not to have the sense to get in out of the rain."

◆

Dev couldn't sleep that night. It had nothing to do with the rain and everything to do with pain. It went deeper than broken bones and torn tendons. It throbbed in the emptiness inside him.

He tossed back the sheet and sat on the edge of the bed.

Aided by the blue-white light from the wavering flashes of sheet lightning, he reached for his Levi's on the nearby chair and pulled them on. Without a shirt or shoes, he tip-toed down the stairs to the front door.

The screen gave its usual yowl as he opened it onto the porch. It was still hot, despite the rain, but the smooth wooden planks were dry and cool against his bare feet. He went to the railing and leaned against a support beam, listening to the distant rumble of thunder. In moments, another ripple of sheet lightning undulated through the belly of the dark clouds as they lumbered over the mountains.

"So, it kept you awake too?"

Startled, he saw July in the shadows where the porch made its bend to the west side of the house. She had her camera in hand and was wearing those silk shortie pajamas. The spasms of lightning sparked the embers in her eyes and lit the gold in her hair, flickering across it like an unsteady, white-hot flame.

And he said, "No, it wasn't the storm that kept me awake."

Chapter Seventeen

Thunder rumbled again and the sheet lightning rippled in the distance behind the old poplar trees, giving them an eerie stance. July aimed her Nikon and captured their ghostly images before moving down the porch toward him. "Is your shoulder hurting?"

He couldn't bring himself to confess that she was the reason he'd lain awake listening to the wind buffet the shingles and rattle the window panes.

He laid his hand on the sling. "I guess I overdid it."

Closer now, a flash of ribbon lightning illuminated the darkness; the Nikon's shutter clicked almost instantaneously. July made a few adjustments and turned the camera toward him.

"Hey, don't waste your film on me." He laughed, raising an outstretched palm in objection. "I'm not even dressed."

July looked over the top of the Nikon. "I noticed."

The flirtatious glow in her eyes sent a rush of heat to his loins and a lightning bolt of longing to his heart. "So, you're enjoying my pain?"

Her laughter again, sweet and pure. "Of course not. But you're a good subject for a photographer. It's all those hard lines and angles. They're even more pronounced in this blue light." *Click. Click.* "All of you Summers men are good subjects. Maybe because you're cowboys, and cowboys exude pure masculinity and exemplify the mystique and romance of the Old West." She spoke as if she were writing one of her articles. "Or maybe because you're part of a dying breed."

He didn't miss the facetious tone in her voice. "What you're saying is that we're out of touch and out of time. Obsolete. Like yesterday's computer."

"Maybe. If you were in New York or L.A. But not here."

"Well, don't be doing any *National Geographic* stories on us, okay?"

"What? And deprive all those people from reading about a famous rodeo cowboy and his family?" The lightning shuddered through the grumbling clouds. *Click. Click.* "I just need to find a theme. Trust me, it'd be great. I see something on the order of a man and his grandson holding onto their land in the face of an adverse economy and a fading way of life."

He shook his head. "Too nostalgic. *Way* too overdone."

"How about an aging bull rider returning to his roots to start a new life?"

He lifted an eyebrow. "Aging?"

"Nicely," she amended with a smile, wondering if she should tell him about the story Eric wanted her to write, but it didn't seem the right moment. She didn't want him to think she was here just to get a story, because she wasn't.

He said, "How about a photographer's unexpected confrontation with the harsh reality of ranch life in Nevada?"

She wrinkled up her nose. "The harsh reality of life. Period. But, on the brighter side, all this rain will break the drought and be good for the crops, right?"

A gust of wind forced them to plant their feet more firmly on the porch's weather-worn deck. It flattened July's thin pajama top against her breasts and sent a spattering of rain clinging to the mat of hair on Dev's bare chest.

He forced his eyes to her face. "Actually, it should have come weeks ago. It'll ruin the hay if it keeps up."

She tucked a strand of wind-blown hair behind her ear. "I thought it was supposed to be good for hay."

She stood only eight feet away. His primal instincts urged him to close the distance; his common sense reined him back. They'd been safe at the Bull Horn; here, they were much too close to the French doors that led to her room, her bed.

"When the hay's been cut," he absently explained, "and the ranchers are waiting for it to cure so they can bale it, they don't want rain. Some of them are in that position now."

"Oh, I knew that," she replied with a hint of self-mockery.

"Did you now?" he bantered.

"I might have grown up in the heart of Albuquerque, but I learned a lot about country life from Buck's parents. They didn't farm, but they had to buy hay to feed all those expensive horses. Finding the best quality from the right person was a standard topic of conversation at the dinner table. Money was never an object with the Joneses. You couldn't even begin to keep up with them."

Dev sat back against the railing and folded his arms across his chest. An occasional drop pelted his back but did little to cool the fire that burned within. "Do you stay in touch with your uncle's family?"

"Not much." Her voice was without regret. "Once I was gone, none of them seemed to care what happened to me. They were relieved to see me go."

"I can't imagine that."

"My uncle treated me good, but his wife had never wanted to take me in, and when he wasn't around, she never missed an opportunity to put me in my place."

"Sounds like Cinderella and the wicked stepmother. How about the cousins?"

"They followed their mother's lead."

"How will Buck's parents feel about you leaving him?"

"They'll be delighted. They never thought I was good enough for their precious son because I didn't have the proper pedigree. They don't keep anything on that place that doesn't have a blood line dating back to Adam and Eve."

He nodded, fully understanding. "Yeah, the few times I was there, I thought they seemed way too proud of themselves." When he spoke again, he tried to sound noncommittal. "So when will you go back to Albuquerque to settle things with Buck and get your belongings?"

She turned her eyes to the crackling storm. There was no mistaking the heartache in her voice. "There's nothing there I want or need."

"Nothing? A woman who travels that light is suspect."

The teasing quality in his voice pulled her away from the painful memories. She flashed a smile. "I had some books I'd like to keep. And a great leather jacket with fringe and beadwork. Oh, and my saddle."

"All the important things in life."

His eyes still teased, but her mood had turned serious. "I don't want to wear out my welcome, Dev. Maybe it's time for me to move on."

Yes, maybe it was, but he couldn't bear the thought of not having her here, regardless of the damage she was doing to his heart. "Don't even think it, lady. You're welcome here for as long as you can put up with us. Besides, Granddad would be sorely disappointed if you left. He likes your company more than he likes home-cooked food."

"Or Toll House cookies?"

"His ultimate weakness," Dev fondly conceded. "He never did own up to why he was all skinned up. I think he might have fallen off his horse and didn't want to admit it."

"Yes, he was pretty embarrassed." July immediately regretted the unintended disclosure, remembering too late that Baxter had shared the story in confidence.

Dev was quick to catch the slip. "So it *was* a horse."

"He swore me to secrecy. He didn't want Jake to know. He's afraid Jake will figure out a way to keep him off his horses, maybe even put him in a retirement home."

"Hey, I'm not going to say anything to Dad. I'm here to look out after Granddad, not get him into a world of shit. Besides, giving unnecessary information to Dad is opening yourself up to being gutted. Do you know how it happened?"

Looking at her bare toes, July divulged the story about the sage hen flying into Dinky's face and catching Baxter off-guard. When she finished, she said, "Please, don't let on that you know. I don't want him to lose his trust in me."

Dev turned back to the railing. "One of us should have been here with him."

July laid a hand on his shoulder. "You're here now, Dev. That's what matters."

Thunder filled the silence that fell between them. Dev's senses were aroused by the sensation of her touch on his bare skin—hot, ambivalently soft yet strong, familiar yet unfamiliar.

"Yes, I'm here, July. And so are you. But what will you do if Buck shows up with more promises?"

She started to turn away. He caught her hand. "You can talk to me. Don't you know that by now?"

She sat down in the porch swing and stared out at the black sky. "I won't go back, but I *am* worried that I might fall flat on my face without the security he offered."

"Sometimes security can cripple a person. It can make you become complacent and too willing to accept your circumstances."

"Yes, and it takes a lot of courage to walk away from it when you have no family to turn to. It's like being a jackrabbit trapped in the headlights, not knowing whether you should plunge into the darkness to the left, or the right, or keep going straight ahead, one jump ahead of the beast bearing down on you."

"You can make it on your own, July. You're a wonderful photographer and writer. You don't need Buck. As for a family, we're here for you, if you want us."

"That means so much to me."

"I know it's hard, July."

"I should be grateful, I suppose, that we didn't have children to complicate things."

"Maybe so. My divorce would have been a lot easier if it hadn't been for the custody battle over Dusty—which I lost, of course, being the irresponsible rodeo cowboy that Mica made me out to be. But I can't imagine life without Dusty, even though I don't get to see her much anymore."

"Buck didn't want children," July offered. "They would have forced him to grow up and think of someone besides himself. I doubt he would have been able to handle sharing the spotlight."

Dev studied her features in the storm's erratic light. "Do you still love him?"

She curled one leg under her and rocked the swing with her other foot. She seemed to be picking her words carefully, or maybe she wasn't certain of the answer. "No. Any feelings I have left are more of regret and wasted time. Not love."

She left the swing and walked to the end of the porch, leaning out over the railing and into the storm that now seemed to be

moving away. She looked frail and vulnerable. Her shoulders began to shake.

"July, I'm sorry. I shouldn't have—"

With a sob rising in her throat, she turned to him, and he
took her into his arms. She buried her face against his neck, hiding her tears. "I don't know why I'm crying. It's not like I regret
leaving him. I just feel so…lost. So empty."

Dev stroked her hair and when her tears had subsided, he
cupped her chin in his hand and wiped the lingering moisture
from her cheek. "Everything is going to be all right. Life has a
way of working itself out."

"Oh, Dev, does it? Despite all the stupid decisions we make
along the way?"

"Maybe *because* of them."

She laid her hand against his cheek, cupping the side of it as
she looked sorrowfully into his eyes, and he wondered if that look
meant that she knew where his heart was but that she could not
follow. Then she placed a light kiss to the corner of his mouth and
hurried to her room.

He stood on the spot a full five minutes, aching to follow her.
In the end, he trudged back to the loneliness of his own room, to
that dark place where sleep still eluded him and he could do nothing but ponder the gentle, tortured way she had whispered his
name.

◆

In her room, July closed the French doors but left the drapes open.
She crawled under the covers and watched the receding play of
lightning. She heard Dev enter the house through the front door
and go upstairs. She closed her eyes. Sleep was elusive. She tossed
and turned and got tangled in the sheets. She imagined Dev holding her, whispering to her, making sweet love to her, making everything all right.

She flung back the covers and sat up, groped in the darkness
for the lamp switch. The golden light illuminated the truth of
things, the reality of her life, and the dangerous foolishness of her
lustful dreams.

She should leave. She had burdened the Summers family with
her presence long enough. She pulled her bag from the closet and

began yanking clothes off the hangers and stuffing them into the bag. She couldn't see clearly for the tears filling her eyes.

Then suddenly she collapsed on the floor and wept. She didn't want to go. She loved it here. She loved all of them in their own way. She couldn't keep running for the rest of her life. But she couldn't stay hidden here forever either. She had to make a move. She had to prepare for the divorce battle that would ensue, but she needed strength—strength and courage to face Buck and his parents and not let them intimidate her, not allow them to destroy her as she knew they would try.

But if she stayed, what would she do about her feelings for Dev? She could see herself without Buck, but she could not see herself without Dev. He had always been there, like a candle in the window lighting her way in the darkness. She didn't want to love anyone again for a long, long time. To love on the rebound was a mistake—everyone knew that. Yet this feeling for Dev wasn't a sudden development. It had lain dormant for years. Could she walk away and always wonder where it might have taken her if she had nurtured it?

He might have kissed her today had she not panicked and ran away. Then tonight, she'd opened the door again, thinking she was ready—she had wanted to feel his lips on hers—but he hadn't walked through the portal. Was it because she was still Buck's legal wife, or because she was giving mixed signals that left him, like her, not knowing which direction to turn? Or would he hold onto honor to the bitter end when she herself felt the only thing left of her and Buck's marriage was a piece of paper.

"Shit," she muttered, rubbing the tears off her face with her hand. "How do you expect him to know what to do when you don't even know what you want him to do."

She pulled the room's only chair over to the French doors, bundled herself up in a blanket, and there she remained, staring out into the darkness until dawn.

Chapter Eighteen

Holding onto the banister, Baxter eased his old legs down the stairs that were getting harder to navigate. Every morning this past year, as he'd made the trek to the kitchen, he had wondered if he should have kept the downstairs bedroom. To this day, though, it was impossible to step into the room without thinking of Cecilia. It was impossible to sleep in the big bed he'd shared with her without remembering their youth and whispered endearments in the night.

It was so long ago. The young, vigorous man he'd been was gone and as far away as if he had been in another lifetime, as if he'd been someone else entirely. Now he was just old and unimportant in the big scheme of things. He'd lived his life and was now waiting to be with Cecilia again. It was a sad truth that the world belonged to the young who were still full of hope and dreams. At his age, he had neither. Yet he went on, because that's what a man did.

The aroma of brewing coffee caught him at the bottom of the stairs, helping him put aside memories of the past and focus on what had to be done today, which was doctoring the cattle. The rain had stopped and it would be dry by noon.

When Dev and July had gotten back from town yesterday, he'd told them about the cow he'd found with a sore foot and the calf whose watering eye could develop into something worse if not treated. He hadn't wanted to pull Ern and Kurt off the fence and he figured that, with July's help, he could do it. He hadn't been in favor of Dev trying to help and risk a setback. But the kid had been adamant, and the truth was, it had been a good long while since he and Dev had done anything together. It would be almost like old times.

When he walked into the kitchen, July stood near the electric griddle, fork in hand, turning a dozen strips of sizzling bacon. Cooking next to them were six eggs. Two pieces of toast popped from the toaster. She retrieved them and smeared them with softened butter. She did it the way he liked it, not letting the toast get cold before she applied the butter. She offered her usual bright smile and "Good morning, Bax. Did you sleep well?"

He returned her greeting and told her he had slept fine. He took his place at the table just as she set his breakfast in front of him on a big ironstone plate. He reached for the salt and pepper. He was sure going to hate to see that girl go.

◆

Baxter headed the Ford into the mountains, bouncing along on a two-track, century-old wagon road that wound through the sagebrush. Over the years, it had widened somewhat from the treads of many tires. In the bed of the pickup, an exuberant Cappy thrust his head out past the edge, oblivious to the dust, intent on the wind in his face and the thrill of movement.

July sat next to Baxter, seeing a hundred photograph opportunities, but Baxter had work to do so she didn't ask him to stop and indulge her.

Below eye level, on the dashboard, was the ever present roll of toilet paper. Next to her left knee, Baxter's age-spotted hand rested on the gear shift knob. Dev sat on her other side, his shoulder rubbing hers. He seemed comfortable with the intimacy of the position as he kept his eyes on the rutted road and made occasional comments to Baxter about the cattle and the range and how the rain had brought it back to life.

July knew that parts of the West were in a drought. She'd taken many photographs of its effects on the people and the animals who inhabited the land. Two of her photographs had been featured in *Heart of the West* when they'd done a story on it a couple of years ago. As a photographer, though, she often felt like a child looking at candy through a window. You arrive on location fresh out of an air-conditioned car, decide on the mood you want to portray, set up the shots, take them, then rush off to get them developed or down-loaded into the computer, and you never get into the picture yourself. You remain a world apart.

Today would be different. Today she would be involved.

Sandwiched between Dev and Baxter on the worn-out bench seat, she enjoyed the heat of summer and the hot rush of the wind blowing from one open window to the other as it loosened strands of hair from her ponytail and slapped the end of the toilet paper roll against the cracked windshield.

They crossed five cattle guards and opened three wire gates before they reached the old mountain cabin. Tucked back in a small aspen grove, it was rustic and low-slung and appeared to have sprouted from the soil like a mushroom. Baxter had kept it in good repair and neat as a pin. The range, refrigerator, and hot water heater ran off propane. A gas generator provided power to pump water from the well and supply electricity to the house.

They left their coffee thermoses and cooler on the table then went back outside. Dev collected the medicine box. July and Baxter followed, bringing lariats and saddlebags bulging with livestock paraphernalia.

What they found on the other side of the barn was an empty corral and two broken poles that had once been the gate. Several sets of bovine tracks led off into the sagebrush. Baxter made straight for the hole in the corral. "Why did they bust those poles down? I gave them plenty of hay when I left yesterday."

Dev made an attempt to gather up the broken poles with his good arm, noticing they were weathered and gray, brittle and run-down, like everything else on the place.

"I've been meaning to replace them," Baxter said, reading Dev's mind. "Guess I'll have to now."

"It's okay, Granddad. I can start making repairs around here as soon as my shoulder heals. I know you haven't had time to do it all yourself." He was too kind to mention that Baxter was too old to keep up with everything.

"Are those your cows?" July pointed to the northwest.

The men followed the direction of her outstretched arm and spotted the two Hereford cows and their black-bally calves about a quarter of a mile away.

"That's them. Let's catch the horses and bring 'em in."

They caught a sorrel gelding named Sam for July. He was an older quarter horse but still nimble on his feet. Dev was itching to ride a beautiful three-year-old bay named Banjo, but Baxter said he needed to be ridden down some more. "I named him Banjo for good reason, son. He's strung pretty tight. Wait until you're healed, okay?"

"Then I'll ride Dinky."

Baxter made another feeble attempt to keep Dev on the ground. "July and I can get them in, son."

"I'll be fine, Granddad. Sitting in a saddle won't strain anything."

"That pony can step right out from under you, if he's a mind to."

Dev laughed. "Don't worry, he'll have to work hard to lose me."

Knowing Dev's mind was made up, Baxter straddled another of his favorite mounts, an Appaloosa named Dan. "I'll circle around them to the left," he said, gathering the reins. "You and July go down the road toward the draw. They'll want to make an escape to lower ground so you'll have to head them off."

As Baxter suspected, one of the calves panicked when it saw them closing in. It split for the draw on a dead run. Its young mother released a startled bawl and trotted after it. The older cow turned in the opposite direction toward the mountains with her calf, thinking she could disappear in the aspen trees. Baxter headed Dan through the sagebrush as fast as was prudent in order to get around her.

Dev and July kicked their mounts into a lope toward the draw to turn the calf and its young mother. Dinky and Sam knew what they were supposed to do and stretched their necks into the wind. The calf skidded to a halt just as they reached the draw right in front of it. Dinky thwarted its attempt to bolt past them, and it raced back to its mother who watched the riders with her head thrown high, prepared to bolt if they came closer.

They moved toward her until she retreated and trotted back to the older cow and calf, which Baxter and Dan had lined out toward the corral. The old bossy was feeling the pain from her attempted escape and now hobbled along on three legs with the fourth held high off the ground.

Baxter wrangled all four animals into the corral without further assistance. July was fascinated as his horse maneuvered around the cattle, cutting in and out and preventing their every attempt to break away. Back in the yard, she dismounted, tied Sam to a hitching rail, and retrieved her camera from behind the seat of the Ford. Switching the regular lens to a telephoto, she began snapping pictures of Baxter and Dan in action.

"Look at him," she marveled to Dev. "You would never guess he's almost eighty. Has he ever competed in any cutting events?"

"Granddad was not much on competing, although he did do some local rodeos in his younger days, mostly fairs and informal gatherings of area ranchers. There was seldom money involved. The families would get together, and the women would bring food. It was a way for young people who lived in the country to have a social outing and meet the opposite sex. Granddad met my grandmother at one of those rodeos. She was from a ranch over in Ruby Valley. They worked side by side to make this place work. I think the only time he left here was when he did his stint in the army."

At the corral gate, the calf ran in after its mother and sought out her udder, deciding that all the stress called for some comfort food.

July joined the men in the opening where the poles had been broken. Baxter and Dan pushed the four bovines into an adjoining pen and closed the gate. He rode up alongside July and relaxed in his saddle, crossing his forearms over the saddle horn.

"That would have been a lot harder if you two hadn't been here to help me. I sure do appreciate it."

July grinned at him. "Now what?"

"Your first lesson in veterinary medicine."

They drove the cows into a separate pen, leaving the calves in the larger one. From there, they forced the cows into a long, narrow alley constructed of green metal stock panels. The alley led to a metal squeeze chute of the same color. It was an apparatus with handles, adjustable sides, and a head catch—or stanchion—that opened enough to trick the cattle into believing freedom waited just beyond. When they stuck their heads through the narrow opening, the sides of the catch closed down on their necks in front of their shoulders. The sides of the chute could then be manually adjusted inward or outward against their bellies to hold them snug while being treated.

For the cow with the sore foot, doses of an antibiotic were given. July was anxious to help, so Baxter explained all the procedures to her, showed her how to fill the syringe from the dark brown glass bottle, and even offered to let her give the shot. She declined, preferring to let him and Dev handle that part of it while she took more pictures.

When the cow was doctored and released back to the pen, along with her calf, Baxter swung into his saddle, roped the calf with the bad eye and snubbed it to the post in the center of the corral. Using another lariat, Dev caught one of the calf's hind feet, took a dally around the saddle horn, and stretched the rope enough to keep the calf from going anywhere.

"Okay, July," Baxter instructed from atop his horse. "This is where you come in. Get the pinkeye medicine from the saddlebags. It's the small white plastic bottle."

July took a couple of quick pictures and set her camera outside the corral in the grass. With plastic bottle in hand, she bent in front of the frightened calf. She took a few seconds to pet his face and croon some comforting words. "We're not going to hurt you. This medicine will make your eye better."

"He can't understand a word you're saying," Dev bantered.

"He's just a baby. Look at the fear in his eyes."

"Then get him doctored, Firecracker, so we can let him go back to his mother."

She came upright with her hands on her hips. She pretended to be indignant, but there was a sparkle in her eyes. "What did I tell you about that, Dev Summers?"

His grin broadened. "Sorry."

"Say it like you mean it."

Their eyes locked for a few moments, toying and teasing with the other and forgetting about Baxter who sat watching the flirtatious play between them.

"Okay," Dev conceded. "I'll never call you that again."

"Thank you."

Satisfied, she returned her attention to the calf. "So what am I supposed to do?"

"Aim it at his eye and give the bottle a good squeeze."

"Is it going to hurt him?"

Dev chuckled. "It might sting a little, but not for long."

She squeezed the bottle, and a bright yellow powder spurted out into the calf's eye. He blinked but didn't seem to mind it.

"Okay. That ought to do it. We'll check him in a few days. Now stand back and we'll let him go."

After they had the calf returned to his mother, Baxter asked July if she'd like to ride Dinky. Never having ridden a cutting horse before, she was delighted.

"See if you can cut them apart again," Baxter suggested.

The men moved to the sidelines. July handed her Nikon to Dev and asked him if he'd take some pictures of her. In the saddle, she tugged her hat down tighter onto her forehead and nudged the little horse toward the cows. With the pleasure of a good challenge, Dinky and July settled into the task; Dinky with ears and eyes alert, his feet nimble and eager; July with a smile on her face and her hands light on the reins. His first strong lunge to the left nearly unseated her. She released a note of startled laughter then tightened her knees against the saddle fenders, soon realizing she was only along for the ride because the horse didn't need any guidance from her. In no time, she was moving in perfect rhythm to the gelding's smooth side-to-side maneuvers as he blocked the cow's every movement. After a few minutes, the cow tired and whirled for the chute.

Job done, Dinky relaxed. July reined him toward the gate, and he pivoted smartly on his back legs. With a mile-wide smile, she dismounted. "Now that could be habit forming."

Baxter was grinning too, happy to see her enjoying herself.

"Well, the fun's over. We need to fix the corral," Baxter said, recoiling his rope. "I've got some spare poles out behind the barn."

While Baxter rode Dan out of the corral, Dev handed the Nikon back to July and started gathering up the veterinary supplies.

"Hey, I'm sorry about using the F-word again. I'm too used to hearing Dad and Seth call you that."

"The F-word? How clever. And if you meant it, you'd wipe that annoying grin off your face."

He ran a hand over his mouth, but the smile wouldn't quite go away.

"Men." She rolled her eyes and walked out of the corral, draping her camera over her shoulder.

Dev stayed behind, enjoying the sway of her hips in the form-fitting blue jeans, and fighting the painful need to see if there was room in them for two.

◆

Baxter was old and his eyesight was failing, but he wasn't blind. From what he could see, there was a powerful attraction between Dev and July. He knew that stubborn kid too well, though, and figured he'd let July get away unless there was a way to haze him in the right direction. He had tried getting them together with the grocery shopping trip, and then again three days ago when they'd doctored the cattle. Since then Dev had spent every waking moment out in the machine shop, tinkering with the Ford as if he believed he could get it back into superb running condition. Well, maybe it was time for another talk.

When he got there, Dev had torn the carburetor out again.

"I hope you have that back in by tomorrow, son. We need to doctor those cows again. Follow up on the antibiotic."

"July wouldn't have to go."

Baxter sauntered over to the Ford and looked at the engine, trying to act nonchalant. "Why don't you admit the way you feel about her?"

Dev's head came up and his eyes narrowed. "What's that supposed to mean?"

Baxter shrugged. "It means what it means."

"I don't know a man alive who wouldn't be attracted to her, Granddad, but we're only friends. As for tomorrow, she wouldn't have to come along. I'm sure she has business to tend to and would like some time for it. We can doctor those cattle."

"Cecilia always liked getting out of the house. July's no different."

Baxter removed the pack of cigarettes from his shirt pocket and went through the motions of lighting one. Sometimes the things he did forty or fifty years ago were sharper in his memory than the things he'd done last month. Lately, his days with Cecilia had come into focus, especially some of the ones he'd spent with her in the cabin, making love. He didn't have to try too hard to make the memories almost tangible. He could feel her skin, smell her perfume. He could still hear the bedsprings on the brass bedstead squeak beneath their weight.

On those hot summer days, the afternoon sunlight streamed in through the open window and slanted across the patchwork quilt and across their young, naked bodies. His had been muscular and tan; hers slender and soft. He could hear her laughter as they talked of the future. They'd occasionally go silent, listening for automobile engines gearing down for the hills, bringing visitors up the dirt road. If that happened, they'd scramble for their clothes, and he'd hurry back outside so no one would know he'd shucked his work for a few precious hours with Cecilia.

There were times these last few years when he felt as if she were close by, as if she were in the shadows watching and waiting for the moment when it was his time to join her on the other side. Then he knew she'd reach out a hand and take him there, leading him to heaven like she'd always done.

"I think it's you who can't get too far away from her." Dev's words brought Baxter back to the present.

"Maybe neither of us can." Baxter propped his foot up on the front bumper. "Are you in love with her yet?"

The comment set Dev back so hard that he turned away and feigned interest in the carburetor. "Hell, Granddad, aren't we all?"

Baxter knew he was pushing too hard, but time was running out for him. He had one more thing he wanted to accomplish before he died, and he hadn't felt this strongly about anything in twenty years. "So what are you waiting for? Women like her don't come along every day. Don't be afraid to get back in the saddle, son. Give her a good reason to let go of the past."

"I'm not afraid of getting in the saddle. I'm afraid of getting thrown out of it. Hell, I can't believe we're having this conversation."

"Why? Because I'm an old man? Well, someday you'll be ready to die, the same as me. At least I had your grandmother for a good portion of my life, and I have those memories. I don't want to see you spend your life alone and lonely. You don't enjoy those one-night stands."

The screwdriver in Dev's hand slipped; he released a string of cuss words.

Baxter didn't seem to notice and kept right on talking. "I hate to see you end up like Jake, knowing you let the right one get away."

Dev put the screwdriver aside. His granddad was flat-out serious. He was, in essence, giving him permission to fool with a married woman, and it was more than unnerving. "I don't know if Dad even realizes it."

"Even if your dad were to take a notion to find someone to settle down with, he'll have missed the best part."

"And what is the best part, Granddad, because I think I've already missed it."

"No. There's still time for you. The best is simple. It's all about growing old with the woman you love. If you marry a woman when you're both young, neither of you will ever get old in the other person's eyes. Right up until she died, your grandmother always told me I hadn't changed a bit. And she never did either."

Baxter looked at his boot toe. "Things always seemed more stable when she was here. She was able to bring calm to chaos. Her presence could fill empty spaces. People gravitated around her. She held us together."

"Like July?"

He nodded.

Dev went back to the carburetor. Baxter lit another cigarette and smoked it a third of the way down before dropping it to the concrete floor and pressing it out with his boot toe. "Well, I'll let you get back to your work. I'm going to see if July needs help with something."

◆

The next morning, Dev thought it ironic that Granddad got up claiming to have a headache that wouldn't stop.

"Have you tried aspirin?" Dev asked.

"Hell, I've tried Excedrin. I think I'm going to have to lay down until it goes away. Must be this heat."

"What about doctoring those cows?"

"You and July won't have any trouble taking care of them."

"I thought you said I shouldn't be doing ranch work."

"You proved me wrong the other day. That arm isn't going to slow you down none. And take the horse trailer. Bring Dan and Dinky home. They need more riding than they're getting. It'll be something you and July can do."

It was hard enough as it was to stay away from July. Look at what had almost happened the last time they'd spent the day together. They were like lightning and grass in a drought year. And the old man knew it.

Chapter Nineteen

All remnants of the previous rainstorm were gone. At the cabin, Dev and July stepped from the pickup into stifling heat. There was no breeze to cool their skin. It was silent except for the insects buzzing in the tall grass and the birdsong filling the nearby trees.

This time the cattle were where they should be, lazing in the shade of the corral poles. After saddling Dan and Dinky, Dev and July separated the animals for a second treatment. They went about their business with no difficulties. By the time they finished, the sun hung at high noon.

Dev suggested they take their lunch and ride up higher in the mountains. "There's a lake with an incredible view. It's one of my favorite spots on the ranch."

July transferred the food from the cooler to the saddlebags. Dev rolled up a cotton blanket for the picnic and tied it behind July's saddle. After he had secured the saddlebags behind his own saddle, he slid his granddad's old .30-.30 Winchester into the gun scabbard. At the twinge of apprehension entering July's eyes, he said, "It's just a safety precaution."

"Are there grizzlies?" Her gaze lifted to the mountains rising not far behind the cabin. "That's one animal that really frightens me."

"None that I know of. I'm more concerned about mountain lions. But don't worry. I doubt we'll see anything larger than a deer."

Trusting him to protect her, she swung onto Dinky. They headed for their destination down another dusty, two-track road that became circuitous and steep.

July's qualms about wild animals were soon forgotten as they left the road and followed alongside a stream, rushing crystal clear over a rocky bed. From there, they rode single-file down a narrow, winding game trail through sagebrush and aspens, which gave way to pine trees, rocky outcrops on the hillsides, occasional granite walls that rose nearly perpendicular, and lush meadows painted with a rainbow of wildflowers. Mule deer grazed the mountain meadows in knee-deep grass, watching their passing without fear. More streams tumbled down canyons, fed by year-round snowfields on the peaks above. They startled small animals: a porcupine, two rabbits, chipmunks, and a pine grouse. Once they heard a rustling in a pocket of pines but didn't see what had caused it. Dev thought it might be a moose or elk, or even a black bear, all of which were adept at remaining hidden.

They moved their sure-footed horses out onto a rocky ridge and followed its spine until it opened up to a cirque in the mountains, and there in the grassy bowl was the sparkling, crystal clear Sapphire Lake. They paused to gaze down at its incredible hue, indeed the color of its namesake, enjoying the silence around them disrupted only by birdsong, the cry of a hawk circling overhead, and the hum of insects in the grass. From this position on top of the mountain ridge, they could also see the valleys stretching out below in all directions and blue bands of cordilleras fading into the horizons. In a not-too-distant valley, a band of horses leisurely grazed.

"Mustangs?" she asked.

"I've heard there are still some in this country, but more than likely they belong to a neighboring rancher."

July wanted photographs and used her telephoto lens until something, perhaps an inner sense of being watched, caused the leader of the band to set the others into motion, racing them eastward over more hills and out of sight. Lowering her camera, she stood motionless, absorbing the vastness into her soul.

"Are we still on Summers land?"

"Everything we've ridden over today is Granddad's, but his property line ends at the top of this mountain, then it starts getting into the high country of the Jarbidge Wilderness. If you go up farther, there's the old ghost town of Jarbidge."

"I'd love to see it and find out some of it's history. It might make a good story."

"The name comes from a Shoshone word meaning 'monster that lurks in the canyon.' There is an old legend that Indians confronted this creature and chased it into a cave where they blocked it up with rocks and boulders. Some say its ghost still walks the mountains."

The wind came up, pressing against her and tousling her hair about her shoulders. It wasn't a cold wind, but she shivered as she looked about, laughing nervously. "So that's the real reason you brought the gun."

He laughed. "We can pack into the wilderness one of these weeks if you want to go all the way to the ghost town."

"After telling me a story like that? Oh, what the heck. Let's do it." Then she spotted a vehicle sending out a plume of dust along one of the many roads and trails that crisscrossed the valley floor below. She pointed, drawing Dev's attention to it. "It's so small from up here, like a toy. What an incredible place."

She remounted, and they sat in their saddles for a few more minutes soaking up the peaceful panoramic view of the snow-capped mountains that rose even higher and more rugged in the distance. The mid-summer heat was heavy and stifling even in this higher elevation, and they noticed thunderheads had mounted the western horizon but were too far away to be an immediate threat.

They rode their horses the rest of the way down to the water's edge, skirting a tangle of willow bushes that grew as tall as their heads and too thick to get through. The lake was open on three sides and offered a grassy place to rest. Indian paintbrush, columbine, and lupine all swayed in the gentle breeze next to the water's edge in bright contrasting colors from deep blue-purple to orange-red; dark pink wild roses covered low-growing bushes. Dev chose a spot where a small grove of aspens had taken root. July spread the blanket closer to the water but still in the shade.

He settled next to her on the blanket. With the wind blocked from the cirque, the air was still and the sun burned hot on their backs. Overhead, two hawks floated in the sunlight's golden glow while crickets chirped in the grass and dragonflies darted near the water. Frogs croaked from the dense willows and ate bugs that congregated over stagnant havens near the water's edge.

Reclining to his elbow, Dev said, "When Seth and I were kids, we used to come up here and go skinny-dipping."

"So you and Seth were close when you were kids?"

"We were. And sometimes Granddad would come with us."

"Somehow I can't see Baxter skinny-dipping."

"Oh, he never went that far when we were around. He always wore a pair of cut-off Levi's. He was a good swimmer. He's the one who taught us. He was still strong and muscular in those days."

Dev started to pull off his boots and socks. "That water is too inviting to pass up. I'm going in." He removed his sling and shed his shirt.

She laughed at him. "You must be a doctor's worst nightmare. You never follow orders."

"My shoulder is healing. Besides, I'm just going to float around, nothing fancy. You know, a little physical therapy. If my arm starts to hurt too much, I'll sit in that shallow pool on the edge. Seth and I put some flat rocks in there when we were kids and built them up like a seat. When you're sitting, the water only comes to your chest." He reached for the zipper on his Levi's but stopped short, giving her a seductive lift of his brow. "Turn your head, darlin'."

She tilted her head saucily. "Oh, I don't know. I came along for the scenery, and it looks as if it's about to get very interesting. It might even be worth a picture or two. Maybe something for *National Geographic*. They're really keen on naked natives."

"Whatever turns you on." His grin waned as his eyes took on a smoldering glow, captivating hers with sexual suggestion. She had seen the look while they'd danced at Win's and again on the veranda during the storm. She understood it. Felt it. The heat outside seemed to have gone inward, but her inner voice kept reminding her that he was an old friend, and she shouldn't gamble with the only solid thing she had left.

He turned his back to her and started to take his pants off.

Laughing, she did the right thing by closing her eyes and lowering her head to her knees although she fought a nasty little devil inside who urged her to peek. But she didn't look up until she heard him plunge into the water and let out a yowl followed by, "*Damn!* I don't remember it being this cold."

As he moved into deeper water, she caught glimpses of his firm, bare buttocks, strong thighs, and the recent scar that ran ragged across his lower back.

When he'd reached the middle of the lake, he stopped and turned around to face her, keeping himself afloat with his good arm. He flashed a devilish grin. "Come on in."

It did look cool and inviting, and she wished she'd brought a swimsuit, or even some cut-offs and a tank top. "You just said it was cold."

"Once you get past the initial shock, it's fine. Feels good."

"I'll bet you can't stay in there five minutes."

"Bet I can stay in longer than you."

"Oh? And how much will you bet?"

He thought about it for a second. "Fifty bucks."

"Okay, fifty bucks it is."

It was good to see the Dev she remembered from the old days. She wanted to get in there with him. It didn't matter that the challenge in his eyes also contained a glow of seduction. It didn't matter that she knew she was headed for deep water.

"All right, cowboy. You're on."

She reached for her boots. Pulled them off. Followed them with her socks. Propped them next to the bank in the tall grass. Stood up and released the button on her jeans, then the zipper, knowing she was behaving recklessly. It was something she would have done when she was seventeen. Something she should have known better than to do at the age of thirty. Still, she couldn't stop.

"Close your eyes. I don't do exhibition."

He laughed and turned his back on her, always the gentleman.

The jeans came off, the shirt, but she wasn't quite bold enough to remove her champagne-colored bra and matching bikini panties. Holding her arms out for balance, she stepped into the pool and jerked her foot back. "This isn't cold. It's ice!"

He turned over in the water and watched her with a big grin.

"Dev Summers! You weren't supposed to turn around until I said so!" Her arms went up in a crisscross over her breasts as she plunged in.

"Looks like something from Victoria's Secret."

"You would know, of course."

His laughter was a hearty roar of delight that brought a reprimanding scowl from her.

"You talk about Seth being a bad boy. He can't hold a candle to you."

"You didn't go skinny-dipping with him, did you?" His smile wavered.

"It's okay for me to do it with you, but not him?"

"That's right."

"Hypocrite."

"Well, did you?"

"No, we stayed fully clothed."

His smile returned. "What you're wearing is no more revealing than a bikini. Don't get so upset."

"It's still my underwear, you jerk."

He laughed again as he watched her pick her way forward. The lake bottom sloped gradually toward its center. She didn't stop until the water slid over her breasts. It was so cold, she could barely take a breath. "I feel like a Popsicle. How did you stand to swim in here all afternoon when you were a kid?"

"A kid's sensors are like his brain—not fully developed."

"I'm sure I won't feel a thing once I'm numb."

"Seth and I had a lot of fun in here after we'd been putting up hay or building a fence somewhere for Granddad. We would get so dirty and tired."

He could remember it well even though it had been two decades ago: Dad off on a drunk so he wouldn't have to help; Seth, a kid of thirteen, gazing out across the acres of hay bales that weighed as much as he did, looking like he was going to cry; and Granddad in the distance, baling up more.

There's miles of it, Dev. We'll never get it up.

Just take it one bale at a time. One day at a time. We'll go skinny-dipping tonight. That'll be fun.

Will you tie a rope to that old tree like you promised?

Sure.

Dev looked at the lone aspen tree spreading its branches over the edge of the lake. Because it stood separate from the grove, it had grown outward instead of upward and had developed nice, sturdy branches. It wasn't very tall and its white bark bore the black scars from their initials carved into its skin. The thick, cotton rope they'd used to propel themselves farther into the water no longer dangled from the broadest branch; it had long ago disintegrated when they'd ridden away to become men.

"Why did I let you talk me into this?"

July's words brought him back. She was floating languorously, drifting closer to him. The sensual movements of her long, slender legs beneath the water gripped his fantasies.

"I didn't talk you into anything," he said lightly.

He was right, of course. She had entered the water of her own volition, albeit his challenge, and she hadn't felt this alive for years. She began swimming with slow, steady strokes that helped to warm her up. She didn't know how long she swam with Dev not far away, watching her and tossing out a remark now and then. It wasn't long before she returned to shore.

"I guess I owe you fifty bucks," she said with teeth chattering. "I've got to call it quits."

Out of the water, with her back to him, she hurried to the sun-warmed blanket and pulled it up around her shivering body.

Then she scooped up her clothes and, holding the blanket around her shoulders, picked her way through the rocks and grass to a stand of willows where she stripped from her wet underwear and hung it on the branches. She used the blanket and the sun to finish drying her skin before getting back into her clothes. By the time she returned to the lake, Dev was out of the water and fastening his jeans. His shirt, used for a towel, was in a wet wad in the grass. She draped the blanket over a tree branch, and he did the same with his shirt.

She felt awkward now that the crazy intimacy of skinny-dipping had passed. For the sake of regaining the safe ground of normalcy, she suggested they eat their lunch. They got the saddlebags with the food and settled down to eat, making small talk but mostly sitting silent, enjoying the warmth and beauty of the high country. After Dev finished, he laid back, adjusting the saddlebags so he could use them for a pillow without the buckles gouging his head. July sat cross-legged next to him and was startled by the soft touch of his hand on her back.

"Let's take a nap. The heat and the food are making me drowsy." Making a motion to her with his hand, he said, "Rest your head on my chest."

While a voice inside her warned that the water was still deep enough to drown in, she consented to the intimate position and laid against him, shifting her body until she was comfortable. Together, they gazed up at the clear blue sky and the distant clouds, and it seemed natural for him to put his arm across her waist and natural for her to place her hands atop it.

They fell asleep that way and neither stirred until over an hour later when a rumble of thunder woke Dev. He opened his eyes and saw the blue-black thunderheads boiling above them and felt the sudden drop in temperature.

July slept, her head turned now so her cheek was pressed against his bare flesh. Her hair had nearly dried and was warm against his chest.

Another low rumble of thunder told him he could not tarry any longer to savor her nearness. Gently he touched her cheek, whispering, "July. Darlin'. We need to go."

Chapter Twenty

It took July a moment to gather her bearings. She saw the black clouds and smelled the oncoming rain just as Dev said, "We'll have to ride hard to outrun it."

Working together, they gathered the remnants of their lunch, the damp blanket, and wet clothing. With everything tied down, they swung into their saddles and left the lake as swiftly as the rocky terrain would allow. The horses sensed the coming storm and were anxious to run. The wind rose as the clouds surged closer; thunder rumbled, low and deep. Dev mentally counted the seconds until the lightning flashed and calculated the center of the storm at two miles away and moving fast. By the time they got down off the ridge, it was one mile away. They raced as fast as they dared across the open sagebrush ridges where they were dangerously exposed to lightning bolts. Into the stands of pines, they felt somewhat safe. By the time they reached the lower elevations and the protection of the aspen groves, they felt the first drops of cold rain on their backs.

As they emerged onto the two-track dirt road, the sky opened, drenching them in seconds. The road hadn't turned to mud yet so they kicked their horses into a gallop the last quarter of a mile. They rounded the corner of the yard and skidded to a stop in front of the barn. Lightning and thunder crashed simultaneously, shaking the earth.

Dev leaped from his saddle and ran to the big wooden door, swinging it wide for their entry. The rain battered the barn's wooden shingles and board-and-batten walls, but it was a secure, dry haven that made July feel safe again. Releasing a sigh of relief that they'd survived the treacherous ride down the mountain, she stepped from the saddle to the packed dirt floor.

"That was too close for comfort."

"Let's get the horses taken care of and get into the cabin. The way the temperature's dropped, I'll have to build a fire and get you warmed up. You're shivering."

"I'm okay, really."

Another boom of thunder told them the storm was right overhead. They removed saddles and replaced bridles with halters, and while Dev pitched grass hay into a manger, July used handfuls of straw to dry the horses' backs.

Dev slung the saddlebags over his shoulder. Ready to make a dash for the cabin now, they paused in the doorway. "You go on," he said, lifting his voice above the roar of the rain pounding the ground and lashing the barn. "I'll be right behind you."

A bolt of lightning cracked the sky in a dozen new pieces. July stepped back, reaching for him. Her attempted smile was more of a grimace. "If you don't mind, I'd rather die with you."

He smiled at her dry humor, but she could tell he enjoyed the excitement of it all, the rush of adrenalin. They stepped out of the barn. She stayed under the overhang until he had the door latched. "Ready?"

With his hand gripping hers, she took a deep breath and nodded. They sprang into the rain, leaping puddles and splashing mud onto their jeans. Another bolt of lightning struck at a knoll a hundred yards away as they bounded up the cabin steps to the shelter of the porch. July huddled close to him while he opened the door and ushered her inside.

Safe at last, they removed their hats and hung them on the hat rack; the rain poured off the brims and onto the floor. Their clothes were plastered against their bodies.

"Let's get into something dry, and then I'll build a fire. We always keep spare clothes in the bedroom closet."

With their clothes dripping a trail of water across the hardwood floor, Dev led the way to the bedroom where he found dry shirts and jeans. "You can take the bathroom," he said. "There are towels in there to dry off with. I hope those jeans aren't too big for you. They're an old pair of mine."

"Anything dry will do."

He got a towel for himself before she closed the door. When she came out a few minutes later, he was lighting kindling in the fireplace. She noticed he had abandoned the sling again, and she hoped his shoulder wouldn't suffer for it later.

"Still cold?"

She hugged herself, rubbing her hands up and down her arms. "A little, but the dry clothes are heaven."

"Looks like they fit you well enough." His approving gaze warmed her from the inside, while the first blaze of fire brought warmth and a cheery glow to the knotty-pine walls and ceiling.

"There's tea or coffee, or hot chocolate, if you want some."

"Hot chocolate sounds good. How about you?"

"The same."

She started water heating on the gas range and emptied a packet of chocolate mix into a stoneware mug for each of them. When she had the drinks ready, she carried them into the living room. With the fire now roaring, she set the mugs on the hearth to allow them to cool enough for sipping.

She said, "This is crazy—building a fire in August and drinking hot chocolate."

"Maybe, but it's not unheard of. I've seen temperatures in these mountains dip to freezing any time of the year. It's not unusual for it to drop dramatically during a storm like this if it's a system coming out of the north."

"Should we call your granddad and tell him we'll wait until the storm quits to head back so he won't be expecting us."

"That's a good idea." He left her side long enough to get his cell phone from the saddlebags in the kitchen. He got a signal strong enough to put the call through and relayed news of the storm, ending with, "It might be for the best. If we decide not to, I'll let you know."

When he hung up, he said, "Granddad said that if it doesn't clear off pretty soon, we should spend the night rather than fight a muddy road after dark."

July's first thought was of the one bed in the cabin, but Dev, apparently thinking the same thing, was quick with a solution. "I'll take the sofa. You can have the bed."

She went to the window and watched the rain sluicing down the panes. The lightning had subsided, but the rain was settling in. The rain had changed the road's gray, dusty surface to a black, slick quagmire.

Dev joined her. "Do you mind spending the night?"

Her eyes took in the view. "No. It's all so beautiful, even in the rain."

She rubbed her arms as if still chilled, so he reached over to the sofa and removed the small lap blanket folded across its back. As she turned around to him, he swirled it over her shoulders, drawing it closed in the front. Without thought, he enveloped her in his arms to give her some of his warmth. They'd been so close all day, it seemed natural now for her to lean against him and rest her head on his chest.

"Mmm, you're like a toasty little heater."

He chuckled. "At your service, ma'am."

He turned her toward the fire and drew her down next to him on the large Navajo rug. He retrieved the throw pillows from the sofa to rest against, and they sipped their drinks and stared into the comforting flames.

"It's nice next to the fire; I might sleep right here."

His lack of a response made her turn to look into his eyes where she saw something akin to pain. "Dev, are you all right? Is it your shoulder?"

He couldn't speak for a moment. When he did, his voice sounded ragged. "No, my shoulder's fine. It's you, July. I can't keep pretending—"

With a look of agony in his eyes, he released the emotions he'd held in check for ten years. He took her cup and set it on the hearth next to his. When he turned back to her, the desire he'd held in check for weeks exploded inside him. He cupped the back of her head with his hand as his mouth came down hard over hers. He pressed her back onto the rug, enveloping her in his arms.

His breath came hard; his words ragged. "If you want me to stop, tell me now."

She lifted her body toward his. Her eyes glowed dark, sultry and urgent. "Don't stop, Dev. Don't ever stop."

"Oh, God...." He buried his face in her neck, her hair, and he held her in a fierce embrace, wanting her to be right where she was until the end of their lives. "It'll be all right, July. I promise." He didn't know if what he said was true, but he did know that the line they were about to cross would bring changes to their lives forever.

"Say this is only the beginning," she whispered, holding onto him in a desperate way. "I don't want it to begin and end in the space of a few moments." Her eyes searched his for the answers she needed and wanted to hear.

"There will always be a tomorrow for us, July, as long as you want there to be."

There was no turning back. No time to think of consequences. He had waited too long to kiss her. Too long to make love to her. Years. Goddamn *years*. He might pay the fiddler tomorrow, but with her in his arms today, the emptiness he'd carried forever flowed out of him and was replaced with sweet joy. He had waited a lifetime for this singular moment of ecstasy that made the reason for his existence come clear at last. That reason was nothing more complicated than to love and be loved by this woman, whom he'd carried in his heart since the first moment they'd met.

Her lips parted, summoning his long and thorough kiss that savored and tasted and weakened any argument or thread of common sense. No part of her beautiful face or graceful neck escaped the starved pressure of his lips while anxious hands removed the barriers of clothing until they both lay naked and vulnerable before the fire and before each other, prepared to take their chances with the consuming desire that was bound to leave its consequences on their hearts. His hands molded to her flesh, memorizing her soft, womanly curves. Where his hands went, so went his lips, stamping his love on nearly every inch of her body. Her skin was hot now from the heat of the fire and from his lovemaking. Her hair had taken on a golden fire of its own as the dancing light from the flames played across it. He filled his hands with her breasts and then took their softness into his mouth. She moved against him, circled his hardness with her hand. He nearly came undone by her touch. It had been too long since anyone had loved him. Much too long.

He laid her back into the pillows, leaving a trail of kisses across her stomach and down to the core of her being. She whispered urgently, "I want you, Dev. I need you."

His need was so intense, it was impossible to be gentle. He rose over her, plunging himself into the wet heat of her body that welcomed him and then closed tightly around him. The ancient dance of love began, rocking them fiercely to its beat until they reached a searing consummation.

But it was only temporary satiety. As soon as he could breath, Dev lifted her into his arms and strode to the bedroom. Still embroiled in the heat of passion, he laid her down in its center, coming down with her. The fire began anew and in only moments, he was inside her again, pleasure mounting to a roaring firestorm that exploded, scattering into a million sparks that fell into smoldering embers like a star shower around them.

She was as needy as he, and her cries rose into the silent surroundings as her back arced to meet his thrusts and her fingers dug into his shoulder blades. He felt nothing but the sheer power of their union.

At last they fell into a calmness and lay deceptively dormant in the tangled bed sheets for an immeasurable space of time, realizing the storm outside had long ago rumbled away. Dev pulled the cord on the window drapes, and they watched the sun sink behind the mountains and the colors fade to dusk. They watched as the light and dark of the long shadows fused, blending in much the same way as their hearts and bodies had become one.

They watched until the breath of desire fanned them to life again. This time they moved slower, playing with the sensations, dragging them out as they pleasured each other, until they collapsed in utter exhaustion and complete satisfaction. Even then he could not find it in himself to release her, to feel the coolness of the night attempt to slide between them.

July slept, and Dev curled himself around her, holding onto her as if she were his lifeline. Only then, in the stillness, with the old grandfather clock ticking off the seconds of their lives, did he silently curse himself for not using protection. He told himself it didn't matter if she got pregnant with his child. It would be all the more reason for her to stay with him. It might be the *only* way he could keep her. Deep in his heart, though, he didn't want her if it was out of obligation alone. He'd traveled that road before. This time, he wanted love for the sake of love. And only her love would do.

◆

Around midnight, as the moon rose above the eastern mountains, July was awakened by the eerie, ululant cry of coyotes not far away in the mountains. Otherwise, the world both inside and out was utterly silent and silver-cast beneath the ghostly blue-white light that made its way through the window, past the open curtain and onto the bed.

Dev lay on his back, having fallen into a deep and contented sleep. She rolled to her side, propped herself up on one elbow and studied his handsome features in repose: the straight nose, the firm male lips, the tanned skin stretched tautly over distinctive cheekbones and a strong jaw. She fingered a strand of his short dark hair and traced the white line of an old scar that cut through the hair on his chest—and wondered how it had happened. A bad bull, no doubt, or a renegade bronc. She rested her head on his chest and listened to the steady, sure thump of his heart beneath her ear. He stirred and brought his arm around her before falling back into his dreams.

She felt a bond with him she had never felt with Buck. He had been in the shadows of her life for as long as she had been with Buck, but she knew him in ways she could never know Buck.

Yet, fear lurked in the shadows and threatened the beauty of this long-awaited commitment. It surged inside her, making her want to hold onto him forever, to never cease being a part of him for even the space of a breath. Did she dare to believe that she would not soon find herself alone again? Did she dare to believe that what she and Dev shared in these isolated moments away from the world would survive the harsh climate of reality? The inevitable confrontation with Buck?

There was a world out there that drove wedges between people. She wanted to believe it did not have to be so, but she had only her own unsuccessful experiences with which to formulate her beliefs. And so, fear grew, climbing up around her like a knot of writhing snakes, making her press closer to Dev in the darkness until he woke and she was calmed by the gentle assurance of his hands and lips. She breathed a sigh of relief at his unerring touch, for when he was consuming her, fear could not.

She rose over him and slowly explored his hard, muscled body with her own, inhaling the masculine scent of him, tasting it and remembering it. As her lips grazed the most intimate parts of his body, his eyes darkened with desire in the moonlight. His grip on her shoulders tightened until the low growl of need rose up in his throat.

She captured him in the slick, hot center of her being and watched him with hooded eyes while she took her pleasure. When she cried out with release, he turned her into the pillows and made his own climb to paradise and beyond. The unselfish give and take brought tears to her eyes that Dev wiped away with his kisses.

The night chill forced them to draw the covers over their shoulders. "I could stay here forever with you," she whispered. She was thinking, *every care of the world seems to fall away in the peacefulness, as if nothing exists beyond us and this cabin and these mountains.*

"Nothing will change when we leave here." He kissed her mouth again, thoroughly. "Nothing will come between us."

But she knew by the passionate way he held her that deep in his heart he, too, feared the ugly realities of the world would ultimately tear them apart.

Chapter Twenty-One

Dev and July spent the last hot breaths of summer together, riding the range, mending fences, and checking the cattle. Oftentimes, Baxter would join them. The companionship they gave him brought joy to his lonely life and made him happier than he had been since Cecilia had been alive. They didn't let on to him, or anyone, about the true nature of their love affair, but Baxter saw the change in them the morning after they spent the night alone at the cabin. He was pleased to see Dev's spirit return along with his lust for life.

Both he and Dev had been surprised when July had confided in them one day that she'd filed for divorce from Buck, and the lawyer would be sending the papers for her to sign because she didn't want to go back to Albuquerque to do it. She also told them about her editor's request for a feature on their lives and asked their permission. Baxter didn't feel as if he'd done anything special in his simple life to warrant a story, but after he thought about it for awhile, he decided it could do no harm. Dev hadn't been so sure, preferring to retire from rodeo without a fuss, but even his manager thought the piece would be a good way to cap off his career. His manager also felt they needed to make his retirement official with a press release, which Dev told him to go ahead and do.

July was daunted by the task of writing about the Summers men. She wondered if she was too close to the subjects to be objective. But she rejected the idea of the story going to someone else who would come out to the ranch, take a few pictures, ask lame questions, collect inaccurate information from old articles, magazines, and other rodeo contestants, and end up with a perception that would be far from the truth. She had grown protective of them, particularly Dev and Baxter, and she wanted to control what went into print.

Around the first of September, the three of them brought the bulls home from the mountains, having completed their summer breeding duties. One of the bulls, a five-year-old Angus, had given them considerable trouble.

"He gets meaner every year," Baxter said. "It's time to sell him before he hurts somebody. He won't be much good on the range anyway at his age."

As it was, the bull had charged Dan, nearly unseating Baxter. If the horse hadn't been so nimble, it could have been hurt and Baxter along with it.

"You ought to get one of the rodeo stock contractors, maybe Leo Mercer, to come out and take a look at him," Dev suggested. "If he'd buck, you could get more for him than if you sold him in the sale ring."

Baxter liked that idea. Mercer had used their arena many times to buck prospective rodeo stock from the surrounding area, so he didn't think he would mind bucking some for Baxter.

When the work was at a lull, the three of them attended local rodeos and fairs, went fishing in the streams, or took the boat over to Wild Horse Reservoir.

Along the way, Dev discarded his sling for good but continued the physical therapy program in Elko. He no longer went to bed thinking about the next go-round, the elusive gold buckle, or the World Championship. The world receded in the hours after Granddad went to bed, and Dev could steal into July's arms once again. Nothing existed beyond the glow of the lamp that illuminated their lovemaking and exposed their souls. Dev didn't ask where their relationship was going. There was peace in the darkness as they held each other and whispered their secrets, their dreams, and the innermost fears and joys of their hearts. They existed for each other and nothing else.

Nothing had ever been more right.

◆

In mid-September, Dev stood on the porch with his hands in his back pockets and watched July and Granddad head for the range.

He had half a notion to forget the physical therapy in town and go after them. He didn't like the trips to Elko if July wasn't with him. The bad part was, she never missed a chance to accompany Granddad. Dev knew it was the work that kept the old man going, that gave him a reason for getting up each morning, so he didn't try to stop him.

When the Ford was no longer in sight, Dev went back inside, cleared the table and put the table scraps in Cappy's bowl by the back door, even though Cappy wasn't there to eat them. Even he refused to stick around when the opportunity presented itself to go with July. He would see her skip out of the house, toting a mini-cooler in one hand and a jacket in the other, and he would jump into the bed of the pickup without being told, his stub tail wagging and his eyes glowing with anticipation. He idolized July. You could see it in his eyes when she filled his bowl with too much food, crooned to him too often, and patted him on the head when he hadn't done anything special. The stupid dog was as lovesick as every other male on the property.

Mumbling disgruntlements at being left behind, Dev plunged the breakfast dishes into the soap suds and thought of July in the pickup, laughing at Granddad's stories; stories he'd been telling all his life but that she had never heard. The old man loved having someone new to tell them to.

Dev was finishing up the last pan when he heard a vehicle pull into the driveway. Hoping to see the Ford return for whatever reason, he stuck his head around the curtain and peered out the window.

His heart sank.

Jake and Seth had returned. And not far behind was Mica.

"I guess it was about time for those two to come back—and most likely with their hands out," he muttered to the empty kitchen.

But with every shadow comes a ray of sunshine. Before Mica's pickup and stock trailer came to a complete halt, Dusty leaped from the passenger side and hurried toward the house.

He was drying off his hands as his daughter stepped inside and paused in the foyer. When she saw him, she suddenly appeared unsure of what her next move should be.

"Well, come here," he motioned, ending the indecision.

A grin burst across her face as she rushed into his embrace. "Dad! I'm so glad you're all right."

"I'm better now. Hey, how long can you stay?"

She stepped back, still holding onto his forearms. Uncertainty filled her eyes again. "I hope you won't be as mad as Mom is, but I want to stay for a while, if it's all right."

It caught him so off-guard he couldn't speak.

She misinterpreted his silence as disapproval. "Mom said you might not want to put up with me." She started to pull away, but he caught her hand.

"Of course I want you here. I just never expected it to happen." He pulled her into his arms again and gave her a bear hug. "But what about your barrel racing?"

Again, she looked unsure. "I want to quit for a while. Go to a regular school this fall. Live with you. No more home schooling. Mom says it's stupid, but I wanted to ask your opinion."

"It's not stupid at all, Dusty. I think it's a wise decision. What are you now? A sophomore?"

"No. A junior." She seemed to be holding her breath for his answer. "But it's okay if you don't want me to. I might be able to stay in the apartment in Elko and go to school there."

"Without your mother? Now, that would *not* be a good idea."

"Then I can stay here?"

"You better believe it."

"Oh, Dad, thank you! I love you."

Something turned over inside him now that he'd had a minute to look at her closer. She wasn't a little girl anymore. She'd grown into a beautiful young woman who held a resemblance to his mother, even though most people said she looked like him.

"Maybe it's a good thing you're staying here with me," he added. "It'll give me a fighting chance to fend off the boys."

Dusty pulled away. A guarded look entered her eyes. "Boys are overrated."

Dev's gut knotted. Had her innocence and young girl's dreams been compromised by Mica's indiscretion with her multitude of lovers as he'd feared it would? Or had something personal happened to make her jaded toward the opposite sex? He didn't even want to think that she might have already lost her virginity to some jerk who'd told her lies and made empty promises.

She headed to the refrigerator, changing the subject. "We drove all night, and I'm hungry. Do you mind if I eat something?"

"You can eat whatever you can find."

"Mmm, bacon and eggs sound divine."

The front door opened again, and the other three clomped in with duffle bags in hand. Mica dropped hers in the foyer and sauntered into the kitchen, looking him over the way she would a prospective new horse.

"So, you're on both feet. Jake and Seth made it sound as if you could barely hobble around."

"I've had a lot of time to recover."

Mica was still an attractive woman, albeit too skinny, but the road, the booze, the cigarettes, the men, the sun, the nights without sleep, the fast food—they were all taking their toll. A year ago he'd seen some premature gray in her black hair. Now the gray was covered with dye, but she still wore it long and loose. She hadn't lost her figure either. From a distance she could pass for a twenty-year-old. Close up, though, the age in her eyes and the sunbaked skin became evident. And she'd always been a walking billboard for every Western wear manufacturer in the country. Today she wore a pair of black Rocky Mountain jeans that fit like a glove. A tight, hot pink Cruel Girl T-shirt with a low, scoop neck stretched tautly across her full bosom—the only fat on her body.

He felt nothing for her anymore, though, except perhaps pity and irritation. It was unfortunate that she was caught in an addictive trap of night life, the road, and men. He'd always regretted the lack of a stable home life for Dusty.

She surveyed the kitchen. "Where's July? Don't tell me she's already got you fixing her breakfast in bed?"

"Yeah, big brother." Seth laid a good-natured slap to Dev's back. "Have you made it with her yet?"

Dev's gaze shot from Seth to Dusty. He didn't want his daughter to hear such a conversation. She responded with a shrug of her young shoulders and an all-knowing look in her eyes. "It's okay, Dad. I know about the facts of life."

Dev shouldn't have been shocked by Dusty's apparent maturity, considering the way she'd been raised around older people in the adult surroundings of the rodeo and life on the road with Mica. She didn't even seem embarrassed by the topic of conversation, but he knew that many of her generation thought nothing of premarital sex and had engaged in it many times and with multiple partners by the time they were her age. Still, he didn't want *his* sexual relationships discussed in front of her.

"July's gone with Granddad to check on the cattle," he said, refusing to respond to the question. "I have some physical therapy on my shoulder today so I had to stay here."

"And stand kitchen duty?" Mica smirked. "Did you break your backbone too? I thought she was supposed to be here to keep the house."

"She isn't our housemaid. She's a guest. And eating and cleaning are all part of life, Mica."

"It's not part of *my* life."

"No, I guess it wouldn't be."

She wasn't moved by the barb; she had spotted the fresh coffee. After helping herself to a cup, she settled at the kitchen table with a Marlboro. Jake and Seth joined her with cups of their own, which drained the pot. None of them volunteered to make more.

"I'll bet this isn't what you planned when you decided to retire," Mica goaded, no doubt trying to make him feel stupid and impotent in front of his daughter, but she failed because he knew all her tactics. Besides, he had July now; July who encouraged him to stay at the ranch and take care of his granddad and his heritage. She had said just the other night, "You're lucky to have this place. Hold onto it as long as you can. It'll be here when everything else is gone."

Dev pulled himself back to the present company. "I expected to do dishes, Mica, along with life's other mundane chores."

Dusty intercepted the uncomfortable silence that descended over the room. "How much longer do you have with the physical therapy, Dad?" She laid three slices of bacon onto the ridged microwave plate, covered it with a paper towel, and popped it into the microwave. With efficiency that impressed Dev, she turned to the range to scramble up a couple of eggs in a small cast-iron skillet. She asked if the others wanted any but seemed to know already that they were happy to subsist on coffee and cigarettes.

"I know the routine," he replied to Dusty, "so I don't think I'll go back after today."

"Will you do what you're supposed to do?" Mica again.

"July will make sure I do."

His easy, fond mention of her brought a storm to Mica's brown eyes. "You'll never get her away from Buck," she stated flatly, taking a deep drag on her cigarette and blowing the smoke out the side of her mouth toward the ceiling. "He was her first love. She'll go running back to him when she gets bored with you and gets over being mad at him. Or when he swallows his damned pride and comes after her. All he has to do is turn on the charm and say he's sorry. He knows she's here, by the way.

"They're both trying to force the other's hand," she continued, all-knowing. "It's a game they play. Buck told me so. Every time he's unfaithful and she's found out about it, she's gone out and found somebody else, just to get even. I'll bet you didn't know that, did you? I'll bet you thought you were special."

Mica's words made his blood run cold. He didn't believe her. He didn't *want* to believe her. He thought about the way he and July were when they were together, and he couldn't believe her heart didn't belong to him. She had filed for divorce. That had to mean something.

He hated that niggling look in Mica's eye as she gauged his reaction. "July and I are only friends," he lied with a face as straight as a gambler's. "She needed a place to go, and I provided it. When she's ready to leave, I won't stop her."

Feeling that he needed another cup of coffee in the worst way, he started another pot brewing.

"I suppose you think you know her intentions?" Mica blew another coil of smoke out the side of her mouth.

"One way or the other, it's her business, not mine and definitely not yours."

"My, aren't we touchy?" She took another sip of coffee. "I'm beginning to understand why you want to stay at the ranch and get all domestic."

"Yes, and it'll be pleasant when you ride away into the sunset again."

Without another word, or the much-needed coffee, Dev left the kitchen by the back door. He didn't quit walking until he'd reached the corral. He sat down with his back against a post and prayed they'd all hit the road again real soon. All of them, that is, except Dusty.

He was still there thirty minutes later when his daughter found him and settled next to him. "Don't let Mom get to you, Dad. I don't think she would have brought me here at all except she was curious about you and July."

"Why should she care if I find someone else?"

"I don't know that she does care, as long as it isn't July. She's jealous of her. Always has been. She can't figure out why men lose all common sense when July walks into a room, like she was Marilyn Monroe or something—those are Mom's words, not mine. But I think deep down inside she still loves you."

"She loves every man she meets—at least for awhile."

"And none of them love her, in the end."

Dusty's sad and wise observation caught Dev by surprise, but it couldn't drive away the decade of bitterness that had poisoned his heart. "She's done it to herself."

Dusty nodded in solemn agreement.

Dev was amazed at how astute his daughter was for her age and how she could see right through her mother but still accept her for the way she was and still love her deeply. It was almost as if the mother/daughter roles were reversed.

"I'm glad you'll be here for awhile," he said. "I've missed you."

She grinned and leaned her head against his shoulder. "I've missed you too. I'd like to stay with you and Granddad forever. I'm tired of the road."

"I thought you liked barrel racing."

"I do. I did. I don't know. It gets old living out of that pickup truck, racing from one place to the next, and I'm bored running barrels day in and out and having Mom bitch at me when I don't win. I did a little cutting competition to try something different, and I enjoyed it. I might do more of it. It's more useful on the ranch anyway. One reason I'd like to go to a real school is because I'm not doing so hot in some of my subjects, and there's a lot of the stuff like algebra and geometry that Mom doesn't understand. I've been able to pass with the tutoring help of one of the cowboys who's a math genius, but I'd like to do better so I can get accepted into college. And no more rodeos for awhile."

"Not even on weekends?"

"No. I want to be able to stay in one spot and make some friends, go to school dances, movies, ball games." She looked down at her boot toes. "And I want to spend time with you, Dad."

"I'd like nothing better." He looked at her small hand resting on her knee, realizing that in a few years he'd be giving that same hand in marriage to some kid wet behind the ears and no doubt penniless. He hadn't had a chance to know who she was or to be a father to her. He was grateful that he was going to get that chance now.

He placed his hand over hers. "I'll talk to your mother, but you know she always wants to do opposite of what I suggest."

Dusty's brows came together. "I'm not going back. She can't make me." She jumped up and tugged on his hand. "Come on. Let's go for a walk."

She linked her arm with his, and they walked in quiet companionship along the road that wound around and through the property. They were almost back to the yard when Dusty asked if he would be doing the farming as well as raising cattle.

"I'm going to continue to contract the farming. We have a lot of land that's been idle for years, and I'd like to see it back into production. I'd also like to increase the number of commercial cattle and start a small herd of registered stock, both horses and cattle. It'll mean more recordkeeping but more profits."

"I'd love to help you."

He met her eyes that were the same color as his. "It's a lot of work, Dusty."

"So was barrel racing. I can handle it."

Dusty took in the view past the pastures, the hay fields and the rolling sagebrush hills all the way to the wilds of the Jarbidge Wilderness. Her voice was laced with desperation. "I'm serious, Dad. I'll shovel out the barn every day, but I don't want to be with

Mom anymore. Don't get me wrong—I love her—but I hate what she does to herself, and I don't like the company she keeps. She gravitates to the worst kind when there are plenty of nice guys on the circuit. I wish she could see that they don't respect her. The ones she hangs with are crude and foul-mouthed. I hate being around them."

Dev sensed she was picking her words, holding something back, and his worst fears came to the fore again. "Your mother's friends haven't been bothering you, have they?"

She was hesitant to talk about it. "Not so much. It's more the way they look at me sometimes, or maybe it's something they'll say. Especially Duane Tarpley. I'm not ready for what they want."

Dev pulled up short. His eyes narrowed. "She's hanging around Tarpley?"

She looked away, shifting uneasily. "No. He's been hanging around me, wanting to go on dates and stuff ever since I turned sixteen—I think he's like twenty-six or something. Mom says I should be flattered because he's one of the best bronc riders on the circuit. But I don't like him, so I told him I couldn't go out with him because you wouldn't let me date until I was eighteen. He didn't believe that so I told him he better leave me alone or you'd kick his butt."

Her last comment cooled his rising anger. He chuckled. "You told him that?"

She gave him a sidelong, unsure glance. "Well…yeah. I had to think of something. Was that…not all right?"

Dev laughed as he put his arm across her shoulders and gave her another hug. "That was exactly right."

Back in the yard, they saw Mica walking toward them. Dev recognized the battle stride and braced himself for the inevitable confrontation.

"Go on up to the house," he said to Dusty. "Your mother and I need to talk."

Mica had strode within earshot. "You bet we do, sweet cakes. Beginning with your irresponsible decision to retire."

Chapter Twenty-Two

Dev waited until Dusty was out of earshot. "It's your behavior, not mine, that needs to be examined."

"*My* behavior?"

"Yes, Mica, like this crap about Tarpley trying to date Dusty, and you doing nothing to set him straight. He's ten years older than her, for Christ's sake. That's statutory rape. What's the idiot thinking? What are *you* thinking?"

"So you're calling me an idiot too?"

"If the shoe fits."

"Listen, Dev. Duane can have any girl he wants. And I know him well enough to know that he wouldn't force himself on Dusty if she said no."

"And I know Duane Tarpley too. It's never occurred to him that any woman *would* say no. We're talking about our daughter. She's still a kid. She needs to be protected from users like him."

"So what if he's older than her? It won't matter in a couple of years. He's on top and raking in the money. She could be part of that."

"And maybe some of it would trickle down to you?"

"You're such an asshole."

"Think what you will, Mica, but Tarpley wouldn't want anything from Dusty that he can't get from hundreds of other women, yourself included. He's not the settling kind."

She latched her thumbs in the front pockets of her jeans. "This is not what I came to talk to about," she said with disdain. Leaning her shoulder against the barn with an air of cocky self-confidence, she jacked a boot heel against the weathered wood. She was sexy in a trashy sort of way and knew her effect on men, but she couldn't get to him anymore. He had long ago left behind the young man who'd had more testosterone than brains.

"Then what do you want, Mica?"

"I want to discuss the real problem, which isn't Duane Tarpley, but *you* for quitting the circuit and putting the same stupid idea into Dusty's head."

Wasn't it just like Mica to back away from an argument in cool indifference after she had made him raging mad, but she was right—the issue with Tarpley was a moot point as long as Dusty stayed at the ranch. "Dusty wants to go to school. She's tired of barrel racing and home schooling."

Mica shook out a Marlboro with angry hands, lit it, and took a drag before saying, "She's quitting because you did. Don't you realize what that did to all of us—to Jake and Seth, and now to me and Dusty?"

"I can't help that, Mica. It was time for me to move on. I wasn't going to wake up one morning and look in the mirror and see Jake Summers staring back at me. I'm not going to be him.

"As for Dusty," he continued, "maybe she thought we would be disappointed in her if she quit. Now she knows it's okay to pursue other interests. She's got her whole life ahead of her. You need to understand that she might not want the same thing as you and I wanted."

"She's a damn good barrel racer. She's stupid to throw that away. She has the ability to make it to the top."

"It won't matter if it's not a passion she wants to pursue. And right now she needs a break. Hell, Mica, she's been barrel racing since she was old enough to ride a horse."

Mica threw her cigarette into the dirt and ground it out hard with her boot toe. "Quitting right now isn't an option, damn it! She's bringing in money that pays the bills!"

"It pays for your booze and cigarettes, you mean."

"It pays the entrance fees and the gas and groceries, you son of a bitch." Her voice turned shrill. "I don't have another way to make a living. Rodeo is all I know."

"I give you child support. Money shouldn't be an issue."

"Yes, and it'll end if she comes to live with you." Her eyes cut through him.

"I'll keep sending you money, Mica. Maybe you should try investing some of it in your future or learn something besides barrel racing."

"Don't tell me what to do with my life. I don't want to sit at a goddamn desk in a cubicle typing letters and answering phones, or slinging hamburgers at some two-bit café in a two-bit town filled with two-bit men! I like my life, and I'm not going to be like you and quit because I'm not at the top of my game right now."

Dev was tired of the argument. She wasn't going to shame him into changing his mind. "You can barrel race until you're seventy if you want to, but don't place all the responsibility on Dusty. She's a kid. The bottom line is, she's winning and you're not. You're jealous of that, but not so jealous that you won't pocket her success."

Resentment boiled in her eyes. She started back to the house.

"Is that a yes or a no?"

She swiveled on her boot heel; her narrowed gaze pierced him. "If she prefers you over me then I don't want the little shit hanging around. She's beginning to be a handful anyway."

"Christ, Mica. You're missing the point, as usual. It's got nothing to do with Dusty not wanting to be with you."

"Oh? I think it does."

"Don't start hating her. She wants a break. She wants to spend some time with me. I'm her parent too."

"Fine. I'll let her stay with you for awhile to pacify the two of you, but she'll get sick soon enough of being stuck in the middle of nowhere. Now, this conversation is over. I'm going to unload her shit so I can get the hell out of here."

"Have her put her things in the room next to mine. Seth's in there right now, but he can sleep out in the trailer for no longer than he'll be here."

"What's wrong with Cecilia's room?"

"July's using it."

She was incredulous. "You gave Cecilia's room to July?"

"Granddad did. She's a guest. He had no idea you'd be showing up."

"Dusty won't like being relegated to second position. And July better not try to tell her what to do while I'm gone."

"It's you who doesn't like second position, Mica, and July's not the bossy type. Besides, Dusty's so glad to be home she'll sleep on the floor and not complain. Will you get the rest of her things from your apartment?"

Her eyes, as sharp as the edges of obsidian, sliced into him. "I have another rodeo. I don't have time to go to Elko and get the rest of her damn shit and then turn around and bring it all the way back out here."

"All right, then leave a key to your apartment."

"Dusty has a key."

"Fine. Great."

He watched her stalk to the house. He needed to cool down, to work her out of his system again. He started by going inside the barn and straightening up the tack. A few minutes later, he sensed he wasn't alone. He looked up to see Dusty in the doorway with tears streaming down her face. At the same time, he heard Mica's pickup roar to life and speed away.

He put his arms around her and tried to lighten her mood. "Hey, what's this? Your mother isn't even out of the yard and already you regret staying with me?"

She pressed her face against his chest. "She called me a spoiled little shit and said I'd better not change my mind because I couldn't go with her now even if I wanted to. She even took my horse."

Dev smoothed her hair and closed his eyes against the raw emotion that roller-coasted through his body. He had known all along that his decision to retire would have far-reaching effects, but he had never dreamed it would cause a rift between Mica and Dusty. Goddamn, he hadn't meant for this to happen. Was he going to have to go back to riding bulls to get everybody off his back?

"Don't take it personally," he soothed. "She gets upset when things don't go her way. She'll cool down."

"I don't want her to hate me."

He held her tighter. "She's your mother. She couldn't hate you if she tried. She doesn't want to lose you, and she's upset thinking she might."

"You'd never know it by the way she acts."

Several minutes later, she wiped her tears with the palm of her hand. "Like Mom always said, crying won't get you anywhere.

I'm sorry to have acted like a baby. Is there anything in here I can help you with?"

Dev knew Dusty's hurt went deep. He could only hope it would eventually heal. "You could clean and oil that old side-saddle that belonged to your great-great-grandmother. July's been itching to use it."

"Wow. I'd like to try it out too."

Eagerly, she gathered saddle soap, leather conditioner, and a clean cloth from the shelves. While he made a few minor repairs on the tack, they exchanged small talk. It was wonderful to have her around, but he had to admit he was a little scared. Dusty hadn't been quite six years old when he and Mica divorced. He hadn't spent much time with her since. They didn't know each other very well, but he was committed to being the father she had always needed and wanted. He would do his very best to make sure she didn't regret her decision to come home.

◆

"The physical therapist thought you were cute, Dad," Dusty said from her side of the pickup and between spoonfuls of an extra thick strawberry milk shake. "But I think she was a little distressed to find out you had a teenaged daughter."

Dev shrugged, amused by his daughter's observations. "She'll get over it. Besides, I'm not going back. I can do those exercises by myself now."

"I'll make sure you do."

He gave her a lop-sided grin. "Just what I need—a mother."

She laughed and went back to her milk shake. They drove in silence the last few miles to the ranch. Dev wondered if July and Granddad were home yet. Another concern crowding to the forefront of his thoughts was how he was going to be alone with July when the house was full of people. At the same time, he wanted to be a better example for Dusty than Mica had been, but he couldn't teach his daughter morals if he showed none himself.

"They're not here yet," he said with obvious disappointment as he stopped the pickup in front of the house.

Dusty opened her door and got out. "Good. That means I can hurry and fix supper for them. I want to surprise July and show her I won't be a nuisance."

He grinned at her. "So you can cook something besides bacon and eggs?"

She opened the rear door and reached into the back seat for the grocery bags that were stacked on top of her clothes from the apartment. "Sure. I do all the cooking—all that gets done, that is. I'm pretty good with lasagna."

Dev reached in from the other side and dragged out two bags by their plastic handles. "Granddad's favorite," he said, tongue-in-cheek.

"Granddad will learn to like it."

"You know what they say about teaching new tricks to old dogs. He's set in his ways. He prefers steak, mashed potatoes, and gravy."

"I don't know how to fix that old-fashioned stuff."

"Then we'll have to teach you. But you go ahead and get started on your lasagna, and don't worry about Granddad. Since he's as old as mashed potatoes and gravy, he'll have enough manners not to complain. I'll bring in the rest of your things."

"Can I share the room with July?" She looked up at him hopefully.

Dev nearly choked. "No. No, I think she needs her privacy. She's got articles and things like that she's working on."

"But I don't want to take Seth's room."

"He won't mind. He stays out in the trailer or the bunkhouse half the time anyway so he can sleep off his drunks."

"Don't bet on it. I think they're broke and hoping you'll spot them another loan."

"Didn't Seth win anything?"

She made a pinched face. "A little, but he and Jake were trying to bum money off Mom on the trip over here."

Dev didn't like to hear that. He had hoped his dad and Seth could make it without him. If he had to support them, he'd go through his investments faster than his dad could go through a bottle of Jack Daniels. He'd also hoped for Seth's success because his brother needed it to build his confidence and boost his moral. He was afraid Seth was on a dangerous downhill spiral that wouldn't end well.

"Don't worry." Dusty laid a hand on his forearm, somehow

knowing what he was thinking. "He and Jake aren't your responsibility. They're grown men, for Pete's sake."

"Why do you call him Jake instead of Grandpa?"

She shrugged. "He says it ages him to be called Grandpa.
Now, don't stress about any of this stuff. I'm going to get started
on the lasagna."

◆

Jake was on his way to a damn good drunk, feeling surly as hell
when Dev and Dusty walked into the house with their arms full
of groceries. After Mica had gotten all in a huff, he'd offered to
take her upstairs and show her a good time. She'd called him a
stupid loser and told him to go find somebody his own age. He
had pretended her words hadn't cut to the quick. He'd ignored
Seth's simpering smile of satisfaction, and then he'd hauled in a
six-pack of Coors from the supply in the trailer and settled down
with it on the sofa. Three cans into it, he'd opted for something
harder and removed his dad's Christmas bottle of Jim Beam from
above the refrigerator.

"I'll have some of that," Seth had said, reaching for it and
plopping next to Jake on the sofa. Jake had held it out of his reach
and told him to drink the Coors. Seth had grumbled for a few
minutes about him being a selfish bastard, but he'd accepted the
Coors, found a rodeo airing on satellite TV, and was criticizing
every rider that came out of the chute, as if he could do a better
job himself.

Now Dev was back, and Jake wasn't in the mood to talk to
the person who was to blame for his life falling into a shit-hole.

Dusty went into the kitchen, but Dev stopped and gave him
a disapproving glare that bordered on pity. It was the pity that
made Jake lift the bottle of Jim Beam to his lips again.

"Figured you'd be eating Mica's dust," Dev said, matter-of-
factly.

Jake wiped his mouth with the back of his hand and kept his
eyes on the TV. "The only reason to follow that woman is to get a
piece of ass. She wasn't exactly in the mood for being generous
after doing the tango with you."

Dev's eyes turned hard, his voice lowered. "I'd appreciate it
if you'd watch your mouth when Dusty's around."

Jake shrugged. "She knows her mother's a whore."

"Christ, Dad, you haven't been fooling with Mica, have you?"

"What difference would it make if I had? She's been rid of you for ten years. It's no different than somebody going after their step-sister, or marrying their dead brother's wife. Hell, she isn't any blood kin of mine."

"Her daughter is your granddaughter."

With insolent eyes boring into Dev, Jake lifted the bottle again and said nothing.

"When are you leaving, Dad?"

Jake was taking pleasure in putting Dev's shorts in a knot; it was payback for him walking out on them. Christ, the kid was such a disappointment. He never would have figured Dev for being the quitter. Seth, yeah. But not Dev.

"I'll go after I see July."

"You've got no business with her."

"It wasn't business I had in mind."

"Stay away from her, Dad."

Jake scraped him with his gaze. "Seth and I were right. You *have* been sleeping with her."

"Which is all the more reason for you to give it up."

Jake sneered. "Well, I'm glad to know you still have some balls. I was beginning to wonder." When Dev said nothing, he took another hit of whiskey and added, "I think I'll stay awhile. Maybe help with fall roundup. That was one job I never minded. Of course, we could get out of your hair if you'd spot us a few thousand. Seth lost his place on the tour. He'll have to work his way back into position again."

Dev was silent for a long moment before he spoke. "I'm sorry to hear that, Seth."

"Yeah, sure you are."

"No, I am."

"It's no big deal. I'll get back in." Seth looked back at the TV, trying to pretend it didn't matter, but the disappointment was clearly written on his face.

"Okay," Dev continued, "there's a couple of things we need to talk about, and it might as well be now. First off, Dad, I can't let you and Seth take my truck anymore. If you need money for a down payment on one of your own, we've got some fencing that needs to be done. I'll pay you if you want to work."

Jake's blood began to boil. Damn the kid for pulling the pickup out from under them. He seemed determined to make sure they failed. Christ, he had more money than he knew what to do with. A few thousand sure as hell wouldn't break him.

"And I guess you'll be magnanimous and pay us minimum wage."

"Minimum wage is better than no wage."

"Where's all the money you've got stashed away?"

"Not accessible to you, even if I took the notion to give you a hand-out, which I won't."

"You sorry little prick."

"Sober up, Dad. Then we'll talk."

Jake exhaled, long and slow. He knew when he was defeated, but, goddamn, he never had liked to crawl. "All right. Where's the goddamn fence that needs fixing?"

"Cougar Ridge."

"Cougar Ridge! My good God, that country's straight up and down and nothing but rocks!"

"Your point?"

Jake swallowed a chunk of pride. "Oh, all right. We'll do it for what the other hired hands make."

"Hey, where did the plural come from?" Seth objected. "I'm not going to fence that goddamn country for any amount of money. I've done this kind of shit with you before, and I'll be the one doing all the work while you sit on a rock barking orders."

"I figured as much." Dev started for the kitchen.

The sound of a vehicle in the driveway drew Jake's attention. "That must be July and Dad coming back." He stood up, losing interest in Jim Beam, rodeo, and honest work. He headed for the kitchen window. "They've brought some of the horses. I'd better go take care of them; she'll be tired."

Dev grabbed his arm and swung him around. "I'm warning you, old man. Stay away from July or I'll kill you."

Jake shook himself free of Dev's grip. "You've threatened to kill me before. Until you do, I'll do as I damn well please."

Chapter Twenty-Three

Despite what Dev thought, and what he himself had insinuated, Jake had no intention of doing anything but talking to July. He didn't care if she and Dev had a thing going. She wasn't the type of woman a man would want for a fling anyway. It was just that she had a way of grounding him, and he needed that right now. He was angry that things were out of his control, and Dev wasn't going to let him take back the reins.

She saw him and smiled. "Jake. You're just the man we wanted to see."

His gaze shifted suspiciously to Baxter. The old man was unloading the horses, not paying him any mind. That didn't mean anything where Baxter Summers was concerned. Now, if July had said "I" instead of "we," his whiskey wouldn't have gone sour in his gut. Maybe he should have stayed in the house.

"What's up?" He managed through a constricted throat.

"One of Baxter's heifers got over the fence and is in with the neighbor's bulls. We tried cutting her out today but she wore out our horses, and Baxter went off without his rope. He said you used to be good with a lariat, but he didn't think you'd be interested in trying to catch her."

Baxter came around to the pickup and joined them. "July made a bet that you could rope her. I bet you couldn't. It doesn't matter, Seth can do it if you don't want to try."

July had given him a vote of confidence. It didn't matter what his dad thought. His dad had never believed he could do anything so he ignored those needling blue eyes.

"I hope you didn't bet a lot, Dad."

Baxter made a show of being skeptical. "You haven't had a rope in your hand for what? Twenty years?"

"Let me worry about that. You two go inside. Dusty's here. She's fixing supper and anxious to see you both. I'll take care of the horses."

"Dusty?" July's eyes widened. "I haven't seen her for years."

Baxter was suspicious. "Is Mica here, too? That woman makes my ass ache."

"Oh, come on, Dad. She has some redeeming qualities."

"By God, none that anybody would notice."

"You can relax. She got into a fight with Dev the minute they laid eyes on each other. She left."

Baxter hitched up his worn Levi's and made a triumphant snorting sound. "Good. If I never see that woman again it'll be too soon."

After July and Baxter headed to the house, and Jake had turned the horses loose in the pasture, he strode with a purpose to the barn, found a lariat, and started throwing it at a snubbing post. If July thought he could catch that renegade heifer, then, by God, he wasn't going to let her down.

◆

July would have recognized Dusty anywhere. She didn't resemble Mica very much; there was more of Dev in her. As July gave Dusty a hug and told her how much she'd grown, she was stabbed with that old pang of wanting a child of her own, and she wondered if she might be carrying Dusty's half-sister or half-brother. She and Dev had more than once allowed passion to consume them along with all common sense.

The love she had for him gripped her hard. Yet, there was something too good, too perfect about it, as if it was destined to end, but not because she or Dev wanted it to. There was a disturbing feeling of transience surrounding them that frightened her, as if something would inevitably tear them apart. The gnawing fear sometimes made her hold him more tightly in the night, determined to commit to memory everything about him, every nuance of touch, taste, and smell. With him, she wanted to erase every trace of Buck that lingered on her skin and in her memory, wiping it away until those years with him existed only in the foggy haze of another lifetime long past.

"I've made lasagna," Dusty said proudly. "I hope you like it."

"I'm sure I'll love it. How did you know I wouldn't feel like cooking?"

Dusty lifted her shoulders in a half-shrug and spoke with experience and wisdom that belied her age. "I know how tiring it is to be on a horse all day, or on the road." She instructed everyone to sit down. She sent Seth to find Jake, who came in, gobbled down the food then hurried back outside. Seth was curious to see what he was doing and left the table as soon as he had two more helpings of lasagna and three thick slices of French bread, toasted and smothered in garlic salt and Parmesan cheese. Baxter, as Dev had warned, wasn't crazy about Italian food, and even though he complimented Dusty on her cooking skills, he ate only one small square and filled up on bread before retiring to the living room to watch the news. Within minutes, his rattling snores rose above the commentator's voice.

"You go relax, July," Dusty insisted. "Dad and I will clean up. I was wondering, though, if you could show me some of the pictures you've taken. Dad says they're really good."

"I'd love to share them with you."

July lifted her gaze to Dev's, wondering if they would ever be alone now that the house was full, but she saw seduction in his eyes above the knowing half-smile.

"All right. If I'm not needed, I'm going to soak in a hot tub. Baxter wore me out today."

"From the sound of those snores, he wore himself out too," Dev said.

July walked past him, touching his hand as she went. It was only a split second of contact, but in it was a promise of love as soon as the night was theirs.

Two hours later, when she heard the tap on her door, July called out, "Come in," only to have Dusty step inside rather than Dev whom she'd expected. She was a little disappointed but truly didn't mind spending time with his daughter.

She closed her journal and sat up in the middle of her bed.

"I won't bother you if you're working on that article about Dad and the others," Dusty said. "Dad told me about it."

"No, I was recording the day's events in my journal. It helps me formulate what I want to include in the article. I hope he's okay with it. I dropped a lot of baggage on him when I came to visit." She motioned to the bed. "Sit down."

Dusty flopped on her belly at the foot of the bed, grabbed a throw pillow, and propped herself up with it. "Don't worry. Dad likes you—a lot."

July laughed, finding it embarrassing to talk to Dusty about her relationship with Dev, even though it didn't seem to bother Dusty one bit. She leaned over to the night stand and took out the pictures she and Dev had taken of each other cutting cattle, and scenes from on top of the mountain the day they'd ridden to the lake. She handed them to Dusty, who, unlike some people, seemed to recognize and appreciate the nuances of photography.

"You're so good, July. I've always liked photography, but I've never had a good camera. We buy the throw-away kind in Wal-Mart once in a while."

"We could go out one day and take some photos if you'd like. I can give you some pointers. I use both film and digital, but we'll start you out with film."

"That would be so fun. I wouldn't mind taking some photography classes in school. Speaking of school—I'm scared to death I'll be a social misfit and won't have any friends."

July propped the bed pillows up against the headboard and got comfy against them. "I doubt that. You've lived your life around a lot of people and in the public eye. You'll do fine."

Dusty looked through all the photographs July had taken and then went back to the ones of Dev again, spreading them out on the bedspread. "Dad is something, isn't he? We were close when I was a kid; I remember riding on his shoulders and tagging along beside him everywhere he went. Then one day it ended, and I felt so lost. Talk about withdrawal pains," she said, laughing at herself, but the pain was still evident in her eyes. "I whined to Mom all the time about 'Where's Daddy? I want my Daddy,' and she would get mad and tell me he was gone and wasn't coming back. I would throw temper tantrums because I wanted him, not her, and one day she spanked my butt good. She said I was stuck with her and that I wouldn't be seeing much of him ever again and to get over it."

"Didn't he get visiting rights?"

"I was supposed to get one weekend a month with him, but Mom never planned her schedule around it, even though he always did, and she would whisk me off because she had another rodeo to make. I didn't even get to be with him in the summer because Mom convinced the judge it wouldn't be good for me to travel with a bunch of men all over the country chasing rodeos. It was okay to do the same thing with her though.

"If we happened to be at the same rodeo," she continued, "I always made sure I went behind the chutes to see him and watch him ride. When he was done, he'd buy me a hamburger and cotton candy, and we'd laugh and talk until Mom hauled me away. I know there were times when Dad needed to hit the road, too, to make the next rodeo, but he would always act as if it was no big deal. Jake and Seth would pull him aside and say, 'We need to go, Dev. You can see her later.' But Dad stood his ground. I imagine he missed a lot of rodeos and got a lot of speeding tickets because of me, but he never pushed me aside. When I got older, Mom avoided the events where he was riding. Then he moved into professional bull riding, and I was lucky to see him a few times a year."

Dusty forced herself to brighten. "But I'll be with him now. It's going to be really fun."

She started to gather up the photos, but July selected two of the best shots of Dev and handed them to her. "You can have these."

Her eyes got wide. "But these are the best ones, July. You might need them for your article."

"I might, but I can print more."

Dusty got up from the bed, still staring down at the pictures. "Gee, thanks."

"You're welcome."

"Well, I'd better go to bed. I'm looking forward to seeing if Jake can rope that heifer tomorrow. He's always bragging about how good he is, but that's about all it amounts to."

"Oh, I think he can do it," July said confidently.

"I hope you're right or we won't be able to live with him. He'll go on a drunk for a week."

"What if he *does* rope her?"

Dusty pursed her lips, considering the possibility. "Oh, he'll go on a drunk for a week—to celebrate. Any excuse, you know. Sometimes I wish he'd grow up, but there seems no chance of that." She opened the door and paused on the threshold. "Thanks again for the pictures. See you in the morning."

◆

Dev was relieved that July had taken Dusty's arrival in stride. Still, he wondered what truly went on in her mind. Would she get tired of his family and their constant needs, and one day decide to leave without warning, without a word of good-bye, the way his mother had? The way she herself had left Buck? It wouldn't surprise him for a woman to get fed up with wading through the shit that was always knee-deep around this place. It seemed that just when he got one stall cleared, the next one was full. Now he had Jake and Seth to contend with again, getting drunk and underfoot and feeling sorry for themselves. Not to mention Dusty wanting to monopolize July's time.

Since the day at the cabin when they'd first made love, Dev had looked forward to going to her room every night and allowing her to sooth away all the pain, frustration, and disappointment of a lifetime. Things were changing again. He couldn't be alone with her, and he felt time racing away as if one day he would wake up and there would be no tomorrow.

To add to it, it seemed his dad never slept. Even now, at midnight, he could hear the old man rummaging around in the room across the hall, no doubt looking for a bottle of booze he'd hidden in the closet. Then he heard his dad's door open and close, heard him head down the stairs. Damn it! All hope of going to July was gone now.

◆

As soon as Dusty left the room, July waited for Dev, and while she waited, she turned on her laptop and opened to the article. She had bought a small tape recorder a few weeks ago, and today Baxter had told her stories of how things had been when his grandfather and father had been alive. She wanted to put the stories into a transcript for easier accessibility and then get him to tell her more about his own life and times. She would not be able to use even a fraction of what she had, but the stories provided the history and background she needed to give depth to the final piece.

It also gave her an appreciation for the land that she might not have had otherwise, and for the heritage that Baxter had been trying so hard to hold onto. She could see now the poignant reality that the land, which had been in his family for over a hundred years, might not last beyond another generation unless Dev had a son, or a son-in-law, who would carry on. Another sad reality was that the face of ranching had changed so much in a hundred years that Baxter's grandfather, if he were to see it today, would not recognize it. Many of the big spreads had become dude ranches in order to survive, others had fragmented into sites for vacation homes and weekend recreational playgrounds for the nation's rich city dwellers.

Men like Baxter who lived by the old ways were a dying breed trying to survive inside fences that continually kept shrinking. They were out of time with the world, and sooner or later the world would demand they catch up or be left behind. The young bloods, like Dev, with modern ideas were the only hope for any semblance of this life to continue. Something had been lost that was impossible to get back, and that saddened her. Even now, people like her could only live that life of the open range vicariously through the memories of old men like Baxter.

Her ears perked at the sound of a creaking stair. She knew which one it was—the third from the bottom—and it squealed every night when Dev snuck down to see her.

She set aside her work, but the footsteps went past her room. The front door opened, closed. The porch light came on. Thinking Dev had decided to come through the French doors, she slipped on her robe, drew back the drapes, and stepped out onto the veranda to meet him. She was surprised to find Jake settling into the swing with a plastic bag from a western wear store.

He heard her and turned. In that split second, she saw wrenching pain in his eyes that cut to the soul. Then it was gone, hidden behind his usual roguish smile.

"Don't look so disappointed, Firecracker."

She pulled the robe around her, tied it. Forced a laugh. "Disappointed? What do you mean?"

"That I'm not Dev."

She hoped the blush that burned her cheeks wouldn't be noticeable in the muted yellow glow of the porch light. "He *has* been the only one around. We come out here quite a bit in the evenings to talk."

His eyes held that knowing look. "It's not evening. It's midnight."

She leaned against the veranda railing. She and Dev were lovers so she wouldn't deny it. She wouldn't justify it either. "Actually, I'm glad to have a minute alone with you. I wanted to talk to you about something."

His eyes said he didn't believe that, but he humored her, although caution edged into his words. "Oh, and what do you want to talk to me about?"

"An article I'm writing about the Summers men."

His eyebrows rose. "About us? Why?"

She told him more about it and the magazine that wanted it. "I'd like to do a serious interview before you leave again."

He relaxed. "Well, sure. I can do that."

"Now, what brings you out here at this hour? Something in the bag? Something you don't want to share with anyone else? Or maybe it's a new pair of boots you wanted to break in for roping that heifer tomorrow?"

Reminded of his bundle, Jake looked down at the sack. His tone was unmistakably facetious. "Yeah, it's new boots all right, and I'm so thrilled with them that I couldn't sleep so I came down here just to open the bag and stare at them, run my hand over the pretty leather."

She grinned, going along with the sham. "Like when you were a kid and got your first pair?"

"You got it."

"Seriously, Jake. What's in the bag?"

He patted the space next to him on the swing and tried to sound mysterious. "Sit down and I'll show you."

The swing was long enough that she was able to put a foot of space between them, but being so close she could smell the whiskey on his breath and see the tell-tale glaze of it in his bloodshot eyes. There was more in his eyes than liquor, though. There was that twinge of pain she'd glimpsed earlier. That hint of gut-wrenching sorrow. He tried to conceal it with cynicism.

"Are you ready?"

At her nod, he opened the bag. She didn't know what she had expected to see, but certainly not the pile of gold buckles glittering back at her beneath the porch light. Her breath caught in her throat.

Pleased by her reaction, he removed the one on top. "This was the last one I won, my last World Championship." He handed it to her and allowed her a moment to examine it before he took out another. He showed her each one and told her the story behind winning it, about the bulls or horses he rode that had helped him. Sometimes he had other anecdotes about cowboys and cowgirls, or clowns who had saved his neck. The buckles piled up in her lap until she had to use her free hand to keep them from sliding off.

"I was the best in my day. It's hard to let that go." He started putting each buckle back into the bag. "I had them on my dresser, but I'm going to sell them."

"Oh, Jake, no. Don't do that."

"Hell, it doesn't matter anymore. I need the money."

"What do you mean, it doesn't matter? Your grandchildren will want these."

"Dusty's seen 'em, and she'll probably be my only grandkid. I don't think she quite understands that I used to be a hell of a cowboy. All she sees is a middle-aged loser."

"Then be the man you want her to see."

He weighed her words without looking at her, but he seemed determined not to be deterred from his intent. He put the last buckle in the bag. "That damn kid left me in a hell of a bind. Christ, he could rodeo for another five years."

"Don't hold it against Dev for moving on with his life, Jake. Maybe you should too. You could get a job, or come back to the ranch the way Baxter's always wanted you to."

A *ha-rumph* escaped his throat. "Nobody is going to hire a

broken-down cowboy crowding sixty. As for the ranch, I could never work with the old man."

"Maybe you both need to try harder to get along."

"Tell him that."

"He'd be willing if you were."

"You know him so well, do you?"

"He might be hard—a man has to be to live out here—but I know he's not mean-spirited or spiteful. I suspect he's mellowed a lot in the last twenty years. I think he would want his son to share his life."

"Only on his terms."

She was losing patience with him, and it angered her that he blamed both of his failed father/son relationships on Baxter and Dev. "Jake, get real. How long do you think the money from these buckles will last, providing you can even pawn them? You're trying to take the easy way out, and you don't have to. You have options. You have talent."

"Talent? Hell, my only talent is—*was*—riding broncs and bulls. Nobody would loan me a dime. I don't even have any credit. I know—don't say it—it's nobody's fault but my own, but it doesn't change the fact."

July shook her head in disbelief. "You know, people who wallow in self-pity annoy the hell out of me." She forged on despite the flare of anger in his eyes. "It's the same thing I told Seth. You have the expertise to teach others how to ride. You could open one of those rodeo training schools; you could start roping, competing at rodeos; you and Seth could team rope—you don't have to get down off your horse to do that; you could hire on with a stock contractor as a pick-up man. The bronc and bareback riders depend on them as much as the bull riders depend on the clowns. The possibilities are endless."

She saw a flicker of interest. These were things he had never seriously considered for whatever his reasons. "Nobody expects you to ride bulls your entire life," she continued. "That was part of your youth. I know you love the rodeo, but it's time for you to find new goals, a new career. Nobody is going to think you're less of a man. You'll still be a World Champion All-Around Cowboy. That's something nobody can take away from you."

He looked across the veranda where the light from the porch faded into the darkness. He released a heavy sigh that sounded a lot like defeat. "These buckles are all I have to show for my life. Because of them, I let Molly get away. Just looking at these things reminds me of everything I did wrong. Of everything I lost and can't get back, including the respect of my family."

"A person has to earn respect, Jake, but your family is waiting to give it to you." She felt sorry for him that he couldn't let go of the young man's quest and face his own mortality. "Promise me you won't sell those buckles. Put them away for Dusty and any other grandchildren that might come along."

Jake rocked the swing with a stocking-covered foot. "Yeah. Okay." His jaw lost its jut of defiance, but she wasn't convinced he meant it.

She moved to the French doors; it was time to go. "Oh, and my bet still stands that you'll catch that heifer tomorrow. Don't prove me wrong."

She slipped into her room and locked the door behind her. She drew the drapes closed then sat down on the edge of the bed and opened her journal again.

> There is a feeling I've carried with me from the time I was a child. A feeling that there was always something better waiting beyond the horizon, just out of my reach, and if I could get to it, I would be free.
>
> You're like that, too, aren't you, Jake? We're all like that. Always wanting what we can't have. Living with our restless hearts, our restless feet, our impossible dreams, when everything we've ever needed is right there inside ourselves.

Chapter Twenty-Four

From the perimeters of the pasture, July and the others watched Jake ride out toward the heifer and bulls, his rope coiled and ready. July had seen into his soul enough last night to imagine how frightening it must have been for him to go out and defend his titles; how humiliating when he'd started to lose; how deflating when he'd never risen to the top again. And how he'd tried to be young again by going after young women to prove he still had his virility.

Today, though, she saw a determined set to his jaw to prove himself in another way. To her relief, he was sober too. She started taking pictures of him, hoping to use one in the article.

When that heifer saw him coming, she got right in the middle of the bulls and started milling them around. She saw Jake adjust his loop and a wild, ready-to-take-flight look sprang into her eyes. Those bulls didn't feel any particular sentiment toward her since she wasn't in need of their services anymore. Being pasture bulls, they parted and trotted off, making room for Jake to get closer to her. But she stuck to them like glue. After all, it had worked for her yesterday.

She ran between two of the bulls and Jake reined his horse right behind her. He let sail with his loop but it hit her on the back. He tried three more times. She was cagey enough now to see the shadow of the rope and duck before it hit her. She dove under one of the bull's thick necks and packed herself tight alongside him, determined to use him for a shield.

"There's more than one way to hog-tie you," Jake hollered at her. He went around to her back end and tossed the loop on the ground right in front of her hind feet. He didn't have to wait long.

She stepped right into it. He pulled it tight and wrapped a dally around the saddle horn. She tried taking off again, but he turned the gelding and dragged her backward toward where July sat astride Stripe, taking pictures. By the time he got there, he was wearing a mile-wide grin.

"Where do you want this renegade, Dad?"

Baxter had his arms crossed over the saddle horn, a smile on his lips. "We'll take her home and then to the sale ring. I won't have a fence jumper in the herd; she'll have them all doing it before it's over with. Seth, put a rope on her head so Jake can take his off. We'll have to lead her back."

Seth made a loop and sailed it over the heifer's head. He took a dally and waited for Jake to loosen his lariat and give it a few shakes so it would fall off the heifer's hind legs. In charge now, he headed home, but the heifer set her front legs in the dirt and decided it would be better to choke to death than to submit to the pressure on her neck. The others got behind her and hazed her with ropes toward the neighbor's corral. From there, they'd haul her back to the ranch in the stock trailer.

"I think this calls for a celebration," Jake announced. He twisted in his saddle so he could see July. "How would you like to do some dancing over at the Bull Horn tonight? Bring Dev too, if he's a mind to have a little fun."

July turned to Dev, knowing he preferred not to drink with his father, and yet he said, "If July wants to."

"All right, Jake. I guess we're on."

Baxter released a snort and threw on the damper. "Drink until your heart's content, Jake, but keep Seth sober. He said he'd ride that bull tomorrow for Leo Mercer."

Seth grinned and slapped Baxter on the back. "Hell, Granddad, don't worry about me. It wouldn't be the first time I've ridden with a hangover."

"Maybe that's the reason you're always on the ground when the buzzer sounds," Jake countered.

Seth turned his back on the barb. "Are you coming with us tonight, Granddad? Kick up your heels a little?"

"Bars are for young people and old drunks," Baxter responded. "Since I'm neither, I thought Dusty might be interested in a checkers marathon." He looked over his shoulder at Dusty riding up alongside him. "What do you say?"

"Sure, Granddad. You might have beat me the last time we played checkers, but I'm a lot better now."

In good spirits, they headed home fanning out in a horizontal line with the recalcitrant heifer dancing on the end of Seth's rope. The sun eased behind a ragged cloud and sent fingers of golden light falling down over them.

July hung back, lifting her camera to snap the shot.

◆

"The only thing missing was the loudspeaker," Jake said in that boastful way that grated on Seth's nerves. "It was like being in the arena again."

Seth was behind the wheel, driving and listening. Dev and July were in the back seat being damned cozy. Hell, you'd think the two of them were in love the way they'd started holding hands and gazing into each other's eyes. It wasn't fair that women always gravitated towards Dev. It pissed him off.

"Hell, you didn't do anything so great, Dad," he snapped. "You just laid your loop on the ground and that heifer stepped right into it. I'm the one that roped her."

"And you never would have if I hadn't dragged her away from those bulls."

July leaned forward and patted them both on the shoulder. "Like I said, you two should consider team roping."

"Hell, we'd never live that down," Seth quipped. "Bull riders taking up team roping. Shit."

"Why not? It takes just as much talent," she insisted.

"A man has his pride, for Christ's sake."

Seth didn't like the thoughtful look on Jake's face or the serious way he responded, as if for once in his life he wasn't trying to be witty. "Maybe she's got a point. At least being out there doing something is better than standing on the sidelines watching. I've been on the sidelines too damned long. I know one thing. If you don't start getting your ass down on those bulls, that's where you'll be too."

Seth had heard enough about his shortcomings. "If you're going to take up roping, Dad, you'll have to find another partner or go it alone."

A rabbit darted out in front of the pickup and Seth jerked the wheel. It threw them all to one side. The pickup trembled but held the road.

"Damn it, slow down," Dev warned. "You could have rolled us."

"I was in control."

"You're never in control," Jake growled. "This road isn't the interstate."

Seth held his boot to the gas pedal, pushing the speedometer to sixty-five. The gravel and dust spewed out; the back end fishtailed. "What's in your craw? You've never cared before if I drove fast."

"Maybe you ought to let me or Dev drive until you cool off."

"I suppose you're both better at that too."

"You said it."

Seth hit the brakes. The Ram skidded to a halt on the gravel, turning sideways in the road. Seth threw open the door and jumped out. "Screw you, old man! I don't blame Dev for quitting. He probably did it to get away from you. You're always hounding and driving to win, win, win. Nobody ever does anything good enough to suit you. I can get along without you! I can do something else. It's *you* who needs *us*. You aren't good at anything but bossing people around, crowing about all your past accomplishments and drinking yourself into blind stupors. Well, go to hell! I'm not riding any more goddamn bulls for you or anybody. Those rodeo guys come out tomorrow and you can ride that sonofabitchin' Angus yourself. Show us all how it's done."

Seth hit the driver's door with the flat of his foot, slamming it shut, and kept on walking. If he noticed the dent, he had no remorse.

He heard July calling him to come back. "Come on, Seth. You can't walk all the way back to the ranch."

"I don't see why not." He didn't know why he didn't keep going, but he stopped and let her catch up to him.

"It's close to five miles."

"Five miles isn't much to a man who's seen a hundred thousand every year for his whole goddamned life!"

"Your feet will blister in those cowboy boots."

"I'm not going anywhere with that bastard again."

"This won't accomplish anything."

Seth swiped at a rock with his boot toe then took a hip-shot stance with his hands on his belt. He glared at Dev and Jake standing by the truck, waiting to see what he was going to do. "Everybody thinks Dev's the only warrior in this family. Well, I've had my share of broken bones and pulled ligaments. Dad thinks I'm nothin'. That I don't matter at all."

"I'm sorry, Seth. I wish he would be more understanding."

He pushed his hat to the back of his head and looked down the never-ending road, wishing that somewhere along its length might lie the balm that could sooth his inner anxiety. But he'd been on every road in the West more times than he could count, and he hadn't found it yet.

Christ, he was a grown man but he felt like bawling. The frustration of his entire life welled up in the back of his throat and into his eyes, choking him and blurring his vision. He jerked his hat down and turned his face away so July wouldn't see the moisture.

"Come on back to the truck," she coaxed. "We were going to celebrate, remember?"

"There's nothing to celebrate. It didn't take any skill to catch that heifer. Dad dropped the loop on the ground and she stumbled into it. I'm sick of listening to him."

July laid a gentle hand on his back and spoke so only he could hear. "It made him feel important again. Can't you understand that maybe he needed a boost to his ego, the same as you do? He's been living in the shadows right along with the rest of us."

Maybe she was right, but some shadows were a hell of a lot deeper than others, so deep that the sunlight could never penetrate them. God, was there something in this world he could do besides fail? If there was, he didn't have a clue as to what it would be. All he wanted was to be free. He didn't like being tied down to anything or anybody. He supposed he was too much like the old man for his own good. He doubted he could settle down to a regular job even if he had a woman like July to come home to every night. He knew he'd get restless and it would end with her leaving, just the way their mother had left all those years ago, just the way *she* had left Buck. Women like July needed stability, and men like him and his dad couldn't give it, or at least he didn't think so.

Releasing all the pent-up anger in his chest with a heavy sigh, he looked into her eyes. What he'd give to find a woman like her, somebody real and true at heart. But it was just as well that she was in love with Dev. He was too big of a loser himself to be worthy of a woman like her.

"How can you be so forgiving of him, July?"

"We're all trying to find our way, Seth. He's no different."

"You seem to have found yours."

She knew that look in his eyes and what he was insinuating. "Yes, I did find what I was looking for, and I'll do what it takes to hold onto him."

He nodded, swallowing hard. "You might not believe me, but I always did think you and Dev made a good pair. I'm happy for the two of you. Honest."

She thanked him. He took her by the elbow and led her back to the truck. This time the old man had the sense to keep his mouth shut.

◆

Inside the Bull Horn, couples filled the hardwood floor, dancing to the music from a country band. Seth and Jake, having mended their fences, went off to flirt with a table of women over in the corner. Dev and July paused inside the establishment, fingers entwined. A man got up from the slot machine nearest the door, kicked it, and said to nobody in particular, "Goddamn machine took my rent and two months' car payments. I'd shoot a hole in it if I had a goddamn gun." Then he stalked off to the bar and ordered a Bud Lite.

Dev fished a quarter from his pocket and handed it to July. "You can't be in Nevada and not play the slots."

As soon as she'd pulled the handle, the reels spun, and when they stopped, there were identical symbols lined up across its face. Lights flashed and quarters clattered into the metal tray. Caught unprepared, July tried to catch the overflow, but it filled her hands and kept coming. Dev pulled off his hat and put it under the cascading quarters. He hollered over to Win, "Hey, we've won the jackpot!"

Win was already on his way to offer assistance.

The cowboy at the bar who had lost his month's rent and two car payments, took his hat off and beat his head against the counter.

"One more quarter. Just one more goddamn quarter. I'd shoot myself if I had a goddamn gun."

"I knew that machine would let loose one of these days," Win said. "I'll get the full amount together and hold it til you're ready to leave."

"I ought to give it to that poor man at the bar," she said. "I think he's about to be sick. It's mostly his anyway."

"Oh no you don't," Win objected. "He'd throw it into another machine and lose it again. He understands the rules of gambling, and he doesn't expect you to give him anything."

With the excitement over, the band started playing a lively tune. July threw herself into Dev's arms. Her sparkling eyes were so alive, so happy.

"What are we going to do with the money, Dev?"

"We?"

"It was your quarter."

"Let's see." He tenderly traced her cheek with his knuckles and whispered close to her lips. "We could use it on a honeymoon in the Caribbean, or Hawaii."

A slow smile moved her lips. "A honeymoon?"

"I don't know if they allow cowboy boots on the beach, but, yes, as soon as your divorce is final let's get married and find a deserted stretch of sand."

"What if we could find a deserted island?"

"That would be even better."

He kissed her, long and thoroughly, only distantly aware of wolf whistles above the music. The crowd closed back around them and they faded into their own world again, closing their eyes to the din and the strobe lights, focusing inward on their bodies slow-dancing in perfect unison.

Then suddenly Dev was yanked away from her. A fist came up from nowhere and landed an uppercut to his jaw. It sent him reeling backwards into the dancers. Women screamed. Men swore. He lost his footing and landed on his back in the middle of denim-clad legs and cowboy boots. The band stopped playing. Another hush fell over the crowd as it parted, leaving him alone in the center of the dance floor.

"Get on your feet, Summers. We've got a score to settle."

Chapter Twenty-Five

Dev pushed his hat out of his eyes and saw Buck Jones standing over him. He hoisted himself to his feet, aware of the silence that had fallen over the crowd. Through the buzz in his head he thought he heard Win say, "You boys settle your differences outside."

If Buck heard the warning, he ignored it. "You told me she wasn't here, you lyin' piece of shit."

Dev tasted blood. "What if I did, Jones? You've been lying to July and cheating on her since the day you married her."

"Nobody steals from me."

"You didn't care enough to close the door behind you."

Buck glared at July. "She just got some things wrong and now she's coming home. Isn't that right, July?"

"She's not going anywhere with you."

"Boys, take it outside."

They ignored Win a second time. "You'll have to stop me, Summers, and I think old Satan beat your balls into the dust right along with your try."

Jones turned for the door with July in tow.

Startled by her unexpected capture, July tried to wrench free of his grip. "Let me go, Buck. I'm not going with you!"

Dev took a running leap onto Buck's back. The impact broke Buck's hold on July's wrist and sent the rodeo star headlong to the hardwood floor with Dev on top of him. People scattered, pressing themselves against the tables and walls. Women screamed and scrambled out of the way, hiding behind men who fought the battle from the sidelines, punching thin air with clenched fists and shouting advice.

Dev and Buck leaped to their feet, circling each other like wild dogs. Buck swung. Dev ducked, coming up with a fist to Buck's stomach that doubled him over. Another punch to the mouth sent him skidding across the floor again, this time on his back.

"You boys get out of my bar!" Win hollered, trotting to the doors to throw them wide. "You'll force me to call the cops!"

Buck came up off the floor like a raging bull. He charged Dev, hitting him in the midsection with his head. The force of the impact sent Dev backward through the open doors, the swinging doors, and out onto the sidewalk. He landed hard on his back. His head made contact with the sidewalk, leaving him stunned. The concrete tore through his shirt sleeves and into his elbows. The crowd followed, still shouting encouragements, but Dev couldn't tell whose side they were on. Maybe they just wanted blood and anybody's would do.

He and Buck wrestled on the sidewalk, first one on top then the other, taking punches when they could. Their breathing became labored, their aims off kilter as they struck air and muscle, bone and concrete. Blood poured into Dev's left eye, out his nose and into his mouth. He was losing the force behind his punches. Then Jake pulled Buck off, and Seth hauled Dev to his feet. Instead of egging them on now, the onlookers were silent, waiting for the next scene.

Dev couldn't see Win through the stream of blood blinding him, but he heard him say, "You stupid bastards would have killed each other."

"Damned right." Buck gasped for air. "And I am...going to...kill him. Let me go."

Dev's legs felt like they might buckle. His shirt sleeve soaked up blood, and his head pounded like holy hell.

Buck was in no better condition. His shirt remained on only by one shoulder seam while blood poured from his mouth and nose. He felt his front tooth with his tongue and released an enraged roar. "Goddamn you! You knocked my tooth loose!"

He staggered toward Dev again. This time it was July who interceded before Buck could get close enough to make contact. With both hands on his chest, she pushed him away. "Stop it, both of you! Damn it, Buck. You need to leave."

"Not 'til I kill him." But the fight had gone out of him, and he allowed July to hold him back.

"Get out of here, Buck. We're through."

"You don't mean that."

"Yes, I do."

"No, by God. I'm not leaving without you."

"It's been over between us for a long time. You sealed it in Ricky Holladay's trailer with whoever it was you were screwing."

He blanched. "How did you–?"

"How did I know? I nearly walked in on you."

"It didn't mean anything."

"Don't make this harder than it has to be."

He looked even more pained but couldn't manage another swing. It was all he could do to stand upright. "Jesus, July, don't do this. I...love you."

The words seemed to catch in his throat. Dev's heart sank as he watched July's emotional struggle at hearing Buck's public admission. Mica's declaration came back to him. *You'll never get her away from Buck. She'll go running back to him when she gets bored with you. All he has to do is say he's sorry.*

Dev spit a mouthful of blood. "Don't listen to him, July."

Buck must have seen an inkling of indecision in her eyes because he persisted, his voice softening into sweet cajolery. "I told you before, honey, it was just sex with all the others, and only then because I wanted you and you weren't with me. I thought of you all the while."

July's back stiffened. "You can't get it right even when you try." She clenched her fists at her sides, wanting to drive them into his face, not once, but again and again for every woman, every lie, every broken promise he'd taken at her expense, and now to say he was thinking of her all the while he was screwing the whole lot of them. She wanted to finish punching out his goddamn tooth. She forgot about the audience watching them air their private pain.

"What did you think, Buck? That I would forgive you forever for your lies? That I didn't need love? That I wouldn't take it if it came to me? That I wouldn't go looking for it? Did you believe that? *Did you?*" She shoved him backward with both hands;

he struggled to keep from falling. "Did you think you were such a prize that I'd put up with anything to keep you?"

He tried to catch her hands but she pushed again. "I...I don't know, but you have to believe me when I say I love you."

"I don't believe anything that comes from your lying mouth. You're too late, Buck. Way too late." She turned and ran down the sidewalk, rounded the first corner and disappeared.

Dev took a few steps after her but found he couldn't make his body respond.

"I'll go," Seth offered.

Dev caught his arm. "No. Give me a minute. I'll be all right."

Jake placed a hand on Buck's shoulder and swiveled him about-face. "Get in your truck, you sorry little bastard." He picked up Buck's hat from the sidewalk and plunked it down on his head, backwards and sideways.

Buck smacked Jake's hand away and righted his hat, becoming aware of the onlookers who were listening to his life as if it were a soap opera.

He took a step out into the street; his eyes locked with Dev's again. "Don't think you've won, Summers. I won't sign those divorce papers. I won't make it easy for you. You won't get the best of me."

"Get the hell out of here," Seth said. "He already did get the best of you."

Buck backed away for five steps, then turned and wobbled down the street toward the parking lot. When he was gone, Seth said, "You whipped the ever-lovin' shit out of him, big brother. Another punch, and he would have been down for the count."

Somebody held Dev's hat out to him. He thanked the unknown cowboy and positioned the hat over his throbbing head. Somebody else, maybe it was Win, handed him a towel to wipe the blood off his face. He didn't see who it was because his eyes were on Buck climbing into his pickup. He watched until he was certain Buck wasn't following July. He didn't know if he'd had the upper hand, but he was too weak to argue the point. He was glad that his dad and Seth had intervened.

The others filtered back into the bar. The music started up again, along with the voices and laughter. For the people inside, the battle was now just fodder for gossip. Dev headed down the sidewalk, ignoring the pain surfacing in every joint and muscle. He figured he ought to stop at the hospital and see if he'd cracked his skull, but first he had to find July.

"Do you want us to help you find her?" Seth offered.

"Thanks, but she couldn't have gone far. I'll take the truck and look for her."

A few minutes later, Dev turned the pickup around the neon-lit corner where July had disappeared. Following along it, he caught up with her several blocks down. She saw him and stopped, meeting his gaze with tear-filled eyes.

The traffic was light at this late hour. He left the truck double-parked, engine running, door hanging open as he got out and pulled her into his arms.

She said, "I'm sorry you got hurt again, and because of me."

"Believe me, darlin', it was more than worth it."

He helped her into the pickup. By lifting the center console unit upright and locking it in place, it formed a bench seat and allowed her to sit next to him. They drove in silence through the darkened, quiet streets and found themselves at the fairgrounds and the parking lot behind the rodeo grounds.

"Let's walk for awhile," he said. "I need to cool down."

The September night had a chill to it so July put her jacket on and linked arms with him. They moved toward the corrals, bucking chutes and bleachers. Most entrances were locked up, but they found a way around them and, with their boots echoing in the stillness, climbed to the top of a set of weathered, wooden bleachers that were isolated at the end of the arena.

They settled three rows from the top. He straddled the seat so he could scoot in next to her and enclose her in his arms. She relaxed against his chest, and the pain in his heart eased because he knew nothing had changed between them. Her green eyes glistened with tears in the soft starlight as she attempted to wipe them away with the heel of her hand. His embrace tightened as he kissed the top of her head.

While he held her, he looked out over the silent, dark arena and felt a familiar twist in his gut, a yearning to be down there in the middle of things again with the lights blaring along with the announcer's voice and the deafening applause and roar of the audience. He felt that rush of intoxicating pride that came when he knew he was riding high. He could understand why his dad had been trying so hard to hold onto it for so long. It was power and strength and youth, and no man ever wanted to give that up.

No matter how hard he denied it, he would miss the excitement of the rodeo, the competition, the satisfaction of trying, and the camaraderie of the other cowboys. But that part of his life was behind him forever. He couldn't go back; he had no choice but to bid it farewell. A deeper, more altruistic purpose now filled his soul, and that purpose was to love the woman in his arms for the rest of his days and to be the sort of man who deserved her love in return.

Dev kissed her tear-stained cheeks. "I love you more than life, July. I hope you will always remember that."

She ran a hand along his cheek. "And I have never loved anyone until I loved you. What I felt for Buck was nothing. There is this tremendous pain inside me...can you understand?"

He ran a hand across her back in a way that said he understood every ache in her heart, every disappointment in her life, every empty room that was never filled.

"I always have."

She buried herself deeper in his embrace and pressed her head against his heart. "That's why I love you the way I do. My only regret is that we couldn't have been here, at this moment, years ago."

"We *were* here, July. We've always been together, in a way."

They sat in silence, holding each other and staring out into the darkness below the star-littered sky. They stayed there until they found their centers again, and until July was strong enough to go back. Hand in hand, they walked down the bleachers, back across the fairgrounds to the pickup.

July convinced Dev to drive to the hospital where he was examined, stitched up, and given pain pills for his headache. The doctor told him he had a slight concussion and that he needed to stay off bulls and out of fights for a few days.

Dev gingerly put his hat on over his throbbing head. "Believe me, Doc. I've been trying."

The battle had left a sorrowful pain in both his and July's hearts. True love should not be subjected to reproach and shame. There should be sanctuaries to protect it. They searched for theirs and found it outside of town away from the city lights and traffic and intrusion of strangers. In the warm darkness of the truck, they held tight to each other like two people who had traveled too many miles and who would not, by choice, travel another alone. There was no fear now that the whispered promises made during midnight's illusion might be broken by dawn's reality. Some might condemn them, call them adulterers, but there would be no regrets in their hearts.

The glowing numbers of the digital clock told them their time had to end. As Dev started the pickup, July stayed tight against his side. Outside, the sky's glittering dome connected with the earth's perimeters like an inverted bowl. It fit snugly to every horizon, even adhering to the ragged teeth of distant mountains. It reminded her of how perfectly she fit with this man whose love she knew was true.

Much later, at dawn, as Dev lay sleeping next to her in the soft lamplight that spilled across Cecilia's bed, she took out her journal and wrote:

My Darling Dev,

> *You may never read this until I am gone—many, many years from now, I hope. There are words worthy of paper and that is what I write tonight. I want you to know that I have found in you a bottomless well of love. I think I have loved you since the beginning of time. If we are entitled to more than one life, then I know I will find your soul again and again in lives to come. You are my soul mate, the half that makes me whole. I do not regret my desperate flight nor will I ever, for at the end of that long, lonely journey, I have at last found home.*

◆

But with the dawn comes those feared intrusions; those ill winds that oftentimes blow, gentle and innocent at first, dressed in disguise but carrying the power to change life forever.

Chapter Twenty-Six

Y ou're too damned old to be riding that bull," Baxter set his coffee cup down so hard that its contents spilled onto the green linen tablecloth. July came behind him with a paper towel and tried to soak up the spill, while Jake refused to back down from the decision he'd made. Even Dusty joined in, trying to talk him out of it, to no avail.

"If Dev and Seth won't ride that bull, then that only leaves me." He glared at his offspring, but both sat unmoved by his attempt to shame them into action.

After yesterday's argument, Seth was immune to his father's needling. "You've been aching for years to show us how it's done, so here's your chance."

"Leo will bring somebody to buck the bull." Baxter was getting more irritated by the minute. "He always does. He doesn't even know you boys are here."

Jake sat with his elbows on the table, cradling his cup in his hands. July saw apprehension, maybe fear, in those aging eyes bloodshot from last night's binge and lack of sleep. Her nerves knotted. He *was* too old to be riding bulls.

"I'm going to ride, damn it."

"Oh, hell," Baxter snapped. "I'll take the damned bull to the sale ring. It's not worth somebody getting hurt just for a few extra dollars."

Dev stood up. "Christ, I'll ride him. It's not about money. It never has been."

"You're in no shape after last night," Dusty objected, but Dev had already headed out the back door.

Jake's shoulders relaxed but his talk was still big. "I said I'd ride that bull, and I will."

July's temper flared. "Damn it, Jake! You finally backed him into a corner, didn't you? You know his arm isn't healed. Last night's fiasco with Buck weakened it even more. A few jerks on that bull rigging and it'll go again. Not to mention the concussion."

"He's healed. Quit babying him. He needs to get back on or he never will, and that concussion isn't nothing."

She threw the coffee-soaked paper towel in the middle of Jake's bacon and eggs. "You make me sick. Just goddamn sick." She stormed out of the house, hurrying to catch up to Dev. Breaking into a jog, she caught his arm and forced him to halt. "Don't you see what he's doing?"

"Of course I do, but he's going to get himself killed to prove a stupid point."

"What about you? Your arm won't hold up to it, Dev. And what about the concussion? The doctor said—"

"I know what he said." Dev paced in a tight circle. "But I'm damned sick of swimming upstream. I'll give the old bastard what he wants."

The words of encouragement and understanding she wanted to speak were cut short with the arrival of a white Chevy pickup.

"There's Mercer," Dev said, watching as the rodeo stock contractor brought his rig to a halt not far from where he and July stood. Sitting on the bench seat next to him were two men in high-crowned cowboy hats. One was Will Reid, Leo's ranch foreman. The other was Buck Jones.

The hair on Dev's head prickled. "That son of a bitch has the gall to step foot on this ranch."

Buck sauntered around the pickup and leaned against the hood. It was with extreme satisfaction that Dev noticed his purple and blue striped shirt blended real well with the bruises on his face and black eye. His top lip was puffy and split mid-way from center to corner on the left side, but the other corner was still mobile. It curled upward, revealing the tooth Dev had nearly knocked out, a tooth that would have to be replaced eventually. Dev had his own share of battle scars from last night, but he decided Buck had gotten the worst of it.

"What are you doing here, Jones?"

Buck's eyes locked with Dev's in cool disdain. "Oh, did I forget to mention last night that I'm doing a favor for Leo? I ran into him before our little altercation at the Bull Horn. He told me about Baxter wanting to buck a bull. Since I was here anyway to take July home—and since none of the Summers men can ride a stick horse these days—I offered to do the job." Even as he said the words his eyes remained on Dev, refusing to acknowledge July who stood by with a cold stare.

Leo looked embarrassed by Buck's fractious remark and offered a handshake to Dev, letting him know that Buck's opinion was not his. "Heard you'd retired and were injured to boot. I didn't know Seth would be here."

Dev had always liked Leo, a man who had been on the circuit when Jake had been on top. He'd quit riding broncs when he'd damaged his neck severely at the age of thirty and been advised by doctors to quit riding or risk ending up in a wheel chair. It was then he had started his own stock contracting business. He was a good, fair man, and Dev wouldn't hold it against him because of the company he had with him today. The man had had no warning when he'd taken Buck up on his offer last night that he was about to be tossed into a lion's den.

Dev accepted the proffered handshake. "I have retired, Leo, and my shoulder's not as reliable as it could be, but I can ride that bull. He's just an old pasture bull who likes to throw his weight around. I doubt he's the performer you're looking for."

Buck inserted himself again. "Well, hell, I came out of my way to do this. I'd be right upset if I couldn't at least test that bull's potential. Besides, Leo needs a person who can get the most out of him."

"Be my guest, Jones," Dev replied, "if you want to risk getting busted up and missing your chance at the million-dollar jackpot. In case you hadn't noticed, there's no Justin Sportsmedicine Team waiting in the wings to patch you up."

"You said yourself, he's just an old pasture bull."

"Tell you what," Leo said, trying to make light of the rivalry between the two men. "I always like to see if a bull will buck more than once. Otherwise, he isn't much good to me, so it would be fine if you both want to ride him."

"I plan to ride him too," Jake said, arriving from the house followed by Seth, Baxter, and Dusty.

Leo shook Jake's hand. "Hell, there's no need for you to do that, Jake. One benefit of age is that you can let the young ones handle the risky business and not feel bad about it."

"I've wanted one last ride for over fifteen years, Leo."

"Well, I wouldn't want it to *be* your last ride."

"Don't talk him out of it," Buck said. "I'd like some serious competition."

"In case you missed something, Buck," July inserted, "there isn't any money or titles involved. Not even a gold buckle."

He took her chin in his hand, squeezing too hard. "Oh, there's more at stake than meets the eye, little darlin'." Then he left her, swaggering toward the corrals.

Everyone was obliged to follow except Jake who hung back with July until the others were out of earshot. "Could you do me a favor?"

Glaring at Buck's back, July rubbed at her chin, wanting to scrub away the feel of his hand on her skin. She was angry at the entire situation and at these stupid men for the stupid things they did, and at herself for feeling compelled to witness their folly. She was furious at Buck for being here. What did he hope to prove, or gain, after last night's fight? There was one comforting fact though. For the first time in her married life, she had no inclination to forgive him or go back to him. She wondered what she had ever seen in him and why she'd been so honor bound all those years to make the marriage work when Dev had been here all along. God, if only she'd known the love she'd been missing.

She remembered Jake's question. "What favor?"

He didn't seem to notice her irritation, or if he did, he thought he could smooth it over. "Could you take a picture of me? I'd like to have one to add to my collection."

"One last moment of glory?" she accused.

"Maybe, but why fault me?"

She shook her head, feeling helpless and wishing there was something she could do to stop Dev, to stop them all. This whole thing was billowing out of proportion, being driven by rivalry, by each of them trying to prove something. And she had a sick feeling she was the root cause.

"You're going to get yourself killed."

"There's worse ways to die."

"Did you know about Buck? Did you ask him here hoping I'd go back to him? Did you think that with me gone, Dev would return to the rodeo?"

He seemed genuinely offended. "I wouldn't do a thing like that, and that's the honest-to-God truth. How was I to know Buck had talked to Leo? As for Dev, he made his decision to quit long before you came along."

For once, July believed him.

"Come on," he cajoled. "It'll turn out fine. You'll see."

July wished Jake would come to his senses. But, like the others, maybe even more so, he had an image to uphold, and pride so powerful it might be the death of him someday. Sometimes a man had to be a man, and the best thing she could do was let him prove his point, or try.

"All right. I'll take your picture. Just stay on the damn bull long enough for me to aim and shoot."

His lips spread into a wide, boyish grin. The old bravado returned. "Look at it this way, Firecracker. You'll go down in history as being the photographer who got the picture of six-time World Champion, Jake Summers, on his last ride."

She shook her head. "I don't know why I ever thought you had redeeming qualities."

He was riding high now, knowing that despite her chastisement, she cared what happened to him. He had her blessing so he ignored the barb. "Hurry now. Leo won't wait."

Anxious to be in the spotlight, he followed the others. July watched him for a moment, feeling a strange foreboding settle over her before returning to the house for her camera.

She was both angry and sympathetic toward Jake. For as much as he got under her skin, she understood him. She understood the weaknesses and shortcomings he was trying to hide and all the painful baggage he'd been hauling around for decades. It didn't mean she condoned what he did, or had done, or how he behaved, but she realized he was a lonely, misguided man crying out for love, even if his situation had been brought on by the choices he, himself, had made. They were all products of the roads they had opted to travel.

At the corrals again, she made the appropriate light and aperture settings. By the time she had settled in a good location atop the pole corral, they had the bull in the chute.

Dev, Seth, and Buck stood behind the chute putting on their chaps and arguing over who would ride first.

"You'll rip your shoulder all up again," Seth was saying to Dev. "I can ride him. You don't have to prove anything."

"Oh, but he does," Buck countered. "He has to prove to July that he can ride circles around me."

Seth's disdainful eyes locked onto his nemesis. "We've always known he could do that, Snaggletooth. The only thing you've ever done better is strut and crow."

Ignoring Seth as if he didn't exist, Buck directed his next remark to Dev. "Don't waste your time trying, Summers. The real contest today is between me and your old man. Now, *he* was good. You can't stand in his shadow, and you never will."

Dev was tempted as hell to finish knocking out Buck's dangling tooth. Wouldn't the ladies love him if they could see him now? But the little bandy rooster was already on his way to the gate. Mercer handed him his Kevlar vest and mouth guard, which he gingerly put in place over the loose tooth.

Knowing someone would need to drive the bull out of the arena as soon as Buck hit the dirt, Dev untied Dinky and swung into the saddle. Baxter straddled Dan, and Seth opted to handle the gates.

Dev trotted Dinky to one side of the arena, then folded his arms over the saddle horn to wait. He didn't know what Buck thought he could prove. Nobody was taking score. There were no prizes to be won—no prize, that is, except July. His gaze was drawn to where she sat on the top pole of the corral with the sunlight backlighting her golden hair and giving it the appearance of a halo. Something twisted inside him, as it always did when he looked at her, and he knew it was the love he had for her. A love so powerful that sometimes it could be painful. In that moment, he knew with certainty that he could never live without her.

A curse from the chute pulled his eyes back to Buck and the Angus bull. Frightened over the strange confinement, the bull threw back his massive black head every time Buck's legs brushed his sleek hide. Wild-eyed, he pawed the dirt and lunged head-long into the confining rails, looking for an escape.

The bull finally settled, panting in blind terror that could be deadly if it exploded into rage. Buck eased down onto him, lowered his bull rope and waited for Mercer to bring the other end back up to him from under the bull's belly while Reid handled the flank strap. He pulled the rope tight over his rosined glove, wrapped it, pounded his fist into it, tightened and wrapped it again, then secured the loose end. He was so practiced, it took only a few seconds. He scooted forward until his hand was snug against his groin, lifted his arm into the air and gave the nod.

Seth yanked the gate open. The frantic bull saw his freedom and blasted into the small arena. Two seconds into his flight he remembered Buck on his back. Wanting to be shed of him, as well as the flank strap, he leaped straight for the sky, twisting his muscled body into a sideways arc. He came down hard and dove forward on his front feet and started whirling one way and then the other, but Buck held his seat like the champion he was.

Reid blew a whistle and the eight-second ride ended. Buck leaped free, landing on his feet. The Angus whirled, blew snot, and came for Buck with his head down. Buck scrambled up the pole corral to safety and kicked the bull in the face.

"You ain't nothin' but an old piece of shit."

Baxter and Dev hazed the bull out of the arena and closed the gate behind him. Dev loped Dinky over to the bucking chute so he could ride next, but he found Jake in place, waiting for Mercer and Reid to prod the bull through the alley a second time.

"Damn it, Dad, you don't have to do this."

Dev could smell his dad's fear—the bull was ranker than any of them had expected—but from the stubborn set of his jaw, it wasn't going to stop him. Jake pulled his hat down tight on his head and refused to look at Dev. He crammed a boot on either side of the narrow chute, sticking his boot toes out between the rails. Still lean and muscular, he looked thirty years old balanced up there—as long as he kept his face in the shadow of his hat brim.

"It's like riding a bike." The words sounded more like self-assurance than arrogance. "Once you learn, you never forget how."

"Let it go, Dad," Dev warned.

Jake twisted from the waist and hollered over to July, "Got your camera ready, Firecracker?"

July hadn't wasted any of her digital memory card on Buck. Enough other people had already done that over the years. She had shot several pictures of the others to check her lighting. Now, as Jake proceeded to prove he was still a champion, that old nervous feeling coiled in her stomach. The fear for a cowboy's life. The helplessness when one got hung up in the rope or battered by a bull's massive head and horns.

This wasn't the time to frighten him. The others were already questioning his decision and his ability. What he needed was someone to believe he could do it, because he wasn't going to back down. So she gave him a wide smile and all the confidence she could muster.

"I've got you covered!"

Jake's grin was replaced with a bulldog expression as he turned his attention to the bull.

"Put the face guard on." Leo's brow knotted with concern.

"I've never ridden with any of that crap, and I'm not going to start now."

"Don't be stubborn, Grandpa." This time it was Dusty speaking. She had found a spot closer to the chutes and wore a worried expression.

Jake shook his head. He was going to ride the way he'd always ridden. Not even his granddaughter could change his mind. "I'll be fine." He gave her a broad grin. "You've never seen your Grandpa ride, have you?"

Baxter rode up alongside the chute. "Damn it, Jake. You don't have anything to prove."

Jake kept himself focused on his bull rigging.

July started snapping shots when he dropped his bull rope down along the bull's side. He went through the same motions that Buck had before him. He moved forward, pressing his groin into his hand, settling down. The Angus's flesh was quivering; so was Jake's.

"Stubborn, goddamn...." Baxter wheeled Dan away.

Jake nodded and Seth jerked the gate open.

This time the Angus started whirling and bucking the second he was in the arena, but Jake fell into the rhythm. Seconds ticked by as he clung tenaciously to the broad, spinning back. The whistle sounded. He didn't seem to hear, or maybe he was afraid of falling beneath the beast's deadly hooves, knowing how hard it would be for a man his age to scramble out of the way.

Seth, Leo, and Reid raced forward, trying to get the flank strap off so the bull would quit bucking and allow Jake the chance he needed to leap clear. From his perch near the chute, Buck hollered, "E-e-e-haw, ride 'em, cowboy!"

Suddenly Jake was flung to the right. He fell to the ground not far from July's position on the pole corral. The bull's back hooves caught him in the back; the front ones came down on his head. He crumpled and lay sprawled, unconscious.

Dev and Baxter rode in cautiously behind the bull and hazed him toward the gate by waving their arms and shouting, but the Angus had gone that way once before and had no intention of being bucked a third time. He escaped to the other side of the arena on a high-headed trot with the riders and Reid, Seth, and Mercer on foot right behind him. Buck even made a half-hearted attempt to help by shouting at the bull, but he stayed close to the chute and safety.

With the bull cornered at the other end of the small arena, July left her camera at the base of a post and both she and Dusty ran to help Jake. He was deathly still. Blood poured from a gash on his head. July felt for a pulse, but her own heart was pounding so fast and furious she wasn't sure she would be able to differentiate between the two.

"Damn it, Jake, why did you do this?" she implored, even though she knew he could not answer.

Dusty placed hands on either side of her grandfather's bleeding head. "Is he alive?" Her voice bordered on panic.

"I've found a pulse," July announced, "but we'd better call 9-1-1."

Dusty sprang to her feet. "I'll do it." In seconds, she had scaled the corral poles and was running across the yard as fast as she could go.

While July waited, she glanced up to see the others still having trouble getting the bull out of the arena. Cornered, it whirled toward Dev and Dinky. Baxter shouted and waved a coiled lariat to get the animal to turn. The men on foot tried to distract him but stayed close to the pole corral in case they needed a fast escape.

Dev nudged Dinky in closer to the bull. "Okay, Granddad, let's see if we can force him toward the gate. Everybody, watch yourselves. He's on the fight."

"Yeah, boys," Buck hollered from his position next to the exit gate. "Get him over here and I'll take care of him."

Seeing himself boxed in with no apparent way out, the bull suddenly charged Dinky, hitting him hard in the front leg. With a scream, the buckskin was knocked back onto his haunches, nearly unseating Dev. The Angus charged past the incapacitated horse to the open arena then stopped short, taking in the handful of men trying to haze him. He paced in a circle, pawed the earth and threw the loose soil over his back. He whirled; July came into his view.

Dev's heart fell, realizing in that instant what the bull would do. "July! Get out of there! Now!"

She looked up just in time to see the bull charging. There was no time to weigh her options. The beast would kill both her and Jake if she didn't do something fast. Jumping to her feet, she started waving her arms as she moved away from Jake.

The bull took the bait. With lowered head, he veered straight for her. She turned and ran as hard as she could toward the bucking chute, drawing him away from the unconscious Jake. But ten feet short of safety, the gigantic head caught her, flinging her headlong into the heavy corral poles. She didn't feel the pain, just the force of the impact before everything went black.

◆

The bull whirled away from her and faced the others racing toward it like a thundering army of attacking warriors, screaming desperate profanities and waving hats and coiled ropes. It saw the open gate to the alley and fled through it.

Jake, across the corral, was regaining consciousness.

July wasn't.

This time Buck came running. The amusement was gone from

his face as he dropped to his knees in the dirt alongside the others. While Dev and Seth felt for a pulse, Buck started to gather her up. "I'll take her to the hospital. To hell with waiting for an ambulance. It could take an hour to get here."

Dev's arm shot out across July's body and grabbed Buck by the shirt front. "Don't move her, you stupid son of a bitch! Her back could be broken, or her neck."

Buck tried to get Dev's hands off him, but they were like clamps. "She's my wife, Summers. It's not for you to decide what we'll do with her."

"Touch her again and I'll kill you."

"Dev's right," Leo said. "You'd better not move her."

"What happened?" Jake staggered over to them, collapsing to his hands and knees. Blood still pumped from the head wound, down his neck and into his shirt collar.

Dev lashed out at him. "She tried to save your sorry ass!"

Jake sat back on his heels, looking like he'd been kicked below the belt. He crawled a few feet away and vomited in the dirt.

Dusty came running back from the house. "They're on their way!" Then she saw that the scene had changed and confusion strained her young face.

"Call them again," Baxter advised, remaining calm but grim. "Tell them we need a life-flight instead of the ambulance."

She didn't ask questions but ran for the house again through a blur of sudden tears. Seth was not far behind, running to get blankets to cover July.

At last, silence settled over them. They'd done all they could think to do. Now began the long wait for the paramedics. Leo and Reid watched the sky and listened for the sound of the chopper. Jake held July's head between his hands as tears escaped his eyes and trickled down his dusty, blood-stained cheeks. Baxter and Seth knelt at her booted feet, each with a hand on one of her ankles. Buck held one of her hands; Dev the other. It was as if by holding onto her, they could keep her spirit from floating away, as if by sheer willpower and silent prayers they could keep her with them. She tried to regain consciousness, mumbling, "Is Jake all right?"

"I'm fine, July. Fine."

"Dev—"

"Don't talk," Buck interceded, leaning over her until she could see only his face before her. "Lie still, honey. I'm here. Buck's here."

By the time the chopper landed thirty minutes later, there was no response from her at all.

Chapter Twenty-Seven

The life-flight helicopter lifted into the sky and swung toward the setting sun, rushing July to Elko General Hospital, and leaving the others standing numbly in its swirling dust. Buck was the first to move, asking Leo to drive him to the hospital. They squealed from the yard, spewing gravel, and hit the main road before the helicopter had gained full altitude.

With Seth behind the wheel, everyone except Baxter piled into the Ram. The old man held back, placing his hands on the passenger door's open window. "I need to see to Dinky."

Dev had to choke back tears, not only because of July but because of his granddad's horse. "I'm sorry, Granddad. I shouldn't have allowed the horses in the arena, especially since he charged Dan that day at the cabin. But he—"

"I know, son. We've herded that bull for years on horseback and with other cattle. He's a range bull, for God's sake. I didn't give it a thought either." Baxter looked away, clearly dreading what lay ahead. When he turned back, his eyes searched Dev's face with a look that said he knew the thoughts tormenting his grandson's mind. "She'll be all right, son."

Emotion closed Dev's throat; he couldn't respond. Jesus, what if he lost her?

"Call me as soon as you hear anything," Baxter said, stepping away.

When the pickup reached the main road, and the chopper was little more than a glint of silver in the sky, Baxter headed for the house. With hands that shook, he removed his Winchester from the gun rack. The fear for July's life engulfed him. There was nothing he hated worse than being helpless, unless it was feeling responsible when things went bad. And he blamed himself for this, all of it. He should have sold that bull when they first pulled him off the range. He should have put a stop to bucking it when Jake had gotten the notion to ride, when Buck had come along and egged him on.

With cartridges fully loaded, he strode back outside. As he walked toward the holding pen, he allowed the anger and pain to engulf him. He needed it to complete the task at hand. He climbed halfway up the corral and swung a leg over the top pole. Half-sitting on it to balance himself, he levered a cartridge into the chamber.

At the sound, the bull whirled. Still on the fight, it tossed its head and blew snot. With a throaty rumble, it pawed the earth until a cloud of dust encircled it and drifted into Baxter's eyes. It charged, hitting the heavy pine poles. The force of the impact barely stunned it. It shook its head and lathered itself into another frenzy, as if it believed Baxter had inflicted the blow.

Baxter pulled the bandana from his back pocket and tried to wipe the dust from his eyes, but the bull kept stirring up more. It charged a second time with such force that the impact nearly toppled Baxter into the pen. As he grabbed the pole to right himself, he watched his bandana flutter through the air toward the bull, who promptly pawed it into the ground. The rage in the brute's eyes insinuated that he wouldn't hesitate to do the same thing to Baxter if given half a chance.

This wasn't the first time Baxter had seen an animal go crazy, and there was only one thing to be done about it. He anchored the Winchester firmly against his shoulder. Without hesitation, he sighted down the barrel to a spot between the bull's gleaming black eyes, and he pulled the trigger.

The bull dropped to its knees then hit its haunches hard. It fell to its side, muscles twitching and extremities jerking.

Baxter climbed down into the pen and didn't stop until his boot toes touched the bull's shoulder. He levered another bullet into the chamber and placed the gun a few inches from animal's thick skull. He fired a second round and watched with a mixture of emotions as the life ebbed from the black eyes and the body lay still at last.

"That first one was for July, you dirty son of a bitch. The second one was for me."

Baxter left the pen and walked into the arena where Dinky was still standing with head drooping and front leg off the ground. The gelding looked at Baxter with a terrible pain in his eyes, and something else—a knowledge—as if he knew his fate would be the same as the bull's. But Baxter leaned the Winchester into a crotch of the fence and went over to examine the leg, verifying his worst fear.

He ran a hand along Dinky's face, then removed the saddle. He had raised the horse from a colt and had broken him to ride. He couldn't kill him anymore than he could kill a member of his family. He had heard of amazing things vets could do nowadays for horses with broken legs.

Baxter stood for a moment longer next to the horse, wondering if he was making the right decision. Then he started for the house to call the vet. Before he could leave the arena, though, he was brought up short by the sight of July's camera resting against a corral post. With a pain so deep in his chest he could barely draw a breath, he bent and gathered it up.

◆

The wait at Elko General Hospital wasn't long. Dr. Jack Carranza, the emergency room doctor, had bumped all other patients and sent July into x-ray upon her arrival. Based on what he'd seen, he had immediately put her on another life flight to Saint Mary's Regional Medical Center in Reno.

The Summers family knew Dr. Carranza well. He had treated all of them numerous times and was familiar with them on a first name basis. While he explained July's condition, Dev sifted through the medical jargon and pulled out the bits and pieces he could understand. "...no time to waste...head trauma...a skull fracture...blood clotting on the brain... swelling...she'll be in the hands of one of the best neurosurgeons in the country...the emergency room staff has been put on alert... she'll have priority the second the chopper touches down...if anyone can save her life, Dr. William Reynolds can."

Buck chartered a private plane to Reno, not offering to share the flight with any of them. They couldn't get another on such short notice, so, once again, they crowded into the Ram. They headed west on Interstate 80, hitting a cruising speed of ninety miles an hour, arriving in Reno a few hours later.

At Saint Mary's, they were directed to the OR waiting room. Because of the late hour, the room was empty except for Buck who had found a corner and was nervously flipping through an issue of *Sports Illustrated*. The Summers family wound their way single file around the rows of chairs to see if he'd heard anything. He hadn't.

Dazed and exhausted, they settled down to wait. Jake was clearly in pain now. While en route, Dusty had wiped away most of the dried blood from his head and face with paper towels and bottled water she'd bought at a gas station. She still couldn't convince him to go to the emergency room.

The five of them took turns pacing up and down the hallway as if movement could dissolve time. They called Baxter and learned that he'd turned Dinky over to the vet, who was encouraged that he would be able to put a pin in the broken leg and believed it would heal well enough that the horse could be used for simple pleasure riding. He would never be able to cut cattle again.

Although the surgery ended shortly after they arrived, it still seemed an eternity before Dr. Reynolds walked into the waiting room, looking grim and exhausted. They rose as he positioned himself in the center of their semicircle. After introductions, he said, "She's holding her own. The surgery to relieve pressure on her brain went well. There were some internal injuries—bruised kidneys and two broken ribs but no evidence of internal bleeding. Her spine and neck are fine and no other bones are broken. The skull fracture remains the most critical injury." He hesitated, taking a breath before adding, "However, she had lapsed into a coma before we got her to OR."

Buck turned livid. "A coma?"

"Yes, and I'm sorry to say that's not all. She lost the baby she was carrying."

Buck's eyes snapped to Dev's. "A baby?"

"She was about a month along." Dr. Reynolds continued, trying to give reassurance. "Also, be aware that with broken ribs, the onset of pneumonia is always a possibility, but our main concern is the head injury. If we can keep the swelling down and the blood flowing to carry oxygen, we're confident she won't experience any brain damage."

While everyone allowed themselves to digest the report, Buck shifted uneasily, sliding his hands into the back pockets of his Wranglers. "You're saying that's a possibility?"

"Her situation is critical, Mr. Jones. She's very fortunate to still be with us. However, the brain scan shows good blood flow. As I said, a lot depends on keeping intracranial pressure at a safe level. It's not a given that she'll have brain damage, but it is a possibility you should be aware of."

"Look, Doc—" Buck's eyes skewered Dev again, "if she's...if there's not a good chance that...what I'm trying to say is...she has a Living Will. Her worst fear was being kept alive by a bunch of machines if her mind was gone. If that's what she's facing, maybe we should consider—"

"Damn you, Buck," Dev took a threatening step toward him. "Don't you dare—"

Dr. Reynolds diplomatically intervened, but he made it clear that he didn't want to discuss a Living Will at this point. "A team of doctors put in a monumental effort to save your wife's life, Mr. Jones. It's too soon to know what course her recovery will take, but as long as there's cerebral blood flow and brain activity, there's hope. I seriously discourage you from rushing into a decision to remove her from life support and nutrition. It's not appropriate to take such action at this point. I've seen people with head injuries worse than July's come out of comas with no disabilities whatsoever."

Buck's temper flared. "And what if she isn't so fortunate? What if she ends up being a vegetable for the rest of her life?"

Reynolds breathed a weary sigh. He was tired and losing patience with Buck. "Every case is different. All we can do is watch and wait and do everything medically possible for her. Give us a chance to do our job. I don't anticipate a significant change for awhile, so this might be a good time for all of you to go home, or to a hotel, and get some rest." He took in Jake's shirt and head, both matted with blood. "And you should go to the ER, Mr. Summers. As for updates on July's condition, feel free to call the nurse's station any time. You'll be notified, of course, if anything changes."

He shook hands with everyone again and departed. Buck didn't wait for comments from the Summers family and stalked out of the waiting room. While he might have been finished with them, they were not finished with him.

Dev told Dusty to stay in the waiting room. He, Jake, and Seth caught up with Buck in the elevator. Sensing trouble from the dirty and bloody cowboys, the other occupants exited before the elevator doors slid shut.

As soon as it began its descent, Dev pressed the Stop button and brought it to a jerking halt between floors.

Outnumbered and backed into a corner, Buck still had the audacity to goad them. "What's this? A persuasion team to change my mind? Well, let me tell you again—I *have* the legal authority to make the decision, and you can't do a damn thing about it. She has a Living Will, and I'll use it if necessary."

"I'm warning you, Buck."

"You'd better quit threatening me, Summers, or you'll find yourself with a restraining order."

It was all Dev could do to keep from putting a fist in the center of Buck's face. "What's this really about? Are you trying to get even with July for walking out on you? Or would you rather see her dead than see her with me?"

"It was lucky she lost that bastard kid she was carrying."

Dev slammed him up against the elevator wall. "I might have known you don't give a shit about her."

"Under the circumstances, I don't owe her anything, and I won't pay for her damn hospital bill or take care of her if she comes out of this an invalid. I'm going to sue Baxter's ass since this happened on his property. I hope he has some damn good liability insurance."

"Just get the hell out of her life, Jones. We'll take care of her *and* the hospital bill. You never loved her. All that talk at Win's was bullshit. You just wanted to stroke your ego, see if she'd come running back so you could hurt her again." He set Buck away from him, as if releasing something vile.

"She sealed her own fate when she took up with you."

"You can blame her, Buck. You can blame me. But if you look back far enough, you'll see that this entire road leads right back to you. All your cheating and lying. It was a lot of miles you put between yourself and July. Miles that she couldn't erase no matter how hard she tried."

"It's not my fault she got injured. If you'd been any kind of a cowboy, you wouldn't have let that bull get past you. And if Jake hadn't been such a glory-monger, he would have had the sense to stay in his crib and nurse his bottle of Jack Daniels."

It was Jake's turn to grab Buck by the shirt front. "You selfish little prick. I ought to kill you myself." Seemingly afraid he'd do just that, he released Buck with a force that slammed him against the elevator wall.

Buck smiled in his typical sneering way as he smoothed his shirt with the downward stroke of a hand. "You accuse me of being selfish, but you're no better. None of you are thinking of July or what she might have to deal with if she survives."

"She deserves a chance, and if you try to enforce that Living Will without just cause, we'll see who wins this go-round."

"The only way you'll stop me is to kill me, and you'll never get away with that."

Buck reached for the elevator buttons but Dev's hand clamped down on his wrist. "Don't be so sure, Jones. I know places in this state where only the coyotes could find your body."

The deadly threat in Dev's eyes brought a flicker of apprehension to Buck's face. Then Dev released him and set the elevator into motion. When the doors opened, Buck shouldered his way out, swaggering past them as if his position on top of the world had never been challenged.

◆

Maybe Dev *was* only thinking of himself. My God, was Buck right? Was it unfair to July? He knew that if he was in her position, possibly facing brain damage, he wouldn't want to be kept alive by well-meaning individuals who couldn't let go.

While the others slept, he peered down the long highway unable to dismiss what Buck had said—that July's accident *was* his fault. It made him sick to admit it was true. Sure, Jake might be at the root of what had happened, but if he himself had been on his toes, he would have anticipated the bull charging and he would have been ready to head him off. If he hadn't been so determined *not* to ride, then his dad wouldn't have felt compelled to. If he hadn't suggested bucking the bull in the first place.

If. If. If.

And what of the baby he and July had created in love, now gone? Lost forever. He hadn't known. Had she? She'd wanted a child for so many years. He wanted nothing more than to be the one to give her that gift. Now, would they get a second chance?

A groan from the back seat drew his attention. In the rearview mirror, he saw his dad awkwardly shift positions. Dusty had gotten him to the emergency room after the confrontation with Buck. He'd been diagnosed with a cracked rib, along with contusions and a mild concussion. It had taken a fancy row of stitches to sew up his head.

In the passenger seat, with a rolled-up coat between her head and the passenger window, Dusty stirred from her slumber long enough to open her eyes and sleepily ask, "Are you okay, Dad? I can drive if you need a break."

"No, I'm fine." His eyes were tired and bloodshot, belying the words, knowing it would take booze or pills for him to sleep. He couldn't help but wonder what she thought of him now that she knew about the baby.

"Maybe we should stop and get something to eat," she said. "You haven't had a bite since it happened."

The others had bought some snacks, but Dev had had no appetite. "Unless you want to stop, I'm okay."

"You need food and rest."

"I'll be fine." He reached across the seat and patted her knee, hoping to reassure her. "Go back to sleep."

Her young eyes pitied him, yet understood with a wisdom that went beyond her years. "I'm glad you and July are in love, Dad. And, hey, she'll be all right."

Looking at her, Dev's heart ached to return to innocence and youth, to the place where hope and faith had dwelled. But he had lost it all, and a thousand other things, somewhere on those million miles of highway. He feared there was no getting any of it back; just as there was no getting July back, if not for the grace of God.

◆

Dev took July's room and let Seth have his, but he lay awake for hours with the darkness punctuated by flashbacks of the accident. He feared the ring of the telephone and the dreaded news it might bring.

He regretted the return to the ranch to bring the others home and get fresh clothes for himself. He should have let them take the truck. He could have walked the short distance from the hospital to a hotel. He could have taken a taxi to buy clothes in Reno. His mind had been so numb at the time, though, he hadn't thought things through. Reynolds had said to go home, and like obedient children, they'd all piled into the truck and done just that. Never mind that home was four hundred miles away.

He rose from bed to pace the floor and, in the dark, knocked something off the night stand and onto his foot. Groping, he found the lamp switch. Its soft glow shone on the object: July's journal. It had come open, and in her neat hand he easily saw the words, *My Darling Dev,* leaping up at him.

He would never have intentionally read her private thoughts, but the words were written to him, for him. What had she said? He had to know. Retrieving the book from the floor, he sat back on the bed, and began to read:

You may never read this until I am gone....

◆

Jake sat on the edge of his bed in the dark, in his underwear, slump-shouldered and angrily swiping at the tears streaming down his face, but they kept coming and coming, and he couldn't stop them. My God, what kind of a man bawled like a baby? A scared man? Yes. A man so scared that his hands shook and his legs wouldn't hold him.

What if July died? Or what if she lived but was brain damaged? He wouldn't be able to live with himself either way. She was a good woman, a good person, and she didn't deserve this. She had cared about him. Knowing that had made him believe it wasn't too late to turn a corner, to start a new life. If she died, there would be nothing to keep him from digressing right back to what he'd been for too damn long: a man with no direction, no future, no purpose.

This was all his fault and he would carry the blame for the rest of his miserable life. Not only would he never forgive himself, but Dev would never forgive him either. Losing July would put a chasm between them that could never be spanned.

He ought to put a bullet in his head. He ought to do it right now. He couldn't stand this debilitating pain, this gut-wrenching guilt. He didn't want to live. He didn't deserve to live.

He reached for the lamp and flicked the switch, opening the darkness. He came to his feet and strode to the closet, holding his breath against the pain in his cracked rib. His gun was in here, somewhere, stashed on the top shelf behind his belt buckles and hats. He shoved things aside, groping and cussing. The damn thing was here. He knew it.

But it was not the gun he found. It was the cool, slender neck of his secret stash of Jack Daniels. His fingers curled around the familiar feel of the glass. Saliva leaped onto his tongue and into his mouth, forcing him to swallow. He licked his lips. A drink would fix this, at least for now. If he got stone-cold drunk, he wouldn't think about her, the guilt, or what might happen tomorrow.

With a shaking hand, he unscrewed the lid and lifted the bottle to his lips. At that moment, he caught his reflection in the mirror; his stomach turned over from the shock of what he saw. The man before him was not the man he had always imagined himself to be. He didn't recognize this person who looked like an old derelict, standing there in rumpled underwear, hair on end, sagging skin, staring back at him with bloodshot, weeping eyes. This person who was weak and useless and repulsive.

His face twisted with contempt as rage boiled over inside him. He drew his arm back and hurled the bottle, smashing to pieces the man he hated with all his heart.

◆

Haunted by the words July had written, Dev fell asleep with the journal in his arms and tears burning his eyes, only to be jerked awake by crashing noises and shattering glass in his dad's room overhead.

Yanking on his jeans, he was met in the upstairs hall by Granddad and Seth. Granddad, wild-eyed in his plaid bathrobe, flung open the door to Jake's room.

They found him sitting on the edge of the bed in his underwear with his head in his hands and tears streaming over his cheekbones. The glow from the single lamp cast his angular, unshaven face in high relief, giving it a jaundiced appearance. Scattered around him on the floor were his gold buckles, his trophies, a broken bottle of Jack Daniels, and shattered glass from the dresser mirror. The overpowering stench of sweat and whiskey bit their nostrils.

"My God, Dad. What the hell—"

Chapter Twenty-Eight

Get out! All of you, just get out and leave me alone!"

"We're not going anywhere until you tell us what's going on," Baxter said.

Jake's head pounded so viciously it hurt to think, to talk, to object. "Damn it, I had to show off for her, okay? I had to be a big shot—the best damn bull rider that ever lived. Now she might die, and it's because of me! Jesus. What have I done?"

Baxter walked into the room, crunching glass under his rubber-soled slippers, and placed his hand on Jake's shoulder. "The doctors haven't given up hope. We shouldn't either."

"Hell, they don't know. And now that damn Buck doesn't even want to give her a chance...I ought to kill him." Jake wiped at his eyes, but the tears continued to seep out, making him furious that they wouldn't stop.

"You'd have to stand in line to kill Buck," Baxter said grimly. "He hasn't done anything yet, so get some sleep."

"I can't. I just keep seeing her...like that."

The guilt was overwhelming, and not just because of what had happened to July. All his sins, past and present, came home to haunt him. Or maybe it was this foreboding about July's condition that had a clamp on his chest so tight he could barely breathe.

"She risked her life for me. I didn't deserve to be saved," he muttered. "I didn't deserve it at all."

He lapsed into silence, barely aware of Seth and Dev sweeping and vacuuming up the glass and soaking up the whiskey with a mop. Then the vacuum clicked off, and, into the heavy silence that followed, he dropped his conscience.

"I can't run from it anymore."

"Run from what, Dad?" Seth asked in a gentle tone.

"The mistakes. The memories. All of it. Not just this thing with July, but the past. I was so arrogant, just like Buck. I thought I could do anything I wanted."

He thought about all the times he'd tried to drink away the pain until he passed out. Now, after a lifetime, he had regained consciousness. He stood face to face with the truth. He couldn't hide in the bottle anymore or on the rodeo circuit, or in some woman's bed pretending that time had stood still and Molly was still waiting for him in Clover Valley, or that he was young and would get a second chance at love like that. He was the reason she was gone and would never be back. He was the reason July might die. And all because of pride and ego and the inexplicable need to be a champion forever.

The pounding in his head felt as if it might split his skull wide open. "I didn't mean to do this to you, Dev. I didn't mean to be such a sorry excuse of a man. Didn't mean to take things out on any of you. I was the weak link in this family, and I'm to blame for everything that's gone wrong with us. Can you ever forgive me?" He looked up into Dev's face with pleading eyes.

Dev stared back at his father, possibly seeing him for the first time. The man looked old and pathetic, worn down and worn out. In that moment, Dev felt more sorry for him than he did himself, but most of what his dad had said was true, and there was no getting any of it back.

He put a hand on his dad's shoulder. "You weren't the only one who made mistakes, Dad. All we can do is go forward and try to do better the next time around."

Drained of strength and emotions, Jake had no more to say. They left him alone to return to their rooms. Downstairs, standing in the center of July's room, Dev understood now more than ever why Granddad avoided this place where he had shared the most intimate part of himself with the only woman he had ever loved. What was to become of this room? Would it have to be locked up with the memory of yet another lost love?

He laid down on the bed and settled his head in the center of July's pillow. Her perfume lingered on the pillowcases and brought her image even sharper to mind. He closed his eyes and fell into a transcendental state so deep that he could feel her fingertips on his skin. In this room, in this darkness, he could feel her arms around him. He could hear her whispered words and low, sensual laughter. Here, he could hold onto her forever. And never, ever, let go.

◆

The next morning, Baxter announced that he was going to Reno with Dev, and that Seth and Dusty had volunteered to take care of Jake and keep the hired hands focused on rounding up the cattle.

At the hospital, Dev and Baxter found July's condition hadn't changed but was at least stable. After a discussion with Dr. Reynolds, Dev was given permission to see her in the ICU. "Buck's with her now," Reynolds said. "I've told the nurses it's all right for you to visit her. Since Buck is her only family member, I felt she might benefit from a close friend." From the knowing look in his eyes, and the information that had been disclosed about the miscarriage, it was evident he suspected that July's connection with Dev was much stronger than the one she had with her husband.

Buck emerged in less than five minutes, angry and agitated.

He grabbed his hat from an empty chair and placed it on his head. "July wouldn't want this. I'm going to have my folks Fed-Ex that Living Will. To hell with what that doctor says."

"Don't back me into a corner, Buck," Dev warned. "I'll stop you, one way or the other."

As Buck swiveled on his boot heel, his eyes narrowed to slits. "Go see for yourself, Summers, then tell me I'm wrong."

When the syncopated rhythm of Buck's boots on the immaculately clean hallway had faded away, Baxter stood up. "Go visit her, son. I'm going to call our lawyer and see if we can do anything to stop that little weasel, or at least throw up a roadblock that might buy time for July. We're not her blood kin, but she was living with us and had filed for divorce from him. There might be something that can be done."

Although he had prepared himself for the worst, Dev was still set back by what he saw when he went into July's room. The glow was gone from her face, leaving it ghostlike. The fragile skin beneath her eyes appeared bruised. The surgical team had wrapped her entire head, except her face, in heavy bandages with a drain protruding. Beneath the bandages, he knew her hair was gone; Reynolds had said they'd had to shave it. Even her body beneath the blankets did not seem to have the fullness and vitality he remembered on those many nights they'd lain in each other's arms. The only noise in the room was the soft whirring and murmuring of the many machines as they intravenously fed her and monitored her progress.

He reached across the bed rail and rested his hand alongside her cheek. He was comforted by the warmth of her skin and the faint pulse throbbing under his thumb. Although there was no indication she was aware of his touch, and regardless of what Buck had said, he felt her spirit in the room.

He kissed her cheek then spoke softly next to her ear, "July, it's me, Dev." Although the words were barely audible, they still sounded ragged and hoarse and too loud in the hollow, sterile atmosphere. "You gave us quite a scare, darlin', but everything is going to be all right."

He continued to caress her cheek while he studied her face for a response, any response at all, even the fluttering of an eyelid. For a moment, he fell back into that morning at the cabin when she was so full of life.

They had forgotten to close the curtains, and the sunlight came into the bedroom in its full glory, waking July first. He woke when the bed gave up her weight, and he watched her with sleepy eyes as she rummaged through the closet and came out with an old flannel bathrobe that belonged to Granddad. She pulled it on as she left the room, saying, "It's a beautiful morning. I'm going out on the porch to take some pictures."

He was obliged to follow. By the time he got outside, she was walking across the rain-soaked grass in slippered feet, snapping pictures of things he would never have thought worthy of film, but he already knew she could make the simplest things tell a story all their own through the eye of a camera. He enjoyed watching her; the way she moved, the way the sunlight turned that mane of hair to golden fire, and the way she simply enjoyed the moment as if each one was a new wonder to behold.

When she returned to the porch, he was waiting in the swing

with a fistful of wildflowers plucked from around the edges of the yard. He drew her onto his lap and handed her the flowers. She curled up against him, lifting the bouquet to her nose.

"I'm surprised the flowers are still blooming."

"They look a little ratty," he admitted.

She laughed and kissed him on the nose. "It's the thought that counts." Then she sighed, tucked her head down onto his shoulder and looked wistfully out at the mountains. "I could stay here forever. Just me and you. Let's never go back."

He burrowed his hand under the warmth of her hair and cupped the back of her head while administering kisses to her neck. "Mmmm, I'm all for that."

They sat for an hour holding each other closely to ward off the morning chill until the sun warmed their faces, soaked up the dew, and committed last night's storm to memory.

"If only we had stayed there like you wanted," he said now, taking her hand in his, despite the tubes and IV. He lifted it to his lips, pressing a kiss to the long fingers that curled over his. He wondered if he had imagined the ever-so-slight tightening of her grip.

He thought about all the things they had talked about doing, like making the pack trip into the Jarbidge Wilderness and to the ghost town. He'd wanted to fix that old sidesaddle she'd loved so much, and had even planned to get the buggy and sleigh into shape so they could use it on romantic summer and winter excursions. They had intended more moonlight rides. She'd wanted babies, and he had wanted to father them. There was so much they hadn't done. Their lives together had just begun.

He pulled in a ragged breath and tried to capture the surgeon's optimism. "Dr. Reynolds says you'll be out of here in no time. As soon as you're better, we'll go to the cabin. It'll be just the two of us and a cozy fire, maybe a bottle of your favorite wine. I don't know if you even like wine. But there's always hot chocolate."

Despite his attempt to be positive for his sake and hers, a deep ache started in the center of his chest and radiated to every inch of his body. My God, what would he do if he could no longer touch her or hold her in his arms? The threat of tears began to burn his eyes just as the ICU nurse, named Kimberly, appeared at the door. "I'm sorry, Dev, but your time is up."

He swallowed the lump in his throat as he lowered July's arm back to the bed. He kissed her cheek again and forced himself away before the escalating emotions crumbled his resolve.

In the hall, he paused to collect himself. He had just moved away from her door when he heard his name called. He turned to see Kimberly coming toward him holding two bags with the hospital's name stamped on them. She held out the larger one. "These are the clothes she was wearing when she arrived. Her husband told us to throw them away, but we thought she might not agree about the boots."

Dev took the bag, happy to have any part of her.

Kimberly hesitated with the smaller bag, as if she wasn't sure she should hand it over. Finally, she said, "When they shaved her hair, they put it in this bag. It's something they do when there's that much of it. They like to leave it up to the family to decide whether to dispose of it. Her husband didn't want it either."

Dev set the larger bag on the floor and opened the smaller one. Her hair lay in a neatly twisted length held together by rubber bands at each end. Suddenly he felt as if someone were ripping out his heart. My God, how many times had he buried his hands in that golden mass? Was this all he was to have of her?

He felt the nurse's hand on his arm. Through a blur, he saw the sympathy in her eyes.

"I was afraid it would upset you. Would you like to sit down?"

With one hand, she gathered the large bag from the floor. With the other, she led him to a chair in a secluded alcove behind a large potted plant. Gripping the small bag, he nodded his appreciation. It was all he was capable of doing.

◆

As days passed, the swelling in July's brain began to recede. She was removed from the respirator and was able to breath on her own, but she still did not respond to commands or the routine tests for pain. The bandages were changed and then removed, exposing the red, raw incision arcing the right side of her head and the staples and stitches that held it together. In the days since the surgery, her hair had begun to grow back, although it was barely visible.

Buck brought the Living Will but was restrained from enforcing it by her ability to breath without the respirator. Dev thought she had responded to him several times, but the doctors and nurses warned that the activity he was seeing could be nothing more than the body's reflexive movements and not necessarily an indication that she was coming out of the coma.

Buck scoffed at Dev's "wishful thinking" and criticized Dr. Reynolds for keeping her alive. "I told you this would happen," he lashed out. "She would have been better off if you'd have let her go in the beginning when you knew there was no hope of her ever coming out of this without brain damage. You and this hospital just wanted the money."

Dr. Reynolds insisted on optimism, and even though it was clear that Buck Jones was challenging his patience, he refused to back down to his belief that July would recover.

Dev and his family clung to the healing power of time, because hope and time were all they had. Buck's parents flew in long enough to take one look at July and announce that the only humane thing to do was enforce the Living Will.

Dev had hoped to see some compassion from Mrs. Jones at least, but the woman with the hard eyes and stubborn jaw was more determined than Buck to cancel July's life as if it were no more than an ill-timed hair appointment. He got the impression that Buck's parents placed July in the same category as an injured pet that needed to be euthanized. They were convinced that even if she came out of the coma, she would have severe brain damage or be in a permanent vegetative state. They clearly did not want their perfect lives burdened by an invalid, for legally she was still their responsibility.

The three of them brushed past Dev on their way out of July's room to "have a talk with that doctor." They acted as if they didn't know Dev, as if he hadn't once been a friend of Buck's. It left him feeling more powerless than he had ever felt in his life. He could only hope Granddad's lawyer would come through with something in time to stop them. He didn't know who was wrong and who was right; he only knew that July's life was in the hands of people who did not love her; people who seemed determined that she should pay with her life for loving him.

Dr. Reynolds told Dev and Baxter to take a break from their bedside vigil and go home for a day or two. When questioned about the Joneses wanting to enforce the Living Will, he replied, "I'm sorry. They've made the decision to pull life support. But her case has to go before the hospital board. They must review it and make a determination based on the medical indications and doctor recommendations. And I certainly won't recommend it. The board also has to agree that there's no chance of recovery. It's unlikely they'll make a decision for several days. With your lawyer in the mix, it will slow things down even more. Don't worry, nothing will happen until you get back."

It was already late when they gathered their bags from the Silver Legacy Hotel a few blocks away and started the drive home. Hours later, Dev fought exhaustion as they turned off the state highway onto the county road. His spirits fell even more when they pulled into the yard and saw Mica's pickup and horse trailer parked by the front gate. He had hoped she would get side-tracked by a new boyfriend or four flat tires, or maybe a blown engine. It would have been too much to ask for her to stay away at a time like this. Curiosity would have gotten the best of her though; no doubt the news about July was all over the rodeo circuit by now.

"Hell," Baxter said, as Dev brought the Ram to a halt in front of the house. "Why is she here? That woman makes my ass ache."

Dev couldn't help but smile. The old man said the same thing every time Mica came to visit. "Maybe she wants to help."

"Yes sir. Maybe she's made a reformatiion, but I wouldn't hold my breath."

Forced to face the inevitable, they found everyone around the kitchen table, discussing July's condition over brownies, coffee, and Coke. Mica held her drink in one hand and a Marlboro in the other, squinting through the curling smoke. Her lips and eyes pinched with what appeared to be genuine concern, even though, to Dev, the gathering looked more like a party.

"Jake told me about the Living Will. God, Dev, I can't believe Buck would do such a thing if her doctor is against it."

"It's true."

"He must be anxious to get back on the tour before he loses his chance at the PBR title and that million-dollar jackpot."

Her statement confirmed a nagging suspicion. "I figured something was driving him to put closure on this."

Mica pressed her cigarette out in the ashtray. Her tone softened from its usual bravado. "Dev, there's something I need to say."

He thought he saw sorrow in her eyes. It was an emotion that startled him. She seemed uneasy about voicing her thoughts but plunged on. "What I said before about July, you know, finding other lovers every time she and Buck had a fight. It wasn't true. I wanted to hurt you, and I'm sorry. She's a good person. I honestly hope she makes it through this."

His throat constricted. Struggling to hold himself together in front of everybody, and desperately needing to be alone, he gathered his hat and jacket from the foyer and left the house by the front door.

Mica carried coffee cups to the sink and announced that they should all go to bed and get some rest. Instead of heeding her own advice though, she stood at the kitchen window and watched Dev walk across the yard like a man without direction. Cappy followed him at a respectable distance as if he sensed Dev's solemn mood and wanted to console him in some way.

Despite their endless fights and the irrevocable words they'd used to hurt each other, Mica felt sorry for this man who had once shared a part of her life; this man who had fathered her only child; this man who was so desperately holding onto hope for the love of another woman; this man she had tossed aside for the sake of fickle fun with good-time cowboys like Buck. Yet she knew, in a sad sort of way, that she and Dev had never been right for each other. There could be no going back, and she accepted that. She only wished she could do something to comfort him, for she still loved him in her way.

Seth came to stand next to her. For once, he, too, was solemn. "I hope he's going to be all right."

"One thing's for certain," she said softly. "He's got his hand in a suicide wrap again. And this time there's no way out."

◆

Dev was back in the truck before dawn, leaving a note to the sleeping family that he needed to be with July, and that he'd call later when he thought they were awake.

As he made the long trek westward again, he drove in silence without the company of the radio. The dark hole in his heart widened to illimitable proportions, sucking him down into it and destroying any hope that there would be a happy ending at the end of this lost highway.

His thoughts drifted back to the day he and July had driven up from Arizona and how both of their directions had changed so dramatically overnight, bringing them together after ten years. Was it fate? Luck? How could it be fair that it would all end now, leaving him to spend the rest of his life without her? Had it truly never been meant to be?

Arriving in the city, his stomach knotted as fear took a new grip. How would the hospital board rule on her condition? That they might agree with Buck and his parents, drained the energy from him, making him wish there was a way he would never have to face that possible decision. Was there a way he could just take her away and continue to care for her himself?

In her room, with hat in hand, he stood next to her side. Like sleeping beauty, she lay peacefully in her slumber. He bent and gently kissed her lips, but she didn't stir.

He whispered, "I'm here, July."

If he wasn't mistaken, she released a sigh, almost as if in contentment.

Having fallen so deep inside his despair, he could not muster the strength to carry on his usual light, one-sided conversation with her. Instead, he went to the window and opened the blinds so the afternoon sunlight could angle down into her room and push the dreariness to the corners. He called Granddad to tell him he'd arrived safely and let him know his room number at the Silver Legacy.

With a heavy heart, he set his hat on the floor and pulled up a chair next to her bed. He took her hand in his and held it for a long while until drowsiness consumed him. He leaned forward, resting his head on the edge of her bed where he drifted to sleep.

In the dream, he could feel her fingers caressing the side of his face with a touch so light it could have come from a breath of wind, or the passing of a ghost. He heard her call his name, and he turned and saw her standing there, smiling and holding out her arms. He stepped into her embrace.

Then it ended, and he was awake, letting the dream go as he became aware of the bed sheet beneath his cheek. In those seconds as he shed the dream and came to full consciousness, he became acutely aware of her fingers against his face.

At first, he thought it was a remnant of the dream. Still half asleep, he turned his head, gathered her hand in his and placed a kiss to her palm. Her fingers curled over his, as they had done before, but this time he lifted his head to look at her. She was watching him.

"July?"

In an instant, he was to his feet, gathering her into his arms and choking on tears of relief and joy.

He didn't see Buck, in the doorway, turn angrily away.

Chapter Twenty-Nine

July's room became the scene of celebration for everyone who had been involved with her care. Dr. Reynolds did an initial exam and was pleased that her cognizant and motor skills did not seem to be impaired. She couldn't remember the accident, or even the moments leading up to it, but Reynolds assured her it was the mind's way of protecting itself from the trauma, and she might never remember it.

Dev called the ranch to report the good news so the family could come to see her. Buck couldn't be reached, and his parents, who had returned to Albuquerque, didn't know his whereabouts, nor did they seem happy about her recovery.

The flurry of activity quickly tired July. After everyone had left the room except Dev, she was barely able to keep her eyes open, but she held tight to his hand and confided, "Before I woke, there was this endless highway, and I was traveling down it, trying to find you. There was something I had to tell you. Something urgent. I was so worried that I'd lost you."

"I've never been far away, July. And I never will be. But now I should go and let you rest. Doctor's orders."

Her grip tightened on his hand and a frightened look came into her eyes. "I'm afraid to sleep, Dev. Afraid the next time I wake up, I'll find that twenty years have passed."

He lifted her hand to his lips, trying to ease her fears. "And if that happens, darlin', I'll still be right here."

She relaxed. Her eyes caressed him. "God, I love you. Did I tell you that before?"

"You did, but I never get tired of hearing it." He bent to kiss her lips, murmuring, "And I love you. I always have, and I always will."

When he rose and looked down at her face, she was asleep with a faint smile on her lips.

He felt such relief, such joy, as if the weight of the world had been lifted from his shoulders. With the release of anxiety and fear, he was overcome by complete exhaustion. She was out of danger now and in good hands. He could go to his hotel room and sleep.

He drove the short distance to the Silver Legacy. By the time he had parked in the garage and walked through the palatial lobby to the elevators, he felt the full extent of the long ordeal. He leaned against the elevator wall as it carried him to his room on the thirtieth floor. He wished he'd opted for one of the spa suites; the in-room hot tub would sure feel good about now, but he could fill the bathtub with hot water and soak in that. Then he'd call up room service. For the first time since July had been hurt, he actually felt like eating.

The room was dark, just as he'd left it, with the drapes pulled back. Through the expansive windows, the city lights glittered below the ragged line of the Sierra Nevada Mountains, thrusting up into the night sky beneath the fading red glow of sunset. He walked across the dark room and stood at the window, allowing any remaining tension to drain away.

Suddenly, like a stealthy spider, a prickly feeling crawled up his spine. He turned his head and saw the man sitting at the table in the dark corner, a cowboy hat shoved to the back of his head.

Dev reached for the switch on the nearby lamp, figuring to grab the lamp itself if he needed it for a weapon. But the intruder didn't move as the muted glow opened the room's darkness and shone upon the all-too-familiar face.

"How in the hell did you get in here, Jones?"

"I overheard you telling Baxter what room you were in," Buck said, sounding uncharacteristically subdued, almost troubled. "I'm staying here, too, two floors down. I wanted to talk to you—in private—and I figured you'd never do it willingly. So I told that young desk clerk that I was you, and that I'd left my wallet in the room, with my key in it. I gave her all the information she needed to verify identification, even your license plate number. Apparently she wasn't the one who signed you in, or she can't tell one cowboy from another. Anyway, she called a security guard to let me in. I made a show of looking for the key while he waited in the doorway, but I produced my own key from my shirt pocket, flashed it so he could see it was a Silver Legacy key card, and he went on his way."

Dev was trying hard to contain his fury. "So you've proved you're a liar *and* a con man. What do you want? It had better be good, Jones, because I can have your ass for breaking into my room."

"Hey, I'm sorry, like I said, it was the only way I could think of to discuss July and the whole Living Will thing. Hear me out."

"The Living Will is a moot point, Jones. July came out of the coma this afternoon. The hospital's been trying to reach you. Why haven't you been answering your cell phone?"

A guarded expression entered Buck's eyes. "Come on, man. Don't make jokes about something like that. I didn't see any change in her the last time I was there."

"Call the hospital if you don't believe me."

Buck contemplated him and what he'd said. "Assuming you're not lying, how is she? Does she know what's going on? Can she talk?"

"Do you mean, has she suffered brain damage?"

"Yeah, I guess that's what I mean."

"Don't be afraid to speak right up, Jones. I'm glad to see you're so overjoyed that she's going to live."

"First off, I'm still trying to decide if you're telling me the truth or a cruel joke. Secondly, you might not believe this, but seeing July attacked by that bull and watching her struggle to live has taken a toll on me. It's been brutal. I love that woman, regardless what you or anybody else might think. It would kill my soul if she didn't come out of this with all her faculties intact."

"Spare me the bullshit."

Buck took a deep breath, as if trying to contain his temper. "Okay, but I need to know if she's all right before I go over there. I need to prepare myself if she isn't."

"There doesn't appear to be anything wrong at this point."

He gave a sigh of relief. "That's good. Real good." But he seemed far away as he looked out the window again at the lights of the city.

"You still don't seem too happy about it. I would have thought you'd run out of here immediately to go see her."

Buck pulled himself back from wherever he'd been. "No, no. It's not that. I'm nervous about seeing her. I shot my mouth off a lot, but this accident has made me realize I was wrong. It's awkward, you know, now that she's filed for divorce, and things were so ugly between us before this happened. I don't want to upset her. I don't suppose…you'd go over with me? I want to wish her well, tell her good-bye and good luck. Then I'll be hittin' the road."

Dev was unsettled by Buck's behavioral turnaround. That he would ask him for a favor was completely out of character. He couldn't help but wonder what the little bastard was up to, but his own mental capacities had shut down from exhaustion. He'd been looking forward to that long soak in the tub and then a solid meal, damn it. But he didn't trust Buck alone with July. Didn't trust what he'd say or do. She was in a vulnerable state; she might believe whatever bullshit he told her. If it would mean protecting July and getting Buck the hell gone, then he'd have to take his chances that Buck was, for once in his life, sincere.

"All right," he said wearily. "Let's go."

In the parking garage, Buck followed Dev to his truck and climbed into the passenger seat. Dev put the vehicle into reverse and turned to look out the side mirror when something hard came down on his head, sending him into the steering wheel face first. For a second or two, he stared at Buck in disbelief then spiraled into unconsciousness.

◆

He came to with a start and found himself slumped down in the passenger seat against the door. A handgun was pressed into his ribs, and Buck was behind the wheel. When he tried to move away from the discomfort of the gun's muzzle digging into his flesh, he realized his hands were tied behind his back.

Buck leaned toward him. His top lip curled into the smirk that Dev had come to know and hate. "Hey, old buddy. You look like you got broadsided by some old bad-assed bull."

Dev's head throbbed fiercely. He felt something warm and wet crawling down the side of his face. Blood. His hat was on the floor of the truck under one foot. He glanced out the window, hoping someone might have seen Buck's attack, but rows of empty cars were all that occupied the gray, dimly-lit garage.

"What are you doing, Jones?"

"Taking control. I saw that heart-wrenching scene in the hospital when July came out of the coma. That moment when you pulled her into your arms brought everything into focus for me, and I knew I had to get you out of the picture."

"You were there when she—?" Dev closed his eyes against the sharp stabs of pain ricocheting through his head.

"Yeah." Buck gloated over Dev's surprise. "I was standing in the doorway. Touching, Summers. Very touching."

Dev lifted his shoulder in an attempt to swipe at the blood dripping off his jaw.

"Jesus, man, you're bleeding like a stuck hog. It's going to ruin these nice leather seats. What a shame." He turned the truck out of the parking garage and into the night.

"Why didn't you come in when you saw she was awake?"

"I had to have some time to think things over. I honestly figured she'd never come out of that coma. Seeing her reach for you the way she did, well, it just got me right in the gut. I was prepared to lose her; I figured she was already gone. But I wasn't prepared to lose her to you, and I'm still not."

"Everything you're saying is bullshit, Jones. You knew before the accident that she was divorcing you. Isn't that why you came to Nevada? To win her back?"

"I sure as hell didn't come to ride no damned old pasture bull." Buck navigated the truck through downtown and headed for the interstate. "When I saw the two of you all over each other at the Bull Horn, I knew things wouldn't be as easy as I'd thought, but I was up for the challenge. Then, thanks to your old man, she ended up in a coma."

"Give it up, Buck. You've lost her."

"I've never lost anything in my life, Summers. And, as long as July is going to live, I'm sure as hell not going to lose her—or my money—to the likes of you. With you gone, she'll come back to me. She always has. There'll be no divorce, and my bank account will stay intact."

"I don't want your damn money and neither does July."

"What do you take me for, an idiot? Even if she signed something forfeiting her share, her hotshot lawyer would send that scrap of paper through the shredder and make damn sure I came out stripped of everything. If she had just died, it would have made it all a lot simpler, but now it looks like you're going to have to disappear in one of those places where only the coyotes will ever find your stinking body."

Dev's eyes focused on the gun resting in Buck's lap. Buck's intent settled in with cold realization. He meant to kill him.

"Even with me gone, she'll divorce your ass."

"No. She won't give up all that money. Do you honestly think she would have jumped from my bed to yours if you hadn't had as much money as I do? I gave her everything she ever wanted; I made her rich. She was nothing when I found her, and she'll be nothing again if she tries to make it on her own. She'll remember that when I take her home to Albuquerque."

He veered into the empty parking lot of a wholesale carpet store that was closed for the night. Putting the truck in park, he reached over to Dev, unsnapped his shirt pocket, and fished out his cell phone. He turned it off and tossed it on the dashboard. Squealing the tires, he drove back onto the street. In minutes, he had merged onto the interstate, crowding the speed limit at eighty miles an hour.

While the lights of the city were left behind, Dev's mind raced to figure a way out. He had no idea where Buck was taking him, but maybe he'd have a chance to escape, or maybe he could talk Buck out of it.

"The law will discover soon enough that July filed for divorce, Jones. The threat you made against me at the Bull Horn won't go unnoticed. You'll be the first person they question about my disappearance, especially when the law sees how anxious you were to enforce her Living Will. Do you think nobody will get suspicious when neither of us shows up tomorrow morning?"

"I'll go to the hospital tomorrow and say I spent the night in my room with a bottle of booze because I was devastated over the decision I had to make to let her go. I'll be recovering from a hangover that kept me sick and in bed all morning, but I'll be elated that she's come out of the coma. And I won't know a damn thing about your whereabouts. They'll find your truck back in the parking garage with the keys in it and your blood all over the seats. They'll surmise you came to a bad end by some thugs who wanted your money. They won't have any way to pin it on me."

"That's as flimsy as hell."

"Nobody can refute it."

Dev didn't mention to Buck that there were surveillance cameras everywhere nowadays, probably even in the parking garage. He said, "There might be people who saw us leave together."

"Yeah, like the little desk clerk who can't tell one cowboy from the next? For your information, she wasn't at the desk when we walked by. Hell, Summers, with the number of people milling around that place, nobody paid any attention to us. People in this town are only thinking of having a good time."

"You hope. And I suggest you don't use that gun because they'll be able to trace the bullet."

"Only if they find your body, and that's not likely. I remember a place we went to once when we were riding in that Jarbidge country behind your ranch back in the good old days. I believe you called it, 'Hell's Back Door'."

Dev's heart sank. Coyotes would not even be able to find a body in that Godforsaken place. The "door" was actually a narrow fissure between sheer rock walls. It was a few yards wide and maybe a hundred yards long. Nobody seemed to know how deep it was. According to the old-timers, the bottom had never been found; it might go all the way to hell itself. One thing was certain. Whatever fell into it, would never make it back out.

Dev leaned his head back and closed his eyes.

"Hey, Summers. Don't fall asleep. With that knock on the head you might not wake up, and that would really mess up my plans. I want to hear you scream when you take your little tumble into hell."

Dev had no intention of sleeping, but he wanted some time to think, to plot an escape. Besides, tilting his head back helped ease the pain.

They spoke very little on the long drive, and stopped only

once on a lonely side road to take a piss. Buck secured Dev's hands to the side mirror, then released one so he could tend to business. When he was finished, Buck shoved him back into the truck at the end of the gun.

Buck grew increasingly edgy the closer they got to the ranch. When he turned off onto the two-track road that led to the cabin, he continued to drive too fast, tossing Dev from side to side. Several times he hit the brakes for pot holes and cattle wandering in and across the road. Dev was flung into the dashboard with no way to brace himself except with his feet pressed against the floorboard. Dev had hoped they might see someone on the road that would recognize his truck, but the only lights cutting a path through the night were their own.

It was four a.m. when Buck stopped the truck in front of the cabin and hauled Dev out by the scruff of the neck. With the gun in his back, he forced him to the corral. The horses had been dozing, but they began to mill about when they saw the men coming toward them through the darkness. Afraid the horses would escape through the open gate that led to the adjoining pasture, Buck grabbed Dev by the arm and dragged him along as he rushed to block their exit.

"You can't mean to go into the mountains in the dark," Dev said.

"The horses can see well enough by starlight and moonlight to follow the road through the hills. By the time we reach the higher elevations and the trails, it'll be coming daylight."

Buck shoved Dev to the barn and flipped the switch just inside the door to activate the generator and lights. With lead ropes, they returned to the corral and caught Sam and Banjo.

"I wouldn't take Banjo if I were you," Dev warned. "He's young and inexperienced."

"He doesn't scare me. The rest of what you've got here looks like a bunch of old nags that wouldn't make it up the mountain. What'd you do? Take all your good horses back to the ranch?"

"As a matter of fact."

Buck dropped the truck tailgate, pulled Sam alongside, and ordered Dev to mount. It was difficult with his hands tied behind his back, but he maneuvered onto the metal platform and stepped over into the saddle.

Swinging onto Banjo, Buck collected Sam's lead rope and set the horses into a trot down the dark dirt road. The impenetrable black bulk of the Jarbidge Mountains rose into the lighter sky like the massive shoulders of the legendary monster, waiting for the day's first kill.

Chapter Thirty

Sagebrush hills gave way to aspens that formed dark walls on either side of the road. A phantom breeze swept down the road toward them, blowing dust in its fore. It snatched the autumn leaves from the branches and flung them into the faces of the riders. Banjo spooked sideways, wanting none of it.

Buck had barely gotten him under control when a pack of coyotes, lumbering toward daylight on the ridge above them, released a plaintive chorus of yipping howls, like the devil's children all singing a different song at once. It was a chilling sound that sent the gelding into a crow-hop, head down and back humped.

Sam did an evasive dance, dodging the younger horse's antics. Dev gripped the saddle tighter with his legs to keep from losing his seat. Looking into the black shroud of trees and the underbrush next to the road, he wondered if now might be a good time to swing one leg over the saddle horn, slide to the ground, and disappear into the darkness. Buck didn't have a flashlight; he might not be able to find him. Then his chance was gone as the trail emerged onto the ridge. The land fell away to the left into ragged humps of boulders and a denser darkness; a death plunge. To the right it was uphill, sagebrush, and no good place to hide. He wouldn't get more than a few yards before Buck shot him in the back.

Maybe Buck wouldn't remember the way after all these years. Maybe it would look different in the darkness, and he'd get lost. But his nemesis continued on course until the first gray light of dawn revealed a faint confluence of trails. One trail continued south around a tangle of deadfall; another turned to the east intersecting a rocky stream; a third made a sharp turn around a clump of ancient, heavy-boughed pine trees and up a steep, heavily wooded canyon. Buck hesitated only a moment before nudging Banjo around the pine trees.

Even with daylight not far away, it was still gloomy in the canyon. Most of the stars were gone now, and the moon, a sliver of light hovering at the brow of the western mountains, cast only a weak white glow through the pine boughs.

Banjo became increasingly apprehensive and balky. He didn't want to lead the way into a place he had never been during daylight, let alone in this gray-dawn murkiness of silence and shadows. He started fighting Buck, who in turn cussed him, kicked him, and yanked too hard on the bit. A smart man would have traded the older and more experienced Sam for the lead, who trailed calmly with only his ears twitching as he took in all the sounds of the coming morning.

Banjo jumped a log and nearly jerked the lead rope out of Buck's hand. He pulled in the slack and brought Sam up close again, proceeding with a scowl and profanities, muttering that if the damned horse belonged to him, he'd teach it a thing or two.

"If he's too much for you, Jones, we can always trade," Dev called out derisively.

"Shut your goddamn mouth, Summers. I can handle this piece-of-shit horse."

For another hour, the animals labored up scree slopes, over fallen logs, and around thickets of buck brush and outcroppings of boulders. They traversed open ridges then dropped down into deep wooded basins and clearings where deer grazed in the first soft light of morning and watched them pass by with no sense of alarm. In the basins where the sunlight hadn't quite reached, the horses' flared nostrils picked up the scent of any creatures that might threaten them. They passed several herds of grazing deer, five head of elk, and a small black bear lumbering away into the trees.

It was full daylight when they paused at the base of the final ascent to the rocky spine that converged with Hell's Back Door. The morning sun shown directly onto the short but steep slope that was also a well-used game trail. This branch of the mountains had been thrust up into an escarpment that ran for a considerable distance in either direction. While the cliffs were not high, they were nearly perpendicular. There were very few places where the rock walls gave way to a slope that could be used for passage; this was the only one Dev knew of in the vicinity.

The passage, only a few yards wide and bordered by massive old pines and granite slabs protruding from the mountain, had been ground into loose, soft dirt by the hooves of deer, elk, and moose. In some places the soil was gone, exposing rocks that became natural steps. Most of the underbrush had been trampled until it was short and stunted. There was no obstruction; nor was there much footing.

The slope was a feat in itself for a horse to climb; the animal would have to lunge its way those last few yards up the steepest part while its rider stretched out over its neck as far forward as possible. A person could get off and try to lead his horse, but the animal would overrun him with the momentum necessary to reach the top. Taking the climb on horseback wasn't a smart thing to attempt for anyone except an experienced rider and a fearless horse. Taking it leading another horse was having a death wish. Dev had been up it a few times, as had Sam, but Banjo had not.

Buck dismounted and stared up the slope, gauging what it was going to take to get the horses up.

"I guess you forgot how steep it was," Dev goaded. "Banjo's never been up it; he could balk."

"I'm not interested in your opinion."

"I don't think you've got the guts to carry this through, Jones. Wanting to kill me is one thing; doing it is another. What's your plan anyway? Shoot me, or throw me into the ravine and let me die on impact?"

Buck spun on his heel, grabbed Dev at his elbow where his arm was bent back and yanked him half-way out of the saddle, catching him by the throat before he fell. "I was thinking I'd like to do it with my bare hands. It would be slower. I could watch the life drain out of your eyes." He squeezed, pressing hard until Dev felt himself choking down. Buck released him with the upward thrust of his arm, pushing him back up into the saddle. "We're going up."

He brought Banjo alongside Sam and remounted. Getting a good grip on Sam's lead rope, he kicked Banjo toward the slope. Dev knew his odds of staying in the saddle weren't good. He could press the point, but he was afraid Buck might shoot him on the spot or drag him to the top with the lariat rope that was tied at the saddle's fork.

The horses began their lunging ascent. There was no turning back now. It was Dev's last chance; the moment he'd been waiting for. Using a lifetime of training in the rodeo, he kicked free of the stirrups and flung himself backward into a roll off Sam's rump. He hit the ground on his stomach and face with no way to brace his fall. A lightning sharp pain seared into his shoulders as the momentum, coupled with the steepness of the grade, somersaulted him several more times before he stopped short against the unyielding trunk of an ancient pine tree.

As he tried to breathe and collect his equilibrium, Banjo released a shrill scream. He looked up to see the young horse panic at the steepest part of the ascent. That moment of hesitation lost him his footing. With crazed fear, he started to slide backward into Sam who bolted out of his way, turning downhill and jerking so hard on the lead rope that he yanked it from Buck's hand and pulled him almost out of the saddle.

Even though Banjo's hind feet dug into the loose soil for traction, he could not counter the pull of gravity and the unbalanced rider on his back. He pawed air with his front feet while his back feet and powerful hind quarters tried to get purchase, but he came over backwards in a flurry of kicking legs. His head hit the earth hard as he landed square on Buck, rolling over him and down the hill a dozen yards before he came to a skidding halt with his legs in a knot beneath him. He stopped only feet from where Dev had scrambled out of his way. Stunned, he sat there for a moment before he struggled to his feet and staggered down the hill toward Sam, dazed and shaking.

It had happened in seconds, yet seemingly in slow motion, and was followed by an unnerving silence. Dev got his feet under him and, digging his boot heels into the hill sideways, worked his way up to the spot where Buck lay on his back with his head pointed downhill. One arm was under him; the other rested on his chest.

Dev's first thought was to get the gun before Buck could gain his composure, but he was stopped cold by the angle of Buck's left leg and the ashen color of his face. From the way his foot was turned out, he suspected his leg was broken, probably a compound fracture above the knee. What he couldn't know was if there were internal injuries from the horse coming down on him. Blood trickled from Buck's nose and mouth, and a familiar dull light shone in his eyes. Dev had seen that light before—moments before Tim Roberts had died.

Dev dropped to his knees next to Buck, jamming his boot toes against a rock to anchor himself on the incline. "Untie me, Buck, and I'll go for help."

He swiveled his torso so Buck could reach him, but his nemesis scoffed at the idea. "Untie you? So you can take off and leave me here?"

"If you want to live, you'll untie me."

"What's to stop you from putting a bullet in my head and dropping me in that crevice the way I was going to do you?" The hatred brought a momentary spark of life to Buck's fading eyes.

"Jesus, man. It doesn't have to come to this. Get the rope off, and I'll go for help."

Buck grabbed his tied hands with more strength than Dev thought possible. "I was going to kill you, you stupid son of a bitch! Don't you understand anything? It's over! You won!" He closed his eyes against the pain and continued to swear under his breath.

"It wasn't a damn contest, Buck. It never was."

The trace of a derisive smile twitched at Buck's top lip; his words were barely audible. "Oh, but it was, old buddy. It certainly was." His grip on Dev's hands relaxed. "You'll have to figure your own way out...."

"Hold on, Buck. Hold—"

Before the words had crossed Dev's lips, the last breath of air escaped Buck's lungs in a faint whoosh.

Releasing his own long breath, Dev sat back against the hillside, turning away from Buck's sightless eyes. Time ticked by as Dev waited for the calm of the forest to help him find his center, but he knew he would never find satisfactory answers to what had happened here today.

He had no idea how long he sat there in the dirt before he mustered the fortitude to saw the rope around his wrists against a sharp, jagged outcropping of rock. He was half-numb to the pain in his shoulder and the ragged cuts in his flesh by the time the rope broke and set him free. As the sun stole toward the middle of the sky, he was driven by the need to return to July. That was all that mattered now.

Again, he found strength from somewhere deep inside himself to load Buck's body onto Sam. He used the lariat to tie the body down.

As he tried to calm Banjo and regain his trust, he saw Buck's gray cowboy hat lying a few feet away in the underbrush. A peculiar sense of loss and regret stabbed him as he picked it up and thought of the man who had worn it; the man who had once been a friend; the man who had never learned what was important in life.

"You never understood what you had in July," he whispered. "You never understood any of it."

Solemnly he returned the hat to the place where its owner had fallen. Then he swung into the saddle and started the long journey home, again.

Epilogue

Five Years Later
From the Journal of July Summers

People have told me it was a brave thing I did, saving Jake's life all those years ago. But I've never felt brave. To me, bravery is straddling a wild bronc or a raging bull, and I've never had that kind of raw courage. The bravest thing I ever did—and the most terrifying—was stepping out onto that long Nevada highway in search of what life should be, but hadn't been.

There have been times since that I've thought divine intervention was involved in bringing me to Dev and the Summers men. Not that I gave God much thought in the beginning, but if He happened to pay any attention to any of us, I'm sure He saw us as a handful of misfits who needed a whole bag full of miracles to straighten us out.

I came here like a bird in flight, a frenzied sparrow rushing headlong into the wind, searching desperately for the calm that waited beyond the storm. Leaving everything and nothing behind.

But I wasn't alone and never had been. For even though we were apart, Dev's hand had been around mine from the beginning, holding onto me with all his might. I realize now that he would never have let go, even if I had gone away from him forever. What I didn't realize, was that, all the while, I had been holding onto him too.

July closed the journal and tucked it into her bag. Soon, very soon, she would be in Dev's arms again. It had only been two days since they'd been apart, but it seemed an eternity.

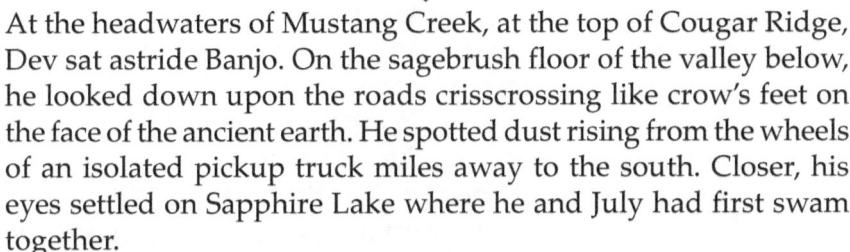

At the headwaters of Mustang Creek, at the top of Cougar Ridge, Dev sat astride Banjo. On the sagebrush floor of the valley below, he looked down upon the roads crisscrossing like crow's feet on the face of the ancient earth. He spotted dust rising from the wheels of an isolated pickup truck miles away to the south. Closer, his eyes settled on Sapphire Lake where he and July had first swam together.

He loved this place, even though everything about a person's life became clear up here. Even though there was nowhere to hide the truth, nor hide *from* it. Up here you could see how the pieces fit together, or didn't. And until they fit, you couldn't find peace, only the torture of seeing the mistakes and the disappointments all laid out before you.

From here, you could see how one decision can have far-reaching effects. Yet, even though the decision he had made to retire from the rodeo had changed many lives as well as his own, he knew now that it had also helped them find their way. Most importantly, it was the road that had brought him to July.

He released his thoughts and gathered his reins. It was time to get back to work. The cowboys he'd hired for the roundup were small and distant down on the flat, bunching the cattle in the draws to drive them into fall pastures. Closer, by the lake, Dusty and her fiancé, Luke, rode their horses side by side. Next to them was Hooley Wilson, Dev's horse wrangler now for three years. They were holding together the heifers that the four of them had spent all morning flushing out of the trees.

He was pleased that he'd been able to bring the ranch back to what it had been when his granddad had been his age. Only Jake and Seth were missing: Seth at the rodeos with his rope in hand, his shelves now filled with trophies, gold buckles, and championship titles, and his heart filled with a woman's true love for the first time; and Jake, slowly winning his ongoing battle with Jack Daniels by immersing himself in the bull riding school he owned and operated in Starr Valley.

Dev missed the rodeo sometimes, but it was in the way a person misses anything of their youth that is taken away by time and age. It is merely something you accept, and then move on.

He supposed there was seldom a day went by that he didn't think of Buck and that fateful day near Hell's Back Door. Buck's fans had mourned the loss of a superstar from what was reported as a tragic accident in the Jarbidge Wilderness. But word had inevitably leaked out from the press that he'd attempted to murder Dev.

Among the bull riders and the other rodeo contestants, the incident was seldom mentioned because Buck was not a man who had made many true friends. Everyone who had known him at all had known him for what he was. It seemed people preferred to discuss the miracle of July's recovery after her heroic act to save the life of rodeo legend, Jake Summers.

Now as he scanned the area below for strays, he saw what he had come to see: the pickup truck making its way along the dusty road to the main gate. His heartbeat quickened with anticipation. Even after five years, July could still do that to him. She was on her way, right on time, just as she'd promised.

He lifted his binoculars to his eyes and watched until the truck stopped at the main gate. When the dust drifted past, July got out from the passenger side to open the gate while Granddad drove through. He couldn't see them, but he knew his boys were in the back seat, strapped in their car seats, probably sleeping.

Dev nudged Banjo down off the ridge. Trotting up to Dusty, Luke, and Hooley, he said, "If you'll move 'em down, I'll drop this fence so we won't have to come back up before the snow flies. July wanted to come up anyway, so would you tell her where I am?"

"Want me to escort her?" Hooley asked. "It's not a good idea for her to be riding up here alone. Not that she isn't capable, of course."

Hooley was still watching out for July in his own way, and he knew the many dangers of being in the mountains alone. Dev knew he'd bring her safely to the lake and then leave them to their privacy.

"I'd appreciate it, if you don't mind."

Nodding, Hooley trotted his horse toward the heifers, raised an arm to get them moving, and started calling out, "Come on now, girls. Let's go."

When Hooley, Dusty, and Luke had the cattle under way, Dev rode back up to the ridge and started letting down the wires from the posts so the weight of the snow wouldn't break them during the winter. He wanted to have it done by the time July got there.

It was a couple of hours before he heard the pieces of rock slip and crunch beneath her horse's hooves, before he spotted the white Stetson bobbing above the sagebrush, shielding her face from the warm September sun. Then she emerged on top of the ridge, dismounted, and tied her horse next to Banjo in the shade of a lone, gnarled tree.

She smiled and waved when she saw him. He quickly closed the distance and pulled her into his embrace, kissing her with the desire she had always incited in him, the desire to not only make sweet love to her, but the powerful need to just hold her for a very long time and lose himself, body and soul, in the comfort of her arms. He had learned long ago how close Death stands to each and every one of them, and he would never take life for granted.

He removed her hat and kissed the top of her head, inhaling the sweet scent of her long, golden hair. He ran a string of kisses along her forehead and down to the corner of her lips before saying, "How are the boys?"

"Glad to be spending the night at the cabin. Anxious to see you. But Granddad promised them a ride on Dinky, so that'll keep them busy until we get back. They'll expect you to play with them. Are you up to it? I know you're tired."

"I'll have my second wind by then."

His heart was light as he continued to kiss her. No matter how weary he was, he always managed to find energy for July and his sons. He knew exactly what the two of them would do as soon as he and July rode their horses into the yard. They would be playing outside on the cabin's porch with their trucks, toy horses, and the new pup. Granddad and Cappy would be sitting close by in the shade keeping an eye on them.

Zack would squeal with delight and come running, covering the uneven ground in miniature cowboy boots and blue jeans, barely able to see out from under Dev's old hat that he refused to give up. He would grab Dev's hand and bounce alongside him, bombarding him with questions until, laughing, Dev would swing the boy onto his shoulders. Zack would clasp Dev's cheeks and ears with his pudgy hands and pretend he was riding a horse.

Quint, only eighteen months younger than Zack, would be slower to come forward. He would wait shyly next to Granddad until Dev motioned for him. Then Dev would put Zack down and give Quint a ride. The two of them would take turns until Dev was worn out and they all collapsed on the grass in a heap.

Sometimes when Dev saw the boys together, he thought of himself and Seth when they'd been that age, and how they'd grown apart. He vowed he would do everything in his power to keep that from happening with his own children.

Sometimes he wondered if his boys would ride the rodeo, but he didn't want to think of the day that they would go away from him and July. He knew it would come, of course, and he would hold onto the knowledge that although the highway would take them away to become men, it would bring them back, just as it had him.

July settled closer to him, circling his sun-baked back in a full embrace. He cupped her face in his palms and covered her lips with his, kissing her as if it were a first kiss, or a last, but savoring her. Always savoring her.

Keeping an arm around her waist, he turned to look again at the view spreading out in the valley below. It was filled with the hopes and dreams that he had once thought were lost to him forever. It was also filled with the memory of roads he had traveled before finding July: long, gray scars reminding him that he never wanted to go down any of them again.

She kissed a spot under his chin in an unhurried way. "I brought some sandwiches. I thought you might be hungry. I also tied a blanket behind the saddle."

She smiled in that slow, seductive way he had come to know so well. Taking her hand, he went to the saddle and untied the blanket, moved a few yards away and spread it on the ground where the autumn sun could warm it.

"I hope you're not in a hurry to leave," he said.

"I've got all the time in the world, cowboy."

She tilted her head back, inviting more of his kisses. Her hat fell onto the blanket, and they followed it down.

About the Author

Linda Sandifer is the award-winning author of thirteen novels. Her stories of the West and its indomitable people have found fans among the ranks of both men and women alike and have been translated into numerous languages throughout the world. She is known for her compelling characterizations, credible detail, and the ability to touch the human spirit. She lives with her husband on a ranch in southeastern Idaho. Visit her website at www.linda-sandifer.com.